Her Happy-Ever-After Family

MICHELLE DOUGLAS
BARBARA HANNAY
SORAYA LANE

MILLS & BOON

All rights reserved including the right of reproduction in whole or in part in any form. This edition is published by arrangement with Harlequin Books S.A.

This is a work of fiction. Names, characters, places, locations and incidents are purely fictional and bear no relationship to any real life individuals, living or dead, or to any actual places, business establishments, locations, events or incidents. Any resemblance is entirely coincidental.

This book is sold subject to the condition that it shall not, by way of trade or otherwise, be lent, resold, hired out or otherwise circulated without the prior consent of the publisher in any form of binding or cover other than that in which it is published and without a similar condition including this condition being imposed on the subsequent purchaser.

® and ™ are trademarks owned and used by the trademark owner and/or its licensee. Trademarks marked with ® are registered with the United Kingdom Patent Office and/or the Office for Harmonisation in the Internal Market and in other countries.

First Published in Great Britain 2016
By Mills & Boon, an imprint of HarperCollins*Publishers*
1 London Bridge Street, London, SE1 9GF

HER HAPPY-EVER-AFTER FAMILY © 2016 Harlequin Books S. A.

The Cattleman's Ready-Made Family, *Miracle in Bellaroo Creek* and *Patchwork Family in the Outback* were first published in Great Britain by Harlequin (UK) Limited.

The Cattleman's Ready-Made Family © 2013 Michelle Douglas
Miracle in Bellaroo Creek © 2013 Barbara Hannay
Patchwork Family in the Outback © 2013 Soraya Lane

ISBN: 978-0-263-92082-6

05-0916

Our policy is to use papers that are natural, renewable and recyclable products and made from wood grown in sustainable forests.The logging and manufacturing processes conform to the legal environmental regulations of the country of origin.

Printed and bound in Spain
by CPI, Barcelona

THE
CATTLEMAN'S
READY-MADE FAMILY

BY
MICHELLE DOUGLAS

At the age of eight, **Michelle Douglas** was asked what she wanted to be when she grew up. She answered, 'A writer.' Years later she read an article about romance writing and thought, *Ooh, that'll be fun*. She was right. When she's not writing she can usually be found with her nose buried in a book. She is currently enrolled in an English Masters programme for the sole purpose of indulging her reading and writing habits further. She lives in a leafy suburb of Newcastle, on Australia's east coast, with her own romantic hero—husband Greg, who is the inspiration behind all her happy endings.

Michelle would love you to visit her at her website: www.michelle-douglas.com

To the Valley Girls
for the support, the laughter and the champagne.

CHAPTER ONE

ARE YOU LOOKING FOR A TREE CHANGE?
Do you long for fresh air and birdsong?
Do you relish fresh-picked produce?
Do you hunger for a gentler pace of life?
RENT A FARMHOUSE FOR $1 A WEEK!
If you're a community-minded family, why not rent a
farmhouse for $1 a week in beautiful Bellaroo Creek?
We can promise you a fresh start and genuine country
hospitality.

CAMERON MANNING PACED from the fence to the empty farmhouse and back again. He checked his watch. The second
hand hadn't moved much from the last time he'd looked.
With a curse, he threw himself down on the bench, squat-
ting beneath one of the Kurrajong trees that screened this
farmhouse from the rest of his property, and drummed his
fingers against his thigh.

Where was the woman?

The slats of the bench, badly in need of a nail or ten, bit
into his back. It would've been more comfortable to sit on
the veranda, but here the deep shade screened him. It'd give
him a chance to contemplate his new tenants unobserved.

He scowled. If they ever turned up.

To be honest, he didn't much care if they did or not. All he wanted was Tess Laing's signature on his contract so he could hightail it out of here again. He had work to do. Serious work.

He leaned forward, steepling his hands under his chin as he glared at the farmhouse. Now that he had the cattle station on the western edges of his property sorted and in the capable hands of an under-manager, and he and station manager Fraser had dealt with all that needed overseeing for the operation of the sheep station and the planting and harvesting of the wheat crop, the only item left remaining was the canola contract.

He needed that locked in.

Once it was he'd be free to leave this godforsaken place. He'd shake off the dust of the poisonous memories that not only plagued his dreams at night but his waking hours too.

He leapt up, a familiar bitterness coating his tongue and the blackness of betrayal settling over him like a straitjacket. For the first time in his life he understood his father's retreat from the world. He recognised the same impulse in himself now. He gritted his teeth. He would *not* give into it.

Blasting out a breath, he glanced at his watch. 3:30 p.m. The woman had said she'd arrive somewhere between two and three o'clock. He slashed a hand through the air. Lucky she wasn't an employee.

Lucky for her, that was. He could fire an employee. He wrenched his gaze from the forty hectares of lovingly improved land that stretched out behind the farmhouse. Land he'd spent the last two years painstakingly improving—turning the soil, digging out rocks, fertilising…backbreaking work. And now…

He seized the contract he'd tossed onto the bench, rolled it up and slapped it against his legs. Once it was signed he could shake the dust of Bellaroo Creek from his feet for good. After that, his mother could deal with the new tenants.

And good luck to them.

He paced some more. He threw himself back to the bench

and kept his gaze firmly fixed on the road and not on those contentious forty hectares. Finally a car appeared at the end of the gravel road, moving slowly—a big, solid station wagon.

Cam didn't move from his spot in the shade, not even stirring when the breeze sent a light branch dancing across his hair, but every muscle in his body tightened. He dragged in a breath and counselled patience. He would explain the inadvertent mix-up to Tess Laing. He would *patiently* explain that a mistake had somehow seen his forty hectares included in her lease on the house. He would get her signature to turn those forty hectares back over to him. End of story.

If the mix-up had been inadvertent—an *honest* mistake. Bile burned his throat. Honesty and his family didn't necessarily go hand in hand. He expected betrayal from Lance. His nostrils flared and his lips thinned. He would never underestimate his little brother's treacherous resentment again. He would never again trust a word that spilled from Lance's forked tongue. But his mother, had she...?

An invisible hand tried to squeeze the air out of his lungs, but he ignored it to thrust out his jaw. Mistake or not, he needed that land. And he *would* get it back. He'd talk this woman out of whatever ridiculous hobby farm idea she'd come out here with. He'd offer her a fair price to lease the land back. He'd make whatever bargain he needed to. His hand curled around the contract. Once he had her signature, Kurrajong Station's obligations would be met. And he'd be free to head off for the far horizons of Africa.

Lance, Fiona and his mother could sink or swim on their own.

The car finally reached the farmhouse and pulled to a halt. He rested his elbows on his knees, eyes narrowed. Would she be some hard-nosed business type or a free-spirited hippy?

Three car doors were flung open and three passengers shot out from the car's interior like bottled fizzy water that had been shaken and then opened—a woman and two children. All of them raced around to the front of the car and bounced from one foot to the other as if they'd been cooped up for too long.

He studied the woman. She didn't look like a hard-nosed businesswoman. She didn't look like a nature-loving hippy either. She looked...

In her red-and-black tartan skirt, thick black tights and black Doc Martens she reminded him of a ladybird. Her movements, though, were pure willy wagtail—light, graceful...cheeky. In fact, she looked like a university student. He sat up straighter. She couldn't be old enough to have two kids!

He turned his attention to the children—a boy of around seven and a girl a year or two younger. He had a vague recollection of his mother mentioning their ages as being a real coup for the school. It was the main reason the committee had chosen this family from the flood of applicants.

A frown built inside him. They might be a coup for the school, but right now they were a disaster for him.

Finally he allowed himself a grim smile as the woman shook out her arms and legs as if she'd spent too many hours in the car—granted it was a bit of a hike from Sydney to Bellaroo Creek—and then moved to rest her hands on the front fence, a child standing either side of her. Her dark hair shone in the autumn sun. It made him realise how brightly the sun shone in the soft autumn stillness of the afternoon.

The boy glanced up at her, indecision flitting across his face. 'What do you think?' He glanced back at the cottage. 'Did you know it would look like this?'

Cam pursed his lips at the edge of disappointment lacing the boy's words. The little girl moved closer to the woman as if seeking reassurance. Cam straightened. If they hated the place they'd happily sign the whole kit and caboodle back over to him! That'd solve everything.

'I had no idea what it'd look like.'

Her voice sounded like music.

She beamed down at the children and then clasped her hands beneath her chin. 'Oh, but I think it's perfect!' She knelt on the ground, heedless of the danger to her tights, to put an arm about each of them.

The little girl pressed in against her. 'Really?'

'You do?' The little boy leaned against her too.

'Oh, yes!'

Cam wondered where she came by such confidence and enthusiasm. She was from the city. What did she know about country living?

Unless she'd known about those forty hectares before times and knew of their value. Unless Lance had already got to her, somehow. Unless—

'Look at the size of the yard. Just think how perfect it'll be once we've mown the lawn and trimmed back that hedge of…' She gestured with her head because it was obvious she didn't want to let go of either child.

'You don't know what it is,' the boy accused.

'I have no idea,' she agreed with one of the widest grins Cam had ever seen.

Plumbago. He could've told her, but something hard and heavy had settled in his stomach. He could've at least mown the lawn for them, couldn't he? He might've been flat out with organising the cattle station, the wheat crop and mustering sheep, but he should've found the time to manage at least that much. He mightn't want these new tenants—his mother had manipulated him superbly on that front—but that wasn't this woman's fault, or her children's.

'But won't it be fun finding out?'

'I guess.'

'And just imagine how pretty the cottage will look once we've painted it.'

She was going to paint his cottage?

'Pink!'

'Blue!'

'Cream!' She grinned back at the kids. 'We'll draw straws.'

He hoped she rigged that one.

The little girl started to jump up and down. 'We can have chickens!'

'And a dog!' The little boy started to jump too.

'And a lemon tree and pretty curtains at the window.' The woman laughed, bouncing back upright. 'And…?'

'And we'll all live happily ever after,' they hollered together in a chorus, and Cam found he couldn't drag his eyes from them.

It was just a house on an average acre block. But it hit him then what this property represented. A new start. And he knew exactly what that meant.

With everything in his soul.

The woman clapped her hands, claiming his attention once more. 'I think we should sing our song to our new perfect home.'

And they started to sing. The children held a wobbly melody and the woman harmonised, and they so loved their song and grinned so madly at each other that Cam found his lips lifting upwards.

'The house loves us now,' the little girl whispered.

'I believe you're right.'

'I love a veranda,' the little boy said and Cam knew it was his way of saying he approved of the house…of their new start.

The woman smiled *that* smile again and Cam had to shift on his bench. 'Right,' she said, dusting off her hands, 'what we need now is the key.'

That was his cue.

He hadn't meant to sit here for so long watching them without declaring himself. He'd only thought—hoped—that a moment's observation would give him the measure of his new tenants. Except… He found himself more confounded than ever.

'That'd be where I come in.'

Both children literally jumped out of their skins at his abrupt declaration and he found himself wishing he'd cleared his throat first to give them warning of his presence.

The little girl ducked behind the woman, her hands clutching fistfuls of the woman's shirt. The boy wavered for a moment or two and then moved in front of the woman, face pale and hands clenched, but obviously determined to protect her. It was a simple act of courage that knocked Cam sideways. His heart started to pound.

The woman reached out and tousled the boy's hair and pulled him back in against her. She kept her voice solidly cheerful. 'Aha! You'll be our emissary from the town.'

Not quite, but... 'I have your key.'

'Good Lord!' She planted her hands on her hips as he emerged more fully into the sunlight. 'Look at the size of you. I bet you're a big help to your mum.'

And beside her both children immediately relaxed, and he found himself careful to keep the smile on his face and to move towards them slowly. 'Actually, I guess I'm your landlord. I'm Cameron Manning.'

She frowned. 'I thought Lorraine...'

'My mother.'

'Ah.' She nodded, and then a cheeky grin peeked out. 'The mother you're such a big help to, no doubt.'

Actually, there was every doubt in the world on that head.

'I'm Tess, and this is Tyler and Kristina—Ty and Krissie for short—and we're very pleased to meet you.'

She held out her hand and he moved the final few feet forward to shake it. With such dark hair—nearly black— he'd thought she'd be pale but she had skin the colour of deep golden honey. Her palm slid against his, smooth and cool. Large brown eyes surveyed him with undisguised intensity as if attempting to sum up the man beneath the bulk.

She smelled of liquorice and cool days, and when he finally stepped back Cam found his heart pounding.

'Can you ride a horse?' Tyler asked, awe stretching through his voice.

'I can.'

'I want to be a cowboy when I grow up.'

'Then you've come to the right town,' Cam said, though he could hardly believe that he spoke them. He hadn't meant to be so welcoming. He'd meant to be businesslike and brisk. But that boy had stepped in front of his mother when he'd thought she'd needed protecting. There were grown men who were afraid to take Cam on physically. At six feet three and sporting the kind of muscles that hard work on the land developed, he understood that reluctance.

He was big and he was strong. Yet, still, this little boy had faced his fear and Cam couldn't ignore that.

'Auntie Tess—' the little girl tugged on the woman's sleeve '—I've gotta go.'

Auntie? She wasn't their mother?

'Right.' She stared at him expectantly. 'The key?'

He recalled how he'd considered talking them out of this property. The contract he'd left sitting on the bench fluttered in the breeze. He considered Tyler's act of courage and Krissie's excitement about chickens and the way Tess had quieted the children's fears with a song.

A new start. He knew all about the need for those.

He fished the key out of his pocket and handed it over.

The three of them raced to the front door of the old farmhouse. Cam retrieved his contract and then stood under the Kurrajong tree and dragged in a breath. Okay, the house was neither here nor there. He had no plans for it. Those forty hectares, though, did matter and he wanted—needed—Tess's signature on the dotted line.

And he wasn't leaving until he had it.

He followed them into the house.

'Bags this room!' Tyler shouted from the corridor off to the right. 'It has a view of the front and I can see who's coming, which is good 'cause I'm the man of the house.'

That almost made Cam smile again, only he remembered how pale the boy had gone when Cam had appeared unannounced.

The toilet flushed, the sound of water running in a tap and then Krissie raced down the corridor too. 'Auntie Tess, this is your room! And this one is mine 'cause it's right next to yours!'

Cam let out a breath as he glanced around. The yard might need some TLC, but the women from the Save-Our-Town committee had cleaned this place to within an inch of its life. The furniture might be mismatched—favouring comfort more than elegance—but there wasn't a single dust bunny in sight. 'Coffee?' he called out, wanting Tess to know he'd followed them into the house.

'Excellent idea,' she called back.

He strode into the kitchen and put the jug on to boil. The farmhouse wasn't fancy by any means, but it had a certain homey charm. He had the impression that Tess would turn it into a home in the blink of an eye.

What on earth was he talking about? He shook his head. She already had, and he wasn't sure how. It took more than a smile and a song to make a home.

Didn't it?

He let himself out of the back door, the contract burning a hole against his palm as he moved down the steps to stare out at those magical forty hectares. She was paying a dollar a week in rent for all that. It was enough to make a grown man weep.

He straightened. He had a canola contract to fulfil—he'd given his word—and he wasn't going to let anyone steal it out from under him. His lips twisted. He didn't doubt for a moment that one person in particular in Bellaroo Creek would try to do exactly that, but would his mother be party to such duplicity?

'You better get that particular look off your face quick smart or you'll give Ty and Krissie nightmares for a month.'

He blinked to find Tess holding a mug out to him. He frowned. 'I was supposed to be making those.' He'd meant to make a stab at the country-hospitality approach first before bombarding her with his demand. Besides, she had dark circles beneath those magnificent eyes of hers. If she'd left two hours from the other side of Sydney this morning she'd have driven for the best part of eight hours.

The least he could've done was make her a cup of coffee. And mow the lawn. And trim that hedge of plumbago.

'No matter, and sorry but I put milk in it before I thought. If you want sugar—'

'No, this is great,' he said hastily. 'Thanks.'

Her lips twitched. 'You didn't strike me as a sugar-in-their-coffee type.'

What was that supposed to mean?

She stared out at the fields and drew a breath deep into her lungs. 'Oh, my, look at it all!'

His skin tightened. His muscles tensed.

'You live in a beautiful part of the world, Cameron.'

'Cam.' The correction came out husky. The only person to call him Cameron was his mother. 'But you're right.' He nodded towards the fields. 'It's beautiful.'

And by rights it should be his. He spun to her. 'There's something—'

'I want to apologise for being late.'

He blinked at her interruption. 'No problem.'

'We had one threat of car sickness.'

He grimaced.

'And I took a wrong turn when we left Parkes. I started heading towards Trundle instead of Bellaroo Creek.'

'That's in completely the opposite direction.'

'That's what a man on a tractor told us.'

He shifted his weight, opened his mouth.

She pointed back behind her with an infectious grin. 'Do you know somebody left us a cake?'

He found one side of his mouth hitching up at her delight. 'That'd be my mother. I'd know her sultana cake anywhere. It's her speciality.'

'Then you must stay for a slice.'

He adjusted his stance. 'Look, there's something I need to talk to you about.'

Her gaze had dropped to take an inventory of his shoulders and he could feel himself tensing up again, but at his words her eyes lifted. She sipped her coffee. 'Yes?'

'It's about that land out there.' He gestured out in front of them.

'Wow! Look how big the yard is!'

With whoops, Ty and Krissie swooped down the back steps and into the yard. Cam winced at how overgrown it all was.

'What kind of tree is that, Auntie Tess?'

She shaded her eyes and peered to where Krissie pointed. 'Tell me?' she shot out of the corner of her mouth and it made him want to laugh. 'Please?'

'Lemon tree,' he answered in an undertone.

She turned and beamed at him. It cracked open something wide inside him—something that made him hot and cold at the same time. Before he could react in any way whatsoever, she set her coffee to the ground, danced down to the lemon tree and the children with her arms outstretched as if to embrace them all. But he could've sworn she'd whispered, 'Smile,' at him before she'd danced away.

'It's a lemon tree!'

The children cheered. They all started rattling off the things they'd make with the lemons—lemonade, lemon butter, lemon-meringue pie, lemon chicken, lemon tea—as if it were a litany they'd learned off by heart. As if it were a list that made the world a better place.

And as he watched them Cam thought that maybe it did.

'Where do you live, um…Mr…?'

He gazed down at Krissie with her blonde curls, and her big brown eyes identical to Tess's, and recalled the way she'd jumped when he'd first spoken. *Smile.* 'You can call me Cam,' he said, making his voice gentle. 'If that's okay with your auntie Tess.'

Tess nodded her assent, but he was aware that she watched him like a hawk—or a mother bear hell-bent on protecting her cubs.

'You can see my house from here.' He led them towards the line of Kurrajong trees at the side fence and gestured across the acre field to his home beyond.

'Wow,' Ty breathed. 'It's big.'

It was, and the sandstone homestead was a point of local pride. 'My great-great-great-grandfather was one of the first settlers in the area. His son built that house.'

'Is it a farm?'

'It is. It's called Kurrajong Station because of all the Kurrajong trees. It's large for these parts at six thousand hectares.' It wasn't a boast, just pure fact.

'What do you farm?'

That was Tess. He eyed her for a moment. He sure as hell hoped she didn't have any interests in that direction. 'Cattle, sheep and wheat mostly.' And just as soon as he had his forty hectares back he'd be branching out into canola. Diversification would ensure Kurrajong's future. And once that was all in place, he could leave.

For good.

'Are we allowed to play in that field?'

Ty glanced up at him hopefully. Cam bit back a sigh. He didn't have anything against the Save-Our-Town scheme in principle. He mightn't want to live in Bellaroo Creek any longer, but his station's prosperity did, to some extent, hinge on the town's ongoing existence. It was just that in practical terms...

So much for his jealously guarded privacy.

Still, they were just kids. They wouldn't disturb his peace too much. And kids would be kids—they'd want to explore, kick balls, run. Besides, he sensed that these kids needed more kindness than most. Rather than declare the paddock out of bounds, he found himself saying, 'You'd better wait till you've made friends with my dog first.'

Ty's face lit up. 'You have a dog? When can we meet him?'

Cam shoved his hands in his pockets and glanced at Tess. 'Tomorrow?'

She nodded. 'Excellent.'

Her cap of dark hair glowed in the sun and her eyes were bigger than they had any right to be. He gave himself a mental kick and turned back to the kids. 'I want you both to promise me something. If you see a paddock with either cows or big machinery in it, promise you won't go into it. It could be dangerous.'

They gazed up at him with eyes too solemn for their age and nodded.

Lord, he didn't mean to frighten them. *Smile!* 'We just want to make sure you stay safe, okay?'

They nodded again.

'And you shouldn't go outside your own yard or this paddock without letting your auntie Tess know first.'

Tess watched Cam as he talked with the children. His initial gruffness apparently hid a natural gentleness for all those smaller than him. Not that there'd be too many who'd be larger! The longer she watched, the more aware she became of the warmth stealing over her.

She shook it off. She wanted this move to be perfect. She wanted to believe that everyone in Bellaroo Creek would have

Ty and Krissie's best interests at heart. She wasn't going to let that hope lead her astray, though. Too much depended on her making the right decisions. She swallowed, her heart still burning at the children's reactions when Cam had startled them—their instinctive fear and suspicion.

She gripped her hands together. Please, please, please let moving to Bellaroo Creek be the right decision. Please, please, please let the children learn to trust again. Please, God, help her make them feel secure and safe, loved.

She relaxed her hands and crossed her fingers. After the initial shaky start, it certainly looked as if the kids had taken to their laconic neighbour. After all, not only did he know how to ride a horse, but he had a dog too. True hero material.

Her gaze drifted down his denim-clad legs and a long slow sigh built up inside her. He could certainly fill out a pair of jeans nicely. With cheeks suddenly burning, she wrenched her gaze away. For heaven's sake, she hadn't moved to Bellaroo Creek for that kind of fresh start!

Besides—she glanced up at him through her lashes—Cameron Manning was a man with something on his mind. She'd sensed it the moment he'd stepped out of the shadows of the trees. She had relaxed a little, though, when he'd handed over the key. She had no intention of handing it back. She'd signed a legally binding lease. She'd paid the first year's rent up front. All fifty-two dollars of it.

The children ran off further down the backyard to explore, but even while she sensed he wanted to talk, she didn't suggest they go inside to do just that. She wanted to keep an eye on Ty and Krissie. She wanted them to know she was nearby. She wanted to share in the joy of their discoveries. She had every intention of smoothing over any little concerns or ripples that threatened their well-being.

That was her first priority. That mattered a million times more than anything else at the moment. Joy, love and hope—

that was what these kids needed and that was exactly what they were going to get.

She shot Cam another half-veiled glance. Still, if he was happy to talk out here… 'I—'

'You're their auntie Tess?'

She blinked.

'Where are their parents?'

Ah. She'd thought the entire town would know their story considering she hadn't been reticent about the details in her application. In fact, she'd shamelessly used those details in an attempt to tug on all the unknown heartstrings that would be reading their application.

They walked back towards the house. Tess swooped down to pick up her abandoned coffee from the grass. She chugged back its lukewarm contents and then let the mug dangle loosely from her fingers. 'Why is your surname different from your mother's?'

'I'm the son from her first marriage.'

Right. She nodded towards the children. 'Their father and mother—my sister—died in a car accident three months ago.'

He stilled. 'I'm sorry.'

He sounded genuinely sympathetic and her eyes started to burn. Even now, three months down the track and a million tears later, she still found condolences hard to deal with. But Cameron's voice sounded low and deep—the tone and breadth midway between an oboe and a cello—and somehow that made it easier. She nodded and kicked herself back into an aimless meandering around the yard.

'Are you interested in farming? In keeping cattle or horses or growing a crop?'

The abrupt change of topic took her off guard. 'God, no!' She hoped he didn't take her horror personally, but she didn't know the first thing about farming. She didn't know much about vegetable gardens or keeping chickens either, she supposed, but she could learn. 'Why?'

'Because there's been a bit of a mix-up with the tenancy agreement.'

Her blood chilled. Just like that. In an instant. Her toes and fingers froze rigid. He couldn't kick them out! *He'd given them the key.*

The children loved this place. *She'd* made sure they'd fallen in love with it—had used her enthusiasm and assumed confidence to give it all a magical promise. Ty and Krissie weren't resilient enough to deal with another disappointment.

And they didn't deserve to.

'I mean, yes,' she snapped out as quickly as she could. 'Farming is exactly the reason we're out here.'

He frowned. In fact, it might be described as a scowl. But then he glanced at the kids and it became just a frown again. 'I beg your pardon?'

She didn't like the barely leashed control stretching through his voice, but he was not kicking them out. 'What I'm trying to say is that I'm fully prepared to learn farming if that's part of my contract.'

She'd gone over the contract with a fine-tooth comb. She'd consulted a solicitor. Her chin lifted. She'd signed a legally binding contract. She *had* understood it. The solicitor had ensured that. She wasn't in the wrong here. A fine trembling started up in her legs, but she stood her ground. 'I'm not going to let you kick us out.' She even managed to keep her voice perfectly pleasant. 'Just so you know.'

'I don't want to kick you out.'

That was when she knew he was lying. Even though he'd been kind to the children. Even though he'd handed over the key. This man would love it if they left.

Didn't he want to save his town?

By this stage they'd reached the back fence. She set her mug on a fencepost, and then leant against it and folded her arms. 'It's been a long day, Mr Manning, so I'm going to speak plainly.'

He blinked at the formality of her *Mr Manning*. And she saw he understood the sudden distance she'd created between them.

'I signed a contract and I understand my rights. If there's been a mix-up then it hasn't been of my making.' She folded her arms tighter. 'Whatever this mix-up may be, the children and I are not leaving this house. We're living here for the next three years and we're going to carve out a new life for ourselves and we are going to make that work. This is now our home and we're going to make it a good home. Furthermore, you are not going to say anything in front of the children that might upset or alarm them—you hear me?'

His mouth opened and closed. 'I wouldn't dream of it.'

He leaned towards her and he smelled like fresh-cut grass, and it smelled so fresh and young that she wanted to bury her face against his neck and just breathe it in. She shook herself. It'd been a long trip. Very long. 'Then smile!' she snapped.

To her utter astonishment, he laughed, and the grim lines that hooded his eyes and weighed down the corners of his mouth all lightened, and his eyes sparkled, the same deep green as clover.

Her breath caught. The man wasn't just big and broad and a great help to his mum—he was beautiful!

The blood started to thump in a painful pulse about her body. Four months ago she'd have flirted with Cam in an attempt to lighten him up. Three months ago she'd have barely noticed him. It was amazing the changes a single month could bring. One day. In fact, lives could change in a single moment.

And they did.

And they had.

She swallowed. The particular moment that had turned her life on its head might not have been her fault, but if she'd been paying attention she might've been able to avert it. That knowledge would plague her to her grave.

And men, beautiful and otherwise, were completely off the agenda.

She snapped away from him. He frowned. 'Tess, I'm not going to ask you to leave. I swear. This house is all yours for the next three years, and beyond if you want it.'

She bit her lip, glanced back at him. 'Really?'

'Really.'

'Still—' she stuck out a hip '—you're less than enthused about it.'

He hesitated and then shrugged. 'My mother has, in effect, foisted you lot on to me.'

She glanced at the house and then back at him. 'Isn't the house hers?'

'Not precisely.' He exhaled loudly. 'My father made certain provisions for my mother in his will. She has the use of this house along with an attached parcel of land for as long as she lives. When she passes the rights all revert back to the owner of Kurrajong Station.'

'You?'

'Me.'

She pursed her lips. He met her gaze steadily. She wanted to get a handle on this enigmatic neighbour of hers. Was he friend or foe? 'Don't you want to help save Bellaroo Creek?'

'Sure I do.'

'As long as you're not asked to sacrifice too much in the effort, right?'

'As long as I'm not asked to give up a significant portion of my potential income in the process,' he countered.

'How will our being here impact negatively on your income?' Her understanding was that the Save-Our-Town scheme only offered *unused* farmhouses in exchange for ludicrously cheap rents. If their farmhouse was unused he couldn't possibly be losing money. In fact, he'd be fifty-two dollars a year richer.

Her lips suddenly twitched. Cameron Manning didn't

strike her as the kind of man who'd stress too much over fifty-two dollars. Not that she needed to stress over money either. It hadn't been the cheap rent but the promise of a fresh start that had lured her out here.

He drew in a breath and then pointed behind her. She turned. 'Forty hectares,' he said. 'Forty hectares I had plans for. Forty hectares my mother had promised to lease to me.'

She slapped a hand to her forehead. 'They were allotted to me in my tenancy agreement? That's the mix-up you're talking about.'

'Yep.'

'And you want them back?'

'Bingo.'

She laughed in her sudden rush of relief. 'Oh, honey, they're all yours.' What on earth did she want with forty hectares of wide, open space? She had a house and a back-yard and a whole ocean of possibilities enough to satisfy her.

She clapped her hands. 'Hey, troops, who's for sultana cake?'

CHAPTER TWO

It took Tess until her second bite of sultana cake to realise she hadn't allayed her sexy neighbour's concerns.

She stiffened. Umm…not sexy. Taciturn and self-contained, perhaps, and, um… She dragged her gaze from shoulders so broad they made her think of Greek gods and swimsuits and the Mediterranean.

Sleep, rest, peace, that was what she needed. The last month had been a crazy whirlwind and she quite literally hadn't stopped. The two months prior had been a blur of pain and grief.

She flinched at the memory and brushed a hand across her eyes. Bellaroo Creek would bring her the rest and the sleep she craved, but peace? She wasn't sure anything on earth could bring her that.

And she wasn't sure she deserved it.

Cameron hitched an eyebrow. 'A penny for them.'

She stiffened again. Nu-huh. But the exhaustion made her silly—an after-effect of the nonsense she'd used all day to keep the children entertained and in good spirits. 'Are you sure you can afford a penny when I'm only paying you a dollar a week in rent?'

His green eyes gleamed for a tantalizing moment. It made him look younger. She dragged her gaze away and rose. 'I'll just check on the kids. The promise of cake should've had them sprinting inside.'

On cue, the pair came racing through the front door. 'We found a lizard,' Ty announced, breathless with excitement.

'Will it bite us?' Krissie asked, wide-eyed.

She directed the question at Cam. He'd obviously become the source of trusted information. Tess's chest cramped as she stared at them—took in their simple wonder.

'That'll be Old Nelson, the blue-tongue,' Cam said, leaning back in his chair, one long, lean leg stretched out in front of him.

Krissie's eyes widened even further. 'He has a name?'

'Wow, awesome!' Ty breathed. 'Will he bite?'

'Only if you poke him or try to pick him up.'

'Can we take our cake outside, Auntie Tess?'

With a laugh, Tess assented. She watched as they left the room and her chest burned. If only Sarah could see them now. If only—

'You okay?'

She jumped, swung back patting her chest. 'Tired,' she said. She sat and forced a smile. She'd become good at that over the last couple of months—smiling when she didn't feel like it—but she could see it didn't fool Cam. She shrugged. 'They've been through so much, but for this moment they're happy and...and that's no small thing.'

He stared towards the front of the house and then glanced back at her. 'They're great kids, Tess.'

She nodded. 'They really are.' And they deserved so much more than life had dished out to them. Focusing on the negatives wouldn't help anyone, though—least of all Ty and Krissie. She sipped tea. Cam had made a pot while she'd sliced the cake. It was the best tea she'd ever tasted.

She lifted her cup. 'This is seriously good.'

'My mother was the president of the Country Women's

Association for a hundred years. Believe me, she made sure her sons knew how to brew a proper pot of tea.'

She made a mental note to join the CWA. But for the moment… 'You want to tell me why you're still so worried about your forty hectares?'

His eyes widened a fraction, but he held her gaze with a steadiness she found disconcerting. 'I had a contract drawn up. I need you to sign it before I can start planting.'

He whipped out a sheaf of papers, literally from thin air as far as her tired brain could tell. He flicked through to the final page and pointed. 'I need your signature here.' He handed her a pen.

She lowered her cup back to its saucer and dropped her hands to her lap. 'I'm not signing anything I haven't read.'

'Fair enough.' He placed the contract in front of her and leaned back.

'And I'm not reading it now when I'm so tired.'

He frowned.

'And if there's something I don't understand, I'll be consulting my solicitor for clarification.'

He was silent for a long moment and the silence should've sawn on her nerves, but it didn't. After a day of chatter and noise in the confines of the car, the silence was heaven.

'You don't trust me,' he finally said, nodding as if that made perfect sense.

'I don't know you. Once upon a time I'd have been prepared to take spur-of-the-moment risks and trust my gut instincts, but I won't now Tyler and Krissie are in my care.' She leant towards him. 'Are you saying you trust me?' She waved a hand in the direction of the back door and his precious forty hectares. 'By all means start planting tomorrow. I'll keep my word. I'll get the contract back to you by the middle of next week.'

His lips twisted but his eyes danced. 'Nope, don't trust you as far as I could throw you.'

Given his size and the breadth of his shoulders, she had a feeling he could throw her a long way if he so chose.

This time it was he who leaned in towards her, and that fresh-cut-grass scent danced around her and it was almost as relaxing as silence. 'But I do need to get started on the planting soon if I'm to meet my obligations.'

'I promise not to drag my feet.' She wanted to be on good terms with her neighbours and the townsfolk of Bellaroo Creek. She just had to make sure she didn't risk the children's futures in her eagerness to fit in.

Without thinking, she reached out and touched his hand. He immediately stiffened and she snatched her hand back, her heart suddenly thundering in her ears. 'I, uh... You said you'd bring your dog around to meet the children. Why don't you aim to do that tomorrow morning some time—say, ten o'clock? I'll try and have your contract read by then.'

'If you need more time...'

Her pulse rate refused to slow. 'No, no, it's obvious that time is of the essence. Besides, the kids will no doubt be up early and we have a midday meet-and-greet luncheon at the community hall, so I should have plenty of time in the morning to go over this contract of yours.'

He rose in one swift motion. 'I'll see you at ten.' And then he was gone.

She heard him say goodbye to the children. She supposed she should've followed him to the door to wave him off, but the strength had leached from her legs and she found herself momentarily incapable of even rising from her chair. She'd spent nearly ten hours in the car today. She was dog-tired. She'd just turned her entire life on its head—hers and the children's. And if this move didn't work out...

She shook that thought off. This move had to work out. In the meantime, she refused to allow her sexy neighbour to unsettle her.

She frowned. He *wasn't* sexy.

She glanced at her empty plate, and then at Cam's and realised he hadn't touched his cake—he hadn't even broken off
the tiniest corner. She hadn't been hungry for the last three
months—ever since she'd received the phone call informing
her of Sarah's car accident. But now…

She stared at the cake. She pulled the plate towards her and
then poured another cup of tea. She devoured both, slowly,
relishing every single delicious mouthful.

The children made instant friends with Boomer, Cam's border collie.

'Will he fetch a ball?' Ty asked, pulling a tennis ball from
his pocket.

Cam's mouth angled up in a lopsided smile as he surveyed
Ty and Krissie and their barely concealed eagerness. 'Believe
me, he'll fetch for longer than you'll be prepared to throw.'
With whoops of delight, the children raced around the backyard with Boomer at their heels.

He had a way of smiling at her kids—and, yes, somewhere in the last month she'd started thinking of them as
hers—that could melt a woman where she stood. 'Morning,'
he finally said, the green of his eyes strangely undiluted in
the mid-morning sun.

'It will be,' she countered, 'if you'll teach me the trick to
making a perfect pot of tea.'

He laughed and it was only then she saw that while his
eyes might be the purest of greens, shadows lurked in their
depths. Shadows momentarily dispelled when he laughed.

He followed her into the kitchen. 'One demonstration coming up.'

He should laugh more often. 'Jug's just boiled,' she said,
shaking the odd thought aside. Cam might well laugh a hundred times every single day for all she knew.

'Did you fill the jug using hot or cold water?'

'Hot. It makes it come to the boil faster.'

'There's your first mistake.' He poured the contents of the jug down the sink and refilled it from the cold tap. 'Cold water has more oxygen than hot. That's key for the perfect cuppa.'

She sat and stared. 'Well, who'd have known that?' Other than a chemistry professor. And a president of the CWA... and her sons.

He sat too, his eyes twinkling for the briefest of moments. 'It's important to be properly trained in country ways.'

'I never doubted it for a moment.' She leapt up to glance out of the kitchen window to make sure the children were okay. When she swung back she could've sworn he'd been checking out her backside.

His gaze slid away. Her heart thumped. She'd imagined it. She must've imagined it. She frowned, scratched a hand through her hair and tried to think of something to say.

'Did you get a chance to read the contract?'

Of course she'd imagined it, but the shadows were back in his eyes with a vengeance and it left a bitter taste in her mouth, though for the life of her she couldn't explain why. 'Yes.' She took her seat again.

'And?'

The contract had been remarkably straightforward. It hadn't asked her to give up her firstborn or sign her rights away to the house and the acre block it stood on. It simply requested she sign over the attached forty hectares of land and to waive her rights to any profits he accrued from the use of the land. Except...

On the table, one of his hands tightened. 'You have a problem?'

She hauled in a breath and nodded. 'I do.'

'You want more money for the lease?'

She hated the derisive light that entered his eyes. She pushed the contract towards him. 'I made my amendment in black ink. That's what I'm prepared to sign.'

Blowing out a breath, he pulled the contract towards him

and flipped through the pages to the end. And then he stilled and rubbed his forehead. 'You don't want any payment at all?'

She rubbed her hands up and down her arms. What kind of people was he used to dealing with? 'Of course I don't want any payment! I'm not entitled to any payment. Rightfully the land is yours. If you want to pay anyone a fee for leasing the land, then pay your mother.'

He sat back. 'I've offended you.'

Why did the wonder in his voice suddenly make her want to cry? Since Sarah's death, the silliest, most unexpected things could make her cry. 'You will if you keep going on in that vein.'

Her voice came out husky and choked. His gaze lowered to her mouth and it gave her a moment to study him. He had a strong jaw and lean lips and she couldn't tear her eyes away. She could keep telling herself that he wasn't sexy, but he was. His eyes darkened. A pulse throbbed in her bottom lip, swelling it and making it ache. The heat in the air between them sizzled with such unmistakable intensity it made her head whirl. With an oath, Cam pushed away from the table. He seized the teapot and started making tea. She closed her eyes. She'd been surrounded by death, preoccupied with it. Life wanted to reassert itself. This—her body's rebellion at her common-sense strictures—was normal.

The explanation didn't make the pounding in her blood lessen any, but it did start to clear the fog encasing her brain.

She jumped when Cam set a mug of tea in front of her, his face a mask. 'I'm sorry. I didn't mean to offend you. I'm just used to paying my own way.'

She wasn't. Not really. Her cold realisation dissipated the last of the heat. She'd always relied on staff or assistants to take care of her day-to-day needs. But she could learn. She *was* learning.

He hooked out his chair again and sat. 'A free ride feels wrong.'

'It's not a free ride. A free ride is if I also did the planting for you. You'd discussed that land with your mother. You had her permission to use it. Like you said, the fact it ended up on my lease agreement was simply an error or an oversight. Cameron, I have no plans for that land. I'm not losing out on anything.'

He didn't say anything.

'Besides, don't knock a free ride. I'm getting one—a dollar a week rent! Who'd have thought that was possible?'

His lips turned upwards, but it wasn't really a smile. 'You've brought two school-age children into the area. You're boosting the school's numbers and increasing its chances of remaining open. The town will think it a very good swap.'

Speaking of children… She rose and went to the window again to check on them. She laughed at what she saw. 'Are you sure they won't wear Boomer out?'

'I'm positive.' He eyed her as she took her seat again. 'They are safe with him. I promise.'

'Oh! Of course they are. I didn't mean…' She could feel herself starting to colour under his stare. The thing was, most days she felt as if she didn't know a darn thing about parenting at all. Maybe she did fuss a little too much, worry too much, but surely that was better than not fussing enough.

That was when the idea hit her.

He leant towards her, his eyes wary. 'What?'

She surveyed him over the rim of her mug. 'You're obviously not very comfortable with me just handing the land back to you.'

'You could make a tidy profit from the lease.'

'Believe me, the one thing I don't need to worry about is money.' Sarah had seen to that. 'But maybe,' she started slowly, allowing the idea to develop more fully in her mind, 'we could do a kind of swap. I'll give you the land…'

'In exchange for what?'

She rose and went to the window again. She loved those

kids. Just how fiercely amazed her. She'd do anything for them. *Anything.* And what she needed to do most was provide them with a positive start here in Bellaroo Creek.

Cam stared at Tess as she peered out of the kitchen window again. She had a stillness and a straightness, even when agitated, that he found intriguing.

And she had the cutest little butt he'd ever seen. There'd probably been a hint of its perfect roundness in her tartan skirt yesterday if he'd been looking, but there was no hiding it in a pair of fitted jeans that hugged every curve with enviable snugness.

And today he was definitely looking!

For heaven's sake, he was male. Men looked at—and appreciated—the female form. It was how they were wired. It didn't mean anything.

But he hadn't looked at a woman in that way since Fiona, and—

With a scowl, he dragged his gaze away. He needed to keep on task. Tess was proposing a deal of sorts. He glanced up to find her watching him, her brow furrowed as if she couldn't figure him out. Not that he blamed her.

'You can take the contract and run,' she said. She walked back to the table, seized the contract, signed and dated it and then handed it back to him. 'Nothing more needs to be said. I don't believe you're beholden to me, not one jot.'

Honour kept him in his seat. Tess hadn't taken advantage of the situation as she could've done. As Lance and Fiona would've done. He did his best to clear the scowl from his face. She'd been reasonable and...generous. 'What kind of bargain were you going to propose, Tess?'

'I want to make moving to Bellaroo Creek a really positive experience for Ty and Krissie.'

She hadn't needed to say that out loud. He could see how much it meant to her. He wanted to tell her how much he admired her for it, but he didn't. He didn't want her to think he'd mean anything more by it than simple admiration. Because he wouldn't.

'But frankly I'm clueless.'

That snapped him back. 'About?'

She lifted her arms and let them drop. 'Everything! I didn't even know that was a lemon tree and yet you heard all our plans for it.'

Something inside him unhitched.

'I don't know the first thing about keeping chickens, but Krissie has her heart set on it. I expect I need a…a hutch or something.'

'Henhouse.'

'See? I don't even have the right vocabulary. And what about a vegetable garden? Other than supposing there's a lot of digging involved, I haven't the foggiest idea where to start.' She frowned. 'I expect I'll need compost.'

And, suddenly, Cam found himself laughing. 'Believe me, Tess, the one thing we aren't short of in Bellaroo Creek is compost.'

She gripped her hands on the table in front of her and leant towards him. 'Plus I need to get Ty a puppy, but is a puppy and chickens a seriously bad combination?'

'They don't have to be.' He leaned across and covered both of her hands with one of his own. She stiffened and he remembered the way he'd stiffened at her touch yesterday and was about to remove his hand when she relaxed. Her hands felt small and cold and instead of retreating he found his hand urging warmth into hers instead.

'So you want help building a henhouse and a veggie patch, and in selecting a dog?'

'It has to be a puppy. Apparently that's very important.'

Cam understood that. He nodded.

'And maybe some help choosing chickens?'

She winced as if she were asking too much, but it was all

a piece of cake as far as he was concerned. 'Tess, helping you with that stuff is nothing more than being neighbourly.'

The townsfolk of Bellaroo Creek would have his hide if he didn't offer her that kind of support. Though—his lips twisted—he expected there'd be quite a few single farmers in the area who wouldn't mind offering her any kind of help whatsoever.

'Then…maybe we can agree to being good neighbours. That's something else I can learn to do.'

He frowned, but before he could say anything she leapt up to glance out of the window again. 'And until I manage to get one of my own, may I borrow your lawnmower?'

'Done.'

She swung around and beamed at him. 'Thank you. Now watch me as I make a fresh pot of tea to make sure I'm doing it right.'

She had the kind of smile—when she really smiled—that could blow a man clean out of his boots. Mentally, he pulled his boots up harder and tighter.

'Why can't Cam come to our party?'

Excellent question. Tess glanced briefly in the rear-view mirror to give Krissie an encouraging smile. 'He said he had lots of work to do.'

'I bet he had to take time off work to bring Boomer around to play,' Ty said from the seat beside her. It was his turn in the front. 'His farm is really big, isn't it?'

'Six thousand hectares is what he said.' And Cameron didn't strike her as the bragging type. He was definitely the state-plain-facts type. 'Which I think is really, really big.'

'So he probably has loads and loads of work to do.'

Was that admiration or wistfulness in Ty's voice? She couldn't tell.

A mother would know.

She gulped. 'Good thinking, Ty, I expect you're right.'

His chest puffed out at her simple praise. Blinking hard, she concentrated on the road in front of her.

It only took three minutes to drive from their front door to the community hall in Bellaroo Creek's tiny main street. Across from the hall stood a row of late-Victorian town-houses—tall, straight, eye-catching, but with all their windows boarded up. Whatever businesses had operated from them were long gone. Once upon a time the town had been prosperous. Tess crossed her fingers. Hopefully they could help make the town prosperous again.

Unhooking her seat belt, she turned to the children. 'Ready?' They watched her so carefully. She knew they'd take their every cue from her. The realisation made her swallow. She had to get this just right.

Krissie leaned forward. 'Is this party really just for us?'

'It sure is, chickadee. Everyone is dying to meet us. They're so excited we've come to live in Bellaroo Creek.'

'What if they don't like us?' she whispered.

Tess feigned shock. 'Do you really think they won't like me?'

Krissie giggled. 'Not you, silly.'

'They'll love you,' Ty announced.

She knew what he was really saying was that he loved her and it made her heart swell and her eyes sting. 'And I absolutely promise that they'll love the two of you too.'

They stared at her with their identical brown eyes—eyes the same as Sarah's. They trusted her so much! She racked her brain to think of a way to make this easier for them.

'You know,' she started, 'it can be a bit awkward making new friends at first, and I bet they're just as worried that we should like them too.' She could see that thought hadn't occurred to either child. 'Sometimes it helps to have something ready to talk about. So...when you're talking to someone today you might like to ask them what their favourite thing about living in Bellaroo Creek is, or if they have a dog, or if they keep chickens.'

Both children's faces cleared immediately.

'Ooh!' She clapped her hands. 'I could send you both on a quest to find out what everyone thinks would be the best vegetables to grow in our backyard.'

Ty squinted up at her. 'Because that's important, right?'

'Vital,' she assured him.

He grinned. 'And you could find out how to make Cam's mum's cake.'

She pointed a finger at him. 'Excellent idea!' She straightened her shirt. 'And I'm going to remember to smile nicely at everyone and remember to say please and thank you in all the right places. Ready?'

The children nodded. They tumbled out of the car and, holding tight to each other's hands, they entered the hall together.

Tess blinked. There had to be at least thirty people in here! As well as one seriously long trestle table covered with more sandwiches, pies, quiches, cakes, slices and biscuits than Tess had seen altogether in one place. The sight of all that food, and all those faces, made her head spin. A hush fell over the crowd.

Thirty people, and yet for one craven moment she'd have given anything to swap ten of them for the familiar reassuring bulk of Cameron Manning. Which was crazy because she didn't know Cameron well enough for him to be either familiar or reassuring. But so far Bellaroo Creek consisted of their farmhouse, their lemon tree and Cameron.

All these people will become your community, your friends, too.

First-day nerves, that was all that this was. Taking a deep breath, Tess beamed about the room. 'Hi, I'm Tess, and this here is Ty and Krissie. We can't tell you how happy we are to be in Bellaroo Creek and how much we're looking forward to meeting everyone.'

A tall, straight woman detached herself from the crowd. 'I'm Lorraine Pritchard, and we're all absolutely delighted that you've joined our little community.'

And just like that the silence was replaced with a hubbub of voices, and the three of them were swept into the heart of the crowd. An older woman—Stacy Bennet, the schoolteacher—whisked Ty and Krissie off to join a small band of children, stopping by the refreshment table to make sure they armed themselves with a fairy cake each first, and thereby winning herself two friends for life.

'The children will be fine with Stacy,' Lorraine told her kindly.

Of course they would. The same way they'd been fine with Boomer this morning. It was just…she hated losing sight of them, even for a moment. Telling herself to stop being so silly, she turned back to Lorraine. The older woman took her arm. 'Come and meet everyone.'

It'd take her longer than a single afternoon to get everyone's names straight in her mind, but they were all so friendly and kind with their welcomes and their offers of assistance to help her settle in that in under ten minutes Tess felt wrapped in warmth. The glimmer of light that had taken up residence in her heart the moment her application had been accepted now became a fully floodlit arena.

She pressed her hands to her chest and blinked hard.

A group of women surrounded her. One handed her a mug of tea, another handed her a plate piled high with food. They filled her in on what produce was available from the general store and how to set up an account there. They shared their favourite online sites for ordering in school supplies, work boots and make-up. When she asked, they told her the date for the next CWA meeting and promised to meet her there.

Several men came up to her too. One to tell her he was her

man if she ever decided to keep pigs. Another to let her know he could help her set up her own home brew if she wanted. Another introduced himself as the soccer coach for the Bella-roo Creek under tens team and told her that both Ty and Krissie were welcome when training started up in another month.

The entire town, it seemed, welcomed them with arms wide open and friendship in their hearts. Her earlier nerves suddenly seemed ludicrous.

'How are you doing, dear?' Lorraine said, coming up behind her. 'I hope we haven't overwhelmed you?'

'This is…' Tess swallowed and gestured around the room. 'It's just something else. I can't tell you how much I appreciate it.'

'Nonsense! We wanted to welcome you to town in style. Now may I introduce my future daughter-in-law, Fiona?'

'Lovely to meet you.' Tess balanced her mug on her plate and shook hands with the pretty young woman. They exchanged pleasantries for a couple of minutes before Fiona, with a glance back behind her, excused herself. Tess turned back to Lorraine. 'Thank you so much for the cake you left yesterday. I can't tell you how much we appreciated it after that long drive.'

'You're welcome, my dear. I'm only sorry I couldn't be there to greet you in person.'

'That's okay, Cameron deputised honourably in your absence.'

Lorraine's head shot up. 'Cam?' Two beats went by then, 'Oh, I'm so glad to hear it.' Her hand fluttered to her throat. 'I've been meaning to ring him, but… Is he well?'

Tess thought about those broad shoulders and long legs and had to swallow. 'He seemed very well.'

Lorraine leaned forward, her eyes eager. 'Yes?'

She blinked. 'Umm… I mean, he obviously works hard, but he brought Boomer around to meet the children this morning, which was kind of him.'

'Oh!' Lorraine clapped her hands together, her eyes shining. 'Oh, I'm so pleased to hear that.'

She was? She continued to stare at Tess as if eager to hear any news about Cam that Tess was willing to share. Tess lifted a shoulder. 'There was a bit of a mix-up on the lease agreement, but we sorted it out.'

Lorraine stilled. 'Mix-up?'

'Something about forty hectares that belong to Cam, or that he was supposed to be leasing from you or something like that, accidentally being on the lease agreement I signed.'

Lorraine paled. 'Oh…no. Are you sure?'

Tess stilled then too because it was evident that something was wrong. Very wrong. She wanted to ask what it was but manners prevented her. She rolled her shoulders. 'Perhaps I shouldn't have mentioned it.' She forced a wide smile, wanting to ease the other woman's evident anxiety. 'But I promise we sorted it out. He's happy with the outcome and so am I.'

A breath shuddered out of the older woman and she sent Tess a smile that signalled her relief. 'I'm very, *very* glad to hear that. If you see him, please give him my love.'

'Of course.' But…why didn't Lorraine give Cam her love in person?

Lorraine stared beyond Tess and suddenly straightened. 'Would you excuse me for a moment, Tess? I—'

Before she could move, however, a man Tess hadn't met charged up and kissed Lorraine's cheek, before turning to survey Tess. 'Would you introduce me to Bellaroo Creek's newest resident?'

Lorraine bit her lip. Finally she shook her head and said, 'Tess, this is my son, Lance.'

Cameron's brother? Tess hastily set her plate and mug on a nearby table and extended her hand. 'I'm very pleased to meet you.' He was prettier than Cameron with his blond good looks and golden tan, but neither his size nor his presence was anywhere near as commanding.

He grinned at her. He had one of those infectious kinds of grins. 'Oh, ho! The single farmers in the district are sure going to be pleased to meet you.'

She laughed. And he had an easy charm his older brother totally lacked.

She'd met men like Lance before—full of fun, but often not much else. On closer inspection, though, the colour was high on his cheeks and she couldn't help feeling his joviality was forced.

'It's great to meet you, Tess. Welcome to Bellaroo Creek.'

'Thank you.'

'And as I'm not the kind of man to let the grass grow under my feet…'

Really? She didn't believe that for one moment.

'I'd like to talk business with you.'

The hair at her nape prickled. She folded her arms. 'Oh?'

'Lance.' Lorraine laid a hand on his arm. 'This is neither the time nor the place.'

He shook off his mother's touch. 'Of course it is.' He bounced on the balls of his feet, a fine sheen of perspiration filming his top lip and his forehead. 'Now I understand, Tess, that you have forty prime hectares on your allotment that are just going begging. I want to make you an offer you can't refuse.'

Several groups nearby stopped talking and turned to listen. Others moved forward.

'Oh, Lance, I can't believe this of you!' Lorraine hissed. 'I think—'

He held up a hand, his eyes glittering. 'I'd like to lease that land from you at very generous terms.'

Someone nearby snorted. Lance ignored it, but Lorraine's hand fluttered about her throat. 'Lance, please,' she whispered.

He rocked back on his heels. 'What do you say, Tess?'

That was when she realised thirty pairs of eyes watched

her closely, waiting to see what she'd say, and instinct told her whatever she did or said now would seal her, Ty and Krissie's fate in Bellaroo Creek, for good or ill.

And she didn't know what would work for or against them.

She swallowed. She hadn't done anything wrong. All she could do was offer Lance the truth. 'I'm sorry, Lance, but I signed a contract this morning leasing that land to Cameron. I understood he had a right to it.'

Cameron was his brother. Surely Lance would be happy for him?

Lance stared at her, the blood draining from his face. 'But…I need that land more than he does. I *need* that canola contract.'

'Cam's spent the last two years improving that land,' somebody from the crowd said.

He had?

'Yeah, back off, Lance. Cam's earned the right to that land,' someone else called out.

Lance swung back to Tess, his face twisting and his eyes wild with panic. 'You've ruined me. You and Cam both.' His voice rose on each word. 'It's what he wants, and you've been party to that!' He stiffened. 'I hope you're happy?'

Happy? She was appalled!

One of the older farmers muttered, 'One can hardly blame Cam for that.' He lifted his voice. 'And it's sure as heck not Tess's fault. So like Stuart said, back off, Lance.'

Lance pointed a finger at her. Tess swallowed. She opened her mouth just as Ty came barrelling up, shaking, his small hands clenched to fists. 'Don't you yell at my auntie Tess!'

Bursting into tears, Krissie hurled herself at her aunt. Tess scooped her up and held her close, dangerously close to tears herself.

Fiona raced up and took Lance's arm. With an apologetic glance at Tess, she led him away.

Lorraine turned to her, pale, her hands shaking. 'Oh, Tess, I'm so sorry. I—'

Hauling Ty in close to her side, she said, 'Just give me a moment,' before leading the children to a quiet corner where she tried to quieten Krissie's sobs. Not easy when her insides were quivering and all she wanted to do was drop her head and cry too.

The luncheon had been so perfect. She'd started to feel like a part of the community. She'd thought everything was going to work out exactly as she needed it to. And then, bam!

Her head reeled. She found it hard to catch her breath. She closed her eyes and dragged air into her lungs. 'Shh, honey.' She rubbed Krissie's back. 'Everything is okay.'

It would be okay. She'd make sure it'd be okay. A setback, that was all this was.

'Why was that man angry?' Krissie hiccupped.

'It's not so much that he was angry as he was upset. He's very worried about some things.'

Her whole body shuddered. 'Is he going to hurt us?'

'No, honey, he's not.' She hugged Krissie close and then touched Ty's cheek. He was so quiet. 'I promise. Okay?'

''Kay,' he murmured.

'The man was being very silly and we don't need to worry about him at all.' She prayed they'd believe her, that they trusted her enough. Time for a brave face. 'You know what I need?' she whispered. 'A lamington. Are there any?'

'Ones with cream in them.'

'Ooh, yum.' She made her eyes wide. 'Let's go look.'

They each selected a lamington, they each took a bite, and then Tess caught Stacy's eye. 'Don't forget,' she whispered before the teacher reached them, 'I need the names of vegetables.'

They were laughing again by the time they reached the group of other children. Tess didn't doubt there'd be more questions tonight, but for now things were fine.

She moved back towards Lorraine and the group of women who surrounded her. 'Are the littlies okay?' one of the women asked her.

Tess hesitated, her gaze darting back to the circle of children. 'I think so.' She swallowed. She'd given an account of Ty and Krissie's circumstances in her application letter. Not a full account, perhaps, but full enough. She didn't doubt that everyone in the room knew about the death of their parents. 'It's just that they've been through so much in such a short space of time... Little things can unduly upset them.'

'An angry man isn't a little thing. Especially when you're five years old.'

Tess had to close her eyes for a moment. *An angry man.* The shaking started back up inside her. Lorraine touched her arm. 'I can't tell you how sorry I am, Tess. Lance has a lot on his mind at the moment, but that doesn't excuse his behaviour.'

Lorraine was obviously appalled

'It wasn't your fault.' But... She twisted her hands together. 'Is there anything I ought to know?'

The women surrounding them discreetly melted away, leaving Tess and Lorraine alone. Lorraine gripped her hands together. 'Cameron and Lance have had the most dreadful falling out, Tess. They haven't spoken to each other in over ten months.'

Ten months!

Lorraine's eyes filled with tears. 'I...I certainly didn't expect any of that fallout to land in your lap, though. I'm absolutely mortified.'

The older woman's heartache tugged at her. But... 'That forty hectares?' she whispered.

Lorraine blinked hard and swallowed. 'I knew nothing about it, I promise.'

The shaking inside her started to slow.

'Tess, I can't tell you how sorry—'

She reached out to clasp the other woman's hands. 'There's no need to apologise further, Lorraine.' She had no desire to make things even harder for the other woman. Especially when she'd gone to so much trouble to welcome them to town so warmly. 'Let's forget about it.' She made herself smile and then turned to check on Ty and Krissie again. She prayed there hadn't been any permanent harm done there.

'Honey.' Lorraine moved in close so they were touching shoulders. 'I understand your concern. Your Ty and Krissie have had a lot to deal with, but…children are remarkably resilient, you know?'

She gave a shaky laugh. 'Are they?' She didn't have a clue.

'Yes, I promise. And I promise they'll be okay. All you can do is love them the best you can…as you obviously do. All of us here in Bellaroo Creek will do our best to become a second family to them. It'll all work out in the end.'

The other women, who'd moved back in closer, all nodded and murmured their agreement.

They made it sound so easy.

Why, then, was it proving so very, very hard?

CHAPTER THREE

CAM WENT TO knock on Tess's front door, but the sound of voices out the back had him redirecting his path around the side of the house.

Tess, Ty and Krissie all sat on a bright blue rug beside the lemon tree. They sat in a row—Tess in the middle—with legs stretched out in front of them and their backs to the sun, and him.

The scene hit him in a place he'd thought he'd locked up for good. For three beats of his heart a gnawing, ragged ache threatened to split him open. Reaching out, he steadied himself against the boards of the house. He'd dreamed of being part of a picture like this once. Ten short months ago, in fact, though it seemed like a lifetime ago now.

A family.

His jaw clenched. Lance and Fiona had stolen this from him.

A boulder of a lump stretched his throat. His temples pounded.

No! He refused to be beguiled by this dream again. He would never again open himself up to the kind of betrayal Lance and Fiona had inflicted upon him.

Filling Kurrajong House with a family, that had all been a ludicrous, out-of-reach dream. He'd found that out the hard way, just like his father. Unlike his father, however, he had no intention of burying himself on Kurrajong Station and stewing in 'what might have beens' and regrets, and waiting for death to come claim him. He'd fill the gaps somehow.

He went to swing away, to retrace his steps to the privacy and solitude of Kurrajong where he could wipe this picture from his mind and replace it with his plans for Africa and adventure, but Ty chose that moment to look up at his aunt. In profile Cam recognised the little boy's frown and the way it changed his entire demeanour. Noted the hunching of his shoulders and the way he curled himself around his knees. Very slowly, Cam turned back.

'What if this isn't a good place?'

Tess tousled his hair, and, although he couldn't see her face, he knew detail for detail the smile she'd have sent the young boy. 'How can this not be a good place? Look, we have a lemon tree *and* sultana cake.' She gestured to the tree and then the plate that shared the blanket with them.

Ty's frown didn't abate. Tess's shoulders started to tighten.

'And what about all the nice people we met yesterday? Cam's mum, Mrs Pritchard, was lovely *and* she gave me her sultana cake recipe. Plus you guys were great and we now have the names for all the vegetables we should plant in our veggie garden. And what about Mrs Bennet? You both told me she's the nicest teacher in the world.'

'Yeah.' Ty grabbed a dandelion out of the lawn and shredded it.

'Suzie was nice,' Krissie volunteered, 'even if she thinks chickens are boring. She said we could come and play in her pool in the summer.'

'Nice.' Tess drew the word out, injecting it with what Cam supposed was the appropriate amount of enthusiasm.

'Mikey and Ryan have dogs,' Ty said, but there wasn't a fleck of enthusiasm in his voice.

Cam shifted his weight. What the hell...?

'What if bad men keep yelling at us?' Krissie blurted out.

'Chickadee, that man yesterday wasn't bad.' She gave Krissie a one-armed hug. 'Like I said before, he was upset, that's all. And remember, people yell for lots of different reasons.'

'You don't yell,' Ty said.

'Believe me, if I saw one of Cam's sheep in my veggie patch, I'd be yelling my head off!'

Neither child laughed.

'But that man yelled at you!' Ty burst out.

Someone had yelled at Tess? Cam stiffened. He stepped into the yard. 'Howdy, gang.'

Both children immediately swung around, fear frozen on their faces. Cold, hard anger lanced through him because then he knew—someone had hurt these kids, had frightened them, and he wanted to find out who it was and tear them from limb to limb.

'Hey, Cam, nice to see you.'

Behind the children's backs, Tess mouthed, *Smile* at him, and it suddenly hit him how intimidating he must appear to these two small kids.

He forced his face to relax into a kind of half grin, although his blood burned and the surface of his skin prickled. 'You guys have the nicest spot in the sun. Mind if I join you?'

'We'd like that.' Tess shuffled over. Both children remained glued to her side. 'Want some sultana cake?'

He glanced at the plate, hunger rumbled through him, but he shook his head.

'Did you bring Boomer?' Ty asked.

Cam kicked himself for not bringing the dog. 'Sorry, mate, I didn't. I left Boomer in charge of the sheep.'

'That is one smart dog,' Tess said, and Cam watched as the worst of the fear and shadows slowly drained from Ty's and Krissie's faces.

'I just dropped by to talk lawnmowers. I have a ride-on and thought I might whizz it around this place tomorrow if that suited you.'

Tess shook her head, her hair so dark and her skin so golden it made him ache in familiar and unfamiliar ways. 'Oh, no, you don't, Cameron Manning. I can mow my own lawn, thank you very much. Though, a lesson in how to operate your ride-on would be greatly appreciated.'

It was obviously important to her to do it herself. He bit down on his urge to argue with her, although it chafed at him. He nodded. 'Right.'

'Woo hoo!' She punched the air. 'I get to use a ride-on mower. How much fun will that be?'

Krissie finally smiled.

'So how did yesterday's luncheon go?' He rested back on his hands, deliberately casual.

'Ooh.' Tess rubbed her hands together. 'There must've been thirty people there.'

'It was a Saturday. Everyone would've made an effort.'

Ty scowled. 'You didn't.'

'No,' he agreed. 'But I really wish I had.' And he meant it.

His stomach suddenly rolled. Why hadn't he gone? Eleven months ago he'd have been there. But since Lance and Fiona... Nausea burned his throat. Despite all his precautions he was turning into a recluse like his father.

No! He snapped the thought off. He was leaving Bellaroo Creek so he *didn't* turn into his father. He'd forge a new life for himself—an involved and engaging life. The kind of life he couldn't have in Bellaroo Creek.

Still... The idea of socialising had become anathema and he'd buried himself in station work, rarely going into town. None of that changed the fact that he wished he'd attended yesterday's luncheon.

Who had yelled at Tess and spooked the kids?

'A bad man yelled at Auntie Tess,' Krissie confided.

'Who?'

Ty scowled again. 'His name was Lance and we don't know if we want to live here any more.'

Lance?

He flicked a glance at Tess and a hand reached inside his chest to wring his heart. The raw grief in her eyes as she surveyed the children made his jaw ache. She glanced up, caught his gaze and tried to smile, but he saw the effort it cost her. That was when he realised she couldn't speak for the tears blocking her throat, and he sensed that crying in front of the children was the last thing she wanted. And probably the last thing either Ty or Krissie needed.

'Oh, Lance!' he pshawed. 'You don't have to worry about Lance.'

Krissie bit her lip. 'He's not a bad man?'

He was a black-hearted traitor, but Cam had enough justice in him still to know Lance would be horrified to find he'd become a bogey man to these kids. 'Nah, he's all hot air, you know? He makes a lot of noise, but he wouldn't hurt a fly. I should know, because he's my little brother.'

Relief rushed into both the children's faces and it hit him then how much these kids trusted him. He didn't know how or why—whether it was a carry-over from all of Tess's positivity when they'd arrived on Friday, or because he'd brought Boomer over to play, or the fact he knew Old Nelson the blue-tongue lizard, but it made his chest cramp. He couldn't let these kids rely on him too much. He was their neighbour, nothing more. But instinct told him he'd need to tread carefully—these kids needed kid-glove handling.

He ached to quiz them more about Lance—why he had yelled at Tess—but the kids needed to take their minds off yesterday's incident. They needed to remember the good things about living in Bellaroo Creek. They needed to be allowed to get on with their fresh start without fear and setbacks.

'Now I don't know if this will be agreeable to you guys or not, but because I worked so hard yesterday, and because Boomer's taking care of things today, I get to take the rest of today off.' He rubbed his chin and pursed his lips as if in a pretence of thought. 'So I was thinking you might like to go and check out some chickens and puppies.'

All three faces on the blanket before him lit up. He immediately tried to temper their enthusiasm. 'Today we only look because these things take a lot of careful thought and planning. It's a big responsibility to own an animal and you need to be very sure that the choice you make is the right one for you, you understand?'

All three heads nodded in unison. It struck him how young Tess was—she couldn't be much older than twenty-five. Too young for taking on all the responsibility she had.

Ty jumped up. 'Can we leave right now?'

He suppressed a grin at the young boy's eagerness. 'You'll need time to get ready. I'll pick you up in an hour. Promise you'll be ready?'

'Yes!' Both children raced indoors and Tess laughed. She actually laughed as she watched them and it lightened the unexplained weight that had settled across his shoulders. To see pleasure in her face instead of fear and grief…

She leapt to her feet. He rose more slowly, finding it suddenly difficult to catch his breath. She grabbed his arm, reached up on tiptoe and kissed his cheek. 'I could kiss you, Cameron! Thank you.'

He went to point out that she'd done exactly that, but he couldn't push a single sound out of his throat. He went to tell her to call him Cam, but his full name sounded so bewitching on those charming lips of hers, he found himself saying nothing at all.

And then she hugged him—hard and fierce—and it knocked the sense and the breath clean out of his body. Every sweet curve Tess possessed pressed against him, and his body soaked up her warmth and vigour. It brought him to aching life and sent a surge of primitive hunger racing through him with the swiftness of a rabbit startled in the undergrowth. A wildfire licked along his veins…carrying the same danger that fire did out here in the bush.

Reason screamed at him to move away. Instead, one of his arms snaked around her waist and he pulled her in closer, hugged her back. His hand rested against the top of her hip. He wanted to move his hand lower, he wanted to mould her against him, wanted her soft and pliant and…

He felt rather than heard her quick intake of breath. She stiffened. A heartbeat passed. A heartbeat in which the fire raging through him threatened all of his control, and then she softened against him.

He let his hand drift down to cup her bottom and lift it against him. She arched into him. He groaned. He couldn't help it.

Her hands drifted down his chest, her face lifted to his, her eyes soft and her lips parted.

He wanted to taste her. He wanted to explore the fullness of her bottom lip and—

For God's sake, she hugged you out of gratitude. She wasn't inviting you to maul her like some low-life sleaze!

He recalled the raw pain he'd witnessed in her eyes a moment before and, rather than snap away, he eased her out of his arms gently. 'Sorry, Tess.' His voice came out raspy and hoarse. 'I forgot myself for a moment.'

She blinked twice before the mistiness cleared from her eyes. Her cheeks flushed bright red. 'Oh! I—' She swung away. 'You and me both. I'm sorry. It's been an emotional morning.'

He shrugged and tried to appear as casual for her as he had for the children earlier. 'No harm done.'

She turned back to him. 'No harm done,' she echoed, her eyes searching his to test that truth. They both stood there awkwardly until she glanced at her watch. 'So you'll be back at around eleven?'

He snapped to and nodded.

'Should I pack a picnic?' She smiled impishly and everything slowly returned to normal—the colour of the sky, the sound of birdsong, the racing of his pulse. 'You wouldn't believe how much food there was at yesterday's do. And somehow most of the leftovers ended up in my car.'

He stared at her lips—they were more plum than rose. Hunger stretched through him as he took in the fullness of her bottom lip. His pulse began to race again. 'Sounds great,' he said, backing up. 'I'll see you in a while.'

He shot around the house and back towards his homestead. It occurred to him that burying himself out on his station for the last ten months might not have been the wisest course of action after all.

Cam's four-wheel-drive pulled up out the front and Tess hauled in a deep breath and locked the front door. Ty and Krissie raced towards the car with all the alacrity of children promised their heart's desire.

Cam had done that. He'd found the perfect way to remind them of all the exciting potential that living in Bellaroo Creek could bring. They'd gone from the doldrums to delight.

But she should never have kissed him. She most certainly shouldn't have hugged him.

And yet, even now, her body throbbed with a primitive hunger. She yearned to explore each and every line of his powerful body—naked. She craved his hands on her again—gentle hands, knowing hands. Oh, so knowing. Her knees quivered before she could stop them.

Enough of that!

She kicked herself into action and moved down the path, sidestepping Old Nelson who currently sunned himself on the cement path. Cam met her at the gate to take the picnic basket from her. He searched her face. She let him—freely and openly. She searched his face too. It was amazing how much information they could convey to each other without a word. He liked how she looked, and he wanted her in the same way she wanted him, but…

They both sighed and nodded at the same moment. Romance wasn't on the cards for either of them. She didn't know his reasons, but she knew her own. She'd been selfish her entire life—selfish and clueless—but not any more.

I won't let you down again, Sarah. I promise.

'Where are we going?' Krissie demanded the minute Cam started the car and eased it onto the road.

'Our first stop is the O'Connell farm. Blue O'Connell has the best layers in the entire district. He has show chickens too. He takes out the blue ribbon every year at the Parkes agricultural show. What's more, his black lab has had a litter of puppies.'

Ty started talking so fast Tess couldn't understand a word he said.

'Steady, buddy.' Cam laughed. 'We've also a litter of border collie pups—like Boomer—to check out as well as some poodles.'

When they reached the farm, the children literally launched themselves out of the car. They both jumped and danced—at least in Krissie's case—and jumped and hopped—in Ty's—with uncontained excitement. Tess watched them and something inside her swelled. To see their faces alive with hope instead of fear, to see them grinning at the unknown farmer who came to greet them rather than backing up towards her with suspicion clouding their eyes, lifted something inside her.

To see them, for just one moment, truly happy. It made her want to weep. It made her hope. It made her think that coming to Bellaroo Creek had been the perfect plan after all.

'Are you Mr O'Connell?' Krissie asked.

'That I am, little miss.'

'I'm Krissie.' She walked right up to the farmer and held her hand out. 'And we're here to see your chickens.'

Sweet Lord, she must want a chicken badly.

Ty hung back for all of five seconds before bursting forward as well. 'And your puppies too.'

'Well, young folk, that's something I can certainly accommodate. Come right this way.' With a wink and a smile for Tess and Cam, he led the children towards the barn.

'Are you okay?' Cam asked, those green eyes of his seeming to plumb her soul.

'Oh!' She pressed both hands to her chest. 'Oh, Cameron, I think they're going to be fine after all.'

He tipped his hat back—a dusty, sweat-stained Akubra. 'Why wouldn't they be?'

She had to swallow before she could speak. 'The last three months have been just awful. And...'

'And?'

Beneath her hand her heart pounded. 'I didn't know if they would ever be happy again,' she whispered. 'I didn't know if I could help them be happy again, but... But your mum was right. Children are resilient.' This was the beginning of the brand-new start she'd been hoping for. Now she just had to focus on keeping them all on an even keel and making sure they felt secure.

'C'mon.' He took her arm. 'I have a feeling you need this as much as they do.'

They found Krissie sitting in a pen with the silliest piece of feathered nonsense that Tess had ever seen perched on her lap. It looked as if it should be worn on some posh hat for Melbourne's Spring Carnival. Krissie raised her big brown eyes. 'This one,' she whispered, hope so alive in her face it stole Tess's breath.

Cam stiffened and opened his mouth. Tess dug her elbow in his ribs. 'Can't you see it's true love?' she murmured, leading him further into the depths of the barn.

'But it's a show chicken. It won't lay a tuppence worth of eggs.'

'And yet Krissie doesn't care…and neither do I.' She wanted to sing! 'Let's find Ty.'

They found him being licked to within an inch of his life by six puppies. Cute, round, roly-poly puppies. When he saw Tess and Cam he picked one of the puppies up and clambered to his feet. He hitched up his chin. 'I thought about it very long and hard,' he vowed. 'This is the absolutest, bestest puppy in the world for me. I don't need to look any more.'

Cam's mouth dropped open. 'We were only supposed to look!'

But she'd started laughing. 'Cameron, you have a lot to learn about children if you really thought all we were ever going to do today was just look.'

They went home with a chicken and a wire cage loaned to them by Mr O'Connell, a puppy, a dog basket, a collar and lead, and plenty of pet food.

And their picnic.

Tess set up a card table in the backyard to keep the food out of reach of their furred and feathered friends, and two camp chairs for her and Cam. Children and animals cheerfully settled on the blanket until they'd finished eating, and then Krissie and Ty set about introducing Fluffy and Barney to the backyard.

Tess selected a pikelet liberally slathered in butter and jam and bit into it, closing her eyes for a moment to savour it. If she didn't stop eating like this soon, she'd outgrow all her clothes. She took a second bite. 'I can't believe that chicken is following Krissie about as if it's a dog.'

'I can't believe you bought a White Bearded Silky instead of a Leghorn or a Rhode Island or…or anything that's a proven layer. You know that thing is going to lay next to no eggs.'

She just grinned at him. 'Have a piece of sultana cake.'

He had a piece of fruitcake instead. 'And a black Labrador?' He shook his head.

'Labrador puppies are the cutest in the world.'

'They don't stop being stupid until they're about four years old. It'll chew everything it can find, you know?'

'That'll teach the kids to pick up after themselves. And while Barney may not prove to be the cleverest of dogs, I suspect he's going to be loving and loyal.'

'He'll never be a working dog.'

'We don't need a working dog.' She polished off her pikelet and licked her fingers. 'Cameron, I know we're breaking every rule of being proper country folk, but look how happy they are.' She found herself grinning like an idiot. 'How can that be a bad thing?'

He glanced at her and those green eyes of his softened. 'It's not, I guess. Not when you put it like that. I just can't help feeling you've taken on more work than you realise. And I'm responsible for that. If I'd known earlier what would happen—'

'I'm glad you didn't! You're responsible for the kids remembering all the good things they wanted from our move to Bellaroo Creek. You're responsible for them being happy that we moved here rather than afraid. Do you always focus on the negatives rather than the positives?'

He didn't answer. His eyes had lowered to her mouth and there was absolutely nothing negative about his gaze. What if he had kissed her earlier? What would that have been like? She swallowed. Heat circled in slow spirals through her veins. She recalled in microscopic detail the feeling of being pulled up hard against him and the need that had roared through her.

The world contracted about them. She touched her lips—lips sensitised beyond measure. Her index finger traced her bottom lip. It swelled and throbbed...until she encountered something sticky.

Sticky? She closed her eyes in sudden mortification. Jam! She had jam all over her face? No wonder Cameron was staring. She scrubbed it off and when she opened her eyes she found him staring straight out in front of him at his precious forty hectares.

She scowled but it didn't slow the thud of her heartbeat.

'Why did Lance yell at you?'

She shifted on her chair. Lorraine had said Cameron and Lance hadn't spoken in ten months. She didn't want to make that situation worse.

'I will find out so you might as well tell me.'

She slumped on a sigh. 'Fine, but I'll only tell you if you fill me in on what's going down with the two of you.'

His nose curled. It shouldn't look sexy. *It didn't look sexy!* 'I'm surprised nobody filled you in about it yesterday. It's no secret.'

His curled lip told her that while it might not be a secret, he didn't enjoy talking about it. She pulled in a breath. 'Whatever it is, it's certainly upsetting your mother.'

He snorted. She didn't understand that.

'Ten months ago,' he clipped out, 'I was engaged to Fiona.'

She stared. Did he mean the same Fiona who... 'Tall, blonde, ponytail?'

'That's the one.'

She stiffened. 'Oh!'

He smiled but there was no warmth in it. 'Exactly.'

They both stared out at the backyard, silent for the moment. 'I, umm...take it,' she started, 'that you and Fiona hadn't broken up before she and Lance...'

'You take it right.'

Ouch!

She opened her mouth to say something, anything that would offer comfort or commiseration, but he glared at her and shook his head. 'Don't.'

Right. She closed her mouth again.

They were both quiet for a long time. Eventually she moistened her lips. 'Lance wanted to lease the forty hectares from me. When I told him I'd already signed the lease over to you he…became a little upset.'

His eyes narrowed, but he still didn't look at her. 'He wanted to lease that land?'

'Uh-huh.'

His nostrils flared. 'I knew he was behind that.'

Um… 'I'm pretty positive your mother had no part in it, though.'

That made him swing to her. 'Oh, really?' His scorn could blast the skin from a person's frame. She darted a glance towards the children. He swore softly. 'Sorry.'

He raked a hand back through his hair. 'Look, I'm still angry that I didn't see it coming, that I didn't see what was happening right under my nose. That he was—'

He broke off. 'I underestimated him. None of that is your fault, though.'

'I'd have said believing in your family was a good thing, not a bad one.'

He didn't reply. She pulled in a breath. 'Look, yesterday your mother seemed appalled and shocked when I told her about the mix-up with the forty hectares. I doubt very much she feigned that.' She bit her lip and then shrugged. 'I liked her.'

His lips twisted. 'And let me guess, despite my brother's bad behaviour you like him too?'

She thought about that for a moment. 'Hmm, no, I'm not convinced I do. I don't much like being yelled at. He owes me an apology and until I receive one he's a…' He'd stolen Cam's fiancée! She tilted her chin. 'He's a weaselling, snivelling, black-hearted swine.'

Cam stared at her, his jaw slack, and then he threw his head back and laughed. The sound rippled through her, warming her all over. Both Ty and Krissie glanced across at them and grinned. It made Tess realise what little laughter they'd had in their lives these last few months. And probably quite a while before then too if the truth be told.

Oh, Sarah.

At the thought of her beautiful dead sister any desire to laugh along with Cam fled. 'Cam, about your mum...'

His face shuttered closed. 'She's made it clear where her loyalties lie.'

'She loves you!' She couldn't keep the shock out of her voice.

'Then she has a funny way of showing it. Besides—' he rounded on her '—this is none of your business.'

'You should talk to her.'

He didn't say anything. She clenched and unclenched her hands. Lorraine's loyalties were obviously torn—she didn't want to lose either son. Tess understood that, but...

She leaned across and touched his arm. 'I'm serious, Cameron. I think you need to speak to her. I think the farm is in trouble. Big trouble. I think she needs you.'

The same way Sarah had needed her. Only, Tess had let her down and now she had to live with that knowledge for the rest of her life.

'Trouble? What makes you think that?'

She didn't want Cam making the same mistakes she had. 'Lance said he needed that canola contract. He implied the farm was in danger.' She bit her lip. 'He thinks you want to ruin him.'

Cam shook his head. 'I don't much care what Lance thinks any more.'

She understood that, but...

He turned to her. 'Look, Tess, the problems associated with my mother and Lance's station is none of my concern any more. Lance has made that clear through his actions and my mother has made it clear by virtue of her silence.'

She chafed her arms against a sudden chill. Three months ago she'd lost her sister. She'd do anything—*anything*—to have Sarah back for just one hour. And yet Cam was willing to turn his back on the only family he had? Lance might be a lost cause, but couldn't Cam see how much his mother loved him?

He rose. 'I'll bring the mower around tomorrow.'

'Thank you.'

He called out a goodbye to the kids and disappeared around the side of the house. Tess rose to find a cardigan and snuggled into it until she started to feel warm again.

CHAPTER FOUR

CAM CLEANED THE last of the tack. He glanced at the neatly aligned rows of bridles and lead ropes, and at the newly polished saddles, but two hours' worth of rubbing and buffing hadn't helped ease the itch between his shoulder blades.

With a frown, and a muffled curse that had no direct object, he strode out of the tack room and into the machinery shed to leap on a trail bike and kick it into life. He pointed it in the direction of the northern boundary fence and let loose with the throttle, even though he knew Fraser had trawled along that boundary through the week to check the fences.

He belted along the track for ten minutes when, with another muffled curse, he turned the bike back in the direction of the homestead. Dumping the bike back in the machinery shed, he grabbed several assorted lengths of wood and a roll of chicken wire and threw them, along with his toolbox, into the back of one of the station's utes and, with a final muffled curse, headed next door to Tess's.

He might be planning to sever his ties with Bellaroo Creek, but he couldn't leave a lone woman with two dependent kids to flounder on her own. Not on land he was ultimately responsible for. Not when it was his fault she now had a puppy and a chicken to look after on top of everything else.

Talk to her. That was what Tess had said about his mother. He swiped a hand through the air. His mother would always have a home with him. She knew that, even if she chose to never accept it.

I think the farm is in trouble.

That was none of his business any more. He fishtailed the ute to a halt in front of Tess's cottage and the itch between his shoulder blades intensified. He stared out of the windscreen and shook his head. The thought uppermost in his mind, it seemed, wasn't on building a chicken coop or wondering why his mother refused to come out to Kurrajong, but what Tess might be wearing today—jeans or a skirt?

He rubbed his eyes. When he lowered his hand it was to find Ty and Barney barrelling down the side of the house towards him. 'Hey, Cam!'

He pushed his door open and found a grin. 'Hey, Ty, how's Barney settling in?'

'I love him best of all dogs in the world!'

It struck him then that Ty looked just like any other seven-year-old boy who'd just got his first puppy—carefree, excited, his face shadow-free.

'He's a mighty fine-looking puppy,' Cam agreed, realising he'd helped to make those shadows retreat. The knowledge awed him, humbled him. He reached behind him to scratch his back.

Then Tess came tripping around the side of the house and all rational thought stopped for more beats of his pulse than he had the wit to count. Shorts. Tess wore a pair of scarlet-coloured shorts and a pale cream vest top. Her bare arms, bare legs and shoulders all gleamed in the autumn sunlight. She made him think of fields of ripening wheat, of cream and honey and nutmeg, of spiced apples and camping under the stars. She made him think of his mother's sultana cake—his favourite food in the world. He curled his fingers against his palms to stop from doing something daft and reaching out to stroke a finger down her arm.

'Hello, Cameron.'

He swallowed and then simply nodded, unsure if his voice would work.

'Auntie Tess said Barney did really good for a puppy. We've only had one accident.'

Cam winced. 'I, uh…'

Her eyes danced. 'Apologise again and I'll thump you. That puppy has been a source of pure joy.' She glanced at his ute and then planted her hands on her hips and sent him a mock glare. 'Where's my lawnmower?'

He grimaced. 'My station manager is currently lying beneath it trying to fix a fuel leak.'

'Ouch.'

'It should be fixed in the next day or so.' He didn't want her using it if it wasn't a hundred per cent safe.

She gestured with her head and turned. 'Come and join the party.'

He followed her. He didn't even try to keep from ogling the length of her legs or taking an inventory of the innate grace with which she moved. She was like some wonderful and exotic creature who'd deigned to live among the mundane and the humdrum. A creature whose beauty took one out of the mundane and humdrum for a few precious moments.

He wondered what she'd done for a living before she'd moved to Bellaroo Creek—maybe she'd been a dancer. He opened his mouth to ask, but they'd rounded the house and Krissie sat on a blanket with that darn chicken on her lap and when she glanced up and saw him she sent him a grin of such epic proportions it cracked his chest wide open.

He had to swallow before he could speak. 'Did Fluffy have a good night?'

'She slept in her cage in the laundry, but I think she'd be happier sleeping in my bedroom.'

Tess sent him a bare-teethed grimace that almost made him laugh. One could toilet train a puppy, but a chicken…? 'Well, honey, I've come around to build Fluffy her very own house.'

Krissie's bottom lip wobbled. 'Barney slept in Ty's room.'

He crouched down beside her. 'The thing is, Krissie, chickens aren't like puppies or kittens. They like the fresh air and they like to see the stars at night and be able to come and go as much as they please. So, as much as Fluffy loves you, she'll be happier out here in the yard.'

She stared at him and he held his breath. 'She'll get her very own house, right?'

'That's right.'

'A nice one?'

'One that she'll love,' he promised.

Her face cleared. 'I can show you a picture of Fluffy's dream house!' She plonked Fluffy down on the grass and raced inside.

'Oh, good Lord.' Tess groaned. 'I have no idea what she has in mind, Cameron.'

He had sudden visions of a hot-pink Barbie house and gulped. And then he glanced around. A collection of plastic planters in assorted shapes and sizes battled for space from the back of the house to the lemon tree. 'Where on earth did all these seedlings come from?'

Tess planted her hands on her hips. Sweet hips…long, lovely legs…pretty arms. Cam curled his fingers into his palms again. With a silent curse he uncurled them and shoved them into his pockets. Deep into his pockets.

'Everyone has been so kind. At Saturday's luncheon Ty, Krissie and I mentioned we'd like to start our own veggie garden and asked for advice on what vegetables we should grow.'

He shook his head, but he couldn't help grinning. 'I guess you got your answer.'

She grinned back. 'I guess we did.'

Her plum-coloured lips gleamed temptingly in the sunlight. His heart thumped. He kept his hands firmly in his pockets. The itch started up again with a vengeance.

Krissie reappeared brandishing a magazine. 'This one!' She held it up for them to see.

'That's an awful lot of house for one chicken, Krissie,' Tess said.

Krissie's bottom lip wobbled. 'But we'll get more chickens, remember? Fluffy will need friends for when I'm at school.'

She turned liquid eyes to Cam and they melted him on the spot. He rolled his shoulders, risked removing his hands from his pockets to take the magazine and survey the picture more fully. 'Oh, I think we can manage something like this.' He frantically recalculated the amount of wood in his ute with the amount he still had at the homestead.

'Give me a list of what we need and I'll go into the stock and station store to get supplies,' Tess said, as if reading his mind.

It wouldn't be cheap. He grimaced. He should've found a way to talk Krissie into something less grand and

'We're good for it, Cameron. It isn't a problem,' Tess said, again as if reading his mind, which unsettled him. He normally maintained a quiet reserve that made him hard to read. It had been one of the things Fiona had complained about. But this woman, it seemed, had only to glance at him to know what he was thinking.

But her plump dusky lips curved up with such promise he found he didn't mind at all…or, at least, not as much as he suspected he should.

'Can I help you build it?' Ty breathed, his eyes alight.

'I'll definitely need a helper—a foreman. It's a big job, Ty, and I'll need your help.'

Ty's eyes grew as big as cabbages, his chest puffed out. That awe hit Cam again as he pulled his cell phone from his pocket. Surveying Krissie's dream chicken coop, and doing his best to keep his eyes from the plump temptation of Tess's lips, he placed an order at the stock and station store.

* * *

They spent the afternoon on Phase One of the chicken coop. Tess couldn't believe Cam's patience with Ty or the way her nephew blossomed under his quiet but authoritative guidance. He'd lacked a male role model for so long.

Eventually, though, both children wandered off to check on Old Nelson. And then Ty set about teaching Barney how to play fetch while Krissie fell asleep on the blanket beneath the shade of the lemon tree, leaving Fluffy free to scratch about the yard.

Tess glanced at Cam whistling idly as he nailed boards to the frame he'd built. Something inside her shifted. Ever since that moment yesterday when she'd hugged him, she'd grown increasingly aware of the breadth of his shoulders, of the flex and play of the muscles in his arms, and of the fresh-cut-grass scent that followed in his wake and stirred something to life inside her. Something she desperately tried to ignore.

The sun shone brightly, but not too fiercely, picking out the lighter highlights in his chestnut hair. Fiona had thrown this man over for Lance? Tess snorted. What a loser! The woman quite obviously had her head screwed on backwards. Lance might dazzle with those playboy good looks of his, but when a woman looked at Cam she was left in no doubt that he was all man.

One hundred per cent fit and honed man.

And the longer Tess stared at him, the more that thing inside her stirred and fluttered and stretched itself into heart-beating, mouth-drying sentience.

Thoughts of Lance, though, slid an unwelcome reminder through her. The expression on Lorraine's face—that mixture of anxiety, regret and heartbreak—rose in her mind and she bit back a sigh.

'You want to tell me what's on your mind?'

She blinked, and then realised Cam had caught her out blatantly staring at him. The skin on her face and neck burned. 'Oh…I…nothing.'

'Why don't I believe you?'

He wielded a hammer as if he'd been born to it. She dragged her gaze from muscled forearms lightly dusted with hair, and the pull of lean brown hands. She tried desperately to dispel thoughts of what else those hands might be expert at.

She clenched her eyes shut and counted to five. For pity's sake! She didn't need this at the moment—this wild, desperate ache. She needed to remain focused on the children. On not letting Sarah down. On making amends.

'Tess?'

She went back to tacking chicken wire to the frame of their mansion of a chicken house, the way he'd shown her, but she couldn't resist another glance at him. The brilliance of his eyes struck her afresh. She swallowed and shrugged. 'Oh, I was just thinking about stuff you'd no doubt declare me nosy for contemplating.'

He set his hammer down. 'Like?'

Keep your mouth shut. She set her hammer down too. 'Like how a man who is as gentle with children and animals as you could just ignore that his mother might be in trouble.'

He stiffened as if she'd slapped him.

'I said it was nosy,' she muttered, though she wasn't certain she was actually apologising.

'You're not wrong there.'

Minding her business was the wisest course of action. She knew that. Cam was a grown-up. He knew what he was doing. She swallowed. She used to be really good at minding her own business.

'You must really hate Lance if you haven't spoken to him in ten months.' She shivered. She understood his bitterness. She really did, but… 'How can you stand to live in the same town as him when you bear that much resentment?'

He eyed her for an interminable moment. It made her chest

constrict. 'I'm not planning on staying for that much longer, Tess.'

He hammered in a nail with more force than necessary, and a sickening thump started up in her stomach. 'What?'

He set his hammer back down and glared at her. 'In two months I'll be out of this godforsaken town and Lance can sink or swim under his own steam. I've washed my hands of him and his tantrums and his so-called troubles.'

'But...' Cameron couldn't leave!

'What about your mother?' she burst out.

He picked the hammer up again. 'I expect my leaving will be a blessing for her. With me gone, tensions will ease.' He hammered in another nail. 'Besides, like I told you, my mother has made it clear where her loyalties lie.'

Tess's mouth opened and closed. 'Can't you see her loyalties are being torn?'

'By remaining in the same house as Lance and Fiona she's given them her tacit approval.'

'You mother is not the type of woman who would ever kick her offspring out of her house, regardless of what they've done.' She planted her hands on her hips. 'But that doesn't mean she doesn't love you.' Couldn't he see that? 'Do you really mean to make her choose between the two of you? She's not responsible for the things Lance has done.'

'My leaving means she won't have to choose.'

She glanced at Krissie and an ache exploded in her chest. Cam's anger and bitterness were warping him and tearing him apart. Couldn't he see that? 'Oh, Cameron, it's been ten months.'

He strode around and seized her chin, his eyes blazing. 'And you naively think that time can heal all wounds?'

His fingers were gentle but his voice was hard. He smelled of wood and grass and sweat.

He paused and she swallowed, aching at the pain she sensed behind the flint of his eyes.

He scanned her face and then released her with a shake of his head. 'Why does this matter so much to you?'

She had to take a step away from him. He was too…much. Too much for her senses. Too much for her hormones. And the hardness in him clashed too deeply with the places that grieved inside her. 'I just lost my sister, Cam. I never appreciated her enough. I wish I had but I didn't. And now I've lost her and I can't get her back.'

He paled.

'I have no one now but Ty and Krissie. Don't get me wrong, they make up for everything, but…you have a mother who loves you and I'm jealous.' She tried to smile. He had a brother too, but she left that unsaid. In his shoes, would she be able to forgive Lance?

His eyes darkened, his hand half lifted as if to touch her cheek…and then he wheeled away.

She hunched her shoulders, wishing she hadn't started this conversation. Wishing she'd left well alone. She tried to make her voice bright. 'Where will you go when you leave Bellaroo Creek?'

He turned back. 'Africa. I'm an advisor for a charity whose mission is to increase agricultural production in Third World countries. I've requested a field position.'

'Wow!' She stared at him. 'Just…wow! That's amazing.' She swallowed and chafed her arms. 'What an adventure.'

'I'm hoping so.'

'Is it a secret?'

'I haven't told anyone, if that's what you mean.' He shifted his weight to plant his legs firmly.

She tried another smile and mimicked zipping her mouth shut to let him know she wouldn't say anything to anyone, and she had a feeling he had to fight back a smile of his own. She'd like to make him smile for real. 'We'll miss you, Cameron. You've been just about the best neighbour we city slickers could've had.'

His eyes widened. He blinked and then they narrowed. It made her want to fidget. Did he think she was making some kind of a move on him? Her spine stiffened and her chin shot up. 'You can lose that nasty suspicion right now,' she shot at him. 'Even if I was in the market for something more, I'm not stupid enough to get involved with a man on the rebound.' She folded her arms. 'In fact, I'm starting to think the sooner you leave, the better!'

He grinned then—a true-blue, solid-gold grin that hooked up his mouth and made his eyes dance. For a moment all Tess could make out was the brightness of the sun, the sound of the breeze playing through the leaves of the lemon tree and the force of that smile. She blinked and the rest of the world slowly surged back into focus.

'From where I'm standing, Tess, my suspicion was more like wishful thinking and it wasn't the least bit nasty. In fact, it was pretty darn tempting.'

Heat crept along her veins. She bit her bottom lip in an effort to counter its heavy throbbing. There was nothing she could do about her breasts, though, except to keep her arms tightly folded across them and hope their eager swelling didn't show.

'But I'm severing ties with Bellaroo Creek while you're in the process of establishing them. And while I wouldn't be averse to a purely physical arrangement...'

She shook her head.

'That's what I figured.'

She pulled a breath of fresh country air into her lungs to try to cool her body's unaccountable response to the man opposite; to give herself the space she needed to remember the promises she'd made to herself. 'Romance in any shape or form isn't figuring on my horizon for the next year or two.'

He stared at her, frowned. 'Why not?'

She glanced at Krissie still dozing beneath the lemon tree, and at Ty and Barney wrestling gently in the long grass down by the back fence. 'Because at the moment the children need stability in their lives. Bringing a new man into the mix would freak them out, threaten them.' For the next year or two she meant to focus all her energies on them and what they needed.

For pity's sake! It couldn't be that hard. She'd spent the last twenty-six years focussing on nothing but herself and her music. It wouldn't kill her to put others' needs before her own for a while. In fact, she had a feeling it was mandatory. Anyway, what did she know about romantic relationships? She'd had flirtations, but nothing serious or long-term. She didn't know enough about them to risk Ty's and Krissie's well-being, that was for sure.

'Tess, you're young and beautiful. You're entitled to a life of your own.'

She stared at him. Did he really think she was beautiful?

She started and shook her stupid vanity aside. 'Well, then, hopefully another two years won't make much difference to either of those things.'

'I think you're making a mistake.'

'Ten months,' she shot back. 'I think you're the one making a mistake.'

They glared at each other. 'Speaking of nosy questions…' his glare deepened '…I have one of my own.'

She moistened dry lips. 'Oh?'

He hitched his head in the direction of the children. 'Who hurt them?'

The strength drained from her legs. She reached out but the chicken coop wasn't stable enough to take her weight. She backed up and plonked down on a load of timber Cam had placed to one side, a chasm opening up in her chest. She wanted nothing more than to drop her face to her hands, but if either child glanced her way it would frighten them, worry them, and calming their anxieties was her number-one concern.

Cam swore. She glanced up. With the sun behind her, she

could see his face clearly and the range of expressions that filtered across it—concern, protectiveness…anger.

Who hurt them? Her chest cramped. She'd hoped… 'Is it that obvious?' she whispered.

He eased himself down beside her. 'Not at first.'

She had a feeling he was trying to humour her, to offer her some comfort, but there was no comfort to be had. Not for her.

'Tess?'

She chafed her arms as a chill settled over her, although the sun and the air remained warm. 'Their father,' she finally said. 'It was their father.'

From the corner of her eyes she saw one of his hands clench. She sensed that every muscle in his body had tensed. 'He hit them?'

She nodded.

'And he hit their mother?'

She nodded again.

'The bastard!'

She had to swallow a lump at the pointlessness of it all. 'Oh, Cameron, it's so much sadder than that.' Heartbreakingly sad.

'Did he kill their mother and then commit suicide?'

Her head came up at that. 'No!' The police had been certain. 'It was a car accident.' She swallowed. 'They hit a tree. The police who arrived first on the scene found an injured kangaroo on the road.'

'They swerved to avoid it?'

'I expect so.'

He reached out to clasp one of the hands she had clenched in her lap. 'Tell me the sad story, Tess.'

Why did he want to know? And then she thought about Lorraine, and Lance and Fiona. Maybe something in Sarah and Bruce's story would touch a chord with him. Maybe it would help heal the anger and pain inside him. Maybe it would help him find a way to forgive. Lance might not deserve that forgiveness, but she had a growing certainty that Cam needed to find it inside himself all the same.

His grip tightened and finally she met his gaze. She turned her hand over and without any hesitation at all he entwined his fingers with hers, giving her the silent strength and support she needed.

'As far as I can tell,' she finally started, 'Sarah and Bruce were happy for most of their marriage.' Though God knew she wasn't an expert. 'But two and a half years ago Bruce was involved in an accident at his work where he suffered a brain injury.'

'Where did he work?'

'In an open cut mine in the Upper Hunter Valley. An explosion went off when it shouldn't have. It was all touch and go for a while. He spent four months in hospital and then had months and months of rehabilitation.'

'What happened?' he prompted when she stopped.

She clung to his hand. Unconsciously she leaned one bare arm against his until she remembered that there were still warm good things in the world. 'His personality changed. This previously calm, family-oriented man suddenly had a temper he couldn't control. It would apparently flare up at the smallest provocation.' And then Bruce would lash out with his fists. 'He looked the same, he sounded the same, but he was a totally different man from the one my sister had married.'

'She should've removed the children from that situation immediately.'

Tess stilled. Very gently she removed her hand from his, and went back to chafing her arms. 'We're so quick to judge, aren't we? But how sacred do you hold wedding vows, Cameron? Because my sister took them very seriously. *For better for worse; in sickness and in health.* The accident wasn't Bruce's fault. He didn't go looking for it. He'd simply been in the wrong place at the wrong time. How do you abandon someone who's been through that?' She peered up at him.

'I don't think you'd abandon a woman who'd been through something like that.'

He stared at her and then dragged a hand down his face. 'Did you know about the violence?'

Bitterness filled her mouth and she shook her head. 'I was hardly ever in the country. I was too busy with my career and gallivanting around Europe and making a name for myself to notice anything.'

She'd been off having the time of her life while her sister had been living a nightmare. Sarah had always been so staunchly independent but that was no excuse. Deep down she'd known something had been troubling her sister, only Sarah would deny it whenever Tess had pressed her. Oh, yes, there had been signs. Signs she hadn't picked up on.

Her vision blurred. Sarah had been so proud of Tess's successes, but they were nothing—surface glitter with no substance. Like Tess herself.

'Tess?'

She shook herself. 'I found out about the violence after the car accident, from Sarah's neighbours and Bruce's doctors. From Ty and Krissie.' And from the letter Sarah had left her, asking her to look after the children if anything should happen to her, and leaving her a ludicrously large life insurance policy, enabling her to do exactly that.

She lifted her chin. 'All that matters now is making sure Ty and Krissie feel safe and building a good life for them here. I'll do whatever that takes.'

'Why?'

The single question chilled her. 'Because I love them.' That was the truth. Cam didn't need to know any more than that. She wasn't sure she could bear the disgust in his eyes if she told him the whole truth.

'Miss Laing, there you are! We've been knocking on the front door, but you obviously didn't hear us.'

Tess and Cam shot to their feet as three women came

around the side of the house—Cam's mum, Stacy Bennet and the unknown but well-dressed woman who'd addressed Tess.

Tess urged herself forward and forced what she hoped was a welcoming smile to her lips. 'I'm terribly sorry!'

'It's no matter, dear,' Lorraine said. 'But I want to introduce you to Helen Milton. She's the headmistress of Lachlan Downs Ladies College, which is a boarding school two hours south of here. She's made the trip into Bellaroo Creek especially to meet you.'

Cam rolled his shoulders and remained where he was. Why on earth did Helen want to meet Tess?

'I saw you play when I was in London the year before last. My dear, you have such a rare talent, but it wasn't until I saw you play in Barcelona a few months later that I truly realised it.'

Tess's spine, her shoulders, her whole bearing stiffened. He couldn't see her face, but the fact she made no reply told its own story. He moved to stand beside her.

'Hello, Cameron.'

He glanced down at his mother and his stomach clenched. 'Mum.'

'Oh, no, no, no,' Helen continued, 'you won't be hiding your light under a bushel out here, Tess!'

Tess gripped her hands together, her knuckles turning white. 'Oh, but—'

'You don't mind me calling you Tess, do you?'

'Of course not. I—'

'It'd be a crime for you to bury your talent and I won't allow it.'

Lorraine smiled at him and behind the lines of strain that fanned out from her eyes he recognised genuine delight. 'Tess is apparently not just a world-class pianist, but a classical guitarist of some note too.'

He stared at her. Not a dancer but a musician? It made perfect sense. It explained her innate grace and balance, and the way her whole being came alive when she sang.

She shrugged, colour flooding her cheeks as he continued to stare at her. He nudged her arm. 'Tess, that's really something.'

But she stared back at him with doe-in-the-headlight eyes and he didn't understand, only knew something was terribly wrong. He straightened. 'How about we go inside and I'll put the kettle on?' Tess needed something warm and sweet inside her.

'I can't, I'm sorry—this is just a flying visit. I need to be back at the college by three—I've chartered a plane—but I wanted to introduce myself to Tess while I had a brief window of opportunity.' Helen turned back to Tess. 'Because I have plans for you, my dear.'

'Oh?' Tess's voice was nothing but a whisper.

'Every year we hold a two-week summer camp at the college, and we want you to give music tuition. Heavens, talk about a coup!'

'But…but I couldn't possibly leave Ty and Krissie for two whole weeks.'

'My dear, they can come too. There'll be all sorts of activities to keep them occupied.'

'But—'

Helen's eyes narrowed and hardened. Cam shifted his feet. The headmistress hadn't got where she was today by taking no for an answer.

'Miss Laing, you can't possibly have a problem with wanting to assist the community that has taken you under its wing. Surely?'

'Well, no, of course not.'

His lips twisted. The rotten woman should've gone into politics.

'Excellent!' She took Tess's arm and led her back the way

she'd come. 'I'll email you with all the details. And don't worry, you'll be handsomely reimbursed.'

'How are you, Cameron?' his mother asked, her question stopping him from following.

He rolled his shoulders. 'Fine, and you?'

Her hand fluttered to her throat. 'Fine.'

He shifted from one leg to the other. 'Would you like to come around for dinner one day this week?' The words burst from him. They burned and needled but he didn't retract them.

'Oh!' She swallowed. 'I…I'm afraid this week isn't good.'

'Right.' Exactly the same response as the last time he'd asked her. 'Let me know when your diary clears.'

She opened her mouth, but closed it again without saying anything more. 'I'd better go,' she finally said. 'Goodbye, Cameron.'

'Mum.'

He stared after her and then started in surprise when Ty slipped his small hand inside Cam's. He glanced down. 'You okay, buddy?'

'What did that lady want?'

'I think she wants your auntie Tess to do some work for her.'

'Auntie Tess didn't look very happy.'

No, she hadn't. Why not? If she had a passion for music… Cam cut the thought off and focused on allaying Ty's concern instead. 'I think your auntie Tess is going to be just fine, Ty. She doesn't have to do anything she doesn't want to.'

Ty thought about that for a moment and then nodded. 'Would you like to play fetch with Barney?'

CHAPTER FIVE

CAM STRODE THROUGH the back door of the schoolhouse. If Stacy really wanted to turn that lower field into a play area for the children, they were going to need to talk about drainage, fund-raising and working bees.

He turned the corner and then pulled up short as Tess bolted through the school's front door.

He swallowed. He'd spent two afternoons last week finishing off the chicken coop. Both times she'd invited him to stay for dinner. Both times he'd declined. Since he'd revealed he was leaving Bellaroo Creek, they'd maintained a polite but slightly formal distance.

Which was fine by him. As far as he was concerned the less time he spent thinking about her, the better.

He watched her halt now, press her hands to her waist and drag in a breath. Something was up. Before he could kick himself forward and ask what, she'd set her spine and moved straight for Stacy Bennet's office. 'Hey, chickadee, what's up?'

Before she could enter the office, however, Krissie had hurtled out of it to fling herself at Tess, her face crumpled and her shoulders shaking with sobs. Tess held her against her with one hand while the other caressed the hair back off her face. His gut tightened as he watched her. Her love was evident in every touch and gesture. The set of her shoulders and her bent head told him that Krissie's pain was her own. He had to swallow. He rolled his shoulders, but he couldn't look away.

Krissie's storm was brief. When she finally relaxed her grip, Tess led her back into the office. Had someone frightened Krissie again? Almost without thinking he moved towards the office, halting in its doorway. Tess, Krissie and Stacy all sat on Stacy's sofa, and Tess wiped Krissie's face with a handful of tissues. They didn't see him.

'You want to tell me what happened, chickadee?'

He marvelled at the calm strength in her voice, at her distinct I-can-fix-anything attitude. He shoved his hands in his pockets. Tess Laing was a hell of a woman. He took a step back. She obviously had everything under control. He should leave and give them some privacy. He turned away.

'Do we have money troubles?' Krissie hiccupped.

He stiffened and swung back.

'Heavens, no,' Tess pooh poohed. 'What's brought this on?'

'Mikey said we must be poor if we're renting a house for a dollar a week. And I know that when you're poor bad things can happen.'

Cam stiffened. A five-year-old should be happy and carefree, not constantly glancing over her shoulder waiting for bad things to happen. A five-year-old shouldn't have so little faith in all that was bright and good.

Neither should a twenty-nine-year-old.

He shook that thought off.

For the first time he truly appreciated the task Tess had set herself.

Tess tucked the child under her arm and pulled her in close. 'When you're a bit older I'll explain life insurance policies to you, chickadee. You'll probably learn all about them at school when you're fourteen or fifteen. But I can promise—cross my heart—that your mum and dad made sure that you,

Ty and me would have enough money so we wouldn't want for anything.'

She'd taken the perfect tone, and she had perfect—

He averted his gaze and wished he'd thought to do that before she'd crossed her heart.

He glanced back to see Krissie turn up a hopeful face. 'Really?'

'Really, truly.'

'Daddy too?'

'Daddy too.'

Tess might've taken the perfect tone, but some sixth sense warned him that she was horribly close to tears. Stacy jumped to the rescue. 'You want to know why your aunt Tess wanted to come to Bellaroo Creek, Krissie?'

She stared up at the teacher with solemn eyes and nodded.

'It's because she knew we wanted you all to come and live out here and be a part of our town. Your aunt Tess knows how nice it is to be wanted.'

The child swung to Tess and Tess smiled at her. 'It's true. Don't you think it's lovely to come to a place where everyone wants to be friends with us? And weren't we talking just last night about all the things we like about living in Bellaroo Creek?'

'You like the fresh air.'

'I sure do.' She nudged Krissie's shoulder with a grin. 'And I'm finding I have a big soft spot for sultana cake.'

Krissie giggled. 'And I love Fluffy and Ty loves Barney. And Louisa and Suzie are really nice, and so is Mrs Bennet,' she added with a shy glance at her teacher.

'So you don't need to get upset about anything anyone says, all right?' Tess said.

Krissie pursed her lips and finally nodded, obviously deciding to trust her aunt. 'Okay.'

'How about you run back to class now, Krissie?' her

teacher said. 'Mrs Leigh is teaching everyone a new song and you wouldn't want to miss out on that, would you?'

With a hug for Tess, Krissie started for the door. Cam suddenly realised he still stood there staring. He tried to duck out of the way, but he wasn't quick enough. 'Cam!' Krissie hugged him, grinning up at him with those big brown eyes of hers before disappearing down the corridor to her classroom.

He gulped and turned back to Tess and Stacy. 'Sorry, I was coming in to talk to you about that lower field. I didn't mean...'

'Well, as you're here now you may as well come in.' Stacy waved him in as she walked back behind her desk. 'You've obviously become good friends with your new neighbours if Krissie's reaction is anything to go by.'

The collar of his shirt tightened. He didn't know what to say, so he entered the room and sat on the sofa beside Tess, careful to keep a safe distance between them. 'You okay?' he murmured.

'Sure.' Tess sent him a wan smile before turning back to Stacy. 'Mrs Bennet, I'm so sorry. I—'

'Stacy, dear, please...at least when the children aren't present. And let me assure you there's no need to apologise. There were always going to be a few teething problems. I knew that the moment I read your application and discovered Ty and Krissie had recently lost their parents.'

Tess's breath whooshed out of her. 'That didn't put you off accepting us into town?'

'Absolutely not! We think you're perfect for Bellaroo Creek. And we think our town has a lot to offer all of you too. What are a few teething problems in the grand scheme, anyway? So don't you go making this bigger in your mind than it ought to be. The children will settle in just fine, you'll see. What we need to do now is sort you out.'

'Me?' she squeaked.

'But before we move on to that, I just want to let you know

that if Krissie has another little outburst like that, then we'll deal with it in-house rather than calling you in.'

'Oh, but—'

'Believe me, Tess, it'll be for the best. I thought it important you came today, just so Krissie knows she can rely on you, but from hereon we'll deal with it.'

'But what if—?'

Stacy held up a hand and Cam heard Tess literally swallow. 'Oh, I'm making a hash of it, aren't I?'

His jaw dropped. He turned to her. 'What are you talking about? You've been brilliant!'

'Cam is right, Tess. You're doing a remarkable job in difficult circumstances. I sincerely applaud all you've achieved.'

Tess shot him a glance before turning back to Stacy. Her spine straightened. 'Thank you.'

'Believe me, you can be the natural mother of twelve children and still feel utterly clueless some days.'

Tess stared, and then she started to laugh. 'I'm not sure that's particularly comforting, but it makes me feel better all the same.' She leant forward, her hands clasped on her knees. 'Okay, so what did you mean when you said you needed to sort me out?'

'Do you really think you'll find it satisfying enough just keeping house and looking after the children?'

'Well, I—'

'My dear, I think you'll go mad. So what I want to propose is for you to run a class or two for our OOSH programme.'

'OOSH?'

'Out of school hours,' Stacy clarified. 'The classes would only run for forty minutes or so. The school has a budget for it, so you would be paid.'

Tess opened her mouth, but no sound came out.

'It'll be a great benefit to the community during term time and great for the kids. More important, however, I expect it will help keep you fresh and stop you from going stir crazy.'

Tess stiffened when she realised exactly what kind of classes Stacy was going to ask her to teach—music classes. Cam stared at her and recalled the way she'd tensed up when Helen had co-opted her for the summer school. He frowned. Surely with her experience and expertise teaching music classes would be a cinch. If she had a passion for music, wouldn't she be eager to share it?

He didn't want to ask any awkward questions. At least, not in front of Stacy, but...

Silence stretched throughout the office. Finally Tess smoothed back her hair. 'I know you're thinking of my piano and guitar training,' she said quietly. Too quietly. 'But piano isn't really appropriate to teach to a large group. As for guitar, that will only work if everyone has their own instrument.'

Stacy grimaced and shook her head.

Tess's hands relaxed their ferocious grip on each other. He stared at them, and then opened his mouth. He could donate the funds needed to buy the school guitars.

'I figured that might be the case,' Tess said.

He closed his mouth again, curious to see what she meant to propose.

She pursed her lips and pretended to consider the problem. He stared, trying to work out how he knew it was a pretence, but he couldn't put a finger on it. He kept getting sidetracked by the perfect colour of her skin and the plump promise of her lips.

'I could do percussion classes,' she said. 'It teaches timing and rhythm and the kids would love it.'

'Sounds...noisy,' he said.

'Which no doubt is part of the fun,' said Stacy. 'What equipment would you need?'

'Any kind of percussion instrument the school or the children have lying around—drums, cymbals, triangles, maracas, clappers. Even two bits of wood would work, or rice in a plastic milk container.'

'We can make some of those in class.'

'Do you have recorders?' Both he and Stacy groaned. Tess grinned. 'I'll take that as a yes. In my opinion recorders get a bad rap. They're a wonderful tool for teaching children how to read music.'

'Oh, Tess, that sounds perfect!' Stacy clasped her hands on her desk and beamed at them. 'Can you start next week? We hold the classes at the community hall and there'll always be a parent or four to help out. Would Tuesdays and Thursdays suit you?'

'I'd love to be involved, and any day of the week is fine with me.'

Cam couldn't tell if she truly meant it or not, but he sensed her sincere desire to fit in, to become fully involved in life at Bellaroo Creek. To give back. His stomach rolled. While he was intent on leaving.

'I know you're busy on Kurrajong, Cam, but I don't suppose you'd take a class?'

He went to say, You can take that right, when Krissie's crumpled face rose in his mind...along with the way Ty flinched whenever he was startled as if waiting for a blow to fall. 'I'll teach judo classes on a Wednesday if you think there'll be any takers.'

Tess spun to him. He refused to look at her. He refused to consider too deeply what that meant for his plans. It'd only be a minor delay. It'd only mean hanging around in Bellaroo Creek for an extra month to six weeks. He did what he could to stop his lip from curling.

'I forgot you had judo training. You received your training certificate before you went off to university, didn't you?'

He nodded. Teaching judo had helped pay his way through university.

'Excellent! That'll be another winner. I can't tell you both how much I appreciate it. I'll be in touch to fine-tune the details,' Stacy said. 'Now, Cam, my lower field.'

'We need to talk drainage and fund-raising.'

She sighed. 'Just as I feared. We might have to leave that all for another day,' she said, leading them to the door. 'But many thanks for coming out here and taking a look. Take care, the both of you.'

Cam glanced at Tess as they set off for the front gate. Was she all right? Dealing with Krissie's and Ty's fears and insecurities had to be taking its toll. He didn't doubt for a moment that she loved them, but... She'd essentially gone from fêted musician to a single mother of two needy children in the blink of an eye. It couldn't be easy. Some days it must be bloody heartbreaking and exhausting. 'Are you okay?'

One shoulder lifted, but lines of fatigue fanned out from her eyes. 'Sure.' When he didn't say anything she glanced up, grimaced and shrugged again. 'Some days it feels as if we take one step forward and three steps back.'

He couldn't think of anything to say that didn't sound like a platitude or the accepted wisdom she already knew.

'I know it'll get better with time.'

But how much time? And how ragged would she run herself in the meantime? He glanced at her again and bit back a curse.

'You did that for Ty's and Krissie's sakes, didn't you?' she said, when they reached their cars. She blinked in the sunlight. 'Offering to teach judo.'

He chose his words carefully. 'I think if they feel they can defend themselves, they'll become a little more...relaxed.'

'I don't doubt that for a single moment, but...'

But? He shifted. 'I don't teach fighting as a good or positive thing to do, Tess. Judo is about self-discipline and learning how to defend yourself.'

'Oh, it's not that!' She actually looked shocked by the idea. 'But...' she glanced around as if afraid of being overheard '...I thought you were leaving town?'

He rolled his shoulders. 'I am. That hasn't changed.' He

wanted them very clear on that. 'But there's still a lot of work to sort out on Kurrajong. Hanging around until the end of the school term means I won't be leaving it all for my station manager to sort out.' He gritted his teeth. What was a month?

Besides, it had struck him afresh in Stacy's office that while he was fighting not to turn into his father, that was exactly what he was in danger of becoming. Just like his father, he'd withdrawn from the community and thrown himself into work on the station. Leaving Bellaroo Creek and involving himself in a cause he was passionate about would ensure that history didn't repeat, but in the meantime he had to fight that inward impulse as much as he could. Even if it meant coming face-to-face with Lance and Fiona some time in the near future.

What would that matter? In three months he'd be in Africa.

In the meantime, he would not bury himself on Kurrajong Station with all of his bitterness and shattered dreams. He thrust his shoulders back. He'd get the chance to explore new horizons, stretch his wings, and shake the dust of this godforsaken place from his boots soon enough.

'You know, I'd kill for a piece of butter cake with orange icing right about now.'

He blinked himself back into the present. 'Sorry, Tess, I'm afraid the town doesn't stretch to a bakery.' Though rumour had it that might change in the not too distant future with Milla Brady coming home. One could only hope.

'It doesn't mean I can't make a cake of my own, though.'

True enough. He opened her car door for her. 'You think it'll cheer Krissie up?'

'It may well do,' she said with a shrug, but a cheeky grin peeped through. 'Mostly I just want one because I'm famished!'

He laughed, noting the way her shoulders had started to loosen.

'I don't know what it is about the air out here, but my appetite suddenly seems to know no bounds.'

'Will you have time for a lesson on the lawnmower this afternoon? It's in perfect working order again and I thought I might bring it over.' It occurred to him that it might be a good idea for Tess to have company this afternoon.

'Oh, that'll be perfect! I'll feed you cake, and you can teach me the fine art of lawnmower riding.'

'Deal.'

He tried to ignore the excitement that curled in his stomach as she drove away. He was teaching her how to use the ride-on, that was all. If he was lucky it might stop her from brooding. End of story.

Cam drove the mower into the backyard. From her position at the kitchen window Tess's gaze zeroed in on those impressive shoulders and the strongly defined muscles of his upper arms, and her breath hitched.

She leaned closer to get a better look. She fanned her face. She jumped when the oven timer dinged.

She wrenched her gaze away. It had been an emotional morning. This was a carry-over reaction from that. She shied away from the 'emotional' part of that thought too. It made her insides start to wobble again, and she was getting tired of wobbling, of feeling the ground constantly shifting beneath her feet.

'Come on through,' she hollered before he could knock on the back door.

She pulled the cake from the oven and, although she sensed him standing behind her, she set the cake on the bench and just stared at it, her mouth watering. She needed to let it cool for at least ten minutes before cutting into it.

Longer if she intended to ice it.

When she finally turned to Cam, his lips twitched as if he

could read her hunger, her greed. He nodded towards it, his eyes dancing. 'I'm impressed.'

Something in his voice… Didn't he think that she could bake? She stuck her nose in the air. 'So you should be.'

Then she grinned. 'I've been practising becoming model-mother material since before we left Sydney.' She tapped an old exercise book—Sarah's recipe book—her sister's hand-writing as familiar as her own. 'There's a wealth of hints and tips in this baby.'

'What is it?'

She handed it to him, and then hitched her head in the direction of the yard, grabbing her sunhat as they went. 'C'mon, I'm dying to eat cake so the sooner I learn all I need to about your ride-on mower, the better.'

Barney greeted them with excited barks, leaping up on Tess and practically exploding with delight when she petted him. Fluffy followed behind at a far more dignified pace.

'C'mon, you two.' She scooped the puppy up in one hand and the chicken in her other and popped them both in the chicken mansion out of harm's way. They proceeded to romp down the length of the run together.

Cam stared. 'Who'd have believed it? They've become playmates.'

'I'm convinced Fluffy thinks she's a dog. I'm not sure what she's going to do when we get more chickens.'

'When are you planning on that?'

'Just as soon as I do my research and know what I'm doing.' The last thing she needed was a dead chicken or three. There'd been enough death in the children's lives—and hers—to last them for a lifetime.

'I've some books you can borrow.'

'Thanks, but I have a couple on order at the library.'

Bellaroo Creek had the tiniest library on the planet—full of fat romance novels of which she'd fully availed herself. As part of the Greater Parkes Shire, though, the library had a huge range of books available through the inter-library loan scheme. Her books should arrive within the week.

Cam surveyed her. 'You don't want to accept my help?'

She recalled the heat that had hit her at the kitchen window, the silly flutter in her chest. 'It's not that. It's just the library already has them on order for me.' And she was *not* going to get into the habit of counting on Cam too much. Not when he was leaving Bellaroo Creek. Not when he heated her blood so quickly and assailed her senses so fully she found it impossible to keep her balance around him.

She dragged her gaze from the green promise of his eyes and gestured to the mower. 'What do I need to know?'

He placed Sarah's book on the garden bench Tess and the children had hauled around from the front yard last weekend, and gestured to the mower. 'C'mon, then, up you get.'

He helped her climb on and his hand on her arm was warm and strong. Absurdly, it made her feel strong too.

'Okay, quick overview—handbrake, foot brake and accelerator—' he pointed to each of them '—and this lever here—' he tapped it '—lifts and lowers the cutting blades.'

'Right.' She nodded. It was an auto transmission—easy-peasy.

'People generally run into two problems with ride-ons. The first is stalling the mower because they're trying to set off too fast. The second is setting the cutter blades too low and hitting dirt. So let's work on starting it up and moving forwards first. Ignition is right there.' He handed her a key.

She fitted it to the ignition and it started up first go. She put her foot on the brake, let out the handbrake and then pressed down on the accelerator.

And stalled.

Cam didn't laugh. He just reached over and pulled the handbrake on, hitting her with his heat and the scent of cut grass. 'Okay, let's try that again.'

Even though her heart beat faster, his calm confidence filtered into her.

'Ease your foot gently onto the accelerator.'

She did as he instructed and this time the mower edged forward. She drove to the lemon tree before pulling to a halt again, a ludicrous flush of accomplishment surging through her. She grinned as he strode up to her and he grinned back. It suddenly struck her how sunny it was out here, how clear the sky and how good everything smelled.

He taught her how to reverse. He showed her how to adjust the blade level. 'Okay, show me what you're made of, Tess Laing. Off you go. I want to see you do a lap around the chicken coop.'

She took a deep breath and headed for the chicken coop. She finished the lap, headed for the back fence and then did it all over again.

'Yee ha!' Holding her hat to her head, she lifted her face to the sun and laughed for the sheer joy of it. Who knew a ride-on lawnmower could be so much fun? 'Oh, man, I have to get me one of these!'

She clamped both hands back to the steering wheel as she whizzed around the chicken coop a third time. Barney raced the length of the chicken run beside her, barking madly and wagging his tail. Cam laughed at her, but she didn't mind in the least. This—this mad, fun dash on the mower—felt like freedom.

With the kids having started school this week, she'd started to feel less tense, less…shackled. Until this morning, that was. But…to not have to be on her guard all the time, aware that her every move and word could impact on Ty and Krissie in some unforseen way. That…well, it was heaven.

Not that she didn't miss the children being at home with her, but she relished the downtime from them too. Nobody had told her how much mess they could make, or how noisy they could be, or how grumpy they could get when they were tired or…or just how relentless parenthood was.

And nobody had warned her how much that could take out of a person.

Which went to show what a poor substitute she was for Sarah.

She promptly stalled the mower.

Cam came up, a frown in his eyes. 'What happened?'

She swallowed. 'I, uh, lost my concentration for a moment.' She tried to find that elusive sense of freedom again, but it slipped out of reach. 'Thank you for the lesson, Cameron. I think I have the hang of it now.' She started the mower up again. Something in his eyes made the ache inside her threaten to explode, and she wasn't sure if tears or heat would be the outcome—and she had no intention of finding out. 'I'll just park it up near the house.' She didn't wait for him to say anything, but took off.

She climbed off the mower and checked her watch.

'Somewhere you need to be?'

She suddenly laughed. 'I'm just waiting for that darn cake to cool. I'd planned on icing it, but I'm not sure I can wait that long. I'll put the kettle on in a moment and cut us both a slice. I just want to check the animals' water first.'

Cam settled on the garden bench and picked up Sarah's book. Tess checked the water bowl by the back door and then the one in the chicken coop, letting Barney and Fluffy out to play in the yard.

Cam gave a sudden snort. 'You have got to be joking! Listen to this. "Carrot spaghetti: using a vegetable peeler, create long lengths of carrot to look like spaghetti. Submerge in boiling water for a few seconds and then top with pasta sauce. Children will love it and it's a tasty way to ensure they eat their vegetables."'

She nodded. 'I know. Who has the time for that, huh? Do

you know how long it takes to peel a whole carrot with a vegetable peeler?'

He stared at her. The book dropped to his lap. 'You've tried this?'

'Well…' She heaved back a sigh. 'I just never knew it could be so hard to get kids to eat their veggies. There's loads more tips in there about grating carrot and zucchini and adding it to mince when making rissoles or meatloaf…and grating cauliflower and zucchini into hash-brown mixture and…'

She plonked down beside him. 'Long gone are the days of pulling a frozen dinner out of the freezer and nuking it in the microwave.' And God help her, but she missed those days. A sigh overtook her. 'Do you know how long it takes to grate anything?'

'Hell, Tess.'

She straightened. 'I mean, that's one of the reasons we came out here—so I'd have plenty of time to do exactly that.' Looking after Ty and Krissie was the most important job in the world to her, so what were a few grated carrots between family, huh?

'You're going to send yourself around the twist grating vegetables as if there's no tomorrow.'

It was starting to feel that way, but…

'You know what, Tess?'

She glanced at him and the sympathy and compassion in his eyes made her sinuses burn and her throat ache. 'What?' she whispered.

'I think you need to stop trying to be Sarah and focus on being yourself.'

Her head rocked back.

'And another thing… Why are you so reluctant to continue with your music?'

She froze.

'Why aren't you eager to dive back into your piano and guitar?'

An invisible hand reached inside her chest to squeeze her heart.

'Hasn't it occurred to you that playing again might actually help you manage all your stress and worry?'

'No!' She leapt up. 'You're wrong. So wrong!'

She stood there, hands clenched, shaking, and realised too late how utterly revealing her reaction had been. She forced herself to sit again, doing what she could to hide her panic. 'No.' She moderated her tone. 'You don't understand.'

'Then explain it to me.'

Explain? Oh, that was impossible, but… 'Music consumes me. I… When I play, nothing else matters. For the time being, it needs to go on the backburner until I get a decent handle on my new life.'

All true, but she couldn't look at him as she said it.

He surveyed her for a long moment. It took a superhuman effort not to fidget. 'So you haven't played since you heard about Sarah's accident?'

The yearning rose within her but she ruthlessly smothered it. 'There hasn't been time.' There would never be time. She'd make sure of it. She'd turned her back on that life of selfishness.

His eyes suddenly narrowed. 'Why do I get the feeling you're punishing yourself?'

'Low blood sugar,' she prescribed, jumping up. 'It's beyond time I serve up that promised cake.'

'Tess.'

She halted halfway to the back door and then turned. 'Cam, can we leave this for now? I…I just need to get my priorities straight and my music messes with that too much. I'll sort it out eventually, but in the meantime talking about it doesn't help.'

She hated lying to him. But he was leaving Bellaroo Creek soon… And it was just too hard.

With a nod, he let it be and she could've hugged him. To

stop from doing anything so stupid, she set up the card table and served tea and cake. Cam ate it with the same relish as she did, and it lifted something inside her.

Eventually they both sat back, sated.

'Tess, about grating all those vegetables.'

His tone made her laugh. 'Yes?'

'I don't think it's necessary.'

'No? Well, c'mon, convince me, because, believe me, if I never see another grated carrot for as long as I live it'll be too soon.'

He sobered, that compassion alive in his eyes again. 'Tess, no matter what you do you'll never be able to make up to Krissie and Ty that they've lost their parents. You can grate from now till kingdom come, but it won't make a scrap of difference.'

Her throat closed over.

'And spoiling them in the attempt will be doing them a grave disservice.'

With a superhuman effort, she swallowed. Had she been spoiling them? 'You think I fuss over them too much, don't you?'

His face softened. 'I think when you're feeling more confident, you'll relax a bit more.'

'So...that's a yes, then?'

He remained silent.

She pondered what he'd said. It should break her heart that she couldn't make up to Ty and Krissie that they'd lost their parents. And it did, but it was strangely freeing too. It gave her permission to focus on the things she could change.

She glanced at Cam. He'd put his exciting plans for Africa on hold for a whole additional month for Krissie and Ty...and for her. She started to smile. 'You're saying I'll never have to grate another carrot in my life?'

'That's exactly what I'm saying.'

He grinned back at her and she couldn't help it. She leaned across and pressed her lips to his.

CHAPTER SIX

CAM DIDN'T PULL away. He didn't even hesitate. He greeted Tess's kiss with wholehearted pleasure. One of his hands cupped her face, engulfing her in his warmth. Tendrils of sensation unfurled in her stomach and drifted out to every corner of her body in slow adagios of delight. Waltzing delight.

And then the tendrils became licks of fire. Cam's free hand curved around the back of her neck and he pulled her in closer, his lips moving over hers more fully, more thoroughly, offering her even more delight, making her even hungrier for him.

Greedy to taste, greedy to touch, she slid her hands to either side of his face and she explored the texture of his jaw and the strong column of his neck until her hands and fingers were as alive as her lips. When he licked the corner of her mouth, traced the fullness of her bottom lip, she opened up to him and he dragged her right into his lap as their tongues danced. She wound her arms about his neck as if she never meant to let him go.

She gave herself up to the thrill of being alive and in his arms. Kissing Cameron was like listening to vibrant, wonderful music. Better yet, it was like *making* vibrant, wonderful music. Music that could fill the soul and send it soaring free, and Tess wanted to soar and fly and swoop and twirl with Cameron and never stop.

She slipped her hand between the buttons of his shirt,

needing to touch firm bare skin. His hand slid beneath her shirt, his caress an omen of bliss. And then they both stilled, so unaccountably in tune with each other that they knew.

They knew this had become more than a kiss. It was about to become something a whole lot more interesting…if that was what they chose.

If.

Tess stared up into eyes so vivid with promise that all she had to do was reach out. She sucked her bottom lip into her mouth and tasted him there. Her body clamoured for more, but…

She shivered. Ty and Krissie.

She gave a tiny shake of her head.

She felt the sigh he heaved back, but he nodded his acknowledgement. He went to lift her off his lap, but she held up a hand to forestall him. She dragged in a breath, counted to three…four, and then removed herself under her own steam until she was sitting beside him again.

'I really shouldn't have done that,' she murmured.

He surveyed her with watchful eyes, but didn't say anything. She bit her lip and then shrugged. 'But while I shouldn't have kissed you, I can't find it in myself to be sorry for it.' She frowned, suddenly realising how selfish that sounded. 'I mean, I'm sorry if I made you—'

'Me neither, Tess,' he cut in.

He leaned back, a grin lighting those ecstasy-inducing lips of his and hunger raged through her.

'I don't see why you shouldn't have done it. I don't have a problem if you want to do it again.' He raised his hands. 'Just saying.'

She laughed and shook her head. 'I shouldn't have done it because I liked it too much.'

'And there's a problem with that?'

It was the same as when she played the piano or the guitar—the world receded and the music took over. And until three months ago, she'd let it. Willingly. Gladly. She'd welcomed it. Only now, she knew how selfish that had been. How unfair it had been to those around her.

No more.

She'd let her selfish obsession keep her from Sarah, when her sister had needed her. She couldn't afford to let Ty and Krissie down in the same way.

'There are just too many strikes against us, Cameron.'

'Like?'

'Like the fact I truly believe Ty and Krissie need stability for a while. I don't think it's fair to ask them to adjust to a new man in their lives just yet. Not after everything they've been through. I don't think that's unreasonable, even if you do. We're just searching for…'

'An even keel.'

She nodded. 'I really don't want to mess this up.'

'Strike One,' he murmured.

She glanced down at her hands and then back at him. 'There are other issues too. You have a grudge in your heart that's bigger than forty hectares of golden canola. Until you come to terms with that, there'll never be room in your heart for another woman.'

He drew back. 'I have good reason for that grudge.'

'Yes, you do.'

'But?'

Couldn't he see how much his bitterness, how much holding on to his grudge was hurting him? 'It's just from where I'm standing—sitting—that's Strike Two.'

He didn't say anything.

She couldn't let it go. 'What Lance and Fiona did to you, Cameron, sucks. But…' She gripped her hands together. 'But has it never occurred to you that maybe they never meant for it to happen, that they never meant to hurt you? That maybe they just fell in love with each other? Maybe he's just as appalled by what's happened as you are.'

Cam dragged a hand back through his hair, making it stand on end. She ached to reach out and smooth it back down.

'Look, Tess, all his life Lance has been jealous of me. Jealous that I had a father with a bigger station than his father's. Jealous that I had two homes I divided my time between. Jealous that I did well at sport and at school. You name it—if it was mine, he wanted it.'

He scowled out at the yard. 'If he spent half as much time working towards whatever it was he wanted instead of resenting me for having it, or stealing it from me, then he might have achieved something worthwhile. I thought he'd grow out of it. Hoped he would. For heaven's sake, he's twenty-six years old! I never thought he would go to such lengths, but...'

His hands clenched. 'But it appears he still wants what I have, so, no, I haven't considered the fact that he never meant to hurt me. I know that's precisely what he was hoping to achieve.'

Bile burned the back of Tess's throat at the expression in his eyes.

'He stole all that I most cherished in this world, and he laughed while he did it. Forgiveness, even if he asked for it...'

He broke off, his face growing grimmer. 'This time he went too far. He involved an innocent third party in his nasty little games.'

All that I most cherished. She swallowed, suddenly nauseous. 'Fiona?' The name croaked out of her.

He gave one hard nod.

She swallowed again. 'Forgive me for saying this, but the fact she, um...canoodled with your brother while engaged to you doesn't exactly cast her in the role of an innocent.'

Did he still love that tall, slim woman with the golden ponytail? The thought left a bad taste in her mouth. If her stomach hadn't been churning so badly she'd have grabbed another piece of cake to override it.

'Lance has always had more charm than was good for

him. He knows how to woo a woman and make her believe he's in love with her.'

She leant towards him, though she was careful not to touch him. 'But maybe he really loves Fiona.'

He turned to her then and raised a dark eyebrow. 'When he's finished with her, he'll dump her.' His lips compressed into a hard, grim line. 'He'll break her heart. All just to get back at me.'

That didn't ring true. Oh, she didn't doubt for a moment that Cam believed it, but... 'They looked very together at the luncheon...as in a definite couple. Cameron, it's been ten months. Your mother obviously thinks they mean to marry.'

He didn't say anything for a long moment. 'Even if what you say is true, does that excuse the fact that they betrayed me?'

'Of course it doesn't! But maybe it'd prove that they never meant to hurt you, and that has to count for something.'

'If it were true, perhaps it would.'

She ached for him then, for the pain she sensed bubbling beneath the surface, his utter sense of betrayal. Forgiveness would bring him peace, if only he would consider it. Ten months. Surely that was long enough. But some wounds, she knew, never healed.

She smoothed her hair back, longing to make him smile. 'Do you know you kiss like an angel, Cameron? And that by holding onto your grudge you're depriving some woman out there of the most divine kisses, all because you won't forgive Lance?'

He stared and then a laugh shot out of him. 'I didn't realise you could be quite so persistent.'

'Dog with a bone,' she agreed. Speaking of dogs... She glanced around and then blew out a breath when she found Barney and Fluffy sunning themselves only a few feet away. 'My parents found it one of my less endearing traits.' But it was the reason she'd become such a fine musician.

He leaned towards her, swamping her with his green-grass freshness and all that false promise. She gulped. He didn't mean to kiss her again, did he?

He reached out and traced a finger down her cheek. Her pulse leapt to life beneath it. 'Tess, regardless of what any-one says, you are divine.'

What if she channelled all the energy she'd put into her music into healing this man, into loving him and showing him there was a better way? Would she succeed? Would she—?

She drew back. She didn't have the time or the luxury for those kinds of games. If she only had herself to consider…

But she didn't.

Her skin pimpled with gooseflesh when she recalled the kind of family Sarah had dreamed of having—a wonderful, close-knit family who loved each other, supported each other and did things together. That had all been taken away from her. It had all gone so terribly wrong for her, and for Ty and Krissie too. Tess couldn't let it go bad for them again. Her fingers shook and her throat tightened. She'd failed Sarah once, but she wouldn't fail her again.

Ty and Krissie were the ones who deserved—who needed—all her energy. And she couldn't risk their hearts to such an endeavour. She couldn't let them become so de-pendent on Cam that they'd be crushed when he left.

When he left…

'And Strike Three,' she said, 'you're planning on leaving town. Unless you've changed your mind on that head.' Her heart gave a traitorous jump.

'I haven't changed my mind.' He stared down at his hands. 'Strike Three,' he agreed.

They sat in silence for a moment. 'So lots of reasons not to kiss,' he said, as if double-checking her resolve.

'Yep.' She couldn't keep the glumness from her voice.

Cam rose. 'I think it's beyond time that I made tracks.'

A protest clamoured through her but she bit it back. He was right.

He set his dusty Akubra on top of his head and touched its brim in a kind of salute. 'I'll be seeing you, Tess.'

It had all the finality of an irrevocable goodbye.

'Let's go down this road,' Ty said, pointing to the right.

Krissie nodded her agreement.

Ty held Barney on his lap, Krissie held Fluffy on her lap, and Tess had a picnic hamper on the passenger seat beside her. It was Saturday. The children had completed their first full week of school, and they'd agreed to spend the day exploring the surrounds of their new home.

Tess turned the car obediently in the direction Ty had indicated. All the roads around here seemed to be unsealed, and some of them weren't in the best of repair. This one was no exception, but she didn't mind driving slowly to avoid the worst of the potholes and corrugations. It gave her a chance to enjoy the scenery.

And the scenery was stunning—long stretches of low hills green with wheat and lucerne. Here and there a river or stream gleamed silver-blue amid the landscape. There were ridges of land dotted with scribbly gums and sheep, and brown fields enclosing brown cattle, muddy dams and dandelions. It was warm enough still to leave the window down and the air was fresh and green, if occasionally dusty.

'Fluffy thinks that'd be the best spot for our picnic,' Krissie announced, pointing to a stand of Kurrajong trees up ahead.

The trees formed a natural glade that sloped down to a river. Tess glanced at her watch. They'd been driving for just over an hour, and, if her sense of direction was anything to go by, they should've nearly completed the loop that would take them back into Bellaroo Creek.

They'd taken the road west out of town and the plan had been to circle around and come back in on the town's northern side. According to her calculations, they couldn't be more than a couple of kilometres from the township.

And it was nearly lunchtime.

And she was starving!

She pulled the car to the side of the road. 'Well spotted, Fluffy. This looks like a fabulous picnic spot.' She hoped whoever owned the land wouldn't mind them trespassing. 'Watch out for cows,' she hollered as the children and animals spilled from the car and raced towards the river. 'And don't get too close to the water!'

She was out of breath when she reached them. And, truly, it was the prettiest spot. They all gazed at it in silence for a moment as if to just drink it in. 'Beautiful,' Tess breathed.

Krissie slipped her hand inside Tess's. 'Do you think Cam has a river on his station?'

'I haven't the foggiest, chickadee, but I expect so. You can ask him next time you see him.'

'At judo class!'

Both children were excited by the after-school activities on offer, but especially Cam's judo class.

'Ninja!' Ty executed a high, flying kick that made Fluffy flap her wings.

'Food,' Tess countered.

They spread out a blanket and devoured their picnic—sandwiches, fruit, date scones and bottles of water—sharing it all with Barney and Fluffy. By the time they were finished, Tess wanted nothing more than to curl up on the blanket and doze in the sun.

'Barney wants to explore,' Ty announced.

'Of course he does,' Tess said, suppressing a grin, a sigh and an eye-roll all in one movement. She glanced at Krissie.

'Fluffy wants to sleep.' She sighed.

Lucky Fluffy.

'Right, well, we'll take our picnic things back to the car and put Fluffy in her cage to sleep.' Tess had thankfully had the foresight to pack the cage and some newspaper. She left the rear door of the car up and wound down all the windows. 'Okay, which way does Barney want to go?'

They walked beside the river. With the children and puppy racing off in front of her, leaving her momentarily chatter free, Tess was at leisure to enjoy the peace. After only five minutes of walking, they rounded a bend and a low sandstone and wrought-iron wall brought them up short.

Krissie turned back to her. 'What is it?'

Tess glanced over the fence. It was so overgrown it took her a moment to make out what it was. When she did her stomach gave a queer little jerk. 'It's a cemetery,' she said, watching both children carefully.

Neither recoiled, and she let out a breath.

'Can we go in?'

Shielding her eyes against the sun, Tess followed the sandstone wall around until she found what she was looking for. 'The entrance is over there.' She pointed. If they'd driven a little further on they'd have happened upon this spot in the car—it was the very end of the road. Her lips twisted. In more ways than one, she supposed, but she determinedly left the gallows humour behind as she walked through the gate.

'Ty, Krissie.' She gestured to the children. 'There are some rules we need to observe in a cemetery. It's very bad manners to walk on a grave, so please keep to the paths.' And there were some, even if they were terribly overgrown in places. Someone was doing what they could to maintain this little cemetery. 'If you want to look at the headstones walk beside the graves, okay?'

Both children nodded solemnly. 'What about Barney?'

'Puppies are exempt, young man.'

They turned in concert to find an elderly woman, half hidden in the shade of a Kurrajong tree, sitting on a camp chair beside one of the graves. 'I hope we're not disturbing you,' Tess ventured.

'Not at all, lovey.'

Tess moved towards her. 'I'm Tess Laing and this is my nephew and niece—'

'Tyler and Kristina, yes, I've heard about you folk and I'm real pleased you've come to settle in Bellaroo Creek. I'm Edna Fairfield. I meant to make it to your luncheon, but my knees aren't as young as they used to be. My husband, Ted, and I own a pocket of land just back that way.' She nodded back the way Tess and the children had come.

After shy hellos, Ty and Krissie raced off to explore. Tess sat on the grass next to the older woman and Barney settled at her feet to nap. 'I'm afraid we've been trespassing on your land. I'm terribly sorry.'

'You're welcome to wander through our holding whenever you want, lovey.'

They sat in silence for a while. Tess finally gestured. 'Is this a private cemetery?'

'Lord, no, it's the Bellaroo Creek cemetery, but folks these days prefer to scatter the ashes of their loved ones on the land. Hardly anyone comes here any more.'

'But you do?'

'My dear mother and father are buried just over there.' She pointed to a nearby grave. 'And this here—' she touched the edge of the grave she sat beside '—is where we buried my darling boy, Jack. He was only a tiny tot—eighteen months—when croup took him.'

Tess read the dates on the headstone and a lump lodged in her throat. Edna had been coming here for sixty years to sit by her beloved baby son. 'Oh, Mrs Fairfield,' she whispered. 'I'm so sorry for your loss.'

'Don't you go wasting your sympathy on me, young Tess. Ted and me, we raised three healthy children and sent them out into the world—good strong folk we're proud of. Into every life there comes some sorrow.' She might be old but her eyes hadn't faded and they glanced shrewdly at Tess now. 'I understand there's been some recent sorrow in your lives too.'

She nodded. Into every life... She glanced at Ty and Krissie, carefully walking around the graves. 'I'm thinking, though, that moving out here means we can start focusing on good things again.'

Please, God.

'I don't doubt that for a moment.'

She couldn't help smiling at Edna's no-nonsense country briskness.

'But, lovey—' Edna sighed after a moment '—I can't help wondering who'll come here and tend my Jack's grave when Ted and I are gone.' She shook her head. 'It's a silly thing to worry about, I know, but it doesn't stop me from thinking about it.'

'I don't think it's silly.'

She didn't think it was the slightest bit silly. She went to say more but suddenly found Ty and Krissie standing in front of her. Holding hands, no less! 'Everything okay, poppets?'

'Can we bury Mummy here?' Krissie asked without preamble.

Whoa!

Okay.

Um...

She glanced at Edna. 'Is it still possible to arrange a plot here?'

'I expect so, lovey. Lorraine Pritchard would be the person to ask. She's the president of the Residents Committee.'

'That's Cam's mum,' Ty said to Edna. 'He's our friend.'

'He lives right next door,' Krissie added.

'He's a good young man,' Edna agreed. 'He helps Ted out every now and again. Means we can still manage to keep a few head of cattle on our land.'

He did? Tess stared at Edna. What would she and Ted do when Cam left?

* * *

Cam's farm ute was parked out the front when they arrived back home. Tess parked beside it and tried to school her wayward heart back into its normal pace and rhythm instead of a ridiculous speeded-up staccato.

'Can we play on the computer?'

She eyed her nephew and her heart expanded. Two months ago he'd been listless with no enthusiasm for any kind of play. Understandable given the circumstances, but now it seemed the world held a whole list of endless possibilities.

She climbed out of the car and crossed her fingers, prayed the worst was behind them now. 'As long as you promise to let Krissie have her turn too.'

He nodded.

'Okay, go on, then.'

He was about to race off, Krissie at his heels, when Cam came around the side of the house. 'Hey, Cam.' He waved.

'Hey, kids.'

Krissie flung her arms around Cam's middle and hugged him. Tess couldn't prevent a squirm of envy.

'We found the bestest cemetery,' she announced, releasing him. 'You wanna come play on the computer?'

He blinked. 'Um… Maybe some other time.' He ruffled her hair. 'I have to chat to your aunt about some stuff.'

Krissie ran off and Cam turned to her with a frown. 'What's so hot about a cemetery?'

'They want to inter their mother's ashes there.'

He pushed the brim of his hat back to stare at her. She nodded. 'I know. It took me off guard too. It's all kind of serious, huh?' She twisted her hands together. Once they interred Sarah's remains in the Bellaroo Creek cemetery, there'd be no going back. For good or for ill, Bellaroo Creek would become their home. For good.

'Are you okay with that?'

'Sure.' As long as Bellaroo Creek flourished. As long as the primary school remained open. As long…

She kicked herself into action. Standing still for too long allowed doubts to bombard her. And what was the use in those? Striding around the car, she retrieved Fluffy and the cage.

'So what's wrong?'

She sent him a swift glance. 'Who says anything's wrong?'

'I do. Your eyes are darker than normal and you have a tiny furrow here.' He touched a spot on her forehead, before taking the cage from her.

She folded her arms. How could this man be so attuned to her and yet be so far out of reach? She clamped her lips shut. He *was* out of reach. *That* was the pertinent fact. Everything else was just…wishful thinking.

'Tess?'

She turned away, swallowing back a sigh, and led the way down the side of the house. 'They want to inter their mother's remains in Bellaroo Creek's cemetery, but they've made no mention of their father.'

She plonked herself down on the garden bench and watched Cam as he placed Fluffy into her mansion of a coop. He was a joy to watch. He might be big, but he didn't lumber about like a bear. He moved with the grace of a big cat.

She forced her gaze away, only turning back when he took a seat beside her. 'And that's a problem?'

She thought about it. 'I don't know. Potentially, I guess. We had Sarah and Bruce cremated, but I had no idea what to do with the ashes. A counsellor suggested I let the children be part of the decision-making process, but they were appalled at the thought of scattering the ashes. So…'

'So you brought them with you.'

'They were very insistent that their mother should come with us.'

'But their father?'

'Not a brass razoo.' She shook her head. 'And I couldn't very well leave him behind, could I?'

'I guess not.' He squinted up at the sky. 'I expect they'll need closure at some point.'

'Lord, I hope so.' She grinned at him. 'Because I'm not sure I want Bruce living on the top of my wardrobe for the next twenty years.'

He laughed as she'd meant him to, but he leaned towards her, and that suddenly seemed dangerous. 'And, yet, why do I get the feeling that if that's how long Krissie and Ty need, then that's exactly where Bruce will stay?'

He smelled like cut grass, dirt and fresh air. It hit her that he smelled like Bellaroo Creek. When he went to Africa, he'd be taking a little bit of Bellaroo Creek with him. The thought should've made her smile.

'I met Edna Fairfield.'

He leaned back. 'Keeping Jack company?'

'Uh-huh.'

She eyed him for a moment. He rolled his shoulders. 'What?'

'She has a very high opinion of you.'

'I have a high opinion of her and Ted.'

'They'll miss you if you leave.'

'When, Tess. *When* I leave.'

She shook herself. 'That's what I meant.'

He had exciting, not to mention important, work to look forward to in Africa. He had the promise of adventure before him, the once-in-a-lifetime experience of immersing himself in another culture and sharing his knowledge, and helping make the world a better place. She couldn't begrudge him his dream, but...

She pulled in a breath. 'I liked her a lot. I don't know much about cattle, but...but could you teach me what to do so I can help them out?'

'Nope.'

She gaped at him.

'Lord, Tess, you think I'm just going to abandon them?'

'Well, aren't you?' He was abandoning all of Bellaroo Creek, wasn't he?

'I've told Fraser to keep an eye on things out there, to help wherever needed.'

His station manager? 'It won't be the same, you know?'

'That can't be helped.'

She supposed he was right.

'If you really want to help Edna out, you'll drop out there when her fruit trees are full and pick the fruit for her…and ask her to teach you how to bottle it, and how to make jam. She'd love that.'

'Excellent.' She'd have to find out when the trees came into fruit. Oh, and she'd better find out what kind of fruit trees they were too.

'Plum and mulberry. And you'll be looking at about November.'

The man could read minds.

'And I also think you should come to judo lessons.'

His sudden change of topic threw her like an unexpected rhythm or an atonal jazz riff. 'You mean…participate? Be one of your students?'

'What would it hurt to learn a few self-defence tactics?'

Nothing, she supposed, but she'd never precisely been the sporty type.

'And you're going to be there anyway, bringing Ty and Krissie to the class. So, why not?'

She saw it then, what it was he was trying to do. 'You think Ty and Krissie will feel safer if I know how to defend myself.' Her heart thumped and her hands clenched.

'I think it's a good idea for every woman to know how to defend herself.'

She chewed her bottom lip.

'Come on, Tess, I'm not talking about grating carrots here.'

He was right. 'It's an excellent suggestion.'

'Good.'

'Now what can I do for you?'

He blinked. And for a moment she could've sworn the colour heightened on his cheekbones. Her heart leapt into her throat and it was all she could do not to cough and choke and make a fool of herself. 'I mean,' she rasped out, gazing everywhere except at him, 'I expect there's a reason you dropped by this afternoon, other than to bully me into taking your judo class?'

He leapt off the bench and strode several feet away. 'I wanted to find out what you had in mind for a vegetable garden,' he said, his back to her, and she knew he felt the same heat, the same urgency, that she did. 'I am getting forty prime hectares practically scot-free, after all. I mean to keep my word, Tess. Chicken coop—tick. Puppy—tick. Vegetable garden—still pending.'

'You didn't just build a chicken coop. You built a chicken palace!' As far as she was concerned, he'd well and truly paid off any debt he'd owed.

He turned and squinted into the sun. 'Are you after a, um, vegetable patch on the same sort of scale?'

She laughed at the expression on his face, though she didn't doubt for a moment that if she wanted it he'd do his best to make it a reality. 'Truly, Cameron, I just want a home for all of these.' She gestured to the ragged array of donated pots and planters. 'And whatever else you think might be a good idea to plant.'

'I was sorting through them when you pulled up. You've a nice variety there.'

'The town's generosity knows no bounds.'

'They want you to stay.'

And she wanted to stay. She had to make this move work. She had to. Her smile faded when she recalled the expression on Edna's face when she'd wondered aloud about who would tend Jack's grave when she was gone. A shiver of unease threaded through her.

'You're not having second thoughts, are you?' he rapped out.

'No!'

'But?'

She swallowed. 'But it didn't hit me until today how tenuous the town's survival is. And I've thrown my lot—and Tyler and Krissie's—in with the town's.' What if the school closed? What if the town did die a slow death? What would they do? It would mean more upheaval and that would be her fault.

'Tess.'

She glanced up.

'Nobody can foresee the future. All you can do is make the here and now meaningful.'

Right. She knew he was right.

'And work with the Save-Our-Town committee to attract even more new blood to the area. Okay?'

She drew in a breath and nodded.

He smiled. 'Now are you going to help me measure out this garden bed or what?'

'Aye-aye, sir.' She clicked her heels together. 'Right after I ring your mother. Apparently she's the one I should talk to about organising a plot at the cemetery.'

He dug his phone out of his pocket and tossed it to her. 'She's on speed dial.' Pulling a tape measure from his hip pocket, he moved away to give her a measure of privacy.

She brought up his list of saved numbers. Lorraine's number was the second on the list.

The first was Lance's.

All you can do is make the here and now meaningful.

She stared at Cameron's back as she placed her call.

CHAPTER SEVEN

Lorraine organised a working bee at the cemetery with all the speed and efficiency of a conductor's flourish. 'We can't hold a memorial service there with it looking the way it is! It's beyond time we tidied it up.'

Which was why Tess and the kids found themselves getting ready to return to the cemetery the following Saturday. Tess finally managed to convince Krissie that Fluffy would be much happier staying behind in her chicken mansion rather than attending a busy, noisy working bee. When she rose and turned she found Cam standing directly behind her and her skin flared and her stomach tumbled and a bubble of something light and airy rose within her.

Her heart fluttered up into her throat. She swallowed it back down into her chest and tried to pop the bubble with silent verbal thrusts. *He'll be gone soon.* But her brain refused to cooperate. It was too busy revelling in the undiluted masculinity on display. In low-slung jeans, soft with wear, and a faded cotton twill work shirt—with buttons...buttons that could be undone—he made her fingers itch to run all over him in the same way they did whenever she was near a piano.

She took a step back. 'Hello, Cameron.'

He blinked and that was when she realised he'd been staring at her as intently as she'd been staring at him. Her skin flared hotter. They both glanced away.

'Are you coming with us to the working bee?' Krissie asked.

'Working bee?'

He glanced at Tess. She frowned. Hadn't Lorraine spoken to him? *None of your business.* She cleared her throat and folded her arms. 'The town's organised a clean-up of the cemetery. We're just about to head out there now.'

'I didn't hear about it.'

She unfolded her arms. Well, why not? It—

None of your business. She folded her arms again.

'You have to come,' Ty said. 'It won't be the same if you're not there.'

That was one way of putting it.

Cam smoothed a hand down his jaw. 'The thing is, buddy, I was going to start on your vegetable garden today.'

'But we want to help you do that, don't we, Auntie Tess?'

'We do.'

'And the working bee is for our mummy.' Krissie slid her hand into Cam's. 'Please...you have to come.'

Tess had to choke back a laugh. Talk about emotional blackmail! She clapped her hands briskly. 'Okay, kids, grab your hats and, Ty, make sure you bring Barney's lead.'

The kids raced off.

Cam stared at her. She sucked her bottom lip into her mouth. He followed the action and his eyes darkened. She released it again, her pulse pounding in her throat. She wheeled away to stare blindly at the backyard. 'I don't feel right about you working here without us being around to help. I want to learn.'

'It'll mostly be brute work today.'

'Nevertheless.'

There was a pause. 'Is that a roundabout way of saying you'd like me to come to the cemetery instead?'

'I'd love you to come.' And she meant it. She really wanted him to be part of the working bee, but she wasn't quite sure what that meant. Except she needed to be careful. *Very* careful.

She needed to fight her fascination for this man, or it would all end in tears. If they were only her tears that wouldn't matter, but… She glanced towards the house. 'I think it's only fair to warn you that I expect your mother, Lance and Fiona will all be there today.'

Again there was a long pause. 'You think I'm afraid to come face-to-face with them?'

He stole all that I most cherished.

'I think you've been doing your best to avoid them.' A part of her didn't blame him. She wouldn't want to come face-to-face with the person she loved more than life itself on a daily basis and know they'd chosen someone else. And not just any anonymous *someone else* either, but a sibling. It'd be like ripping a scab off a wound again and again.

She could understand why he wanted to leave Bellaroo Creek. She could even see why he might need to. She couldn't see that cutting himself off from the entire community in the meantime was the thing to do, though. He hadn't done anything to be ashamed of.

'You know—' she planted her hands on her hips '—I think you've made it awfully easy for Lance and Fiona. It wouldn't hurt them to have to see you on a regular basis and feel awkward and ashamed about what they've done.'

He laughed. It surprised her. 'It's nice to have you in my corner, Tess.'

Was that what she was? *You want to be a whole lot more than just in his corner.* She shook the thought off, refused to follow it, tried to focus on the conversation. 'That's your problem with your mother, isn't it? You feel she's not on your side.'

'She's not,' he said bluntly. 'She's always favoured Lance. And, no, that's not jealous sibling rivalry talking, Tess, but…'

Her heart stilled at the expression on his face. 'But?'

'I realised something when we were up at the school the

other day. When my mother left my father, he withdrew into himself. He still managed the farm but he had no social life. He let all his friendships slip; he let his position in the community go. When he died he'd closed himself off so completely that the only person left to mourn him was me.'

She pressed a hand to her chest. 'Oh, Cameron, I'm so sorry.' What a terrible story. And what a sad household for a boy to grow up in. No wonder—

'But I have no intention of following his lead.'

She stared at him for a long moment. 'That's one of the reasons you're going overseas.'

'I might never have a wife and children, but it doesn't mean I can't find meaning in something I'm passionate about. It doesn't mean I can't have adventures and contribute to the world.'

Helping to feed the world would be a huge contribution. Africa would be an amazing adventure. He'd experience the most awe-inspiring things and eventually his heart would heal. Eventually.

'But in the meantime, it's time to stop holing up like a hermit.'

She lifted her chin. 'I think that's an excellent plan.'

He stared at her and then pursed his lips. 'But?'

This is none of your business. She lifted a shoulder. 'Just because things didn't work out with Fiona doesn't mean you'll never fall in love again.'

He shook his head. 'I saw what love did to my father.' His eyes grew grim, dark…shadowed. 'No, thanks, once was enough. I'm not diving into that particular hellhole again. I'll find satisfaction elsewhere.'

She grimaced. Feeding the world was all well and good, but an abstract concept couldn't give you a big fat hug when you needed it. She opened her mouth but he held up a hand. 'Leave it now, Tess.'

She moistened her lips and then nodded. He'd make friends

on his adventure. They'd look after him. For no reason at all, a hole opened up inside her.

'You know,' she started, turning back towards the house, 'I used to be really good at minding my own business.'

One side of his mouth hooked up. 'I don't believe that for a moment.'

The thing was, it was true. She'd been too caught up in her music to notice if anyone had been feeling down or worried. How selfish she'd been! She'd been too self-absorbed to involve herself in other people's problems, in other people's lives. In a way, she'd cut herself off as comprehensively as Cam had.

Her chest burned. Giving up music had been a good thing.

But that bubble of half-happiness half-excitement that had been floating around inside her ever since she'd turned and seen Cameron finally popped.

'Would you like to come with us, Cam?'

'I'll meet you at the cemetery. I'll run back home and collect a few tools first.'

She waved him off as Ty and Krissie piled into the car. She pushed her shoulder back and drew in a breath. A big one. These kids were worth every sacrifice she'd have to make. She'd choose them over music any day of the week—even when they were running her ragged. She'd choose them over a man.

Yes. She slid behind the steering wheel and nodded. This was the life they were meant to be living. *I won't let you down, Sarah.*

Lorraine set the men to work with lawnmowers and whipper-snippers clearing the scrub from around the fence line and mowing the paths. The women and children she set to work clearing weeds from around the graves and scrubbing headstones clean of moss and lichen. Having never been a part of a working bee before, Tess enjoyed the sense of camaraderie with the dozen or so other workers.

As expected, the handful of children eventually took off to play in the neighbouring paddock—eight children, three dogs and two soccer balls. One of the older women kept an eye on them. 'Don't worry yourself,' she'd said to Tess when Tess had wandered over to check on them for the third time. 'We know out here that at least one person needs to keep an eye on the children to avert potential accidents. And it's a treat for me to sit in the sun like this and listen to the littlies.'

With her fears eased, she'd returned to work pulling weeds from around a grave.

Lorraine came up, touched her arm. 'Tess, I want to thank you for convincing Cameron to come along.'

Tess sat back on her heels. 'I had nothing to do with it. I was only surprised he didn't know about it.'

The older woman's hand fluttered about her throat. She glanced away.

'When the children told him, though, he was more than happy to lend a hand.'

Lorraine turned back with an overbright smile. 'All I can say is that it's lovely to see him here.'

Tess met the other woman's gaze. 'Then you might want to tell him that some time.'

She blinked. 'You think he'd...' She swallowed. 'It's his birthday next Sunday, you know? It's one of those birthdays that ends in a zero. Maybe I...'

Tess didn't want to appear too interested. She went back to pulling weeds. 'Are you planning anything special?' Would she like Tess's help?

'Oh, no, I don't think so. I don't think he'd welcome that.'

The older woman's sigh touched her heart. The secateurs suddenly felt heavy in her hands. What would she do if Ty and Krissie were ever at sixes and sevens the way Cam and Lance were? She suppressed a shudder. She'd do everything in her power to make sure that never happened. If it did, she'd do everything in her power to fix it.

But what if that wasn't enough?

'Listen to me rambling on! Time to get back to work.'

Lorraine moved away to oversee more job delegation. Tess glanced around until she found Cam's broad capable bulk, whipper-snipper in hand, cutting a swathe through the long grass on the other side of the cemetery. He looked at ease, comfortable, in his element, and Tess followed his lead, giving herself up to working in the fresh air beneath an autumn sun that wasn't too fierce.

'Hello, I'm Fiona. We met briefly at the luncheon.'

Tess blinked to find the flawless blonde working on the other side of the grave. She suddenly found herself battling the desire to reach out and slap the other woman or to just get up and walk away.

Whoa!

She rocked back on her heels. 'I remember,' she managed, but something in her tone made the other woman flush.

Be nice! 'Gorgeous day for it, isn't it?'

'Yes.' Fiona didn't immediately set back to work, but stared at a point beyond Tess's right shoulder. 'Cam is looking well.'

Ah… 'Well? Gorgeous more like.' She turned to look too. 'That man is a sight for sore eyes.'

When she turned back she found Fiona staring at her. 'Are you and Cam—?' She broke off. 'Sorry, that's none of my business.'

Tess went back to weeding. She had no intention of satisfying Fiona's curiosity.

'Look, Tess.' Fiona set her clippers down. 'What I really want to know is if he's doing as well as he looks.'

Tess glanced up. 'Why don't you ask him some time? I understand you used to be close.'

The flawless skin suddenly flushed pink. 'Oh! You think I'm a right piece of work, don't you?' She sat with a thump on the side of the grave—a cement rectangle with an angel atop the headstone. Tess kept her mouth very firmly shut. 'I never meant for all this to happen. I never meant to fall in love with Lance and cause a rift between the brothers.'

And yet she had. And from what Tess could see, Fiona wasn't doing anything about it—wasn't trying to bridge gaps or make amends.

'I know Cam is the better man.'

That had Tess's head swinging around.

'The thing is, you see, he never really needed me. He's so strong and honourable and…self-sufficient. I can't complain about the way he treated me—he treated me like a queen—and yet… I never felt I'd made much of an impact on him.'

How wrong Fiona had been! She opened her mouth and then snapped it shut again. She had no intention of betraying Cam's confidence.

'But with Lance…'

Fiona turned to glance at Lance and her whole face lit up. Tess's stomach clenched.

'Lance needs me.' She turned back to Tess, her face earnest. 'I feel I can help make him a better man. I don't expect you to understand because you're strong, like Cam.'

Her, strong? That was laughable.

'Taking on your niece and nephew like you have proves that,' Fiona continued. 'But I'm the kind of person who needs to be needed. And that's why I'm with Lance instead of Cam.'

Couldn't she have found a different man who needed her instead of Cam's brother?

A bustle at the front gates interrupted them. 'It's the CWA with lunch,' Fiona explained, rising. 'I'll go lend them a hand.'

'You do that,' Tess muttered under her breath, pulling out a weed with a vicious tug. No doubt the CWA *needed* her. Man, what a flake! What on earth had Cam seen in her?

Other than her flawless skin.

And her perky blonde ponytail.

Oh, and her model-like figure.

She sat back on her heels scowling at the grave, but after a moment she started to laugh. Oh, did she have the green-eyed monster bad or what? Fiona was probably a perfectly nice woman. And to give her credit, she did seem genuinely sorry for hurting Cam and creating a rift between him and Lance.

Though, from what Cam had said, that rift had been widening well before Fiona had come onto the scene.

Mind your own business.

As for the jealousy, she had no right to that. No right whatsoever.

Cam was more than ready for lunch when it was announced. Breakfast seemed like hours ago and he expected they'd all worked up healthy appetites. He joined the throng around the CWA tables and started loading up a paper plate with sandwiches and party pies.

'Hello, Cam, would you like a mug of tea?'

Fiona. He waited for his gut to clench. It did. A fraction. Not as much as he expected, though. 'Thanks.' He nodded.

'Are you well?'

She was obviously trying to make an effort. 'Never better.' He went to ask her how she was, but his arm was suddenly tugged.

'Cam,' Ty asked, 'can I feed Barney a party pie?'

'Sure you can, buddy. Just make sure it's cooled down first, okay?'

And then he found he'd wandered away from the table and he hadn't made the polite enquiry of Fiona after all. With a shrug, he set off for a spot in the shade of a Kurrajong tree.

'Hey, Tess.' Lance called out from his spot in the sun on the other side of the gated entrance from Cam. 'Why don't you join us?'

Cam's gut clenched up tighter than a newly sprung barbed-wire fence. With his back stiff and rigid, he kept moving towards the Kurrajong tree.

'No, thanks,' Tess called back. 'I prefer the view over here.' And then she was sitting beside him on the newly clipped grass and gesturing at the scene spread in front of them. 'It's really starting to take shape, isn't it?'

The woman stole his breath.

'This working-bee idea is really something.'

He glanced around at the clumps of people settling down to have their lunch and his throat tightened. He'd honestly thought, once, that he could make his simple dream come true in this community. Days like today brought the disappointment home to him afresh. And yet…

He couldn't deny it'd been invigorating working in the sun, side by side with people he'd known his entire life. He glanced at Tess—and some he'd known for less than a month.

'Yeah, I guess it is,' he finally agreed. And if she noticed the strain in his voice, she didn't mention it.

I prefer the view over here.

He found himself starting to grin.

'I think this will be the perfect spot to bury Sarah.' She shrugged when he glanced at her. 'Well, to inter her ashes or whatever it's called. You know what I mean. It's a nice spot for a final resting place.'

He supposed she was right.

'What did you do with your father's remains, Cameron?'

'I scattered his ashes on Kurrajong Station. It's what he wanted.'

She nodded and bit into a sandwich. 'That's nice too.'

What about her parents? Were they still living? 'Will your parents come to the memorial service?'

'I doubt it.'

She lowered her sandwich to her plate and he immediately regretted asking the question. 'Forget I asked,' he ordered. 'It's none of my business.'

She shot him a look that made him laugh, and then she shrugged. 'I don't mind. It's kind of funny coming to a place like Bellaroo Creek. You've all known each other so long that you know each other's histories.'

She turned those big brown eyes to him and he had to swallow. He shifted and covered his lap with his plate, and hoped she didn't notice how tightly he gritted his teeth.

'It's nice,' she finally finished.

'You're fitting in brilliantly.'

She flashed him a smile. 'I'm not feeling insecure, but thank you. I know it'll take time, but so far it's going better than I'd hoped.'

That was okay, then.

'My parents are...distant,' she said, picking her sandwich up again. 'Sarah and I actually came from quite a privileged background, but to be honest I'm not really sure why my parents had children. We were raised by nannies.'

The sweet vulnerable curve of her mouth turned down and her slender shoulders drooped for a moment, and an ugly darkness welled in his gut.

'So, to be honest with you, I don't really know them. Obviously they came to Sarah and Bruce's actual funeral.'

But he could see now that they'd provided Tess with no support whatsoever.

'And I very much doubt they'll ever visit us out here at Bellaroo Creek. They've been living in America these last few years.'

He shifted. 'Privileged, you say?'

She nodded.

'So, you could've organised nannies for Ty and Krissie and kept your career?'

'It's what my parents wanted me to do.'

He saw now that Tess had too much compassion and natural sympathy, too much integrity to have abandoned her niece and nephew.

She rolled her eyes. 'Apparently a daughter who's a concert pianist and fêted classical guitarist has more cachet than one who is merely a mother and housekeeper.'

They should be proud of her and all she'd taken on!

'I couldn't let Sarah down,' she said softly.

He reached out and briefly clasped her hand. 'She'd be proud of you, Tess.'

'I hope so,' she whispered, her eyes suspiciously bright. She blinked and then resumed eating. 'We always promised each other that if we ever had children we'd be hands-on parents—the opposite of our own.'

He understood that perfectly. He couldn't imagine having a child and then farming it out for other people to look after. Even the folk around here who sent their kids to boarding school couldn't wait for end of term time.

'She left me a letter, you know?'

'Sarah?'

She nodded.

'She knew something was going to happen to her?'

'I think after Bruce's accident it really hit home to her how life can change in an instant. She said she wouldn't offend me by asking me to raise Ty and Krissie as if they were my own—she knew I would. She told me all the good things I had to offer them. And then she told me about the life insurance policy she'd organised so we'd never have to worry about money.'

'She wanted to be prepared,' he murmured. In case life ever played her another nasty trick. She'd been smart.

'Which is why you should get married and have kids, Cam. 'Cause, the way things currently stand, if anything happens to you Lance will probably inherit Kurrajong Station, and we can't have that.'

He stared, and then he threw his head back and laughed. 'You never give up, do you?'

'Nope.'

He shook his head. 'Sarah sounds like a hell of a woman, Tess.'

'She was.' Her eyes turned misty and faraway and he knew she no longer saw the cemetery and this golden autumn day. 'She was four years older and became a bit of a surrogate mother to me.'

'And you hero-worshipped her, right?' She'd had the kind of relationship with Sarah he'd hungered to have with Lance. He promptly lost his appetite.

Tess laughed. He loved the sound. 'I expect I plagued her half to death. But I remember...'

She leaned forward, her eyes dreamy and distant again. Thirst snaked through him and the longer he gazed at her, the thirstier he became, but he couldn't tear his eyes away. 'What do you remember?'

'Music was my passion.' She sat back. 'No, it was more than that. It drove me, rode me...obsessed me. I would practise for hours and hours, driven to get a piece just right. I'd stay up into the wee small hours, practising and playing and practising more and more. And Sarah would sit up with me, and when I was about to drop with exhaustion she'd put me to bed.'

His heart started to ache. Ty and Krissie had lost their mother, and that was a terrible thing. But Tess had lost a sister—a much-loved sister—and who had held her in their arms and let her cry out her grief?

Certainly not her parents.

Tears swam in her eyes. 'I miss her so much.'

He reached out to touch her cheek, but suddenly a little dynamo in the shape of Krissie burst up between them. Her bottom lip wobbled as she stared at Tess. 'Why are you crying?'

Tess held her arms open and Krissie threw herself into them. His heart clenched when Tess lifted her face to the sun and dragged in a breath to steady herself.

So strong!

'I was just telling Cam about your mum and I got to missing her.'

'I miss her too,' Krissie whispered.

'I know, chickadee.'

Krissie snuggled closer. 'Tell me a story about when you and Mummy were kids like Ty and me. Were you ever naughty?'

'Never!'

Tess feigned shock and Krissie giggled.

'Except—' she winked '—this one time when we were in high school. We both really, *really* wanted to see this movie—*Charlie's Angels*—and we actually snuck out of school early to go and watch it.'

Krissie covered her mouth with both her hands, her eyes wide.

'What's more, we bought the biggest popcorn we could find and the biggest cola you ever did see.'

'Did you get caught?' Krissie breathed.

'No, but we got the biggest tummy aches, which served us right for being such gluttons!'

Tess tickled Krissie until she squealed with delight and then ran back off to find what the other children were doing.

Cam wanted to hug Tess the way she'd hugged Krissie. He wanted to tickle her until she felt better too.

His lips twisted. Who was he trying to kid? He wanted to kiss her until neither one of them could think straight. But that wouldn't make her feel better, not in the long term.

He blinked to find her eyeing him as hungrily as he did her. His skin tightened, but he ignored it. He had to tread carefully around this woman. She'd taken on a lot. She'd sacrificed a lot, and it would be cruel and thoughtless of him to make her life harder. She didn't deserve that.

She deserved to grow roots and be surrounded by a community that would look out for her. She deserved to be loved by a man who could give her security and a loving family. She deserved a man who meant to stay in Bellaroo Creek.

He crushed his plate into a ball. He wasn't any of those things.

But...

There was one more thing she deserved. 'Tess?'

'Hmm?'

'I think you're making a big mistake.'

She swung to him, brown eyes wide and alert. 'About?'

'Giving up your music.'

Her face closed up. 'I haven't given it up. I'm giving music lessons for the school, aren't I? Ty, Krissie and I sing all the time—I'm teaching them to harmonise. As for being on stage—'

'I'm not talking about being on stage. Tess, when was the last time you played the piano or picked up a guitar?'

She flinched. 'What's that got to do with anything?'

'I think it has everything to do with it.'

'You don't know what you're talking about.'

Every instinct he had told him he was right. Sacrificing something that was such a part of who she was would damage her in a fundamental way. Maybe not this year or the next, but eventually. 'Do you think Sarah would approve of you punishing yourself like this?'

Tess went to leap up, but he grabbed her arm. 'I'm not going to let this lie, Tess. I'm going to get to the bottom of it.'

She subsided back to the ground beside him. 'And what do you think you're going to find when you do? Do you think it's going to be pretty or something you can fix? Because it's not pretty and it can't be fixed. So as far as I'm concerned talking about it is pointless.'

'I mightn't be able to fix it, Tess, but bottling it up won't help either.'

She had to look away then because his eyes told her he

only wanted her to be happy. And she knew his questions came from a good place, not a bad one.

'Tess?'

And he wouldn't leave it alone; she knew that too. If he knew the truth then he'd see that she was right. Even if it did change his opinion of her for the worse.

'Sarah asked me to come home at the beginning of December.' She stared at her hands. 'But I had a whole series of concerts lined up and I put her off for a month.'

A whole month!

'Later, when I did get home…' When it was too late. 'I found out Sarah had been trying to set up a second residence and was in the process of moving the children there.'

She'd wanted Tess to come home and help her. But Tess, in her selfishness and self-absorption, had put Sarah off for a whole month. Who knew what they could've accomplished together in a month, what changes they could've made…what disasters they could've averted. Instead of making a difference in her sister's life, she'd chosen to shine on stage instead.

She straightened. But she wouldn't let Sarah down again. She'd look after Ty and Krissie and give them all the love she had, give them the absolute best lives she could. It wouldn't be enough. It would never be enough. But it was something.

'Hey!'

She blinked at the hard command in Cam's voice.

'Did she tell you why she wanted you to come home?'

'No, but—'

'Then you have nothing to beat yourself up about.'

He was wrong about that. 'She asked so little of me over the years.' *She should've come home.*

'She should've been straight with you. Nothing that happened to Bruce and Sarah was of your making.'

'No, but—'

'And whipping yourself into a frenzy of guilt is ludicrous. You didn't cause Bruce's accident. You weren't driving the

car that left the road and hit the tree. Hell, Tess, you're giving these kids a great life. You should be proud of yourself.'

Proud of herself for not being there when Sarah had needed
her? Never!

'Depriving yourself of your music—'

She leaned towards him. 'When I chose my music over
Sarah, music let me down. I let me down. But, worse, I let
Sarah down.' She shook her head. 'I'm not risking that again.'

'Tess, I think Sarah would weep in her grave if she knew
all you'd given up.'

Tears clogged her throat. This time when she leapt up, he
let her go. 'My life has a different focus now and I'm pleased
about that.' *She was!* She pointed behind her. 'I'll go help
clear the food away.'

Tess had been working steadily for an hour when Lance
stormed up. 'You have no right upsetting Fi!'

She stared up at him. 'Lower your voice,' she snapped.
'You upset my kids again and I will have your guts for gar-
ters, got it?'

His mouth opened and closed. He dropped down to sit
on the side of the grave she was working on. 'I, uh…I didn't
mean to appear so…'

She quirked an eyebrow. 'Aggressive?'

He raked a hand through his pretty blond hair. 'I've never
thought of myself as scary to kids before,' he muttered.

'Then maybe you should stop puffing your chest out and
beating it in that ridiculous fashion, and learn some manners.'

She swore his jaw dropped to the ground at his feet. She
didn't doubt for a single moment that the women in his life
mollycoddled him, and she had no intention of joining their
ranks.

Still…

She rose, planting her hands on her hips. 'And I didn't

upset Fiona. I suspect she upset herself. I believe it's called a guilty conscience.'

He turned beet-red and glanced away. Interesting. Maybe he wasn't immune to a guilty conscience either.

'Still, at least it appears you really do love her.'

He swung back. 'Of course I love her.' He gazed to where Fiona worked and his face took on a goofy expression. 'I mean, she's the best girl in the world.' He glanced back at her, the blue of his eyes suddenly bleak. 'I didn't mean to...'

She waited but he didn't go on. 'You're wrong about Cam too. He's not trying to ruin you. I doubt he'd ever stoop to something so petty.'

He squinted down at the ground. 'Cam never was petty. But after what I did, who could blame him for wanting his revenge?'

She let the silence speak for her.

He rose with a sick kind of pallor. 'I wish...'

She ran out of patience with him then. 'For God's sake, stop thinking about yourself for once! Have you ever considered actually apologising to Cameron for your appalling behaviour?'

His eyes started from his head. 'Are you joking? He wouldn't listen. I expect he'd deck me!'

'Then you're a stupider man than I thought.' With that, she turned away sick to her stomach. Cam deserved so much more than what any of his family had given him.

It's nice to have you in my corner.

She set her shoulders. Cam mightn't be here for much longer, but for as long as he was in Bellaroo Creek she had every intention of remaining in his corner.

CHAPTER EIGHT

'SHOULDN'T WE BUY Cam a present if it's his birthday?'

Tess glanced at Ty. 'I think you and Krissie should make him a birthday card. I bought cardboard, glitter pens and stickers.' She'd lugged them all the way from Sydney sure they'd find a use for them, and she set them on the kitchen table now. 'Plus, we are making him the best cake in the world.'

'With cream and jam in the middle and sprinkles on top?' Krissie double-checked.

'That's right, chickadee.'

'And I'm going to take my pin-the-tail on the donkey game,' she added. 'I think Cam will love playing that.'

'I'm sure you're right.'

'I know!' Ty's face lit up. 'I can write him a story. We're writing stories at school and Mrs Bennet said I was good at them.'

'Cam would love a story,' Tess agreed. 'And you can make a proper cover for it out of the cardboard and draw a picture on it.'

Hopefully book and card building would keep the two of them occupied for the next thirty minutes while she worked out how to cut her sponge in half, fill it with jam and cream, and then ice it.

Krissie suddenly rose from the kitchen table to press herself to Tess's side. 'Mrs Bennet's leaving at the end of the year. She's re…re…'

Tess's heart clenched at the anxiety that threaded through her niece's eyes. How she wished she could shield them from everything that worried or frightened them. 'She's retiring.' Tess's own heart clenched then too. 'Which means you'll have a brand-new teacher next year.' Please, God, because if Bellaroo Creek couldn't attract a new teacher to town, and the school closed…

Her stomach churned, but she made her voice cheerful. 'And we'll have to make sure they feel as welcome to town as we did.'

'And then we won't be the newest people any more,' Ty said.

Krissie bit her lip. 'Do you think we'll like her…or him?'

Ty glanced up at Krissie's 'or him', his eyes wary. It made Tess's heart burn harder. 'I'm sure we will.' She sent them both her biggest smile. Reassured, they returned to their card and story making.

'That's the best cake in the world!' Krissie said in awe a little while later when Tess stepped away from the cake to admire her handiwork.

'And that's one super-duper card.' Tess picked it up to admire Krissie's handiwork.

'And I'm finished too!'

Ty handed her the book he'd made. He'd stapled the pages between cardboard and had drawn a…um… She'd challenge even Sarah to hazard a guess about that one. 'It looks just like a proper book!'

That was obviously the right response because Ty beamed at her. 'It's a story about a cowboy.'

'Which will be perfect for Cam,' she agreed, glancing again at the cover trying to make out either a cow or a horse or a cowboy.

She clapped her hands. 'Okay, go wash your hands, put on your party clothes and let's go surprise Cam.'

He'd been here yesterday afternoon, building the bed for the vegetable garden. He hadn't let slip for a single moment that he had a birthday today. He'd said he was going to catch up on his bookkeeping.

On a Sunday?

On his birthday?

Oh, no, no. Tess had decided then and there that the least she could do was make him a birthday cake. Somewhere along the line, that had evolved into a full-blown party. Grinning, she went to put on her pink party dress. A party was exactly what they all needed.

Cameron stilled, cocked his head to one side and then frowned. Someone was knocking on the front door.

Nobody knocked on the front door. Ever. The few people who came out to Kurrajong these days came around the back. Fraser would've tapped on the French doors of Cam's study if he'd needed to discuss anything.

More knocking sounded. He pushed away from his computer with a growl and set off through the dim hush of the house. Since he'd taken a bedroom at the back, he rarely came into this part of the house any more. These big front reception rooms with their picture rails, antiques and high ceilings held the memory of too many shattered dreams. He scowled as he strode through them now. He flung the heavy door open, a bitter reproof burning on his tongue…

A reproof he swallowed at the sight that met his eyes. A sight as colourful as a flock of rosellas and just as cheerful.

'Surprise!' Ty and Krissie yelled, almost in unison, and then they each popped a party popper that covered him in coloured streamers, and for a moment he felt just as colourful—as flamingo-pink and butter-yellow as the girls' party dresses and as purple and blue as Ty's best jeans and shirt.

But then the shadows of the rooms behind touched the back of his neck with cold fingers, mocking him with the ludicrousness of any colour surviving within their forbidding walls, and he pulled the streamers from his head and shoulders, and a hard ball settled in the pit of his stomach.

'Happy birthday, Cameron.'

Tess's smile almost melted the coldness. 'How on earth…?'

She waggled a finger at him. 'You needn't think you can keep something as important as a birthday a secret.'

As far as he was concerned, it was just another day.

'And we wanted to give you a party, because you're one of our best new friends!'

The smile Krissie sent him did melt the coldness. And while he wished with all his might that they'd turn around and walk back home, he managed to cover his lack of enthusiasm with a smile. 'A party?'

Ty held up a bag. 'We brought jellybeans and crisps!'

'And Auntie Tess made you a cake.'

He glanced at Tess, delectable in her pink dress, but her smile had slipped. She'd sensed his discomfort. 'I hope we haven't caught you at a bad time.'

He blinked. He straightened. She was giving him an out? He could tell them he was really busy, promise to drop over to their place in a couple of hours… And Tess would turn the children around and walk away, and leave him in peace?

But when he glanced at the kids with their eager shining faces, he didn't have the heart to disappoint them. He could manage a party in this cold, heartless house just this once. It wouldn't kill him. He dragged in a breath and made himself grin. 'A party sounds like just the thing!'

He was rewarded with a smile from Tess that almost knocked him off his feet.

'Your house is amazing,' Ty breathed, glancing around Cam's bulk. He frowned and edged closer to his aunt. 'It's a bit dark.'

He translated that immediately into, *It's a bit scary.* He kept his voice steadily cheerful. 'Well, with only me living here these days I don't use these front rooms much.'

'Auntie Tess was right,' Krissie whispered to her brother. 'We should've gone around the back.'

'But I wanted to see,' he whispered back.

Cam then found himself pushing the door open as wide as he could, beckoning his visitors inside and turning into the reception room to his left and throwing open the curtains as wide as they would go, so the children could take in the room in its entirety, sans shadows. He strode across the corridor and did the same for the other reception room. The children trailed behind him, oohing and ahhing, their eyes wide and mouths agape.

When Tess saw the dark cherrywood baby grand in the second room, she froze. He took the cake from her before she could drop it. He recognised the fear in her eyes, but there was something else there too, fighting for supremacy. She closed her eyes, but not before he saw raw, naked hunger.

With sudden resolution, he turned back to Krissie and Ty. 'It's been a long time since I used this room, but I think it makes the perfect party room, don't you?'

'Yes!'

He set the cake down on a colonial-style hardwood coffee table. He took the bags of party food from Ty and set them there too. 'Then let's get some plates and drinks and then we can really get this party on the road.'

He led them through the formal dining room with its magnificent table-seating for twelve.

Ty gazed at it in awe. 'You must be able to have the biggest parties.'

'Legend has it that my grandparents threw the kind of parties that people spoke about for years.'

There were photo albums showing these rooms filled to bursting with smiling people, dressed in their best. As a boy, he'd pored over those photographs. He'd yearned to be in those photographs, and he'd sworn to bring that kind of gaiety back to Kurrajong House—a dream he'd finally thought within reach when Fiona had agreed to marry him. His hand clenched. How wrong he'd been. He couldn't re-create the gaiety of that bygone era. Not with the kind of family he had.

But he refused to fade away as his father had done.

'Cameron?'

Tess touched his arm. He stared down at her and had to fight the urge to haul her into his arms and kiss her. Falling into her would chase away the ghosts of the past and ease the hurt of shattered dreams, at least for a little while. If he backed her up against the wall, teased her, seduced her...

He could lose himself in her arms and take all he wanted.

And he wanted all right, no doubt about that, but it'd be a despicable thing to do.

She bit her lip—her plump, delectable bottom lip—and her eyes darkened at whatever she saw in his face. The pulse at the base of her throat fluttered. He wanted to press his lips to that spot and—

'The kitchen?' she croaked.

Gritting his teeth, he swung away. 'This way.'

They collected plates, bowls and cans of soda, and headed back to the so-dubbed party room. Cam opened the two front bay windows. A warm breeze filtered through, fanning the lace curtains, a touch of white against the dark wood panelling. While he did that, Tess and the children put out the party food—a big bowl of crisps, smaller bowls of jellybeans and chocolates, a plate of ginger-crisp biscuits, and even a small cheese platter.

He didn't have much of a sweet tooth, but his mouth started to water.

Tess, with her back very firmly to the piano, placed three blue candles on top of the cake and then lit them. She glanced at Krissie and Ty. 'Ready?'

They huddled in around her and at the tops of their voices sang the Happy Birthday song to him, and the longer it went on the wider their grins grew.

'Blow out the candles,' Tess ordered.

He did and they popped more party poppers. Krissie handed him a card she'd made out of glitter and stamps, and Ty handed him a story he'd written about a cowboy, and Cam found himself laughing and eating jellybeans and playing pin the tail on the donkey…and having a party.

He pulled up short when Fraser and Jenny appeared in the doorway a short while later. 'We came to investigate the noise,' Jenny said.

Cam leapt to his feet. 'Come and join us. Tess, Ty and Krissie, this is my station manager, Fraser, and his wife, Jenny, who manages to keep this place clean and running smoothly.' They'd be Tess's nearest neighbours when he left. It would be good for her to know them.

'Lovely to meet you.' Tess beamed at them. 'And you've arrived at the perfect time. We were just about to play pass the parcel.'

Everyone ended up with a snack-sized chocolate except Cam, who won the final prize of a family block of chocolate.

He stared at it—*a family*. He gazed about the room. At the moment they had all the appearance of a family. His heart started to pound, but he pushed the fantasies away. He wouldn't be beguiled by them. Not for a second time. He knew his own strength. He could survive one let-down, but two? He shook his head.

He couldn't deny, though, that for the space of an afternoon Tess and her kids with their laughter and this party had brought a spark of life back into this cold mausoleum of a house.

Krissie slipped a hand inside his. 'Are you having a good party, Cam?'

'The best,' he assured her. 'There's only one more thing that would make it perfect.'

They all swung to him. Tess planted her hands on her hips. 'What could we have possibly forgotten?'

His heart started to thump. She wouldn't thank him for this. At least, not initially, but... He glanced about the room. She'd given him a marvellous memory to take away with him when he left Bellaroo Creek. Instead of seeing his father sitting here in the half-dark, he'd now see Tess in her pink dress and hear the children's laughter.

'Come on, out with it,' she ordered.

He planted his feet. 'I'd like you to play something for me on the piano.'

Wind rushed in Tess's ears. The room shrank in on her. She collapsed onto a footstool.

No! Cameron couldn't ask this of her. He couldn't. It was too cruel. She'd kept her back firmly to the piano because the lure of it was like a siren song.

She knew he didn't mean to be cruel. He couldn't know about the hole that had opened up in her as big and as dry as the Great Western Desert since she'd packed away her guitar and stopped playing the piano

'I don't play any more,' she whispered, aching to sit at that beautiful piano and to fill her soul with music, but—

She'd turned her back on that life. On that person she'd been.

'I don't have parties,' Cam said, 'but I made an exception today and I don't regret it.' He glanced at the children and then at her again. 'Make an exception, Tess, just for today.'

She glanced at the children then too. The hope in their faces tore at her. Didn't they know that if she'd been a better person—if she'd never played music—their mother might still be alive?

Krissie hopped from one leg to the other, clapping her

hands silently, hope filling her eyes—eyes the same shape and colour as Sarah's. Ty came over to where she sat and pressed his hands to either side of her face. 'Please, Auntie Tess? Mummy loved to hear you play.'

Her heart nearly fell out of her chest. It took every ounce of strength she had not to cry. Cam came across and held out a hand to her. She stared at it, swallowed and then reached up and took it, allowed him to help her to her feet and lead her across to the piano.

'What would you like me to play?' she murmured, once seated.

'Whatever you want,' he said, moving to sit across the room from her in an easy chair.

Her hands shook as she played a tentative scale and she had to suck in a breath at the familiarity, at the need growing in her.

Oh, play that one again, Tessie. I love that one. It makes me feel as if I'm flying above the treetops.

Tuning out the doubts, Tess gave herself up to playing one of Sarah's favourite pieces. It filled her up. It made her feel—for a short time—as if she'd found her sister again.

As ever, the music transported her. When she finished she couldn't tell if she'd played it well or not. The stunned faces in front of her told her it'd been good.

Cameron leaned towards her and she imagined she could feel the strength of his regard and his admiration all the way across the room. 'Superb.' And the expression in his eyes made her feel as if she were flying above treetops.

Then she saw a movement by the doorway. Glancing at Cam, she rose and nodded towards his visitors.

Lorraine. Fiona. And Lance.

All the adults rose, but nobody spoke. Finally Jenny cleared her throat. She glanced at Ty and Krissie. 'Would you like to see where Fraser and I live? It's just out the back,' she added to Tess. 'And I can show you the lambs.'

Krissie and Ty leapt to their feet.

'You could come meet the horses too,' Fraser added, winning over one little boy in an instant.

Tess went to start after them, but Jenny touched her arm with a murmured, 'You might like to stay here.'

Tess didn't want to stay. She didn't want to intrude. But she recognised the vulnerability behind the stiff set of Cam's shoulders and the grim line of his mouth. *It's nice to have you in my corner.* She counted the people in the room. She went and stood beside him. She might not even out the numbers, but she'd give him whatever support she could.

Lorraine finally broke the silence. 'Hello, Cameron.'

'Mum.'

'I wanted to wish you a happy birthday, son, and…' She trailed off as if she wasn't sure what else to say.

Tell him you love him!

'If you really wished me a happy birthday,' Cam drawled in a voice so hard it made Tess wince, 'you'd have left your other son at home.'

'He wanted to wish you many happy returns too.'

'They say love is blind. Where Lance is concerned, you're living proof.'

'Oh, Cam, please,' Lorraine implored.

'Please what?' He rounded on her. He glared at Lance. 'I want you off my property now!'

Lance flinched, but he held his ground. 'I came to say I'm sorry.'

The silence grew so loud Tess wanted to clap her hands over her ears.

'For?'

She glanced up at Cam uneasily. She didn't like that edge to his voice.

'For…for breaking up your engagement with Fiona. The thing is, I…I love her.' He swallowed. 'But I'm sorry we hurt you.'

'Love her?'

Cam's scorn almost burned the flesh from Tess's arms and it wasn't even directed at her.

'The only person you love, the only person you've ever loved, is yourself.'

Lance flinched.

'The only reason any of you are standing here now is because your farm is in trouble and you want me to bail you out.'

'You're right. Ever since you walked away from the management of the farm it's all gone to hell in a hand basket, but that's not why we're here. We're here because...' He halted, but Fiona nudged him. 'Because I've never been the kind of brother you deserved. I'm sorry for that. But I never really thought you'd turn your back on me and Mum.'

'I haven't turned my back on Mum.'

The unspoken words, *but I've turned my back on you*, hung in the air.

Cam shifted his gaze to Lorraine. 'That said,' he drawled, 'she doesn't seem particularly eager to spend any time in my company.'

Although he hid it well, Tess could feel the hurt emanating from him. She moved a fraction closer.

'Oh, Cameron, honey, it's not that I don't want to spend time with you! But you refuse to step foot over my threshold.'

'The threshold where Lance and Fiona reside,' he pointed out.

'It's this house!' she suddenly blurted out. 'I find it so difficult being here.'

They all stared at her in varying states of astonishment.

'You hate this house?' Cam shifted, frowned. 'But, why?'

Her hand fluttered about her throat. 'That's all in the past now.'

'Obviously it's not or you wouldn't find it so hard being here. Why?' he demanded again.

Lorraine folded her arms as if to shield herself, and Tess had to fight an urge to go to the older woman.

'You won't like it, Cameron. It does no good to rake over old hurts.'

'The truth,' he demanded in that hard voice Tess found difficult to associate with him.

Lorraine glanced away. Her gaze drifted about the room and she barely suppressed a shudder. 'I was so unhappy here. I…I married your father with such high hopes…'

She dashed away a tear. Tess's throat thickened. Surely Cameron could see what distress he was causing his mother.

'So you had an affair.'

Lorraine drew herself up at that. 'I most certainly did not! I'd left your father for a good eight months before I fell in love with Bill. I left your father because he was unfaithful to me, Cameron. Not once, but multiple times.'

Cam's jaw slackened. 'But he left that house and land for you to use. Even after you'd married another man.'

'Oh, darling, that wasn't due to unrequited love. It was due to remorse. And guilt.'

Tess wanted to take Cam's arm and lead him to a chair to digest the information, to give him time to think and take it all in.

'That's why I never visit this house. It holds so many bad memories for me—a time in my life where I questioned my very abilities as both a wife and a mother. When I left here I…I thought I would never laugh again. That's why I've refused your dinner invitations, Cameron. I simply can't imagine being in this house and not being overwhelmed again by those old feelings. And since the unfortunate business with Lance and Fiona…well…it's been almost impossible to ask you to dinner at my house. I knew you wouldn't come.'

'Unfortunate?' Cam choked out.

'They didn't do it on purpose, son.'

Cam glared at Lance. 'I don't believe that for a moment,'

he said with soft menace. 'I wonder how long Fiona will stick by you, *brother*, when you ruin the farm and have nothing left to your name?'

Lance paled. 'Things have always come easy to you, Cam. You always had good grades, were great at sport and took to farming like it was bred into your bones, but you have no sympathy for those who don't have the same natural aptitude.'

'I have no sympathy with those who sit back and let everybody else do the hard work.'

'It was hell growing up in your shadow!' Lance suddenly yelled. 'I wanted to be just like you, you know that? It's why I took your things. I was hoping they'd give me the key, the magic, but I failed again and again until I decided to stop even trying. And you want to know what the worst thing was? You let me keep all the things I took, when you could've taken them back so easily. Even Fiona. I know you could probably win her back with a snap of your fingers if you put your mind to it, but this time—*this time*—I will fight back.'

'Hey!' Fiona pushed forward to give Lance's arm a shake. 'No, he couldn't. Why do you have so little faith in me?'

'Because you left me for him, so who will you leave him for?'

The words could've been uttered cruelly, contemptuously, but Cam said them with a weariness that simply highlighted their logic.

She stared at Cam with those perfect blue eyes, and Tess wished she could just disappear into the woodwork. She refused to glance up at Cam. She didn't have the heart to deal with the hunger she fully expected to see in his eyes.

'I really wanted to make things work with you,' Fiona said. 'You had such seductive dreams about turning this house into a wonderful family home, but...'

'But you obviously changed your mind and decided my brother was a better bet.'

She shook her head and her perfect blonde ponytail

swished about her perfect face in perfect rhythm. 'I came to realise those dreams of yours meant more to you than I ever did. I was just some idea you had of the ideal wife and mother. I needed more than that. I needed you to need me, but you're so self-sufficient, Cam, that I started to think you'd never need anyone.' She glanced at Tess. 'Maybe I was wrong about that.'

Beside her, Cam stiffened. She wanted to drape herself across him and tell Fiona to *back off!* That Cameron was too good for the likes of her. She didn't. That would be a crazy, stupid move, and she was darn sure Cam wouldn't thank her for it if she did. But one thing became increasingly clear. She was fed up with just standing here while these three made excuses for themselves.

'I'll tell you all something for nothing,' she stated so loudly it made everyone jump. 'Cameron has made my family's transition to Bellaroo Creek so much easier than it would otherwise have been. He's one of the best men I have ever met and he's a valued friend.'

True, true and true.

'Furthermore, I think he deserves a whole lot better from all of you.'

'Tess,' he growled.

'No, she's right,' Lorraine said. 'I shouldn't have let stupid memories keep me from coming out here to check on you, Cameron, and to make sure you were doing okay.'

'I didn't need checking up on or looking after.'

She smiled sadly. 'And there you go pushing us away again.'

He rolled his shoulders and frowned. 'I'm not pushing you away.'

'Tess is right, though,' Lance said.

'It's why we wanted to come out here and apologise,' Fiona added. 'And to hold out an olive branch.'

Cameron said nothing, but Tess stood so closely to him she could feel the tension coiling him up tight.

'We're kin, Cam.' Lance held out his hand. 'That has to mean something.'

Tess held her breath, hoping, praying that Cam would accept his brother's proffered hand. She closed her eyes when he gave a harsh laugh.

'Your farm must be in a real state. You're welcome here any time, Mum, but, Lance…you can go to blazes. If I shake your hand now, how long before you turn around and stick the knife in again? How long before you try to steal another canola contract out from under my nose? I'm just waiting to find you rustling my cattle next. But stand warned. If I do I'll be contacting the authorities. You've burned your bridges as far as I'm concerned. Now get out!'

'What about me?' Fiona whispered.

Cam planted his hands on his hips. 'What about you?'

The scent of cut grass wafted about Tess. She drew it slowly into her lungs to counter the nausea churning her stomach. Did Fiona want him back?

'Do you accept my apology? Am I welcome in your home?'

Cam sent Lance a cruel, hard smile. 'You're welcome in my home any time, Fiona.'

Lance turned white. He seized Fiona's hand and stormed from the room.

Lorraine pressed a gift into Cam's hand and then reached up to kiss his cheek. 'It was lovely to see you, Cameron. I just hope we haven't spoiled your day.'

And then she left and Tess could feel all the energy just drain out of her body, leaving her limp and wrecked. It must be a hundred times worse for Cam. She moved to a chair, pressed her hands together between her knees. Her pink party dress suddenly seemed totally out of place. She eyed Cam carefully. He hadn't moved. She cleared her throat. 'Are you okay?'

He rounded on her then. 'That was all your doing, wasn't it?'

Her jaw dropped.

He flung an arm out, pacing from one side of the room to the other. 'I should've known little Miss Fix-it wouldn't be able to mind her own business, that she'd need to interfere.'

She shot to her feet. The roller coaster of emotions she'd experienced this afternoon crashing through her now. 'Well, even if I did—' which she hadn't, but she'd rather walk on broken glass now than admit it '—I sure didn't make things worse. Oh, no, you accomplished that all on your own!'

He swung back to her. 'Are you telling me you actually believed that line he fed me?'

She planted herself directly in front of him. 'Yes, I do.' And strangely enough she did. It was only now when he was deprived of his brother that Lance could see all that Cam meant to him, and how much he needed him. 'But even if I didn't,' she suddenly found herself shouting, 'he's your brother and he deserves the benefit of the doubt!'

'Just because you feel guilty about letting Sarah down doesn't give you the right to go meddling in my life! Fixing my situation won't be a form of restitution, you know.'

She sucked in a breath. 'At least I'm not hiding from life.'

'What do you call turning away from your music?'

She clenched her hands. 'At least I'm not afraid to let love in my life. At least I put people first!'

Neither of their voices had lost any of their volume and the walls practically rang with their shouts.

'That's just as well because you know nothing about chickens!'

'At least I know how to throw a decent party! Me!' She thumped her chest. '*Me* has got the hang of country hospitality in under a month. You haven't got the hang of it your whole life!'

'Your grammar sucks!'

'And your manners suck!'

She glared. He glared.

She bit her lip. His lips started to twitch.

She snorted. *'Me has got?'*

He rolled his eyes. 'I can't believe I made that chicken crack.'

And suddenly they were both roaring with laughter.

And then Cameron pulled her right into his arms and kissed her.

CHAPTER NINE

RAW, BURNING NEED blazed a path of fire through the very centre of Cam's being and shot out in every direction. He'd ached to kiss this woman ever since…ever since he'd clapped eyes on her. But he'd burned harder and fiercer with that need since the first kiss they'd shared. And he was tired of fighting it.

He revelled in the sweet softness of Tess's lips and the way they opened up at his demand—so sweet and giving as if she sensed his hunger and wanted to assuage it. So unselfish.

The realisation made him slow the kiss down, gentle it until she could catch up with him. Loosening his hold on her nape, he slid his hand through the dark cap of her hair and caressed the skin behind her ear in a slow circular motion, and then followed with his mouth. A shudder rippled through her, filling him with satisfaction, increasing his hunger, but he refused to speed up to meet that demand.

He wanted Tess with him. All the way. He wanted her smiling and satisfied…sated and delighted. A resolution he nearly lost the battle with when her grip tightened on his arms and she moved in closer to press all her softness against him.

He tugged gently on her ear lobe. She gasped and arched into him. He grinned a lazy grin and did it again. She smelled of jellybeans and cake. Breathing her in was a treat in itself. The grin disappeared when she shifted restlessly against him, one of her hands plunging into his hair, her other arm winding around his neck.

He lost all sense of himself then, all sense of time. His mouth found hers and he fell into her, losing himself in the experience of kissing her, touching her, filling himself up with her essence like a man gorging on some vital nutrient he'd been lacking but had suddenly found.

The hunger built and built until kissing and touching was no longer enough. He needed—

A groan broke from him when she tore her lips from his and wrenched herself out of his arms. She stumbled to a sofa on the other side of the room. Seizing a cushion, she hugged it to her chest.

His chest rose and fell as if he'd spent the last hour roping yearlings. He wanted to stride over to where Tess sat, haul her back into his arms and propel this encounter through to its natural conclusion. He almost did, but common sense reasserted itself. Ty and Krissie were somewhere on the premises. This was not the ideal time for making love to Tess. He bit back an oath. 'I'm sorry. The timing on that could've been better.'

She didn't say anything. He wanted her to look at him, but she didn't do that either.

He dragged in a breath, adjusted his stance and tried to quieten the stampeding of his blood. 'Would you like to have dinner with me tonight? Jenny would love to babysit the kids and—'

'No.'

He blinked.

She plumped the cushion up and set it back to the sofa. 'There won't ever be a good time for us, Cameron.'

'But—'

'Do you think I'm the kind of woman who jumps willy-nilly into bed with men I know I have no future with?'

'No, I—'

She walked across and poked him in the chest. 'Do you want me to fall in love with you so you can then break my heart? Will that mend your wounded ego and make you feel powerful and manly again? Will that show Lance that you're over what he did to you?'

Her eyes blazed with a fire he hadn't witnessed before, but her words left him chilled. 'No!' How could she put such a dreadful interpretation on his desire for her? 'You're beautiful, Tess. I find you fascinating and irresistible. I love kissing you.'

Colour flared in her cheeks. She backed up a step. 'That may well be, but it's been an emotional day. I refuse to be the distraction you need to distance yourself from all that's happened this afternoon.'

He stabbed a finger at her. 'You're more than a distraction!' She was wonderful and warm and she could make him laugh even when he was livid.

She folded her arms and lifted her chin. 'How much more?'

A chill trickled down his backbone. For a short time today this woman had brought his old dream roaring back to life. She'd made him wonder if it were still possible. The arrival of his mother, Lance and Fiona had dashed that, had forced him to face reality again.

'You still have no intention of forgiving Lance. You're determined to hold on to your bitterness. What would it hurt to just let it go?'

His gut clenched. 'How can you even ask that?'

She pressed a hand to her forehead. 'There's absolutely no point to this conversation. You have no intention of staying in Bellaroo Creek anyway, have you?'

He straightened and shoved his shoulders back. He wasn't being made a fool of a second time. Not by Lance. Not by Tess. Not by anyone.

She gave a short laugh, obviously reading the resolution in his face. 'Well, in the meantime I won't let you turn me into some toy you can play with. I might've let my sister down, but I don't deserve that. And the children certainly deserve better.'

He wanted Tess in every way a man would want a woman. If she were free and unencumbered he'd ask her to come to Africa with him. For fun. For adventure. No strings. His chest clenched. Maybe…

He closed his eyes. What was he thinking? Tess was all strings and he wanted no part of that. Besides she wanted the impossible. Forgive Lance? No chance. He made himself take a physical step away from her. His chest hurt, his groin ached, but he held firm.

Without even glancing at him, she headed for the door.

'Tess…' He could hardly speak for the bitterness that coated his tongue and lined his throat.

She turned in the doorway.

'Whatever else has happened, you've not let Sarah down. You love her kids as if they're your own. You're giving them not just a good life but a great life. You've brought them laughter and joy and hope for the future. You never let Sarah down. If you'd known the true state of affairs you'd have returned home as soon as you could. And I don't doubt for a single moment that she knew that. Saying you let her down by not returning home sooner is the same as saying she let you down because she didn't tell you the truth sooner. Nobody let anybody down.'

She gripped her hands together, her eyes wide and wounded. He wished—

He cut the thought off. 'There's only one issue that I suspect would bring Sarah pain. How do you think she'd feel if she knew you'd turned your back on your music because of her?'

The confusion that flared in her eyes made him ache to go to her, to comfort her. But she didn't want the kind of comfort he offered and he could hardly blame her. When she turned and left, he let her go.

Cam avoided Tess's house for the next week. She attended his judo class on Wednesday. When they'd heard she was doing the class, another two mums had signed up too. The three of them had spent the majority of the class in fits of giggles. He hadn't spoken to her one-on-one, though.

Instinct told him she needed time. He sure did. Time to rebuild his defences. Time to reinforce his plans for the future. Time to forget the impact of their kisses. Because after vowing not to, he'd almost fallen under the spell of that old dream again. Tess brought out that old weakness in him, and he was determined to fight it with everything he had.

Out of sight, though, didn't mean out of mind.

And there was still the issue of her vegetable garden. His debt to her wouldn't be cleared until he'd finished that.

The following Saturday he loaded the tray of his ute with all the tools he'd need—shovels, picks, hoes and a generous amount of cow manure—and headed for Tess's. One good day should see the vegetable bed finished. He'd help her with the planting and give her tips on how to look after it.

And then he could walk away. Job done. Debt cleared.

He pulled in a breath when he arrived, and then set off towards the back of her house. *Don't think about that kiss!* Work, that was what he had to think about. Work and digging and—

He rounded the side of the house and then pulled up short, unable to move another step.

Tess and the kids were dancing around the backyard, singing along to a pop song on the radio. And it wasn't just any old singing and dancing. His chest clenched. They jumped and twirled and swooped with abandon. With complete unadulterated joy at being alive. As if this moment was the best moment that had ever existed and they were going to clutch it and hold it close and cherish it and live it before it could slip away.

It filled him with a yearning that almost buckled him at the knees.

Tess's hips swayed and shook in a sexy rhythm and his mouth dried and his blood pounded. Her simple delight in the dance and the way she occasionally caught one of the children's eyes and how their pleasure fed each other's left him breathless. He'd never seen anything like it.

He'd never experienced anything like it.

His heart started to thump and an ache pounded behind his eyes. He would *never* experience anything like it. This kind of exuberance, rapture, was alien to his family.

Duty, responsibility and self-reliance—those were all the things he'd been taught to value. Not joy. And no matter how much he might hunger for the same kind of closeness with his family that Tess and the kids shared, he knew it was beyond his reach.

Fiona had taught him that. Trying to reach for these heights with her had revealed it for the sham it had been. He had to stick to what he did know—duty, responsibility and self-reliance.

Without a word, he backed up a step, turned and headed for his car.

Tess spun around, arms outstretched as the song came to an end, feeling alive and young and grateful for Ty and Krissie's laughter, when a flash of blue disappearing around the side of the house caught her eye.

She acted on instinct. 'Hey, Cam!' She tripped around the side of the house.

He froze. He didn't turn around. Her heart surged against her rib cage. His back beckoned—so strong and muscled. So capable. Her fingers curled against her palms. 'Anything we can do for you?'

'Hey, Cam!' Ty came rushing around the side of the house with Barney in close pursuit. 'Look, I taught Barney how to shake hands.'

Cameron turned to watch the trick. He smiled, but it didn't reach his eyes. 'That's brilliant, Ty. He's one smart dog.'

Those shadows in his eyes chafed at her. They made her want to go to him and offer herself to him, to offer the kind of comfort he wanted from her.

She glanced at Ty and Krissie, planted her feet and remained where she was.

'I, uh…' He rose from patting an ecstatic Barney. 'Thought I might get a start on digging the bed for your vegetable garden.'

Bed? It brought a whole different picture to her mind that had nothing to do with gardening or vegetables. Heat that had nothing to do with the exertion of dancing surged into her cheeks. It took a moment to unknot her tongue. 'That'd be great,' she finally managed. 'If you can spare the time, that is?'

'Right.'

He didn't move. She didn't move. The air between them vibrated with all that remained unspoken.

With a superhuman effort she managed to shake herself out from beneath the heavy, suffocating blanket that tried to descend over her. She clapped her hands. 'Right! Let's help Cam unload his tools.'

They all set to work. Digging, she decided an hour later, wasn't a bad antidote to restlessness. Other than to issue instructions or to check his directions, she and Cam barely spoke. But as they worked side by side together the tension slowly dissipated. She liked having him in her backyard again. She frowned at that thought. He'd been a great friend.

He'd be a better lover.

Whoa!

She pushed the thought away, thrust her shovel into the

ground, and pushed her hands into the small of her back, groaning as her muscles protested.

Cam sent her a grin that filled her to the brim with renewed energy. 'Sore?'

'No wonder you're so fit if you do this kind of work day in and day out. All I can say is thank God it's lunchtime. I'll go rustle up something to eat.'

A short while later they all sat in the sun munching sandwiches and apples.

Krissie glanced up. 'Auntie Tess?'

'What, chickadee?'

'It's a big vegetable garden, isn't it?'

'Well, I'm not an expert on vegetable gardens, but I think ours is pretty much the perfect size.'

'So can we grow marigolds in there too? Will there be room? Did you know they were Mummy's favourite?'

Yes, she did know. Her throat tightened. She swallowed. 'I think there'll be oodles of room for marigolds. I think marigolds will be the perfect addition to our vegetable garden.'

Krissie, Ty, and the animals all ran off to play.

Cam shook his head. 'You can't eat marigolds.'

She couldn't tell if he was vexed with her or not. 'They do look pretty in a vase, though.' And for taking out to a grave. She eased back on the blanket to survey him more fully. 'Do you always choose the common-sense option?'

'I work the land. Planting forty hectares of marigolds instead of canola will not earn me my crust.'

'What a sight it'd be though.'

He suddenly smiled. 'Wait until the canola blossoms.' He gestured out in front of them at the newly ploughed fields that stretched over a low hill in the distance. 'It will be bright yellow for as far as you can see.'

'Magic,' she breathed. Then she frowned. 'But you won't be here to see it?'

He shook his head.

Wouldn't he miss that? Didn't he want to see the fruits of his labour? She bit the questions back. They'd carefully avoided any mention of the personal today, had found a comfortable footing with each other, and she didn't want to ruin it. 'I'll take a photo and have Fraser send it to you,' she said instead.

She was just about to tip the dregs of her mug of tea out when Ty and Krissie came up. She could tell from the fact they walked rather than ran and by the serious expressions on their faces that they'd just 'conferred' about something. 'What's up, chickadees?' She kept her voice deliberately light and cheerful.

'When are we going to have Mummy's...' Ty frowned, obviously searching for the right word.

'Memorial?' she asked softly.

They both nodded and knelt down on the blanket in front of her.

'Well, Mrs Pritchard is organising a plot for us, and I expect to hear from her about that in the next couple of weeks. Then I'll speak to Reverend Wilkinson, who'll perform the service, but he's only out this way every second week.' How long was a piece of string? Things moved at a different pace in the country. 'So I'm expecting it'll be maybe in a month, possibly two.'

'So, sorta soon?' Ty checked.

She nodded.

They leapt up, evidently satisfied. 'But while we're on the subject...' she started, her throat drying.

They stared at her for a moment and then sank back down to the blanket. Her chest clenched. Maybe she should let this subject rest. Instinct, though, told her ignoring it wouldn't be right.

'Okay, chickadees, we need to talk about your daddy.' Ty's eyes grew wide and wary. Her stomach started to churn. 'Do we want to bury his ashes too? Do we want to put them in the same plot as Mummy's?'

'No!' Ty shot to his feet. 'I hate him! He killed Mummy!'

The blood drained from her face. Her hands started to shake. 'Ty, honey, that's not true.' His bottom lip wobbled. He stood there pale and shaking. Her heart lurched and her eyes stung. She wanted to reach out and hug him to her, but she sensed any such movement would send him running. 'That's not true, Ty. I promise you. You know Daddy was sick.' She'd tried to explain it, but, truly, how much were they expected to understand? Especially when Tess could barely accept it herself. 'It was an accident.'

'No, it wasn't! I heard him say he was going to kill her. He drove into that tree on purpose!'

Tears poured down his face. They started to pour down hers too. 'He only said those things because he was sick. He didn't mean them. And I know he didn't drive the car deliberately into the tree, Ty, because he wasn't the one driving—Mummy was.'

His fists clenched. His face turned red. 'No!'

She tried to take him into her arms, but he wheeled out of her reach and raced away. She started to her feet, but Cam's hand on her shoulder stopped her.

'I'll go after him,' he said quietly with a nod towards Krissie.

She turned and found her little niece with her face buried in the blanket and her shoulders shaking. With a lump in her throat the size of a teapot, Tess lifted the child into her lap and wrapped her arms tight around her.

Ty didn't go far. He'd raced around the front of the house to fling himself down full length on the veranda.

Cam sat next to the distraught boy and hauled him into his arms so he could cry against his chest.

His throat thickened as he rubbed a hand up and down Ty's

back, trying to impart whatever comfort he could. So much grief and pain. These kids had been through so much. Tess was doing a great job, but…

He thought back to this morning's image of them all dancing. Tess was doing a *brilliant* job. It was those moments of joy that would help Ty and Krissie through the hardship of their grief and create bonds that would link them together as a family. He ached to take away all their pain—Tess's included—but that wasn't possible. All he could do was offer his friendship and hope it helped.

Tess. His mind rang with her. She was trying to do so much on her own. And she was achieving so much. If only she could see that she didn't have to lose herself in the process.

Eventually Ty's sobs eased to hiccups. A couple of minutes after that he pushed away from Cam's chest to stare up in his face.

'How you doing, buddy?' Cam asked, his chest cramping at the small, tear-stained face. He found himself wanting to protect this young boy from every kind of harm. All of Tess's fussing suddenly made perfect sense.

'Do you think Auntie Tess is right?' he said without preamble.

He'd give away Kurrajong Station in an instant if it'd mean sparing them all of this. He met Ty's gaze. 'Has your aunt Tess ever lied to you about anything else?'

Ty considered that for a long moment. 'No,' he finally said.

'Then do you really think she'd lie to you about this?'

He considered that too. 'She doesn't want me and Krissie to be mad with our dad.' He glared. 'But I am. I'm really mad.'

'Yeah, I get that.'

Ty gazed up at him, eyes wary. 'You do?'

'Sure I do. Your dad hurt you and Krissie and your mum. It'd make me angry too.'

'Auntie Tess said he was sick.'

'I think your auntie Tess is right. And you know what else

I think? I think that your dad would be very glad that he can't hurt you any more.'

'Even though he's dead?'

Cam nodded. 'Even then.'

'You think he loved us?'

'I think he loved you all very much, Ty. I think he just wasn't able to show it any more.'

Ty rested his head against Cam's shoulder. The trust awed him. The warm weight cracked open a gulf of yearning inside him. He closed his eyes. He understood Ty's anger. It was the same as his anger at Lance. Except Ty's dad had been sick. Lance had no such excuse.

Eventually Ty pushed away and climbed out of Cam's lap. He missed the warmth and the weight immediately.

'I'm going to go and give Auntie Tess a hug.'

'I think that's an excellent plan.'

He followed Ty around to the backyard to find Tess and Krissie, now with Fluffy on her lap, talking quietly on the blanket. Tess turned at their approach. Without a word she opened her arms and Ty raced into them.

What if, like Ty and Krissie's father, Lance died in a car accident? The ground shifted beneath his feet. He planted his legs more firmly and bit back a curse. Lance had burned his proverbial bridges. He was nothing to Cam any more.

That assertion, though, didn't ease the burn in Cam's heart.

He forced himself to focus on the tableau in front of him. Tess held Ty for several long moments and then rose, holding him in her arms. She hitched her head in the direction of the house and Cam nodded, settling down on the blanket beside Krissie.

She glanced up at him with those big brown eyes that were identical to Tess's. With a cluck and a flutter, Fluffy freed herself to scratch about in the grass.

Krissie moved closer and curled up against him as if it were the most natural thing in the world. 'You okay, pet?'

She nodded. 'My daddy was very sick, you know?'

'So I understand, honey.'

'It's very sad,' she whispered, leaning into him. 'And I think we should bury him with Mummy and maybe he'll be happy again.'

She was five, but her generosity and ability to forgive stole his breath. 'I think that's a real nice idea, sweetheart.'

He wasn't sure for how long they sat there, but when Tess materialised in front of him, he glanced down to find Krissie fast asleep. Tess went to take her from him, but he shook his head. 'Let me. You lead the way.'

They put Krissie to bed. He followed Tess back into the kitchen. She grabbed two beers from the fridge and handed him one before leading the way back outside again.

'You okay?' he asked. She looked pale and lines of weariness fanned out from her eyes. She looked as if she could do with a nap herself.

She settled on the blanket, stretching her legs out in front of her before glancing up at him. 'Some days I feel as if we're merely lurching from one catastrophe to another.'

He lowered himself down beside her. It suddenly shamed him to think how he'd tried to seduce her last weekend. She had so much to deal with. 'I held Ty while he cried his heart out and all I wanted to do was make things better for him. I know that's impossible. I don't know how you're managing to do all this with such grace.'

She opened her beer. 'I'm not sure there's much grace involved.'

'I think you're doing an incredible job.'

She turned those eyes on him. Eyes the same as Krissie's. He had absolutely no intention of trying to seduce her again, but what if she moved in close and curled up against him the way Krissie had? He couldn't get the thought out of his mind.

He forced his gaze away. 'I will tell you something,' he

managed. 'Nobody could get them through this as well as you are.'

She took a long pull on her beer. 'Some days are better than others. The gaps between the bad days are getting longer.'

He read her unspoken hope that eventually there wouldn't be any more bad days, but both of them knew bad days came and went. Ty and Krissie, as they got older, would simply learn to deal with those bad days more effectively. With Tess's help.

'So…' She studied him. 'Are you okay?' She asked as if she could sense the confusion bubbling just beneath the surface. It reminded him how well attuned they were to each other's moods. It reminded him that he *wasn't* going to attempt to seduce her again.

'Yeah, sure.'

But even as he said the words he knew they were a lie.

He frowned. 'Krissie…'

She watched him closely, as closely as he often caught her watching the children. It made the ache around his heart ease for some unaccountable reason. 'What about Krissie?'

'Something she said…' He scratched a hand back through his hair. 'She said she thought that if her father was buried with her mother, then maybe he'd be happy again.' His frown grew. 'She *wants* him to be happy.'

'Of course she does. He was her father. She loved him.'

'But he hurt her and Ty so badly.'

'Your father was unfaithful to your mother, but does that make you love him any less?'

His mother's revelation had shocked him, had made him rethink all he'd thought he knew about his father—but, no, it didn't affect the love he bore for him.

'I think a part of Krissie remembers the good times before her father's accident, when they were all happy and life was how it should've been. I think Sarah helped keep those memories alive.'

'You've forgiven him too, haven't you?'

She stared down at her beer and nodded.

He leapt up and started to pace. 'How can you? How can you find that in yourself after everything he did to your sister?' He knew she'd loved Sarah. 'And to those kids? I know how much you love them.'

'I don't see why loving them means I should hate Bruce. I can't forget that Sarah hadn't given up on him. I know *she* still loved him. I can't forget all the years he made her happy or their joy when the children were born. They—'

She broke off to stare at her drink. 'He didn't go looking for that accident. He didn't deserve what happened to him. He'd been a loving husband and father up till that point. And I'm proud of Sarah for sticking by him.'

He opened his mouth but she held up a hand. 'Yes, she should've gotten the children away from that situation sooner, but I'm proud of her for having the courage to try to find help for the man she loved. My sister loved him, Cameron. I cannot hate him. I…I just can't.'

He's your brother and he deserves the benefit of the doubt!

He collapsed back down beside her, her words of last weekend echoing through him. He knew precisely where Krissie's generosity and her big heart came from—from her auntie Tess. 'No wonder you think me a hard, unfeeling brute.'

'I think no such thing!'

'Lance.'

Just one word but comprehension dawned in those melt-a-man eyes of hers. 'That's a bit different. You're an adult and so is Lance, even if he has been acting like a petulant teenager.' She smoothed the rug and glanced away. 'He's learning a very hard lesson now, though.'

I think a part of Krissie remembers the good times.

Cam scowled at the ground. There had been good times, but…

'I think it'll probably be good for him in the long run. He

relies too heavily on his charm, and I suspect your mother has shielded him far more than has been good for him. A bit of hard work and a whole lot of worry may make a man out of him yet.'

His head came up. 'Steady on, Tess, he's not that bad.'

There were days when Lance had made life hell. There'd also been days when he'd made Cam laugh until his sides had hurt. It was why Cam had put up with the hell days—because nobody else in the family had ever laughed all that much. That laughter had been worth a lot.

She leaned back, stared down her nose at him. 'Do I hear you defending him?'

Was he?

If anything happened to Lance while he was in Africa… Cam swallowed. What if something happened to him while he was away? Was this really how he meant to leave things?

He frowned and finally cracked open his beer. 'I guess I am.'

She arched an eyebrow. 'Is that significant?'

He dragged in a breath. 'If Krissie can forgive her dad…' He shook his head. 'Lord, Tess, I can't be shown up by a five-year-old, now, can I?'

'It'd be very poor form,' she agreed.

Somewhere inside him a smile started to build. He held his beer towards her. She clinked it in a silent toast.

CHAPTER TEN

TESS WANTED TO leap to her feet and dance. She wanted to hug Cam.

She suspected the dancing would prove the lesser of two evils.

A new calm had settled over him, certain shadows had retreated from his eyes—not all, but some—and his shoulders had lost their angry edge.

She surveyed them and bit her lip. In fact, they looked broad and scrumptious.

Cam cleared his throat and she realised with a start that she'd been staring at them for too long. She snapped her gaze away and lifted her beer to her lips. 'If you want my two cents' worth…' she started before taking a sip.

'Which you'll give me, even if I don't.'

The grin he shot her and the effortlessness with which he teased her filled her with such a fluttery nonsense of wings she was in danger of floating two feet above the ground. She clutched a handful of blanket and held tight.

'What's your two cents, Tess?'

She surveyed him over the rim of her beer. 'I think you should pay your family a visit tomorrow afternoon.'

'Why?'

'The sooner the better, don't you think?'

He stared at her for a long moment. 'And?'

'And I'll be there,' she finally 'fessed up. She wanted to be there when he faced his family too. She wanted to make sure Lorraine, Lance and Fiona didn't take advantage of him. 'Last weekend at your party it was as if it were you against them and the rest of the world. That's not true. You have friends and I think both you and they should acknowledge that fact.'

Also, her being there would create a subtle confusion she was eager to encourage. Cameron might love Fiona to her dying day, but neither Lance nor Fiona had to know that. They had no right to crow in triumph. It wouldn't hurt anyone to think Cameron had well and truly moved on.

It could hurt you.

She shrugged the thought off. She knew the truth—Cam was leaving. Forewarned was forearmed. She could protect her heart.

'I'm dropping Ty and Krissie off at a birthday party and then popping by Lorraine's to discuss the memorial service. Apparently Lance and Fiona plan to be there to offer their...' She shrugged and rolled her eyes.

'Moral support?'

She bared her teeth. 'Something like that.'

He started to laugh. 'So who exactly is helping who in this scenario?'

She couldn't help but grin back at him. 'Why don't we call it a joint effort?'

His grin was slow and easy and it could make a woman's heart kick straight into triple time without any warning at all. 'What time are you supposed to be out there?'

'One-thirty.'

'I have a few things to do in the morning, but...I'll be out there by two.'

'Excellent.'

'C'mon.' He nodded towards the garden bed. 'Time to get back to work.' He helped her to her feet and she tried to ignore the strength of his hands, tried to ignore the heat he exuded, and the fresh smell of cut grass.

She averted her gaze from the strong, lean promise of his back and threw herself into attacking the ground with the assorted instruments of destruction currently within reach.

'Well, Tess,' Lorraine said, leaning back in the padded wicker sofa that graced her generous back patio, 'that should all be remarkably easy to arrange.'

Tess had just outlined the simple service she and the children had agreed upon.

'No Herculean feats to be performed,' Lance said with a smile.

He almost looked disappointed, as if he sensed Tess's reservations about his character and wanted to prove himself in her eyes. Who knew? Maybe he did. But if she needed any Herculean tasks performed she'd ask his brother, thank you very much.

Fiona leant forward to top up Tess's teacup. 'Do have a scone,' she urged, as if unstinting hospitality might melt Tess's reserve.

It'd take more than a scone and a cup of tea. What this pair had done to Cam—

It's none of your business. She had no right holding a grudge against this pair. Especially when she'd been urging Cam not to and—

Her teacup wobbled. None of her business? Everything to do with Cam felt like her business.

Because he's helped you so much, helped you, Ty and Krissie feel a part of Bellaroo Creek.

That was right. That was all it was.

Her heart started to thump. Why, then, when he smiled at her did her heart grow wings? Why when his eyes practically devoured her did she feel like the most desirable woman on earth? Why when she kissed him was it better than making music?

She'd told herself she'd wanted to be here today to support him, but it wasn't the whole truth, was it? She set her tea down before she could spill it. She'd wanted to be here today to prevent Fiona from getting her perfect pretty little claws into him again. She'd wanted to stake her claim.

Because she'd fallen in love with him.

Her heart throbbed. Her temples pounded. Cam had made it clear to her that she had no claim to stake. Hadn't she been listening?

Of course she'd been listening! She seized a pumpkin scone and bit into it viciously. But how could a woman not fall in love with a man like Cam? He had the biggest heart of any person she'd ever met. He did so much for others, and all of it without fanfare. He had the kind of grin that could melt a woman's resolutions in a heartbeat and the kind of physique that could have her fantasising in Technicolor.

He was so…much. He was everything. And she loved him.

The acknowledgement calmed the dervishes careening through her blood. A hard black ache settled in her heart instead. She set her pumpkin scone back to her plate.

Cam rounded the corner of the veranda and found his family and Tess seated in front of him. In the warm sunshine and the filtered light from a wisteria vine, the tableau looked inviting and almost summery—even with the cool of autumn in the air.

Tess, though, looked pale and his heart lurched for her. Organising this memorial service must be hell. She glanced up and her face relaxed into a smile of pure pleasure. It immediately buoyed him up. He couldn't remember any woman's smile affecting him the way Tess's did. Not even Fiona's.

'Hello, Cameron.'

'Tess.'

His mother shot to her feet, delight lighting her face. 'Cam!'

He moved down the length of the veranda and kissed her cheek. 'Hello, Mum.'

Lance stood more slowly. He nodded to Cam and then turned to Lorraine. 'There's some work I should get done in the eastern paddock.'

Fiona jumped up too. 'I'll help.'

There was no denying that they were trying to make room for him, trying to make things less awkward. He appreciated the effort. Tess had been right. They deserved the benefit of the doubt. 'I'd like the two of you to stay, if you don't mind.'

A tremulous smile appeared on Fiona's lips. It left him unmoved and he suddenly frowned. When precisely had he fallen out of love with her? His heart started to pound. Or had she been right? Had he been more in love with his dream of filling Kurrajong Station with laughter and with a family?

Lance sat when Fiona tugged him back down to the seat beside her. His blue eyes filled with a hope he desperately tried to hide, but Cam had always been able to read his little brother.

Until he'd turned his back on him.

He glanced at Tess and she held a hand out to him. He took it without thinking, squeezed it before releasing it to take the lone chair at right angles to her. The only other spare seat was beside his mother. It wasn't that he wanted to shun her. He just wanted to face his family square on during this conversation—read their faces, gauge their reactions.

'You wanted to speak to us about something, Cameron?' his mother asked.

'I've been thinking about your visit last weekend, and it has to be said that I was discourteous and churlish in response to your offer of an olive branch. If the offer still stands, I'd like to accept it.'

'It still stands!' Lance shot to his feet and thrust his hand towards Cam.

Cam rose and shook it. With a nod he took his seat again. He met Tess's warm gaze, recognised her unspoken approbation. It made him push his shoulders back and lift his chin. Her innate generosity and the sacrifices she'd made had helped him see sense. More than that, though, she'd made him believe he was worth more than he'd ever credited before.

He turned back to Lance before he could become too preoccupied with the dusky fullness of Tess's bottom lip. 'This is just a start. It's going to take me a while to trust you again.'

'I know.' Lance squared his shoulders. 'But it's a start, and I'm not going to screw up this time.'

Cam stretched a leg out. 'Now to the financial situation of this station. I'm not just going to bail you guys out. I'm not a bank and I have my own place to consider. But—' he glanced at his mother '—I am prepared to buy a fifty per cent share of the property and to invest in improving it.'

She bit her lip and nodded. It was an acknowledgement, not an acceptance. This was business. This wouldn't be her ideal scenario, but interest-free loans and working for this station gratis were a thing of the past.

He glanced back at Lance. 'Are you fair dinkum about giving farming a proper go?'

'Yes.'

'Then I'm prepared to pay you a wage to train under Fraser for the next two years. If Mum does decide to sell me half the property, and if you prove yourself, I will let you buy back my share of this station for whatever the current market value is.'

Lance swallowed and nodded. 'I accept.' Fiona nudged him and he broke into a grin. 'In fact, I'm darn grateful, but...'

He had to stop his lips from twisting. Here it came. 'But?'

'Cam, I'd rather work under you than Fraser.'

The steel momentarily left his spine. It was the last thing he'd expected Lance to say. It brought home to him the depth of the younger man's resolution. A breath eased out of him. 'I'm afraid that won't be possible.'

His mother leaned towards him. 'Why not, darling?'

'Because I won't be here.' His gut tightened and he couldn't look at Tess. 'I've accepted a field assignment to Africa with the Feed the World programme.'

'For how long?'

'Two years.'

To his right, he heard Tess's quick intake of breath and his chest started to ache.

'When do you leave?' Lance burst out.

'The end of next month.'

And then all hell broke loose as his mother, Lance and Fiona all broke out in loud voices, talking over each other as they remonstrated with him. Tess leaned across to touch his arm. 'Will you stay at least until the memorial service?'

He didn't know when the service was scheduled, but he knew she wouldn't try to trick him into staying any longer. He trusted her. 'Yes.'

'Thank you. It'll mean so much to Ty and Krissie.'

And her?

'And me,' she added as if she could read his mind.

Then she stood. 'Honestly,' she snapped to his family, 'stop all this nonsense. All his life Cameron has looked after you lot. All his life he's done things for other people. Stop being so selfish and think of him for once. He's entitled to follow his dream and you as his family should be supporting him rather than bellyaching at him and making things difficult.'

She was fierce and fabulous and he suddenly wanted to laugh with sheer exhilaration. But when she turned to smile at him he wanted to close his eyes. He recognised what glowed in the gorgeous brown depths of her eyes. Love.

Love for him.

And he had absolutely no intention of accepting it, of returning it, and that knowledge was there in her eyes too.

Bile burned his throat. Why hadn't he taken more care around her? She was the one person in Bellaroo Creek who wanted what was truly best for him—without agenda and without reference to her own needs or desires. He'd rather cut off his right arm than hurt her. A giant vise squeezed his heart. He hadn't meant for it to happen, but a fat lot of good that would do her in the months to come.

He opened his mouth. He wanted to offer her some form of comfort. Only he knew that'd be useless. Worse than useless.

He dragged a hand back through his hair. She'd wanted to be here today to shield him in whatever way she could from Lance and Fiona's betrayal. That all seemed so small and petty now. If only there'd been someone looking out for her!

'Tess is right,' his mother finally said, waving everyone back to their seats. 'Again.'

'Again?' he found himself asking.

'The day of the working bee at the cemetery I mentioned to Tess how nice it was to see you there.' Lorraine bit her lip. 'She said I might want to mention that to you, and it made me suddenly see how...unsupportive I must've seemed to you. Frankly, I was mortified.'

And because of Tess he now knew why his mother had stayed away from Kurrajong Station for all these years.

'She gave me a right set down that day too,' Lance said. 'Demanded to know if I'd ever actually apologised for my appalling behaviour.' He grimaced. 'It was the kick in the pants I needed.'

Cam turned to stare at Tess. She screwed up her nose. 'I tried really hard to mind my own business, but...'

He leaned across and covered her hand with his. 'I'm glad you didn't. I want you to know that all this—' he gestured around the table '—is due to you. And I'm grateful.'

'So am I.' Lorraine rose and embraced Tess. 'My darling girl, not only are you helping save my beloved town, you've helped save my family.'

With her arm about Tess's waist, she turned to Cam. 'Darling, of course you must do what your heart tells you. You've been involved with the Feed the World programme for so long, and I know you've made a real difference in the lives of those less fortunate than us. It's selfish of us to want to keep you to ourselves, but you must never forget that you always have a home here with us.'

He leant across and kissed his mother's cheek. 'I won't forget.' But it was Tess's fragrance he drew into his lungs as he moved away.

'I think it's beyond time I made a fresh pot of tea. Could you give me a hand, Fiona, dear?'

Cam turned to Tess. He wanted to say something—something that would tell her how much he appreciated all she had done, and how sorry he was for the rest of it.

Her smile and the tiny shake of her head forestalled him. 'I think it's all worked out exactly the way it should've, don't you?'

No.

Oh, it had for him and his mother, and for Lance and Fiona, but not for her. Not in the way she deserved.

'I'm mighty glad you came around today, Cam.'

Lance's words reminded him that he and Tess weren't alone. And he didn't want to say or do anything that might embarrass her in front of Lance or cue anybody in on her pain. Tess was like him. She'd not want a broken heart on display for all and sundry to exclaim and pick over. He could at least do that much for her.

He turned to his brother. 'So am I.' And he meant it more than he'd thought he would.

'Say.' Lance pointed, leading him to the edge of the veranda. 'See that colt in the home paddock? Do you think he's ready for breaking?'

Cam watched the colt moving over the grass with an easy

gait and his tail held high. 'Your call, Lance, but I'd be inclined to give him another six months.'

When Cam turned back, Tess was gone. Every atom in his body shouted at him to go after her. He remained where he was. In his heart he knew there was nothing he could say that would make an atom of difference to either one of them. Letting her go was harder than going after her, but it was also kinder.

Where Tess was concerned he'd already done enough harm.

CHAPTER ELEVEN

TESS WORKED HARD at making the memorial service a celebration of Sarah's and Bruce's lives. The scheduled day dawned cold and still, with barely a breath of breeze to stir the leaves in the Kurrajong trees. Cameron's canola had been planted and, while winter had arrived, the blue skies and constant sunshine made her feel as if she, Ty and Krissie were moving into a smoother, calmer period. Truly a new beginning.

Even though she missed Sarah every single day.

Even though whenever she thought of Cameron leaving Bellaroo Creek her heart trembled and her throat would close over.

Still, at least she would know that somewhere in the world Cam was following his heart. If his heart could never belong to her, then she just wanted him happy.

When the day of the memorial service dawned—with Cam due to leave Bellaroo Creek the very next day—Tess bounced out of bed and lifted her chin. She had so much—a home, two beautiful children, and a bright future. Today she meant to count her blessings, not her sorrows.

The entire town turned out for the memorial service. The women wore their best dresses, and while not all the men owned suits, they all wore ties. It touched her to the very centre of her being.

The minister gave a brief but heartfelt sermon. Lorraine led them all in a stirring version of 'Amazing Grace'. Tess, with Ty and Krissie at her side, gave a eulogy—she spoke about Sarah's generosity, her love for her family, and how much she'd have loved Bellaroo Creek. Both Krissie and Ty told a little story about their mum—even their dad. There wasn't a dry eye after that. They ended the service with a recording of Sarah's favourite song—the Hollies hit 'He Ain't Heavy, He's My Brother'.

A wake was held at the community hall. After refreshments and cake had been amply consumed, Tess strode up to the podium and called the room to order. 'Ty, Krissie and I wanted today to be a celebration of Sarah's life and you've all helped make that possible and I want to thank you from the bottom of my heart.'

Without any effort at all, she found Cam's tall broad bulk in the crowd. The smile he sent her warmed her to her toes. 'We miss Sarah every single day, but we don't want to focus any longer on all the bad stuff about missing her, but on how much better our lives are for having known her. Today, you helped us do that.'

She smoothed her hair back behind her ears. 'Something Ty, Krissie and I have taken to doing at dinnertime is naming something that has made us happy for that day or something that we're grateful for. Every single day I'm grateful that Sarah was my sister, but when she died I turned my back on my music. A very special guy here in Bellaroo Creek, though, showed me what a mistake that was. I'm very grateful to Cameron Manning for that lesson. I want to now play you all a piece that was one of my sister's favourites.'

She moved to the side where she'd stowed her guitar case and retrieved the guitar she'd had couriered from Sydney. She hadn't played it in over five months. She slipped the strap over her head, seated herself on a stool, and looked out at the sea of faces staring back at her. 'Sarah, honey, this one's for you,' she whispered.

She met Cam's eyes, drew in a breath at his encouraging nod, and then her fingers touched the strings and magic filled her. She lost herself to it, pouring her heart into the music.

When she finished she smiled at Ty and Krissie sitting on the floor in front of her. And then at Cam. He was right. The music was a gift, and there was room in her heart for it all—for Ty and Krissie, and for the music. She should embrace it.

'I want to invite anyone who'd like to take part, to come up here and share something that's made you happy or that you're grateful for.'

Cam stared in awe.

Tess Laing was the most amazing woman he'd ever met. If Bellaroo Creek could attract another couple of women with her spunk the town would be safe for the next hundred years. It wouldn't just be saved. It'd flourish!

Krissie walked up onto stage to the microphone. 'You should go down there now,' she whispered to Tess, pointing at the crowd, obviously not meaning for everyone to hear, but the microphone picking it up as Tess adjusted it for her.

With a kiss to the top of the child's head, Tess made her way down to the crowd to stand with Ty. Without consciously meaning to, Cam made his way to her side. She smiled at him, turning automatically as if she'd sensed him there. It made his gut clench.

Did he truly mean to leave this woman?

'I want to say that one thing that makes me happy is my auntie Tess. We do lots of fun things together like singing, and we dance around the backyard and colour-in together. She's not a very good dancer...'

Everyone laughed. Cam remembered seeing Tess dance and shook his head. She was a great dancer.

'But she's going to teach me guitar and I love living with her.'

He held Tess back when Krissie finished. 'Let her do it all under her own steam,' he counselled.

'I'm fussing, huh?'

He didn't interfere though when she bent down to encompass the child in a hug once Krissie had reached them. It wasn't until she righted herself, though, that he saw Ty had moved to the microphone.

'My auntie Tess is awesome, but today I want to say I'm happy Cam has been our neighbour. He's shown me how to stake tomato plants and how to nail chicken wire and how to teach Barney to fetch a ball. I'm going to miss him when he goes to Africa.'

There were a few 'hear, hears' from the crowd and Cam found his throat thickening. He lifted Ty up in a bear hug when he rejoined them. 'Thanks, buddy, I'm going to miss you too.'

'Me too?' Krissie tugged on his sleeve, demanding a hug of her own.

'You too,' he said, hugging her close.

Damn it! Did he really mean to leave these kids behind?

'Me three.' Tess leaned across and kissed his cheek. She backed up pretty quick again too, though, and he didn't blame her. Not if the heat threatened her in the same way it did him.

One by one the townsfolk walked up to the microphone to name the things that made them happy—family, a good wheat crop, a clean bill of health, family, friends who rallied around in times of need, good rainfall, grandchildren, family. *Family.* It figured high on everyone's happiness radar. Not a single person mentioned going to Africa—or any other place for that matter. Bellaroo Creek and family, that was what mattered.

Bellaroo Creek and family.

Cameron stared at Tess and the kids. Could he truly leave them? Did he *want* to leave them?

He stared at his mother. She'd miss him dreadfully. He knew that now, even if she was putting a brave face on it.

Family and Bellaroo Creek.

Lance and Fiona canoodled in a corner like the lovesick couple they were and he didn't even feel a pang. Instead he felt hopeful. Lance was keeping his word and working hard. Having finally emerged from under Cam's shadow, he was even showing some natural aptitude on the sheep-breeding programme. And it was obvious he had no intention of breaking Fiona's heart as Cam had feared.

Family and Bellaroo Creek.

Once upon a time that had been his dream too. When it had failed him he'd turned his back on it, proclaimed it impossible. His heart started to thump. But it wasn't impossible, was it? It was within reach if he had the courage to try for it.

He stared at Tess and Ty and Krissie, remembered the laughter and light they'd brought to Kurrajong House, the life they'd sent flowing through it.

That dream of his wasn't impossible. Oh, it hadn't been possible with Fiona, and all he could do was be thankful that she'd realised it in time.

That dream of his was absolutely possible.

If only he wasn't too afraid to reach for it again.

His heart thundered in his ears. Tess had found the courage to embrace her music again. Could he find the same courage within himself?

He shoved his hands in his pockets and stared hard at the floorboards at his feet. What did he truly want? What would he lay his life down for and be glad to do it?

Tess.

That single word filled his soul.

'I'm next!' He pointed to the microphone. Everyone turned to stare at him. He swung to Tess, seized her face in his hands and kissed her soundly. His lips memorised every single curve and contour of hers and she kissed him back with such unguarded love it fed something essential inside him.

He let her go. He squeezed Krissie's and Ty's shoulders before striding up to the stage and the microphone.

Tess watched Cam adjust the microphone while the blood crashed through her veins.

He'd kissed her.

In front of everyone!

What did he mean by it?

Ty and Krissie grinned up at her. She couldn't help but grin back.

Cam cleared his throat. Her attention flew back to his tall frame and those powerful shoulders and lean hips...and long, long legs with their powerful thighs. Her knees quivered and her heart tripped and fluttered.

His gaze wandered about the crowd until she thought he must've made eye contact with everyone. 'I know every single one of you by your full name. I've listened to you recite the things that make you happy, the things that are most important to you, and the message has come through loud and clear— you love your families, your properties and Bellaroo Creek.'

He shifted. 'All I've ever wanted is to grow a big bustling family at Kurrajong Station, but a year ago that dream came crashing down around my ears and I thought it would never happen. That's when I made my decision to leave. I knew it would be too hard living here day in and day out with that dream mocking me.'

Her heart burned for all he'd been through.

'I want to say now that I'm grateful to Fiona for realising we weren't well suited and calling our engagement off before we made a dreadful mistake. I only wish I could've seen that truth sooner.'

He didn't love Fiona? Her hands clenched and unclenched until, to stop their fidgeting, she gripped them together.

'Because now I know what true love is.'

He did?

When his gaze moved to her, she had to press her hands to her heart to make sure it didn't leap right out of her chest.

'Loving someone means wanting them to be happy, even if it means giving up your own dreams. It means supporting them in the things that are important to them, even if you don't understand that importance.' He suddenly grinned. 'Like White Bearded Silkies and marigolds in a vegetable garden.'

Krissie tugged on Tess's blouse. 'Cam loves us, Auntie Tess.' She grinned as if it were the best news in the world.

'Course he does,' Ty scoffed, as if he'd always known as much.

She swallowed. Had she truly thought they wouldn't welcome another person into their lives? It was obvious that they'd welcome Cam.

Except…

Her heart started to wilt. Loving someone meant supporting their dreams. Cam's dream was to go to Africa—to experience the world, to make a difference. She couldn't stand in the way of that.

'Loving someone means risking your heart, even if you've vowed to never do that again, even if you don't feel ready to take that leap.'

He was going to risk his heart for her, wasn't he? She wanted him to. Oh, how she wanted him to, but…

Africa. His dream.

'I want you all to know that I won't be going to Africa after all.'

Applause broke out along with several cheers. Tess couldn't bear to glance around. Her heart had slumped to her ankles.

'I'm going to fight for the life I want. I'm going to fight for my dream. If that dream proves impossible, I'm going to stay here in Bellaroo Creek anyway. I'm not going to turn my back on the town. This is where I belong.'

He climbed down from the stage and made his way directly

to where she stood. Taking both Krissie's and Ty's hands, he led them away to the far side of the room and knelt down to speak to them. With his back to her she couldn't see what he said. She could only see the smiles that lit the children's faces, their decisive nods, and the hopeful glances they sent her way.

She wanted to close her eyes. She couldn't let him do this. When he rose and beckoned to her, she pulled in a breath and moved towards them. With a smile designed to heat her from the inside out, Cam took her hand. 'You guys go join the party again. Your aunt and I are going to talk.'

And with that he led her out of a side door and away from the noise of the hall until they stood beneath the fronds of a pepper tree that partially hid them from view. He stared down into her face, plucked one of the fronds from her hair, but he didn't say anything.

Loving someone means wanting them to be happy.

'When did you realise I'd fallen in love with you, Cameron?'

He touched her cheek with the backs of his fingers. He kept a firm grip on her hand. 'That day at my mother's.'

'It was the day I realised I loved you.' She paused and bit back a sigh. 'I don't think I'm very good at keeping things from you.'

His lips lifted. 'I'm glad about that.'

She gently detached her hand and moved a couple of steps back until she leant against the hard, rough trunk of the tree. He stiffened. 'I hope you mean to tell me what's troubling you now?'

Oh, how she would miss him!

Behind her, she closed her fingers about the rough bark. She dragged in a breath that hurt her lungs. 'All your life you've taken responsibility for other people. For your father when he cut himself off from the world, and for continuing his legacy in providing your mother with a haven if she should ever need it. For taking on the management of the property your stepfather left to her…and even for helping Lance find his feet. You help Edna and Ted Fairchild run cattle so they can stay in the home they love, and heaven only knows how many other people you help out in a similar way. You're amazing, Cameron, a true-blue hero. I swear I have yet to meet anyone with more decency and integrity.'

He adjusted his stance, legs wide and hands on hips, and her heart stuttered in her chest. 'Why, then,' he said, 'am I suddenly not happy to hear this?'

She ached to rush forward and throw her arms around his neck and tell him how much she loved him, but…

He deserved to chase his dreams.

'Because all your life you've taken on everyone else's responsibilities, but now you have a chance to travel and to find out where you truly want to be.'

'I know where I want to be.'

She wanted to believe him, but… 'Do you know how much responsibility it is raising two kids? Do you know how needy and…and…Cam, we—Ty, Krissie and me—we're *not* your responsibility.' She might not have given birth to Ty and Krissie, but they were hers now and she loved them as if she had. 'I know when you look at us you see a single mum with two kids who need rescuing, but—'

'Garbage!' He slashed a hand through the air, making her blink. 'I look at you, Tess, and I see an incredibly strong woman who manages to make me laugh even when I'm feeling my bleakest and grumpiest. I look at you and see a desirable woman I want to take to my bed and make love with thoroughly and comprehensively.'

She pressed hands to cheeks that burned.

He moved in close until all she could smell was the scent of cut grass and hot man, and all she could see was him.

'I look at you, Tess, and my soul sings and my heart is at rest and there's glitter in my world.'

He reached out to touch her face. 'I don't see a woman

who needs rescuing. I see a woman with a safety net ready for me if I should ever fall. Tess, when I look at you I don't see a responsibility. I see my future. I see my soul mate. I see the woman I love.'

Her heart all but stopped.

His hands clenched, his eyes blazed with resolution. 'I don't know how long it will take me to convince you of the truth of that, but I want you to know I'm going to dedicate my life to doing exactly that.'

'But Africa,' she whispered. She wanted him happy. She wanted him to follow his dream.

'To hell with Africa! It was my consolation prize. I'm not running away. I'm not leaving Bellaroo Creek. And let me tell you another thing.' He jabbed a finger at her nose. 'I'm not making way for some other single farmer to make a move on you.' He thrust out his jaw. 'I'm not going anywhere!'

She stared at him. He stared back, his eyes a glowing, gleaming green. 'Africa is not where I want to be. Wherever you are, Tess, that's where I'm going to make my home—whether that be at Kurrajong House, your little farmhouse or in Sydney.'

He meant it. Every single word.

And she could see the exact moment when he clocked her belief in him. His smile was like drought-ridden land coming back to life after vital rain.

He reached out to cup her face. 'Your eyes tell me you're going to say yes when I ask you to marry me.'

She grinned. She couldn't help it. She reached up to touch his cheek, before moving in closer to wind her arms about his neck. 'Yours tell me you've already asked for the children's permission.'

'They gave it gladly.'

Of course they had. They adored Cam as much as she did. 'My eyes don't lie, Cameron. I love you. My heart is completely and utterly yours.'

Just as his was hers. And she meant to treasure it and keep it safe for ever.

He stared down at her as if her words were magic. She moved against him suggestively. 'So, what do you mean to do with your Bellaroo Creek bride once you have her?'

His head dipped towards her, blocking out the sun. 'I mean to make her the happiest woman on the planet,' he murmured against her lips, before he captured them in a kiss of such pure joy Tess felt as if she were flying and swooping among the treetops.

* * * * *

MIRACLE IN BELLAROO CREEK

BY
BARBARA HANNAY

Reading and writing have always been a big part of **Barbara Hannay**'s life. She wrote her first short story at the age of eight for the Brownies' writer's badge. It was about a girl who was devastated when her family had to move from the city to the Australian Outback.

Since then, a love of both city and country lifestyles has been a continuing theme in Barbara's books and in her life. Although she has mostly lived in cities, now that her family has grown up and she's a full-time writer she's enjoying a country lifestyle.

Barbara and her husband live on a misty hillside in Far North Queensland's Atherton Tableland. When she's not lost in the world of her stories she's enjoying farmers' markets, gardening clubs and writing groups, or preparing for visits from family and friends.

Barbara records her country life in her blog, *Barbwired*, and her website is: www.barbarahannay.com

To the town of Malanda, which doesn't need saving,
and to Deb Healy at the bakery for showing me
how beautiful bread is created every day.

CHAPTER ONE

Boutique business opportunity at Bellaroo Creek

Former bakery offered at nominal or deferred rental to help revitalise the town's retail business.

Bellaroo Council, in support of the Regional Recovery Programme, is calling for expressions of interest to occupy and redevelop Lot 3 Wattle Street on a lease or freehold arrangement. Some bakery equipment is included in the assets.

Enquiries/business plan to J. P. Elliot CEO Bellaroo Council, 23 Wattle Street.

MILLA SAT ON the edge of the hospital bed, a cup of tea and sandwich untouched beside her.

It was over. She'd lost her baby, and any minute now the nice nurse would pop back to tell her she was free to go.

Go where? Back to the lonely motel room?

From down the hospital corridor the sounds of laughter drifted, along with the happy chatter of cheery visitors. Other patients' visitors. Milla looked around her room, bare of cards or flowers, grapes or teddy bears.

Her parents were away on a Mediterranean cruise and she hadn't told anyone else that she was back in Australia.

Her Aussie friends still thought she was living the high life as the wife of a mega-rich Californian and she hadn't been ready to confess the truth about her spectacularly failed marriage. Besides, the few of her friends who lived in Sydney were party girls, and, being pregnant, Milla hadn't been in party mode. She'd been waiting till the next scan to announce the news about her baby.

But now...

Milla wrapped her arms over her stomach, reliving the cramping pains and terror that had brought her to the emergency ward. She had wept as the doctor examined her, and she'd sobbed helplessly when he told her that she was having a miscarriage. She'd cried for the little lost life, for her lost dreams.

Her marriage fiasco had shattered her hopes of ever finding love and trust in an adult relationship and she'd pinned everything on the promise of a soft, warm baby to hold. She longed for the special bond and unconditional love that only a baby could bring, and she'd been desperate to make a success of motherhood.

Such wonderful dreams she'd nurtured for her little boy or girl, and imagining the months ahead had been so much fun.

Along with watching a tiny, new human being discover the world, Milla had looked forward to patiently caring for her little one. Chances were, it would be a boy—the Cavanaugh wives always seemed to produce sons—and Milla had imagined bathing her little fellow, feeding him, dressing him in sweet little striped sleep-suits, coping with his colic and teething pains and the inevitable sleepless nights.

She'd pictured trips to the park and to the beach as he grew, had even seen herself making his first birthday cake with a cute single candle, and issuing invitations to other mums and babes to join in the party.

Now…

'Ten to twenty per cent of known pregnancies end in miscarriage,' the doctor had informed her matter-of-factly.

But Milla could only see this as another failure on top of her failed marriage. After all, if the statistics were turned around, eighty to ninety per cent of pregnancies were absolutely fine. Just as two thirds of marriages were perfectly happy.

The irony was, she'd become pregnant in a last-ditch attempt to save her marriage. When that had proved to be clearly impossible, she'd turned her hopes and ambitions inwards. To her child.

She'd been mega careful with her diet, taking all the right vitamins and folates, and, although she'd been through a great deal of stress and a long flight from LA to Sydney, she'd made sure that her new lifestyle included a healthy balance of rest and exercise and fresh air.

And yet again, she'd failed. Fighting tears, Milla packed her toothbrush and wallet into the carryall she'd hastily filled when she'd left for the hospital.

It was time to go, and after one last look around the small white room she set off down the long hospital corridor.

The final years of her marriage to Harry Cavanaugh

had been grim, but she'd never felt this low...or this lost...as if she'd been cast adrift in a vast and lonely sea.

Fleetingly, she wondered if she should let Harry know about the baby. But why bother? He wouldn't care.

In his midtown Manhattan office, Ed Cavanaugh was absorbed in reading spreadsheets when his PA buzzed that he had an important call. Time was tight and the info on his computer screen was critical. Ed ignored the buzzer and continued scanning the lines of figures.

A minute later, he sensed his PA at the door.

'Mr Cavanaugh?'

Without looking up, Ed raised a silencing hand as he took a note of the figures he'd been hunting. When he was finished, and not a millisecond before, he shot a glance over the top of his glasses. 'What is it, Sarah?'

'A call from Australia. It's Gary Kemp and I was sure you'd want to speak to him.'

Gary Kemp was the Australian private detective Ed's family had had hired to track down his escapee sister-in-law. An unexpected tension gripped Ed. Had Milla been found?

'Put him through,' he said, closing down the screen.

Scant seconds later, his line buzzed again and he snatched up the receiver. 'Gary, any news?'

'Plenty, Mr C.'

'Have you found her? Is she still in Australia?' They already knew that Milla had caught a flight from LA to Sydney.

'She's still in the country, but you'll never guess where.'

Ed grimaced. This Aussie detective could be annoyingly cocky. Ed had no intention of playing guessing games, although in this case it would be dead easy to take a stab at Milla's whereabouts. Her tastes were totally predictable. She would be holed up in a harbour-side penthouse, or in a luxury resort at one of those famous Australian beaches.

'Just tell me,' he demanded with a spurt of irritation.

'Try Bellaroo Creek.'

'Bella-who *what*?'

'Bellaroo Creek,' Gary repeated with a chuckle. 'Middle of nowhere. Dying town. Population three hundred and seventy-nine.'

Ed let out a huff of surprise. 'Where exactly is this middle of nowhere?'

'Little tinpot whistle-stop in western New South Wales, about five hours' drive from Sydney.'

'What are you telling me? My sister-in-law passed through this place?'

'No, she's still there, mate. Seems it's her hometown.'

Just in time, Ed stopped himself from asking the obvious. Of course, his brother's sophisticated socialite wife must have grown up in this Bellaroo Creek place, but he found the news hard to swallow.

'Her family's long gone,' the detective went on. 'So have most of the former residents. As I said, the place is on its last legs. These days it's practically a ghost town.'

None of this made sense to Ed. 'Are you sure you have the right Milla Cavanaugh?'

'No doubt about it. It's her all right, although she's using her maiden name, Brady. Interesting. As far as I can tell, she's barely touched her bank accounts.'

'No way,' retorted Ed. 'You can't have the right woman.'

'Check your emails,' Gary Kemp responded dryly.

'This isn't amateur hour, mate, as you'll soon see from my invoice. I've sent you the photo I took yesterday in Bellaroo Creek's main street.'

Frowning, Ed flicked to his emails, opened the link and there it was…a photo of a woman dressed in jeans and a roll-necked black cashmere sweater.

She was definitely Milla. Her delicate, high-cheek-boned beauty was in a class of its own. His younger brother had always won the best-looking women, no question.

Milla's hair was different, though. Pale red-gold, with a tendency to curl, the way it had been when Ed had first met her, before she'd had it straightened and dyed blond to fit in with the other wives in Harry's LA set.

'OK,' he growled, his throat unaccountably tight. 'That's helpful. I see you've sent an address, as well.'

'Yeah. She's staying at the Bellaroo pub. Booked in for a week, but I'm guessing she might think twice about staying that long. It's so dead here, she could get jack of the place and shoot through any tick of the clock.'

'Right. Thanks for the update. Keep an eye on her and keep me posted re her movements.'

'No worries, Mr C.'

Ed hung up and went through to his PA's desk. 'We've found her.'

Sarah looked unexpectedly delighted. 'That's wonderful, Mr Cavanaugh. Does that mean Milla's still in Australia? Is she OK?'

'Yes on both counts. But it means I'm going to have to fly down there pronto. I'll need you to reschedule the meetings with Cleaver Holdings.'

'Yes, of course.'

'Several people won't be happy, but that's too bad. Dan Brookes will have to handle their complaints and he can run any other meetings in my absence. I'll brief him as soon as he's free. Meantime, I want you to book me on the earliest possible flight to Sydney. And I'll want a hire car ready to go.'

'Of course.'

'And can you ring Caro Marsden? Let her know I'll be out of the country for a few days.'

To his surprise Sarah, his normally respectful PA, narrowed her eyes at him in an uncharacteristic challenge. 'Ed,' she said, which was a bad start. Sarah rarely used his given name. 'You've been dating the poor woman for four months. Don't you think you should—'

'All right, all right,' he snapped through gritted teeth. 'I'll call her.'

Sarah was watching him with a thoughtful frown. 'I guess you're going to break the news to Milla about your brother?'

'Among other things.' Ed eased the sudden tightness of his collar. His younger brother's death in a plane crash and the subsequent funeral were still fresh and raw. The loss had hit him so much harder than he'd imagined possible.

'The poor woman,' Sarah said now.

'Yeah,' Ed responded softly…remembering…and wondering…

Almost immediately, he gave an irritated shrug, annoyed by the unwanted pull of his emotions. 'Don't forget, it was Milla who cut and ran,' he said tersely.

Not only that. She kept her pregnancy a secret from

the family. Which was the prime reason he had to find her now.

'I know Milla's persona non grata around here,' Sarah said. 'But I always thought she seemed very nice.'

Sure you did, Ed thought with a sigh. That was the problem. The woman had always been a total enigma.

It was weird to be back. It had been twelve long years…

Milla drove her little hire car over a bumpy wooden bridge and took the next turn left onto a dirt track. As she opened the farm gates she saw a large rustic letter-box with the owners' names—BJ and HA Murray—painted in white.

She hadn't seen her old school friends, Brad and Heidi, since she'd left town when she was twenty, dead eager to shake the district's dust from her heels and to travel the world. Back then, she'd been determined to broaden her horizons and to discover her hidden potential, to work out what she really wanted from life.

Meanwhile Heidi, her best friend, had stayed here in this quiet old backwater. Worse, Heidi had made the deadly serious mistake of marrying a local boy, an error of judgement the girls had decreed in high school would be a fate worse than death.

Shoot me now, they used to say at the very thought. They'd been sixteen then. Sixteen and super confident that the world was their oyster, and quite certain that it was vitally important to escape Bellaroo Creek.

Unfortunately, Heidi had changed her mind and she'd become engaged to Brad only a matter of months after Milla had left town.

But although poor old Heidi had stayed, it was clear

that many others had found it necessary to get away. These days Bellaroo Creek was practically a ghost town.

This discovery had been a bit of a shock. Milla had hoped that a trip to her hometown would cheer her up. Instead, she'd been depressed all over again when she'd walked down the main street and discovered that almost all the businesses and shops had closed down.

Where were the cars and people? Where were the farmers standing on street corners, thumbs hooked in belt loops as they discussed the weather and the wool prices? Where were the youngsters who used to hang around the bakery or the hamburger joint? The young mums who brought their babies to the clinic, their children to the library?

Bellaroo Creek was nothing like the busy, friendly country town of her childhood. The general store was now a supermarket combined with a newsagent's and a tiny post office—and that was just about it.

Even the bakery Milla's parents used to own was now boarded-up and empty. Milla had stood for ages outside the shopfront she'd once known so well, staring glumly through the dusty, grimy windows into the darkened interior.

From as far back as she could remember the Bellaroo bakery had been a bustling, busy place, filled with cheery customers, and with the fragrant aroma of freshly baked bread. People had flocked from miles around to buy her dad's mouth-watering loaves made from local wheat, or his delicious rolls and shiny-topped fruit buns, as well as her mum's legendary pies.

Her parents had sold the business when they retired, and in the short time since it had come to this…an empty, grimy shop with a faded, printed sign inside the dusty window offering the place for lease. Again.

Who would want it?

Looking around at the other vacant shopfronts, Milla had been totally disheartened. She'd driven from Sydney to Bellaroo Creek on a nostalgic whim, but instead she'd found a place on the brink of extinction…

It seemed the universe was presenting her with yet another dismal picture of failure.

It was so depressing…

Poor Heidi must be going mental living here, Milla decided as she drove down the winding dirt track between paddocks of pale, biscuit-coloured grass dotted with fat, creamy sheep. At least Heidi was still married to Brad and had two kids, a boy and a girl—which sounded fine on the surface, but Milla couldn't believe her old friend was really happy.

Admittedly, her contact with Heidi had been patchy— the occasional email or Facebook message, the odd Christmas card…

She'd felt quite tentative, almost fearful when she'd plucked up the courage to telephone Heidi, and she'd been rather surprised that her friend had sounded just as bright and bubbly as she had in her teens.

'Come for lunch,' Heidi had gushed after the initial excited squeal over the phone. 'Better still, come for morning tea and stay for lunch. That way you'll catch up with Brad when he comes in around twelve, and we can have plenty of time for a really good chat. I want to hear *everything.*'

Milla wasn't particularly looking forward to sharing too many details of her personal history, but she was keen to see Heidi again. Curious now, too, as the track dipped to a concrete ford that crossed a small, shady creek.

As her tyres splashed through the shallow water she imagined Heidi and Brad's children playing in the creek when they were older. She edged the car up the opposite bank and rounded a corner, and saw her first view of the farmhouse.

Which wasn't grand by any means—just a simple white weatherboard house with verandahs and a red roof—but it was shaded by a big old spreading tree and there were well-tended flowerbeds set in neat lawns, a vegetable garden with trellises at one end and free-ranging, rusty-feathered chickens.

Her friend's home was a far cry from the acres of expensive glass and white marble of Milla and Harry's Beverly Hills mansion...

And yet, something about the house's old-fashioned, rustic simplicity touched an unexpected chord in Milla.

No need to get sentimental, she warned herself as she drove forward.

Before she'd parked the car, the front door opened, spilling puppies and a rosy-cheeked little girl. Heidi followed close behind, waving and grinning as she hurried down the steps and across the lawn. As Milla clambered out she found herself enveloped in the warmest of welcoming hugs.

After weeks of loneliness, she was fighting tears.

Ed had tried to ring his father several times, but the arrogant old man had a habit of ignoring phone calls if he wasn't in a sociable mood. Which happened quite often, and went part-way to explaining Gerry Cavanaugh's multiple marriages and divorces and why his three sons had been born to three different wives, who now lived as far apart from each other as possible.

Today, when Gerry finally deigned to return his son's call, Ed was in the Business Lounge at JFK, sending last-minute business emails.

'Glad to hear you've tracked Milla down.' His father always jumped in without any preliminaries. 'And you know what you have to do when you catch up with her, don't you, Ed?'

'Well…sure. I'll tell her about Harry.'

'If she doesn't already know.'

Ed was quite sure Milla couldn't know that Harry had died. Even though she'd run away, she would have been upset. She would have contacted them if she'd heard, and come back for the funeral.

'And I'll set up the trust fund for the baby,' he went on. 'Make sure Milla signs the necessary papers.'

'That's not all, damn it.'

Ed sighed. What else had his old man up his sleeve?

'Your main job is to bring the woman home.'

'Home?' This was news to Ed. 'Don't forget Milla was born and bred in Australia, Father. And she still calls Australia home,' he added with a grim smile at his joking reference to the popular song.

'Like hell. My grandson will be born in America.'

'What are you suggesting? That I kidnap a pregnant woman? You want extradition orders placed on your pregnant daughter-in-law?'

His father ignored this. 'You'll find a way to persuade her. You're a Cavanaugh. You have a knack with women.'

Not with this particular woman. Ed squashed unsettling memories before they could take hold. 'Just remember, Father. Milla ran away from Harry and from our family. It's obvious she wants as much distance between us as possible. She's unlikely to come back willingly.'

'Trust me, son, as soon as she hears she's a widow, she'll be back here in a flash. Of course, she won't get a goddamn cent of Harry's money unless she lets us raise the child as a Cavanaugh, as my grandchild.'

'Got it…' responded Ed dispiritedly. 'I'll see what I can do.'

His offer was received with an expressive grunt that conveyed the full brunt of his father's doubts and displeasure.

Ed gritted his teeth. 'Anyway…I've briefed Dan Brookes and everything's in hand as far as the business is concerned, so I guess I'll see you in a couple of days.'

Ending the call, Ed sat staring bleakly through the wall of windows, watching the busy tarmac and the endless streams of planes taking off and landing.

He wasn't looking forward to the long, twenty-hour flight, but he was looking forward even less to the task that lay ahead of him. After all, Milla had returned to Australia because she'd planned to divorce Harry, and she'd clearly been so disenchanted with the Cavanaughs that she hadn't told them about her pregnancy.

It was only while Ed and his father were going through the painful process of sorting through Harry's paperwork that they'd discovered the medical forms.

Slam!

A small missile crashed into Ed, sending his Black-Berry flying. Rascal-faced yet cherubic, a little boy looked up at him with enormous and cheeky blue eyes that peeped from beneath a white-blond fringe.

'What's your name?' the kid lisped cutely as he gripped at Ed's trouser leg for balance.

'Ethan!' A woman dived from the right, sweeping the child into her arms. 'So sorry,' she told Ed, her eyes widening with horror as she saw her son's sticky, chocolate-smeared fingers and the tracks he'd left on Ed's Italian suit trousers.

The kid squirmed in his mom's arms, as if he sensed that his fun was about to end. And Ed couldn't help remembering Harry as an ankle-biter.

For ages after the woman and her boy disappeared, Ed sat, thinking about his younger brother. Milla's unborn baby would probably be just like that kid—an angelic rascal, full of mischief and charm, stealing hearts and creating havoc. Another Cavanaugh…a new generation.

Memories washed over him as they had many times in the past few weeks. Growing up with different mothers, he and Harry hadn't spent a lot of time in each other's company, but his younger brother had always been the wild child, the prankster, the kid who hadn't done his homework, but still passed his exams with good grades.

As an adult, Harry had wasted his talents on gambling and flying his private jet and he'd contributed almost nothing to the family firm. And yet, they'd all loved him. Despite his faults, the guy had been a born charmer.

Ed was the conscientious son, the hardworking eldest, the one who'd carried on the family's business so that all the others could continue to live in the manner to which they'd become accustomed.

Admittedly, their youngest brother, Charlie, the son

of Gerry Cavanaugh's third wife, was still in college. He was a good student, from all reports, more serious and focused, more like Ed. But they'd both known that Harry had always been the Golden Child, their father's favourite, and Harry's son would be the apple of his grandfather's eye.

Ed would have to deal with the full force of his father's wrath if he failed to bring Milla and her unborn baby home.

Sitting at Heidi's scrubbed pine table, drinking coffee and talking nineteen to the dozen, Milla made a surprising discovery. She felt calmer and happier than she had in…ages…

Looking around at Heidi's honey-toned timber cupboards and simple open shelving, at the jars of homemade preserves and pots of herbs on the window sill, she realised that she'd completely forgotten how very comforting a farmhouse kitchen could be.

This room had such a timeless and welcoming quality with its huge old stove pumping out gentle warmth, with Heidi's home-baked cookies on a willow-pattern plate…a yellow jug filled with bottlebrush flowers… dog and cat bowls in the corner…

It brought to mind Milla's childhood here in Bellaroo Creek. She'd been happy back then.

Chatting with Heidi was so very different from socialising in LA, where the women's conversations had been more like competitions, and the topics centred on shopping, facials, pedicures, or gossip about affairs.

Heidi simply talked about her family, who were clearly the centre of her world. She told Milla about Brad's farming innovations with the same pride she displayed when she mentioned her son's success in his first year at school or her little daughter's playful antics.

The conversation should have been boring, but Milla found to her surprise that she was fascinated.

It was all a bit puzzling... Heidi's hair was still exactly the same as it had been in high school—straight, shoulder length and mousey brown. She spent her days working on the farm with Brad and growing vegetables and raising chickens, which meant she lived in jeans and cotton shirts and sturdy boots.

She had freckles and a few lines around her eyes, and her hands were roughened, her fingernails chipped. But Milla, looking at her friend, knew she was as happy as a pig in the proverbial...

'I'm doing exactly what I want to do,' Heidi happily confessed. 'Maybe I'm totally lacking in ambition, but I don't want to do anything else. And it might sound crazy, but I don't have any doubts.'

This was a *major* surprise, but to her even greater surprise Milla found herself opening up to Heidi telling how she'd clocked many, many miles and tried a ton of different jobs in exotic locations, until eventually, she'd arrived in America and fallen head over heels for a charming and handsome multimillionaire adventurer, who had, incredibly, asked her to marry him.

She told how those first years of her marriage had been such a heady time. Harry had so many celebrity friends in his social circle and he'd flown his own plane. 'He used to fly me to Paris for a dinner and a show, or to Milan to buy a dress I could wear to the Oscars.'

Heidi's jaw dropped with a satisfying clunk.

'We would fly to New Orleans for a party,' Milla went on. 'Or to Buenos Aires to watch a polo game. I never dreamed I'd ever have such excitement and fun, such astonishing luxury and comfort.'

'I used to hear bits and pieces,' Heidi said, overawed. 'But I never realised you were living like a princess. Wow! It must have been *amazing.*'

'Yeah.' Milla wished she could sound more convincing. She couldn't quite bring herself to tell Heidi the rest of her story—about Harry's gambling and endless affairs, and if she mentioned the baby she would burst into tears.

Crazy thing was, she'd come back to Bellaroo Creek full of pity for Heidi, but, looking back on her own life, she felt as if she'd achieved next to nothing that really counted. In terms of happiness and self-esteem, she was at an all-time low.

And it wasn't long before she sensed that her friend had guessed. She could see the questions and the dawning compassion in Heidi's eyes. And then, out of the blue, as if they'd never lost their best-friends-for-ever closeness, Heidi jumped out of her chair, circled the table and gave Milla an enormous hug.

'Mills, you have to tell me why you're here on your own and looking so sad,' Heidi said gently. 'And what are we going to do about it?'

CHAPTER TWO

At last…a road sign announced: *Welcome to Bellaroo Creek… Population 379…*

Ed slowed the car and surveyed the cluster of tired houses and the narrow strip of faded office buildings and shops set in the middle of wide, almost featureless plains. It was like arriving on the set of a Western movie. And potentially as risky, he thought wryly.

A new tension replaced his frayed and jet-lagged weariness as he pulled over, took out his phone and punched Gary Kemp's number. He'd given Milla no warning of his arrival—he'd more or less come here to ambush her. It wasn't a pleasant prospect.

'Mr Cavanaugh,' the Australian drawled, recognising Ed's number. 'Welcome to Oz.'

More like Kansas than Oz, Ed almost told him. 'Milla still here?' he asked. 'Still staying at the pub?'

'Sure, her room's booked through till Wednesday and she's still in town, but you're more likely to find her in the old bakery across the road.'

Ed frowned. He'd heard of pregnant women developing food cravings, but he couldn't imagine his slender sister-in-law wolfing down endless strudels.

'Apparently her family used to own the bakery,' Gary

Kemp clarified. 'It's closed now, but she seems to have the keys.'

'OK, that's helpful.' Ed scratched at his jaw, finding a patch of stubble he'd missed during his hasty shave at Sydney airport. 'I'll take it from here.'

'Glad to hear it, Mr C. I certainly don't want to hang around in this hole any longer than I have to. It's probably safer if you and I don't meet. I've just fuelled up on the other side of town, so I'll head off.'

'So the bakery's easy to find?'

'Can't miss it. In the main street, opposite the pub and about three doors along.'

'Thanks.' Ed edged his car forward, cruising into the almost deserted main street where a few battered pickup trucks and dusty sedans were parked. A couple of pedestrians crossed the road at a shuffling snail's pace—a young woman, arm in arm with an elderly, white-haired man huddled inside a tweed jacket.

Further down the street, two women holding laden shopping bags were deep in conversation. A spotted dog slept in a sunny doorway.

Otherwise, the street appeared empty, but despite the lack of people the town didn't look completely neglected. A neat and colourful strip of garden cut the wide street in half, clear evidence that someone cared. There were shade trees, too, and noisy, brightly coloured birds were feeding in the blossom-filled branches.

The taller buildings were no higher than two storeys, but they looked solid and stately and over a century old, signs to Ed that the town had seen better days. Opposite the post office a memorial had been erected to fallen soldiers and there seemed to be a hell of a lot of names on it.

Bellaroo Creek had boasted a bigger population at one time, he decided as he parked a few doors away from the pub and took off his sunglasses, conscious again of his tiredness after the long flight and the five-hour drive on the wrong side of the highway.

Tension nagged and he grimaced. He wasn't looking forward to the task ahead.

He told himself he was doing it for the kid's sake. Now, with Harry gone, Ed's role as the unborn baby's uncle loomed as a greater responsibility, with higher personal stakes. He would cope best if he concentrated on the kid and erased from his memory his fleeting history with its mother.

Frowning, he climbed out of the car and stretched his long, cramped limbs. Across the road, he could see a row of rundown, empty shopfronts in stone buildings that still showed traces of their former elegance. One door was open and above it, in faded green paint, the shop's name, Bellaroo Bakery, was faintly visible.

With an air of determination Ed crossed the road and stood on the sidewalk outside, observing. He couldn't see anyone in the front part of the store, but he listened for voices. Although he planned to take Milla by surprise, he didn't want to embarrass her if she had company.

There was silence, however, so he knocked on the open door.

And waited impatiently.

No one came and he was about to knock again when Milla appeared at the back of the shop, wiping her hands on her jeans. She looked pale and tired, but her delicate features and candle-flame hair were as lovely as ever. And, as always, the sight of her sent a painful dart spearing through Ed.

Her face turned white when she saw him.

'You?' she said softly and her sea-green eyes looked stricken. Her lips trembled, parted and then shut again as if she couldn't think of anything else to say.

Ed swallowed to ease the sharpness in his throat and Milla came forward carefully, almost fearfully.

'Hello, Milla.'

'What are you doing here?'

'I—' He was halted by her fragile air, suddenly afraid that his news would flatten her completely. 'There've been...developments.' *Damn, how clumsy was that?* 'We need to talk.'

'No, thanks.' Green fire flared in Milla's eyes. 'I'm finished with you lot.' She shot him a tight, haughty glare. 'I have nothing to discuss with you or with your brother.'

Turning away, she tossed her next words over her shoulder. 'I know why you're here, Ed. Harry sent you, because he didn't have the guts to come and try to con me himself. But I don't care if he wants me back. I'm done with him. It's over.'

'Harry didn't ask me to come.'

Milla stiffened, half turned towards him again. Her eyes were sharp, her arms crossed defensively over her chest. 'How did you find me?' Before Ed could answer, a knowing light crept into her eyes. 'It was that weasel-faced guy in the pub, wasn't it? He's watching me. He's a private investigator.'

Ed shrugged.

'Cavanaugh money,' she scoffed bitterly. 'It'll buy anything.'

'Milla, I've come a long way and we need to—'

'You shouldn't have bothered, Ed. I know your role in the family. Mr Fix-it. The others are always getting you to clean up after them and to sort everyone's problems.'

At least her voice wasn't quite as harsh as she said this.

And Ed found himself fumbling to explain. 'Well… listen…I had to find you. I knew you couldn't know what's happened.'

She frowned. 'What do you mean?'

'Milla, it's bad news about Harry.'

'Harry's always bad news.' Now she gave a theatrical eye-roll, as if she hadn't heard the seriousness in his voice. 'It took me four years to discover what you and your family probably knew all along.'

'Milla, Harry's dead.'

To Ed's dismay Milla's face turned whiter than ever. She clamped a hand to her mouth and she seemed to crumple and sway.

Instinctively, he stepped forward. The reaction was timely as Milla sagged against him as if her knees had given way.

Horrified, Ed remembered too late that she was pregnant. He should have delivered the news more gently, instead of oafishly blurting it out.

Scooping her into his arms, he scanned the empty shop, but there wasn't so much as a chair. He carried her, trying, unsuccessfully, to ignore her soft curves and the flowery fragrance of her hair. Through the doorway, and at the back of the shop he found a huge cleaned space with, among other things, a scrubbed table and chairs. But already, Milla was stirring.

* * *

'I'm sorry.'

Milla realised she was being carried in Ed's arms with her face pressed against the solid wall of his chest. 'I'm OK, Ed,' she protested, although she was still feeling dizzy. 'Put me down, please.'

He was incredibly gentle as he lowered her to a chair. 'Are you sure you're OK?'

'Yes, thank you.' It wasn't completely true. She was still dazed by the news.

Harry couldn't be dead. It was impossible. She felt sick and faint and she propped her elbows on the table and sank her head in her hands, trying to take the astonishing news in.

Her husband was dead. The man who'd caused her so much initial joy and subsequent pain. Desperately handsome, dangerously charming, hurtful and selfish Harry Cavanaugh. Gone. For ever.

When she'd left America she'd hated him. He'd lied and cheated on her one time too many, and in the worst possible way. In his final act of faithlessness, she'd come home unexpectedly early from an appointment with her obstetrician and found him in bed—*their* bed—with one of her so-called girlfriends.

It wasn't the first time and Milla knew she'd been foolish to forgive him in the past. Leaving Harry had been easy after that.

But now…

Death.

No chance for forgiveness either way.

Milla was aware that Ed had moved to the sink and was filling a glass with water.

'Thanks,' she said as he offered her the drink. She took a few small sips.

'Milla, I'm sorry. I should have been more thoughtful—'

'There's no thoughtful way to break this kind of news. I made it difficult to be found, so it was good of you to come, Ed, to tell me face to face.' She took another sip of water and forced herself to ask, 'What happened? How did Harry—?' But she couldn't bring herself to say the dreadful word. 'How did it happen?'

'He crashed his plane.'

'No.' Milla flinched as she pictured the beautiful sleek and shiny jet—Harry's pride and joy—crumpled. Burned. Harry inside.

'It happened over the Mojave Desert,' Ed said. 'The funeral was last Thursday.'

It was the same day she'd lost the baby. Remembering, she was so overwhelmed she had to cover her face with her hands. Sinking forward, she compressed her lips tightly to stop herself from sobbing out loud.

By the time she was once again under control, Ed was at the side window, standing with his back to her and with his hands plunged deep in his trouser pockets as he looked out into the untidy, narrow alley between this shop and its neighbour.

'I would have come back to the funeral,' she said.

Ed nodded. 'I knew you would have, but we couldn't find you.'

'I'm sorry.' She was. Truly sorry. Despite the many times Harry had hurt her, she still felt something for him, although she wasn't quite sure what that something was.

'Was there anyone else in the plane?'

A muscle jerked in Ed's jaw. 'Yes.'

'Not Julie?'

'No,' Ed said wearily. 'Julie had already been passed over.' He looked down at the floor and his throat worked as he swallowed, as if he hated what he had to tell her next. 'It was Angela.'

A groan broke from Milla. 'Angela Beldon?'

'Yes,' Ed said unhappily.

Another from her circle of so-called friends...

Harry, you poor silly man...

'It must be genetic, don't you think?'

'What's that?'

'The Cavanaugh male's wandering eye.'

Ed frowned. 'You're probably right.' He sighed and turned back to the window, as if he hoped this difficult conversation had come to an end.

He was every inch a Cavanaugh, with the family's typically strong features and broad-shouldered muscularity. An inch or two taller than Harry, he was as dark as his younger brother had been fair, but, like the rest of the family, he had an indefinable masculine ruggedness that inevitably drew admiring glances from women.

That was where the similarities ended, however. Ed was the serious, responsible member of the Cavanaugh clan. *The Good Son,* Harry had dubbed him, but, while Harry's tone had been mocking, there'd been a hint of envy, too.

Milla, for her part, had always been a little in awe of Ed, even a bit afraid of him.

She was nervous now, realising that there had to be more to his sudden arrival in Bellaroo Creek than the delivery of bad news that could have been handled— now that they'd tracked her down—with a phone call.

'I suppose you came all this way to talk about money,' she said dully.

Ed turned from the window. 'It has to be discussed. Apart from anything else, we have to settle your inheritance.'

She shook hear head.

'As I'm sure you know,' Ed went on, 'my father placed certain restrictions on Harry. He made sure it was in your pre-nup.'

Yes, Milla knew that Gerry Cavanaugh had learned hard lessons after being royally screwed by three wives. She had no intention of completing that pattern. 'I don't want Harry's money.'

Ed narrowed his smoky grey eyes as he studied her for long thoughtful seconds. Then he shrugged. 'I know you gave up your right to the money when you left the marriage, but now that Harry's…' He swallowed unhappily. 'Now that he's…gone…you still have a claim as his widow.'

'I said, I don't want any of it, Ed.' She was determined to manage on her own and she didn't want money from anyone—not even her own parents, who would have happily helped her out if she'd let them. For now, she was pleased that her mother and father were safely overseas and unaware of her plans.

Ed's eyes widened as he stared at her, clearly taken aback by her claim. 'Maybe it's too soon for you to think about this.'

Milla felt a stirring of impatience. She wasn't playing games. She was deadly serious. She still had some money in her bank accounts and that was all she wanted.

Most women would think she was crazy to knock back a fortune, and if she'd still had her baby to consider her reaction might have been different. But her take-home lesson from her marriage was that even Himalayan-sized mountains of money couldn't buy the things that really mattered.

Sure, money bought power and glamour and ease and moments of heady excitement, but in her four years of marriage and rubbing shoulders with the mega wealthy she'd never seen evidence that these things added up to genuine, lasting happiness.

She only had to remember Heidi's bone-deep contentment with her seemingly 'boring' life to reinforce this belief.

'If you come back to the States,' Ed said, breaking into her thoughts, 'you and the baby will be much better off.'

Shocked, she looked up swiftly. 'You know about the—about my pregnancy?'

'Yes,' he said gently. 'It's wonderful news.'

So Harry had told them, after all...

'That's why you've come, isn't it? Old Gerry sent you. He wants his grandchild to live in America.'

'It's understandable, Milla.'

'It's not going to happen.'

'Look, I'm sure you need a little time to think this through.'

'It's not a matter of time. There's no baby, Ed.'

'What do you mean? What are you saying?'

Her voice quavered. 'I lost it. I had a miscarriage.'

He looked shocked. 'No.'

'It's the truth,' she said tightly, but she saw doubt and suspicion in his storm-cloud eyes and realised, to her horror, that he wasn't going to believe her.

Damn him.

He was pacing now, clearly baffled and probably angry.

'Ed, this isn't something I'd lie about. I was in a hospital, not an abortion clinic. I really wanted my baby.' Her lips trembled and she drew a sharp breath, but she was determined that she wouldn't dissolve into tears. The fainting spell had been bad enough. She had to be strong to stand up to this man.

'If you don't believe me, get that PI you hired to check out the RPA Hospital. I'm sure he'll be able to ferret out the proof you need.'

'Milla, don't be like that.'

'Don't be like *what*?' Her voice was shrill, but that was too bad. 'I'll give you *don't*. Don't you dare look at me like I'm lying about something that meant everything to me.'

Now she was so mad and upset she was shaking.

'OK, I apologise.' He stood before her, with his hands once again in his jeans pockets, his shoulders squared, his jaw tight, his eyes a battlefield where doubt and sympathy warred.

It was late afternoon and a wintry chill made Milla shiver. Shadows crept across the thick stone sill of the bakery window and spread along the brick walls and the ancient and worn stone floor. In the fading light, she could see that Ed looked deeply tired.

He'd had a long journey from New York and he'd probably driven straight from the airport. He had to be dead on his feet.

'I'm sorry about the baby,' he said quietly.

'I'm sorry you came all this way for nothing.'

The slightest hint of a smile flickered, giving a cynical tilt to his lips, but his eyes continued to regard her solemnly.

It was so not the right moment to remember the one time he'd kissed her. But the memory came, unbidden, bringing rivers of heat rushing under her clothes.

'Maybe we can have a more civilised discussion about everything over dinner,' he suggested.

'There's nothing to discuss.'

'Milla, I'm not the Cavanaugh who stuffed up your life. Surely we can share a meal before I go back.'

Perhaps she *was* overreacting. 'I guess. But there's really only one place in town to eat and that's the pub.'

'I'll need to check in to the hotel. You're still staying there, aren't you?'

Milla nodded. 'Until I get this place cleaned up.'

'This place?' Frowning, Ed looked around the bakery as if he was seeing it for the first time. His steely gaze took in the metal tables, the big gas cooker, the trolleys and baking trays and bins, the massive oven that filled the far wall. Finally, his gaze rested on the brooms and mop and bucket in the corner. 'Are you having the bakery cleaned?'

'In a manner of speaking—except I'm the one doing the cleaning.'

This time, Ed didn't even try to hide his disbelief.

'I'm not only *cleaning* the bakery. I plan to get it up and running again.' Before he could comment, Milla hurried to explain. 'The former owners went broke, along with several other businesses here, and the local council is offering peppercorn rent for people willing to restart. I've put in an application for this bakery and, as far as I know, no one else is interested.'

'I'm not surprised,' he muttered, just loud enough

for her to hear. 'One question.' He stared at her again. 'Why?'

'My family used to own this bakery. I know how to run a place like this. I grew up here.'

Still, Ed looked puzzled. 'So?'

Milla sighed. How did she explain everything she'd seen and felt since her arrival in Bellaroo Creek? How could she explain her longing to do something meaningful after years of unfulfilling luxury and wastefulness?

This billionaire standing before her in his high-end designer-label jeans and polo shirt couldn't possibly understand how the resurrection of this humble country bakery was an important chance to do something positive, not just for herself, but for a whole community.

'The town needs help, Ed. Bellaroo Creek is on the brink of extinction, but a local committee has started a plan to rescue it. Everything hinges on keeping the school open, so they're inviting families to rent farmhouses for a dollar a week.'

'Desperate families.'

'People who want to make a new start,' Milla defended. 'People looking for fresh air and something better than a dark backstreet alley for their kids to play in. A place where people know each other by name and have a sense of community.'

'You've been brainwashed, haven't you?'

'I'm looking for a way of life that makes me feel fulfilled,' she said hotly. 'And this is something I'm determined to do without touching my ex's money.'

His mouth tightened. 'It's a knee-jerk reaction, Milla. You're not being rational.'

'I'm not asking for your approval, Ed.'

'Look, I said I'm sorry about the baby, and I am, honestly, more than you can guess. And hell, I'm sorry your marriage to my brother didn't work out—but I know business and commerce inside out, and I know for absolute certainty that you'll regret this.'

'I really don't want to fight about it,' she said firmly but decisively.

After all, what she did with her life now was *her* business. The Cavanaughs no longer had any kind of hold on her.

However, Ed had no choice but to stay in Bellaroo Creek tonight and the pub was his only accommodation option. 'As you said, we can try for a civilised conversation over dinner.'

'I'm glad you agree.'

'At least we won't be able to yell at each other in the pub dining room.'

'That's a relief.'

'The chef is Chinese,' Milla told him. 'And he's pretty good. I think you'll like his duck with mushrooms.'

Ed's eyebrows lifted and, at last, there was a hint of a smile. 'Duck with mushrooms way out here?'

'Bellaroo Creek has one or two surprises.'

'OK. Sounds good.' He pulled his cell phone from his pocket and noted the time. 'I need to check in.'

It was, at best, a temporary truce, but Milla let out a huff of relief.

'I'll come with you,' she said. 'Unfortunately, Sherry, the girl on the reception desk, isn't as professional as the chef. There are so few people who check in here, she often wanders off to help in the kitchen or the laundry. Sometimes you have to go hunting for her.'

* * *

Five minutes later, having checked the pub's bar, the lounge, the dining room, the laundry and the kitchen without unearthing Sherry, Milla returned to Reception to find Ed in a spindly wooden chair with his eyes shut and his long legs stretched in front of him. He seemed to be asleep, although he looked dreadfully uncomfortable.

'Ed.' She touched his knee and he woke with a start. 'I can't find the reception girl and you look like you need to sleep.'

'I'm fine,' he insisted, blinking and frowning as he got to his feet.

'You're exhausted and jet lagged. I think you should come up to my room.' To her annoyance she felt a bright blush as she said this. 'You can at least have a shower while I track down someone who can organise a room for you,' she went on brusquely.

'A shower sounds good.' Ed yawned. 'Thanks, I won't say no.'

The offer of her room had seemed practical and sensible to Milla until she climbed the narrow staircase with Ed beside her. In the confined space she was super aware of his height and broad shoulders and mega-masculine aura. Her heartbeats picked up pace and her skin prickled and even her breathing seemed to falter.

By the time they reached her room she was ridiculously flustered. When she pushed the door open, she took a necessary step back. 'After you, Ed.'

'Thanks.' He set his expensive leather duffle bag on the floor and stood with his hands propped on his hips, surveying her double bed and the cosmetics scattered over the old-fashioned dressing table, the wardrobe with an oval, age-spotted mirror on the door.

'It's old-fashioned but at least there's an en-suite. The bathroom's through here.' She moved to the louvre doors, newly painted white, and pushed them open. 'It's tiny, but adequate. There's a spare towel on the shelf above the—'

Oh, help.

Why hadn't she remembered that she'd left her undies hanging above the bath? Now her silky panties and lacy bras were on full display. To make matters worse, rosy light from the setting sun streamed through the high bathroom window, gilding the lingerie's creamy fragility.

And Ed was smiling. 'Nice decor,' he said with a grin. But a darker glint in his eyes lit flames inside Milla.

Leaping forward, she hastily grabbed the offending articles, bunching them into a tight ball. If she'd had a pocket she would have shoved them into it.

She kept her gaze safely lowered. 'The bathroom's all yours.'

CHAPTER THREE

ED WAS COLD. As he clambered from a black hole of deep, drugging sleep he opened his eyes a chink and discovered chill grey dawn light filling a strange room. Everything was alien—the shapes of the furniture, the position of the windows.

He had no idea where he was.

And he was cold. Naked and cold. Instinctively, he groped for the bed covers, and as he lifted them he caught a drift of flowery scent. With a jolt of dismay, he remembered Milla.

This was Australia. He was in a hotel in Bellaroo Creek. He'd showered in Milla's bathroom. This was her bedroom.

They were supposed to have had dinner together.

Where was she?

Shivering, he rolled under the covers, relishing the new-found warmth as his mind struggled to sort out his dilemma. Or rather, Milla's dilemma. It was obvious now that he'd come out of the shower last night, seen her bed, and fallen onto it in exhaustion.

With that part of the puzzle sorted, he could all too easily picture the rest. Milla had come back to her room to find him sprawled, naked, on her bed. Out like a light.

No doubt she'd bolted like a frightened squirrel, and he could only hope the hotel people had given her another room, the room that should have been his.

What a stuff-up. Now he would have to start the day with apologies. Never a comfortable exercise.

Groaning, Ed burrowed deeper under the covers, but already the room was growing lighter and he was all too acutely aware that this was Milla's bed. Although the sheets had probably been changed, the floral perfume he always associated with her lingered. Unhelpfully, he also remembered the delicate wisps of her lingerie that had hung over her bath, and, *man*, that was *not* a useful memory for a red-blooded male at this hour of the morning.

One thing was certain. He wouldn't be getting back to sleep.

'Good morning. You're up bright and early.' A leggy blonde in a cowgirl shirt and jeans grinned broadly at Ed as he walked into the hotel dining room. 'I'm Sherry,' she told him brightly. 'And you're our first customer for breakfast. You're welcome to sit anywhere you like.'

Ed, freshly showered, shaved and changed into clean clothes, chose a small table by a window with a view down Bellaroo Creek's empty and silent main street. In a far corner, a wood fire burned in a grate, making the room cosy, despite its emptiness.

'Would you like tea or coffee to begin with?' Sherry asked.

'Coffee, thanks.'

'Oh, you're American,' she gushed. 'Of course you'll want coffee.' But instead of leaving to fetch a coffeepot, she stood beaming at him.

Ed realised she was the elusive girl Milla had searched for last night, but he wasn't inclined to be talkative first thing in the morning, so he made no comment.

'You're not a movie star, or anything exciting, are you?' she asked next.

'Not the slightest bit exciting,' he replied dryly. 'And I'll have scrambled eggs as well as coffee.' He didn't return her smile.

'With bacon and tomatoes?'

'That'd be great.'

'Sausages?'

'Yes, the lot.' He'd skipped lunch and dinner and he was ravenous enough to eat an entire rhinoceros. 'And I'd like toast and orange juice.'

'Right away, sir. I'll get Stu straight onto it.'

She was back quite soon with a steaming pot and, to Ed's relief, the coffee was strong and hot. He considered asking her about Milla's whereabouts, but opted for discretion.

'You can leave that pot here,' he told her.

He was on his second cup when she came back with a laden breakfast plate. His stomach growled gratefully.

'So you're a friend of Milla's?' she asked coyly, remaining by his table as he tucked into his food.

Ed nodded as he ate, but he had no intention of sharing details of his exact relationship to Milla with this nosy girl.

'We're all excited about Milla starting up the bakery,' the girl said next.

This time he looked up, unable to hide his interest. 'So the town really wants a bakery?'

'Of course. It'll be wonderful. But the problem is, bakeries are so much hard work. Poor Milla will have to work dreadful hours. She'll be up at something like three in the morning.' The girl gave a wide-eyed shake of her head. 'Half the town are right behind her and can't wait for her shop to open. The other half think she's crazy trying to do it on her own. They're betting she'll last a month at the most.'

Ed accepted this news grimly, but he didn't encourage further discussion.

'Mind you, I'm amazed Milla bothered to come back,' said Sherry. 'I mean, with her looks, why would she bury herself here?'

Exactly, thought Ed.

By the time he'd finished his breakfast, there were still no other diners, and no sign of the girl who'd served him. He left her a tip and went out into the street, staring across at the bakery and wondering when Milla would show up.

The other half think she's crazy.

Deep in thought, he crossed the road. The scent of wood smoke lingered in the chilly morning air, reminding him, briefly, of visits to his grandparents' farm in Michigan, but he turned his focus to the bakery.

Yesterday, he'd paid next to no attention to it. He'd been preoccupied with his original mission to persuade Milla to return to the States, and then he'd been side-swiped by her news about the baby. Now, he thought about her plan to set up a business here. This ex Beverly Hills heiress wanted to get up at three in the morning in the middle of winter to bake bread. Not just once, but every day.

Impossible.

Half the good folk of Bellaroo Creek were right. Milla *was* crazy. Running a bakery was damn hard work. Intensely physical labour. Certainly too much for a woman of head-turning beauty who was used to the heights of luxury.

This bakery scheme didn't make any kind of sense. It had to be Milla's over-the-top reaction to losing Harry and the baby. Ed supposed it was possible that her hormones were out of whack. She certainly wasn't thinking straight.

That would be his task today, he decided as he stood staring through a dusty window into the murky depths of the empty shop. He had to bring Milla to her senses, had to convince her to withdraw her application before she was committed to something she'd quickly regret.

Almost five years ago, he'd stood by and watched her marry Harry, knowing full well that it could only end in disaster. He wasn't going to let her walk into a second catastrophe.

He wondered what time she came down for breakfast, but the question had barely formed when he heard a sound coming from the back of the shop.

An intruder?

Frowning, he tested the shop's door, and it fell open at his touch. He stepped quietly inside.

'Hello?' he called. 'Is anybody there?'

When there was no answer, he moved forward stealthily. 'Can I help you?'

'Ed?'

Milla appeared in the doorway.

'Ah.' Feeling slightly foolish, he offered her a sheepish smile. 'Hi.'

Hands on hips, Milla frowned at him. 'What were you doing? Why are you sneaking around?'

'I thought there was an intruder in here.' He shrugged. 'And I was sure you were still asleep.'

Milla rolled her eyes. 'I've been up since before six.'

'But you weren't in the dining room for breakfast.'

'I had breakfast here.' She pointed to an electric jug beside the sink in the corner. 'A tub of yoghurt, a banana and a mug of tea, and I'm set for the day.'

Ed gave a shrugging shake of his head.

'I hope you slept well,' she said after a bit.

'Like a baby.' He grimaced and a small silence fell while they both studied the bare concrete floor.

He guessed that Milla was as reluctant as he was to mention the obvious fact that she'd found him last night, sprawled on her bed, sound asleep and stark naked.

'Sorry I missed our dinner date—er—dinner discussion,' he said, steering the conversation away from that particular danger zone. 'I hope the duck was good.'

'It was delicious, thanks.'

'And I hope you were—uh—comfortable last night.'

'I was perfectly comfortable, thanks. In your room,' she added, not quite meeting his gaze.

The air around them seemed to thicken and grow hot.

'Have you had breakfast?' Milla asked, after a bit.

'Sure.' He patted his middle. 'An inelegant sufficiency.'

'I'm sure you were starving.'

'Yeah.' But it was time to remember that he hadn't come here to discuss his appetite. Narrowing his gaze, he said, 'So why are you over here so early?'

'I thought you might want to sleep in, and I needed to make a start. I'm making an inventory of all the equipment that's here, and working out what I still need.'

'Jumping the gun, aren't you? You don't even know if the council will accept your application.'

She made an impatient sound of annoyance. 'I'm quite certain they will, Ed. They're very keen.'

Ed bit back a swear word. 'You're setting yourself up for failure, Milla. You can't do this. It's obvious this town is on its last legs.' He flung out an arm, indicating the empty shop and the equally empty street. 'Where are your customers? The last people who tried to run this place failed.'

'They didn't know enough about baking. Their bread wasn't popular.'

'Are you sure you can do better?'

'Absolutely.'

'Milla, if you really want to work, you could get a job in a top Sydney hotel. The sort of work you were doing before you married.'

'You want me back rubbing shoulders with the rich and famous?'

'Yeah? Why not?' When Ed first met her in London, she'd been a brilliant hostess for VIP guests.

Arms folded, shoulders back, jaw jutted, Milla eyed him with bolshie determination. 'I've had enough of that life, Ed. If I see another spoiled rock star I think I'll puke. I was born and raised in this town. We lived in Matheson Street, but I spent half my life in this shop. Before I started school, I was playing down here with pieces of dough, making my own bread rolls for my lunches.'

A fighting light burned in her lovely green eyes.

'All through high school, I sliced and packed bread each morning before I caught the bus to Parkes. Afternoons, I worked out the front on the counter. Saturdays, I helped my mum to make her famous fruit lattice pies.'

Ed was impressed, but he didn't let it show.

'After I finished school, I started learning the trade properly. I know baking inside out,' Milla said finally.

'And you couldn't wait to get away from it.'

She glared at him. 'I was young and impatient, with a head full of big dreams.'

He nodded his acceptance of this. He supposed she was remembering, as he was, where her youthful dreams had led her—overseas to a wide range of interesting and fulfilling jobs, but, eventually, into the arms of his dangerous young brother.

No point in rehashing that now.

He nudged the conversation back to where he wanted it. 'So, I guess you've written a business plan? You've prepared a break-even analysis and a profit and loss forecast?'

She sent him a drop-dead look.

'Do you know your fixed costs?' he continued. 'The profit you're likely to make from each sale?'

'Go home, Ed. I don't need you marching in here and throwing your weight around, spoiling everything.'

'I'm trying to save you from the misery of starting up a business that's doomed to fail.'

'That's very thoughtful of you.' She lifted her chin and eyed him steadily. 'But I'd prefer a little faith.'

It was then that he saw behind her bravado and glimpsed the vulnerable girl clinging to her last shreds of dignity and hope. And damn it, he felt a flicker of admiration. He quickly stifled it. A good businessman always trusted his head, not his heart.

'Tell me about the equipment,' he said, changing tack. 'What have you got and what do you still need?'

'Do you really care?'

'Give me a break, Milla. Of course I'm concerned.'

She pursed her lips, then seemed to relent. 'OK. I have a big oven that's been here since the nineteen fifties. It's great. No worries there. I have gas cookers, a big bread mixer and a refrigerator and freezer. I'll need more measurers and cutters and things like piping bags and nozzles, but they're not a huge cost. I could do with an orbital mixer, but that can wait.'

'An orbital mixer? What's that?'

'It's good for the smaller things—cakes, cream and icing.'

'I guess you need scales for weighing things?'

Her eyes widened with surprise. 'Yes, scales are very important. Dad used to have a really expensive set. I don't know what happened to them.'

'Where are your parents now? Will they be around to give you back-up support?'

'Heavens no.' A warm smile lit up her face. 'They're on a cruise. The Mediterranean this time. These days, they're always on cruises and good luck to them. They've worked hard and they've earned their chance to have fun.'

Her smile faded, replaced by a look of defiance. 'I need to do this, Ed.'

Deep down, he understood. Milla wanted to throw herself into hard, honest labour, as if it would somehow heal her past hurts.

'What if you fail?' He had to ask this. 'What if you

reject Harry's money and try this—this hare-brained scheme and end up with nothing?'

'That's not going to happen.'

'Milla, how can you be so sure?'

She simply smiled. 'Try all you like, Ed. You're not going to change my mind.'

CHAPTER FOUR

To MILLA'S RELIEF, Ed's farewell was unsentimental. A handshake, a kiss on the cheek.

Unsmiling, he wished her good luck.

'Good luck to you, too,' she said, and he looked at her strangely. 'Good luck with explaining everything to Gerry.'

His mouth tilted in a wry smile. 'Thanks, I'm sure I'll need it.'

The smile disappeared as Ed got into his red hire car and the look in his eyes then made Milla's throat ache.

They both knew this was the last time they would see each other, but she hadn't expected Ed to look quite so bleak. And she certainly hadn't expected to feel bereft, pierced by a sadness that was quite different from how she'd felt when she'd lost Harry or her baby.

As Ed zoomed off down the long straight road she stood on the footpath, watching his red car grow smaller and smaller. When it finally disappeared, she let out her breath with a deliberate whoosh and she waited for the expected sense of relief to wash over her.

To her surprise it didn't happen.

Instead she felt strangely empty.

It was such an annoying, irrational response. Now

that Ed was gone, she was free. Free of the Cavanaughs, free to put her mistakes behind her and to make a success of the rest of her life.

As she went back inside the bakery it didn't make sense that she couldn't stop thinking about Ed. Bizarrely, her thoughts weren't centred on his warnings about her business. She was remembering, of all things, the first time she'd met him when she was working at The Hedgerow Hotel in London.

The job in Knightsbridge had been the pinnacle of her working career. She'd earned it, of course, having worked hard at all the usual jobs that backpackers grabbed when they left Australia. She'd been a barmaid in Kent and a baby-sitter-cum-cleaner in a French ski resort. She'd worked on organic farms in Italy for free meals and board, and eventually she'd ended up in London with a job on a reception desk in a hotel chain.

To her surprise, the position had really suited her. She hadn't minded working different shifts, and handling computers hadn't fazed her. She'd managed to be cheerful and diplomatic with difficult guests and queue jumpers, and she'd quickly picked up that it was worth taking time to deal with all the little things that counted.

As a result, Milla had been promoted quite quickly, and when the manager of the VIP luxury service for the hotel's executive clients retired, she was offered his position.

She'd loved this role and she'd thrown herself into it. She made sure that platters of fresh fruit were available on arrival for VIP guests, and whatever they wanted— even pink champagne in their bathtubs—was accommodated.

As well as arranging beauty spas and massages, it

had been her responsibility to make sure these special guests never had to wait for a dinner table, or theatre tickets, or a clean towel. She had even sent staff out to buy gluten-free bread at awkward hours.

Whether the VIP guests were charming or childish, aloof or overfriendly, Milla had taken their peccadilloes in her stride. Keeping them happy had been a daily challenge to which she'd risen conscientiously.

It was while she'd been working in this role that she'd met Ed. She would never forget the way he'd come striding into the hotel lobby just on nightfall, straight from a transatlantic flight. Tall, dark and dignified in a long black winter coat, he'd sent the hearts of female guests and staff fluttering.

Milla hadn't been immune to his impact. Not by any means. Until then, she'd never met any man who made her heart-rate quicken on first sight, but, despite his attractiveness, she'd made sure her manner was pleasant and friendly, and scrupulously professional.

Ed had come to London on business, of course, working very hard with late meetings and hasty dinners and Milla had facilitated several private, one-on-one hearings with European businessmen that had apparently been highly productive.

'You're an amazing asset here,' Ed had told her when he was leaving. 'I'll look forward to seeing you next time I'm in London.' He was dangerously handsome, especially when he looked into her eyes and smiled.

To Milla's dismay, she'd felt a warm blush that wouldn't go away. 'I'm actually moving on,' she'd told him. 'I think I'm a nomad at heart, and I've been in London for almost two years.'

He didn't try to hide his disappointment. 'Are you going back to Australia?'

'To America, actually. I've been offered a job in California.'

Such a gorgeous smile he'd given her then. 'Which hotel?'

'The Ritz-Carlton.'

'Fabulous. You never know.' Silver sparks had shone in his grey eyes. 'We might meet up again.'

Looking back, Milla could see the way her life had taken a crucial turn that day. She and Ed *had* met up again, of course. He'd made sure of it.

And who knew how things might have turned out if she'd been a little braver?

Ed was troubled as he burned up the miles down the highway. He knew he could never persuade Milla to give up her bakery plan. His efforts to do so had been a total waste of energy. She would almost certainly fail, but no one was going to talk her out of this.

As his hands clenched the steering wheel and his chest tightened he warned himself to let this go. It was Milla's problem, not his. He'd done his duty and she was an intelligent woman with the right to make her own decisions. Her own mistakes.

Again.

Thing was—despite his concerns, he couldn't suppress a niggling admiration. Having spent almost his entire adult life behind a desk or in boardrooms, he could totally understand the appeal of breaking free of the mould.

Heaven knew there'd been days when he'd wished he could throw off the shackles of shareholder expectation and escape the office to climb a mountain or canoe the Amazon, or sail around Cape Horn.

But Milla running a bakery?

No way. That made no sense.

Ed was still a little shell-shocked after seeing her with her hair covered by a scarf as she tackled cobwebs and wielded a mop and bucket. So different from the woman who'd always been so carefully groomed and dressed in up-to-the-minute fashion. So different from the first time he'd seen her working in the London hotel.

That day she'd been wearing a simple but chic black dress, a perfect foil for her pale skin and flame-coloured hair. He remembered her poise and the glint of elegant jewellery as she'd walked towards him with a warm smile.

She'd extended her hand. 'Hello, Mr Cavanaugh. Welcome to The Hedgerow.'

Ed had enjoyed his share of classy women, but there'd been something about Milla Brady that had woken a response beyond the ordinary. He'd been as fascinated by her efficiency as he had by the sheen of her hair, and her beautiful smile.

One evening during his stay, while he'd waited in the private lounge for an important meeting with a business contact from Brussels, he'd invited Milla to keep him company.

With a little encouragement, she'd told him about the places she'd visited in Europe, the sights she'd seen and the people she'd met. Her conversation had been so easy and entertaining that she might have been a high-class hooker.

She wasn't, of course. Ed's discreet inquiries had ruled that out. She was just damn good at her job. But she epitomised, he'd realised, his idea of the perfect woman.

Then she'd told him she was moving to America, and, although he didn't believe in astrology, he was quite sure his stars had been perfectly aligned. The fact that he lived in New York and Milla was going to California was a minor problem. With a brother in LA, Ed could use his out-of-town status as the perfect excuse to invite a woman he hardly knew to a party.

Harry's thirtieth birthday party had been timely. And it had been, of course, a lavish Beverly Hills affair. No expense spared. An orchestra, massive urns with towering flower arrangements, waiters in white coats and bow ties, guests from Hollywood's A-list.

Amidst the expensive gowns, the mirrors, the marble and chandeliers, Milla, in backless cream silk that showed off her moon-pale skin and bright hair, had looked completely at home in the glamorous crowd. And to Ed she'd looked utterly enchanting.

The night had gone well until he'd kissed her.

Even now, he could never look back on that party without a painful stab of self-reproach. He'd always thought of himself as urbane and cool, but he'd handled that night like a ham-fisted youth.

The evening had unravelled when he'd gone to fetch Milla another drink. While he was away, a gaggle of girls from Harry's set had gathered around her.

Returning, drink in hand, Ed had heard their conversation through a small forest of potted palms.

'What do you think of American guys?' one girl had asked Milla.

'I'm reserving judgement,' she'd told them smoothly

and then she'd laughed. 'But I must say, I wasn't in London this long before a fellow kissed me.'

'Those British guys are quick off the mark,' suggested another girl.

'Or American guys are damn slow on the uptake,' joined in another.

Laughter had rippled around the group, and Ed waited for it to die down before he joined them and handed Milla her mai tai cocktail. Even so, there'd been a momentary lull when he arrived, and in the quietness Milla's eloquent gaze had met his.

She must have known that he'd overheard their conversation and its implied challenge, but she hadn't seemed in any way embarrassed, and it had made every kind of sense to Ed to find the first opportunity to lure her out into the moonlit garden.

The grounds of Harry's mansion were perfect for strolling—smooth lawns and winding paths and shadowy pockets of palms or fragrant shrubbery.

'It's so lovely and warm here,' Milla had said as they walked past a lily pond where silver moonlight streamed. 'It reminds me of Australia.'

'Do you miss home?' he asked her.

'Sometimes. Not often. It's ages since I've been back. Luckily, my parents have retired, so they can visit me over here.'

'And how have you found America so far?'

Milla smiled, and her green eyes sparkled knowingly in the moonlight. 'I like my job. America's fun,' she'd said. 'Everyone's so friendly.'

'But the men are slow off the mark.'

She stopped walking. Her silk dress shimmered whitely and her skin looked wonderfully soft. 'It was just silly girl talk, Ed. I was playing along with their game.'

'But it's true, isn't it?' He took her hands in his, holding her cool fingers lightly. 'You haven't been kissed by an American?'

Her eyes became luminous. 'No, I haven't,' she admitted softly.

'That's a crime,' he said.

Her response was a breathless laugh.

'In fact,' he said next, 'I'm quite sure it's a crime in at least seven states.'

His heart was drumming as he settled his hands on her slim waist, which was crazy given that he'd kissed hundreds of girls in the moonlight. But, alone with Milla Brady, he had difficulty keeping his voice steady. 'It's most definitely a crime in California.'

As he leaned in she swayed towards him and their lips met in an easy and friendly hello. Warm and pleasurable and sweet. But within moments, everything changed. Ed had been lost. Lost in her yielding sweetness, lost in her eager response and the warm press of her slim body to his.

He kissed her hard and long and it felt like destiny, as if he'd been waiting all his life for this woman. This night. This moonlight. When he kissed her breasts through the thin silk of her gown, she went a little wild and he was quite sure she would have run away with him then, if he'd asked her, or even if he hadn't asked and had simply taken.

Perhaps she brought out the gallant knight in him, or perhaps he'd been a little afraid of the strength of his own passion… After all, the Cavanaughs were ladies' men, but they never lost their hearts.

On the brink of tipping into madness, Ed broke the kiss, but Milla remained entangled in his arms, her chest heaving against his chest, her head on his shoulder as their ragged breathing slowed.

'I'm not sure *that* kiss was legal,' he said eventually, trying to lighten the intensity of what had passed between them.

Her response was so soft he hadn't caught it, but she was no longer smiling. In fact, she looked worried. Very worried indeed.

After her passionate response, this didn't quite make sense. Ed couldn't think what to say. He'd been quite sure she hadn't wanted to discuss what had just happened, and he certainly hadn't. Small talk seemed somehow impossible, so he'd led her back, walking in silence via a wisteria-scented path, to the safety of the party.

Harry was standing near the door as they came inside. Golden haired, smiling, devilishly handsome, he was holding a champagne bottle. 'I wondered where you'd got to, Ed.'

Harry called to a waiter for two more glasses. 'You two look like you need a drink.' As he poured bubbles into Milla's glass his charismatic smile brimmed with sympathy. 'Beware of my big brother.' He managed to sound both sincere and amused. 'Ed spends too much time stuck in boardrooms and he doesn't really know how to party. He can be a bit of a wet blanket.'

'I'm having a perfectly lovely time,' Milla assured him.

'Are you?' Harry's gaze was shrewd as he studied her and then he'd looked at Ed. 'Hmm,' he said, slipping his arm possessively through Milla's.

Ed felt a prickle of apprehension. *No,* he'd thought. *No. Harry won't. He can't possibly.*

But of course, Harry could and he did.

He gave Milla his most charming smile. 'I should warn you, my dear, Ed peaks early and the night is young.'

She laughed, pulling gently away.

Harry's grip on her arm tightened. 'Besides, it's my birthday, and I demand your charming company for the next half-hour.'

As Milla surrendered and was borne away, she looked back over her shoulder to Ed, shooting him a look of amused bewilderment. 'See you later,' she mouthed.

Watching her leave, laughing at something Harry whispered in her ear, Ed felt powerless. It was Harry's party and there were too many guests to make a scene.

Besides, having witnessed his parents' fights so often during his early years, Ed abhorred family scenes.

His grandmother had sensed this back when he was seven. 'You're going to be our family's anchor, Ed,' she'd said.

It was a vocation he'd taken to heart, but there'd been many times since that he'd regretted his restraint on that fateful evening. He'd known from the start, and with chilling certainty, that Harry had had no qualms about stealing the girl his brother had invited.

And thirty minutes was all it had taken.

CHAPTER FIVE

Paint roller in hand, Milla was poised on a trestle balanced between two ladders when the phone rang. Fortunately, the phone was in her jeans pocket, and she didn't have to scramble down to answer it.

'Milla? Or should I say Michelangelo?' Heidi chirruped. 'How's the painting?'

Milla laughed. 'Believe it or not, I'm actually enjoying myself.' She beamed at the snowy ceiling above her and at the two walls already covered with lovely, fresh paint, the rich hue of thick cream. 'And I'm almost halfway there.'

'Well done.' After a beat, Heidi added, 'But it's a pity the handsome American didn't hang around to help you.'

Milla's heart gave a twist, much to her annoyance. 'Who told you about Ed?'

'A little bird whispered.'

'A bird by the name of Sherry, I suppose.'

'Well, yeah, you know this town's always desperate for a bit of juicy gossip. Sherry was raving on about this American of yours. She said he looked like—'

'He's not mine,' Milla cut in.

'But he looks like a film star, right?'

Milla sighed. She'd been working hard to erase Ed from her thoughts. 'He's Harry's brother, Heidi. He was here on—on family business.' Although Milla had shared the awful news about Harry's death with Heidi, she'd skipped details of exactly how that news had been delivered. 'Now he's well and truly gone. Back in the States.'

'Oh.' Heidi sounded disappointed, but she quickly switched to her usual cheerfulness. 'Anyway…getting back to the subject of painting…do you need a hand? I could come tomorrow. Mum's offered to look after the kids.'

'Gosh, that's very kind of you, but I hope to be done by then. With luck, I'll finish this first coat before lunch today and get the second coat on this afternoon.'

'Wow, you've set a cracking pace. You always were one for a challenge, Mills.'

'I suspect the painting will be the easy part of this particular challenge. I'm sure I'm going to need help closer to opening day. That's when I'll start to panic.'

'I'll warn Mum in advance and make sure we're free.'

'Thanks, you're a doll. That would be brilliant.' After the out-of-whack values in Harry's set, where her friends were constantly trying to compete, it was so refreshing to have a friend who genuinely wanted to help. 'Heidi, I don't suppose you know anything about writing a business plan?'

'Sorry, haven't a clue. Do you really need one?'

'The Bellaroo Council's asking for it. Apparently, it's a requirement for their dirt-cheap rental agreement. I'm afraid I bluffed my way through that bit and told them I'd have a plan within the week.'

'Hmm. I don't suppose they're offering to help you write the plan?'

'Unfortunately, no,' Milla said.

'Well, I could ask Brad. He's done a few business courses.'

'Thanks. That could be helpful. I'd probably only need a few pointers.'

'Why don't you come out to our place tomorrow evening? Kill two birds with one stone. You can talk about business schemes with Brad and we can have a barbecue. It'll be fun. You can celebrate finishing your painting.'

'Thanks. I'd love to.'

'See you around six-thirty?'

'Perfect. I'll bring a fruit pie. I've been practising with Mum's old recipe.'

Heidi laughed. 'Fab. I'll be generous and supply the ice cream.'

Milla was grinning as she pocketed her phone and turned back to work. She was incredibly grateful for the way Heidi had picked up their friendship exactly where they'd left off, as if the intervening years hadn't made a jot of difference.

Now, making her way carefully along the trestle plank to the radio she'd balanced on top of the ladder, she flicked a knob, and found a country and western station. Music filled the shop, one of the happier songs about a rollicking cowboy, and she sang along with it as she ran the roller through the tray of rich creamy paint.

As she spread it in smooth swathes on the wall she realised that she'd told Heidi the truth. She found this painting job unexpectedly satisfying. The worst part had been the preparation and cleaning the dingy old walls with sugar soap, but now it was so rewarding to see the way a fresh coat of paint could revitalise the space.

Once the walls were finished, she planned to scrub the terracotta floor tiles till they shone, and *voilà*! The bakery would look fresh and welcoming again.

Throw in the added fragrance of freshly baked bread and—

'Milla!'

A masculine voice boomed from below.

Milla turned and when she saw who it was she almost slipped.

It couldn't be. It was impossible. Where had he sprung from?

'Hey, don't fall.'

Two strong hands gripped her calves, just below the knees.

Ed. Why on earth was he here? He was supposed to be safely in New York by now.

'You startled me,' she accused shakily. 'You shouldn't creep up on a girl like that.'

'I tried knocking, but you had that music so loud you couldn't hear me.'

Milla was still too shaken to defend herself. 'You can let me go. I'm quite steady, now,' she lied.

Grim-faced, Ed released her, and Milla was at her most dignified as she set the roller back in the paint tray and carefully lowered her butt to the trestle. From this point she could normally get to the floor quite easily, but today Ed was there to lend a helping hand.

The fact that she was still trembling was his fault, of course.

'Mind if I turn the radio down?' he asked.

'Be my guest. Turn it off.'

The music stopped and the sudden silence seemed to fill the shop. But now that Milla had both feet on the ground, she demanded answers. 'What's happened? Why aren't you in America?'

'No drama.' Ed looked annoyingly calm as he stood there, hands resting lightly on his hips as he let his gaze linger on her beautiful walls. 'You're doing a good job,' he admitted grudgingly.

She couldn't help saying, 'I'm happy enough with the way it's going.' But it was annoying to be pleased by his comment when she should have been interrogating him.

Now that she was beginning to recover from her shock it was time to ask questions. 'Get to the point, Ed. You still haven't told me why you've come back. What's the problem?'

There had to be a problem. Why else would he come back all this way?

Ed's throat worked and he shifted his gaze to the street, as if he'd been suddenly gripped by an almost boyish nervousness. 'I—er—stayed to look after a spot of business in Sydney, and I happened to run across a few things.'

Huh? 'What kind of few things?'

Frowning, he squared his shoulders, as if he was deliberately throwing off his initial shyness and returning to his default mode as Mr Serious. 'I found some of the equipment you need.'

At first, Milla couldn't imagine what he meant. 'Equipment for the bakery?'

Ed shrugged. 'You haven't already ordered them, have you?'

Stunned into silence, she shook her head. 'I wanted

to get the place cleaned up first. I was planning to start researching on the Internet this weekend.'

His brow cleared and a slow smile lightened his eyes. 'Well, I found one or two items that might be useful. So I'll bring them in now, OK?'

'I—I guess,' she said faintly. 'Can I help you?'

'No, no. I'm fine.'

There was a ute parked in the street outside, she realised now, and the tray back held several large cardboard cartons. Heavy cartons, judging by the bulging muscles in Ed's arms as he carried them into the shop.

'Will I take them through to the back?' he asked.

'Thanks.' Milla decided that he must have been working out. Or he'd started buying T-shirts a size too small. Either way, the display of masculine strength was almost as distracting as her curiosity about the boxes he carried.

Her eyes popped when she read the first label. 'An orbital mixer?'

'I hope it's the right size.'

'Wow, Ed.' She found a knife and began to cut the packaging tape, whipping the cardboard flaps open. 'It's perfect. So new and shiny.' She'd been planning to investigate second-hand equipment. It was mind-boggling to think that Ed had remembered her passing comment.

She was stunned and grateful...but just a tad worried. Why had he done this? Could it be a new strategy for regaining Cavanaugh control?

But it was hard to suppress her excitement when the next box revealed a top-of-the-range set of bakery scales.

'They're beautiful.' Milla touched a fingertip to the

rim of the shiny steel bowl. 'They're brilliant. Thanks so much.'

The scales were followed by more boxes holding all manner of lovely things—dough dividers, pie cutters, a tiered rack of bun pans.

Milla was quite dazed. 'I can't quite believe this.'

'I happened to come across a warehouse with all this stuff and it seemed crazy to walk past.'

'Which warehouse?'

Ed looked away and mumbled the name of a Sydney suburb, and, despite Milla's excitement and gratitude, she was sure she smelled a rat.

'So you just happened to be walking down a Sydney street and, blow me down, if there wasn't a bakery warehouse right in front of you? I suppose the mixer and scales were on display in the window?'

'Look,' Ed said, jutting his jaw defensively. 'I have no plans to interfere with your new venture, Milla. I know you don't want our money. You made that very clear.'

'So you'll let me pay you for these things?'

A dark stain coloured his neck. 'That's not necessary.'

Milla sighed. 'So what's this about, then? Come on, Ed, spill. Are you going to tell me you're concerned about the demise of Bellaroo Creek?' Sarcasm crept into her voice. She couldn't help it. 'You're doing this for the good of the town?'

He met her acerbic challenge without blinking. 'My grandparents used to live in a small country town like this.'

It was the last answer Milla had expected and she felt caught out. Winded.

She simply couldn't imagine the wealthy, lavish-living Cavanaughs coming from humble roots in a small rural town. The picture wouldn't gel.

Then again, why would Ed make up a story like that?

Warily, she offered him a puzzled smile. 'Well… if that's really what's driving you… On behalf of the Bellaroo Creek Residents' Association, thank you very much, Mr Cavanaugh.'

'You're welcome.' Slowly, Ed returned her smile and their gazes linked and held, and ridiculous tingles zipped and zapped through Milla.

Then Ed nodded through the doorway to the half-painted shop. 'But I've interrupted your work. The paint on your roller will dry out.'

'Yes. I'd better get back to it.'

'I don't suppose you have a second roller?'

Milla's jaw dropped so hard it hurt. How many surprises was this man planning to spring on her? She did have a second roller, but surely Ed didn't really plan to help?

'I'm not going to turn straight around and drive back to Sydney,' he said. 'I don't fancy another five hours on the road today, so I have an afternoon to fill in. I may as well make myself useful.'

Once again, Milla hesitated, torn between her desire to remain stubbornly independent and her gratitude for his apparently good-hearted generosity. And somewhere above and beyond these hovered an extra problem, the problem she'd always had with Ed Cavanaugh. The strong, almost frightening attraction she felt in his presence, and the scary certainty that a relationship with him would take her well out of her depth.

Five years ago, this fear had sent her running into

the supposedly safer arms of his lighter-hearted, fun-loving brother.

And what a mistake that had been.

Now, Milla didn't want to feel attracted to any man, certainly not to Ed. She was making a fresh start as far away as possible from her past mistakes.

Just the same, she knew she shouldn't be in such a stew over one afternoon in Ed's company. This evening he would stay at the pub and tomorrow morning he would be gone again, finally and for ever. Where was the harm in that?

Feeling calmer now that she had this sorted, she reached into the box of gear she'd bought from the hardware store in Parkes. 'It's kind of you to offer to help.' She broke open the plastic packaging and handed him a brand-new fluffy roller and tray. 'Ever used either of these before?'

'Of course.'

She couldn't hold back a cynical smile. 'Honestly?'

'Well…not in the last twenty years.'

It truly was like stepping back in time.

Ed hadn't spent an afternoon like this since he was fifteen when he'd helped his grandfather to paint their barn. Back then it had been fall in Michigan and Ed could still remember the scent of apples in his grandparents' orchard and the gentle lilt in his grandfather's voice as he delivered his homespun philosophies while they worked.

Today, Ed couldn't believe how good it felt to be away from boardrooms and meetings and phone calls and the constant crises and pressure of his Cavanaugh Enterprises. It was such an agreeable change to be working at a task that demanded a totally different kind of concentration.

In no time he was crouching low, taking desperate pains to paint as close as possible to the skirting in a neat straight line. It was unexpectedly rewarding to take as much care with the smoothness of his paintwork as he normally took over calculating a new investment strategy.

When Milla stopped for lunch, they perched on stools at the stainless-steel table at the back of the shop. Milla made thick, tasty cheese and salad sandwiches, which they washed down with mugs of hot tea, and while they ate she explained that she'd moved into the rooms above the shop, and that this area would double as her kitchen.

They chatted about the best positions for the new equipment, and Milla explained the steps involved in producing dozens of bread loaves. She certainly seemed to know the process well, Ed was relieved to note, and although he itched to fire a host of questions to test her business knowledge he held his tongue.

Just as they were finishing their meal, a fat ginger cat stalked regally into the room, his ginger tail waving above him like a flag.

Milla's face was alight as she squatted to scratch the cat's neck. 'Blue, you beautiful boy, how are you this afternoon? Have you had a good morning?'

'Why would you call an orange cat Blue?'

Her eyes sparkled. 'It's an Aussie thing. Goes way back. I guess it shows how contrary we are. We often call redheads Blue or Bluey.'

Ed smiled. 'Were you called Blue at school?'

'Sometimes.'

'So where does this Blue live?'

'Here. He's mine.' Her laugh was light and silky. 'At least, he seems to have made this place his home. He just wandered in one day and stayed.'

'So you've already taken in a stray?'

Her chin lifted. 'Yes, Ed, I have. You got a problem with that?'

He gave a non-committal shrug and Milla returned her attention to the cat, her face soft and loving as she spoke of sweet nothings with him. Watching her more intently than was wise, Ed decided that this was, almost certainly, how she would have looked when she talked and played with her baby.

The baby she'd lost.

Thinking about it now, he felt his throat constrict and he had to look away. She'd hardly mentioned the miscarriage, but it was patently clear that this plan of hers to return to her roots was her way of dealing with her loss.

He was still absorbed by these thoughts when Milla asked, 'What about you, Ed? Are you a cat or a dog person?'

Neither, he almost said, but out of nowhere he remembered carefree summers in Michigan when he and Harry had roamed and fished along the Kalamazoo River. Their grandparents' golden Labradors had been their constant companions and the dogs' loping, loyal faithfulness had added an undeniable dimension to the boys' adventure.

'I guess I'd go for a dog if I had a choice.'

'I like dogs, too, but once the bakery's up and running, I won't have time to exercise one.'

Ed thought about the long hours of hard work ahead of her and grimaced. Had she really thought this through? She couldn't simply dabble at baking, then give it up if she got tired of it. Did she really know what she was letting herself in for?

He might have asked, but he hadn't come here to start another argument. By the same token, he didn't want to think too hard about why he *had* come back to Bellaroo Creek.

When Milla had challenged him, he'd thrown up his grandparents' hometown as a convenient excuse, but he hadn't really been thinking about them when he tracked down the bakery warehouse in Sydney, had he?

His focus had been his concern for Milla taking on this huge task on her own. That, plus his guilty awareness that the Cavanaugh family had let her down badly.

His family owed her.

He said, 'At least Blue will help to keep the mice population down.'

Milla flashed a grateful smile. 'Exactly. And I've decided that every bakery needs a cat.'

Her smile was as fond as a lover's as her gaze followed the tom when he stalked off once more, heading to the back door where a food bowl waited on a sunny step.

The damn cat had no idea how lucky he was.

They got back to painting and the afternoon seemed to fly. It was almost dark by the time they finished. Milla turned on the light switch to admire their handiwork.

'I love it,' she said, gazing with deep satisfaction at the smooth cream surfaces. She could already imagine these beautiful walls lined with racks of freshly baked loaves of smooth golden bread. She would have wicker baskets, too, with an assortment of bread rolls, and she would place pottery urns in the shop's corner, filled with sheafs of dried wheat. It was going to be gorgeous.

She sent Ed a triumphant grin. 'Thanks for your help.'

'I think we've done a great job. It was fun.'

He looked as if he meant it, which worried Milla. She was used to seeing Ed looking buttoned-down and serious in an expensive Italian business suit, busy with his BlackBerry. Today he looked too different, so relaxed, in his dark grey T-shirt and jeans. And way too attractive.

And now she noticed a scattering of fine, cream-toned spots sprinkled through his raven-dark hair. And there were larger splotches on his cheek and shirt. 'Yikes, you've got paint all over you.'

In answer, his gaze rested on her chest and a slow smile warmed his handsome face. 'I see we're two of a kind. Your sweater looks like a Jackson Pollock painting.'

It couldn't be that bad.

But it was pretty bad, Milla had to admit, when she looked down at her paint-splattered front. 'I guess I'm still getting the hang of this painting gig.'

She shrugged. 'And you need to get cleaned up and hop over to the pub. You're welcome to use the sink. There's a towel and soap and at least the paint is water based.'

She might have offered to wash out his T-shirt, but the thought of Ed standing around shirtless brought on a vision of him lying naked on her bed and she was assaulted by a fresh flurry of zaps and tingles.

'I suppose I'll have to hunt for Sherry again,' Ed said as he went to the sink and began to scrub paint spots from his arms. Milla took one look at his muscular forearms and hurried out the back to clean the rollers at an outdoor tap.

When she came back inside, Ed was still at the sink, now with his shirt off, washing his hair. Just as she'd feared, the sight of his powerful shoulders and strong, muscular back was enough to give a healthy woman problems with her breathing.

Ed reached for a towel and dried his face and hair. Then he looked up and grinned at her.

Help. Had he caught her ogling him?

'I'll book a table for dinner,' he said. 'You'll join me, won't you?'

Milla was quite sure that a dinner date couldn't be wise. This was supposed to be her post-Cavanaugh life.

Ed's smile was several versions of engaging, however. 'I promise I won't fall asleep on you this time.'

'If we're to have dinner together, it should be my shout,' Milla said stiffly. 'I'd like to thank you for the equipment and for your help today and…everything.'

He shook his head. 'I need to make up for last time.'

It would be silly to fight over this, but it would help if she understood exactly why Ed was here and why he was being so helpful and friendly. She'd assumed he was trying to keep some kind of control over her, but why would he need to do that now that both Harry and his baby were…gone?

She supposed Ed might be genuinely concerned about her, which was kind, even noble. But she would find his kindness so much easier to accept if she could forget about that long-ago kiss…

Then again, it was plain crazy and unhelpful to think about that kiss now. Ed had probably forgotten it years ago. At this moment, he was calmly waiting for her answer.

'Thank you,' she said as lightly as she could manage. 'I'd love to join you for dinner. Let's hope the duck and mushrooms are still on the menu.'

As soon as Ed was gone, Milla hurried upstairs to the three rooms above the shop that were now her living quarters. In the days when her parents had owned the bakery, they'd only used these rooms for storage and they'd lived in a large and comfortable house two streets away.

Now, however, Milla quite liked the idea of living above her shop. Her needs were simple—a bedroom, a tiny sitting room and bathroom were sufficient. The only furniture she'd bought during her one trip to Parkes were a bed and an armchair, but in time she would paint these rooms in rich, warm tones, and she would shop for a sofa, a bookcase and a rug and other small items to make the space homely.

She had plans for the skinny strip of weedy yard at the back of the building too. She wanted to create a small courtyard, a chicken coop, a veggie patch...

As she pulled her sweater over her head her muscles complained. Her arms were tired from all the painting. A hot shower would help and—

Heavy footsteps sounded on the tiled floor in the shop below. Milla froze. Surely that couldn't be Ed back already?

Hauling her sweater on again, she went to the top of the stairs. 'Who's there?'

'Just me,' came Ed's voice.

It was annoying to feel suddenly anxious. 'What's

wrong?' she called as she hurried down. 'Can't you find Sherry?'

'I had no problem finding her,' Ed said. 'But the pub's fully booked.'

'You're joking.' Milla gripped the post at the bottom of the stairs as she stared at him in disbelief. 'But that's ridiculous. I stayed at the pub for over a week and I was the only guest in the place for most of the time.'

'Apparently there's a rodeo on this weekend.'

'Oh.' Milla winced. 'Yes, that's true.' But it had never occurred to her that the pub might be full. And now it was too late for Ed to set off back to Sydney.

She pictured him spending the night here with her, and a riffle of disquiet that was close to panic made her shiver. 'I should have thought of that—I'm so sorry, Ed—I should have warned you.'

He didn't look worried, however. 'Most of the guests are staying out at the rodeo till late, so I still managed to book a table for us for dinner.'

'But where will you *sleep*?' Her voice made an embarrassing squeak on the final word.

Ed looked mildly amused. 'I'll be fine. Sherry tells me there are rooms in motels in Parkes and that's only an hour away.'

'Oh...yes, of course.' Why hadn't she thought of Parkes, instead of uselessly panicking? 'I'm sorry I can't offer you a spare bed. There's only an old camp stretcher here, and you wouldn't want that.' Ed was used to nothing less than five-star hotels. 'I slept on it for the first couple of nights over here, and it's not very comfortable.'

Ed merely shrugged at this and looked mildly amused. 'If I took the stretcher, I wouldn't have to drive to Parkes. We could enjoy a bottle of wine with our dinner.'

Milla was quite sure she could do without the wine.

But Ed was in persuasive mode. 'You must agree we've both earned a relaxing meal and a glass or two, and I'd rather not drive and risk an encounter with your police.'

What could she say without sounding inhospitable?

'Let me see this stretcher,' he said.

The stretcher would do, Ed decided, although exactly why he was willing to sleep on it was a question he wasn't keen to examine.

Chances were, he'd look back on this interlude in Bellaroo Creek as temporary insanity. But if he was pushed to give an answer, it wouldn't be too hard to justify this return visit. He felt responsible for Milla. After all, he'd introduced her to Harry, and as a result her life had veered way off course. And everyone knew he was a responsible kind of guy.

His desire to hang around here had nothing to do with any finer feelings for the woman. Ed knew better than that. Sure, his blood leapt whenever he saw Milla, but falling for a person who couldn't love you back happened to nearly everyone. He'd learned to accept this particular wound. It was permanent but bearable. A war injury he'd collected on the Cavanaugh family battleground.

Some time back, Ed had decided that relationships weren't for him. They weren't straightforward like running a business. There were no secure, blue-chip investments. Relationships were all about risk and loss, and it was easier to remain an emotional bankrupt.

Discreet affairs were fine. Anything deeper was out of his league.

As for now…his mission was simply to support Milla's goals, to do everything within his means to ensure her success and future happiness.

With that achieved, he could leave Australia with a clear conscience, and he would finally close the door on this less than happy chapter in his life.

And now that Milla seemed to have accepted his plan to stay, she'd changed from looking scared to being re-signed and practical.

'If you're going to stay here, I'll fetch the sleeping bag from upstairs,' she said. 'It belongs to a friend and it's designed for sleeping in the snow, apparently, so it should keep you plenty warm enough. And you'll need to use my bathroom, so go bring your things in, Ed, and I'll get a towel for you.'

She shot him a cautious glance. 'The bathroom's up-stairs.'

'I'll wait till you've finished using it.'

'All right.'

The sleeping bag was duly unrolled and Ed prowled around the downstairs area until the sounds from the shower stopped and Milla called down, 'All yours…'

When he ascended, she was already in her bedroom with her door firmly shut. But the tiny bathroom was filled with her flowery scent, and he was all too con-scious that she'd been in there, bathing.

He shut off his damned imagination before it got him into all kinds of trouble.

CHAPTER SIX

MILLA CAME DOWNSTAIRS in black leggings and elegant ankle boots teamed with a bright, leaf-green knitted top that fell to mid-thigh. It was a simple outfit but with her bronzed-copper hair and pale skin, she looked sensational.

Ed swallowed. 'You look wonderful.' *Like an elven princess.*

To his dismay, she blushed and looked embarrassed. 'Let's go,' she said quickly. 'I'm starving.'

Outside, a blustery wind whipped at them as they ran across the road. The pub's carpeted foyer was warm and welcoming, however, and Milla was tidying her hair, tucking bright curls behind her ear, when her phone rang.

'That's Heidi's ringtone,' she muttered, digging her phone out of her shoulder bag. 'Excuse me, Ed, I'd better answer it.'

'Of course.'

She'd already explained about her friends Heidi and Brad, and he waited while she went to the doorway, where she stood with her back to him, looking out at the street while she talked.

Ed tried not to listen, but he couldn't help pricking up his ears towards the end of her conversation.

'No, that's perfectly OK, Brad,' she said. 'I totally understand. Your farming and marketing plans would be very different from a small retail outlet like mine. Yes, yes, that's good advice. I'll find an accountant. Or a good business advisory firm. Got it. Thanks for letting me know. No worries. Yes, tell Heidi I'll ring her in the morning about the barbecue. Thanks again. Bye.'

As she turned off her phone and slipped it back into her bag, she gave Ed a self-conscious smile. 'Sorry about that, although I guess you're used to taking endless phone calls in public.'

'Endless,' he agreed. 'But over the weekend, I've switched off my phone and I've had my calls diverted to my long-suffering PA. I'm loving the silence.'

'So no withdrawal symptoms?'

'Not even the occasional twitch.'

Milla smiled and they were both still smiling as they went down a silky oak-panelled passage to the dining room where they were greeted by a very wide-eyed Sherry.

'Nice to see you again.' The girl beamed at Ed and shot Milla a look brimming with significance as she showed them to a table near the fire. Their table was set for two with a white linen cloth and starched napkins, shining silver and a small crystal vase of yellow jonquils.

'This is rather elegant,' Ed remarked with genuine appreciation as Sherry went off to fetch their selected wine.

'Bellaroo Creek springs yet another surprise.' Milla looked around at the other diners sitting at equally attractive tables. 'Perhaps the hotel staff lifted their act for the busy weekend.' A small smile played. 'Most rodeo visitors don't need starched tablecloths, but it shows the staff can achieve wonders when they try.'

'As we have discovered today,' said Ed.

She nodded and her smile grew broader. 'The shop's going to look fabulous, isn't it? I can't wait to get the bakery up and running.'

Ed hated to burst her bubble by pointing out that a few painted walls were a long way from a successful business. And he couldn't pretend that he wasn't concerned by her end of her phone conversation.

I'll find an accountant, she'd said. *Or a good business advisory firm.*

It was pretty clear she was seeking business advice, which her friend, Brad, had been unable to provide.

There was no way she'd ask for his help, Ed accepted grimly, but, although this rankled, he wouldn't let it spoil the night.

After the wine arrived, had been tasted and poured, he raised his glass. 'Here's to the Bellaroo Bakery.'

'And to all who sail in her,' Milla responded with a laugh.

It was the first time since he'd arrived in Australia that she'd looked so happy and relaxed. And so beautiful with the firelight reflected in her smiling green eyes.

I'm mad, he thought. *I should get out of here now.*

He paid attention to the menu instead, and they both ordered a Chinese wonton soup to be followed by the famous duck and mushrooms. And while they waited for the food, they drank their wine and talked about their favourite meals and their childhood pets and the similarities and differences between America and Australia.

Over the soup, they tossed around the pros and cons of baking organic bread made from specialised wheat.

When the duck arrived, their conversation was reduced to 'Yum' and 'Mmm' and blissful smiles.

'This is really good,' Ed said, spearing a dark plump mushroom with his fork.

Milla grinned. 'Not bad for the back of beyond.'

'Not bad for anywhere.'

'I hope the chef stays.'

'He might if the "Save Our Town" scheme works.'

'Yes.' Milla's bright smile faded and was replaced by a thoughtful frown. 'I hope it doesn't turn out to be a pipe dream.'

Unable to help himself, Ed asked, 'Is everything OK? With your business? I—I couldn't help overhearing part of your phone conversation.'

The shutters came down on Milla's face. 'Everything's perfectly fine,' she said. 'It—it's nothing I can't handle.' She paid studious attention to the food on her plate.

It was damn frustrating to know that she might have a problem he could easily solve. 'Milla, if it's to do with the business, you know I can almost certainly help you.'

'You've already done enough.' She set her fork on her plate and sat back, lifting her napkin to dab at her lips. 'I don't need your help. Anyway, you have to go back to New York, and I'll be fine. There are any number of people here who can help me.'

'So you admit you do need help?'

Milla sighed. 'Has anyone ever told you, you're like a terrier with a bone?'

'All the time.'

She smiled again then. And Ed smiled back at her.

They seemed to be doing rather a lot of smiling this evening. Her eyes were the clearest green and breathtakingly beautiful, and he sensed a moment of connection that made his head spin.

Eventually, he said, 'So now you know that I'm not going to give up, why don't you just tell me your problem?'

'It's not really a problem.' She looked around at the other diners who were scattered about the room, intent on their own conversations, and not paying them the slightest attention. With a resigned lift of her shoulders, she said, 'It's just that I need to write a business plan. It's part of the council's lease agreement.'

'Hang on. You mean to say, you've moved into the bakery, you've started painting the walls, I'm buying equipment, and you still don't have a proper agreement?'

Milla narrowed her eyes at him. 'This is the bush, Ed. The council trust me. They know I'll get it done.'

'Have you ever written a business plan?'

'You know I haven't, but I'll engage someone who knows how to write one.'

'Like me,' he said quietly. 'I know these things inside out and backwards.'

'You're leaving in the morning.'

'I don't have to.'

It wasn't strictly true. There would be all hell to pay if he stayed away much longer, but Ed had lived his whole life being the conscientious Cavanaugh. Perhaps he could blame being down under for this sudden, reckless reassessment of responsibilities.

'I don't know,' Milla said with a worried shake of her head. 'There's a world of difference between the business dealings of Cavanaugh Enterprises and anything I'm trying to do here.'

'Business is business.' Ed topped up their wine glasses. 'It's simply a matter of scale.'

She seemed to consider this as she watched him cautiously over the rim of her glass. 'So what would you cover in my business plan?'

'Well…for a start, you'd need to show your estimated costs of production, your expected capacity and cash flows, and your break-even point. I guess the council would be interested in the range of your potential market, your sources for materials. The degree to which your business will help the locals. And you'd—'

'OK. OK.' Milla gave a smiling eye-roll as she held up her hands. 'I think you've made your point, Ed. You could write my business plan in your sleep.'

Sherry arrived to take their plates. 'Can I tempt you guys to try our desserts?'

'Just peppermint tea for me,' said Milla.

Sherry pulled a face. 'I'm not sure we do herbals. I'll have to check. What about you, sir?' She batted her eyelashes at Ed. 'Can I tempt you to strawberry pavlova?'

'I'm happy with the wine,' said Ed, impatiently returning to his conversation with Milla even before the girl had left. 'Given half a chance, I could pull a business plan together for you in a day.'

'Do you know enough about this district?'

He shrugged. 'I can jump on the Internet to find any info I need. There'll be government websites with demographics for the region.'

Milla's peppermint tea arrived. 'I found a tea bag,' Sherry said, but she was too busy tonight to linger, which was probably a good thing, given Bellaroo

Creek's hunger for gossip. After she'd left them, Milla took a thoughtful sip of her tea and then set her cup on its saucer with excruciating care.

Her face was super serious as she looked at him. 'Why are you doing this, Ed?'

It was a good question. A damn good question. Milla was probably worried that he had designs on her. But he wasn't a fool. He'd learned his lesson when she rejected him on their very first date.

They'd shared one kiss, a kiss of earth-shattering passion—he'd never experienced anything close to the powerful magic of it before or since. And while she was sitting chastely opposite him now, she'd been wild and uninhibited on that night. A sexy, heart-stopping miracle. He had known then that he'd found someone very special.

And yet...

Ed considered the abysmal way Harry had treated her. And he thought about the angry phone call he'd received from his father two days ago. Gerry had berated Ed, as if he were somehow responsible for the loss of his grandchild...

And Ed knew Milla had every right to ask why he, another Cavanaugh, was here uninvited, offering to hang around and help.

He gave her the simple truth. 'I believe my family owes you.'

His family owed her...

Ed's answer sideswiped Milla. Her teacup rattled against the saucer as she set it down again.

She'd been so sure Ed was here to maintain some kind of Cavanaugh control over her. She'd been certain that his selfish, egocentric family assumed that *she* owed them a debt, simply because they'd allowed her into their hallowed, wealthy midst.

And now, at the mere mention of his family, the memories she'd been trying so hard to bury flooded her thoughts. The long lonely nights, Harry's drunkenness and gambling. His endless affairs.

Her husband had hurt her and let her down in so many ways, and his hard, self-centred mother had always taken her son's side and never supported Milla.

As for Gerry Cavanaugh, Harry's father—he'd practically ignored Milla until he'd learned that she was pregnant with his grandchild, and then he'd sent Ed and a damn PI after her.

Now here was Ed, the one member of the Cavanaugh family who had every right to resent her, claiming instead that they owed her.

'I don't understand,' she said. 'Are you talking about money? My inheritance?'

Ed gave her a long, hard look without speaking. Eventually, she felt flustered and dropped her gaze. What was he implying? That the family should have warned her about Harry? Protected her?

But she'd been a grown woman, free to choose, to make her own mistakes.

And Ed's presence in Bellaroo Creek was a constant reminder of those mistakes. 'I crossed hemispheres to put it all behind me,' she said.

Ed let out a heavy sigh. 'I get that. And to be honest, I don't blame you.'

Across the table, he sent her another sad smile, a smile that made her heart beat faster and raised more questions. Questions she dared not ask.

Milla was relieved that the meal had come to an end. There'd been times when it had felt dangerously like a date, and she was glad to hurry back through the cold winter's night to the bakery.

Again they took turns using the bathroom, a situation Milla found ridiculously intimate, so she was tense as a trip wire when it was time to say goodnight.

'I'm afraid I only have one small heater,' she confessed.

'In your bedroom?' Ed asked.

'Well…um…yes…'

Amusement glittered in his eyes and she feared he might tease her about this, but then he seemed to think better of it. 'I'll be toasty in my thermal sleeping bag.'

'OK, I'm impressed,' announced Heidi as she stood at her kitchen window, supposedly tossing a salad, but mostly staring out into her backyard where Brad and Ed were manhandling steaks on the barbecue. 'I mean, I'm *seriously* impressed.'

'With my cherry pie?' asked Milla sweetly.

Heidi made a scoffing sound. 'I'm sure the pie's delicious, but, man, your *American* is hot!'

'You sound like Sherry,' Milla protested. 'And you should know better. You know he's not *my* American. He's Harry's brother and he's here on business.'

'But whose business?' Heidi asked darkly. 'That's the big question.'

This silenced Milla. She was beginning to wish she'd come up with an excuse to back out of this evening. Instead she'd weakened and phoned Heidi, who had of course insisted that she bring Ed to the barbecue.

'I've sliced the baguette,' Milla said now in an unsubtle bid to change the subject. 'Would you like it buttered?'

'That'd be great,' Heidi muttered impatiently. 'But I'd rather you answered my question.'

Milla sighed as she reached for the butter dish. 'Ed came here to settle family business.'

'But he stayed here to help you with *your* business?'

'He's a control freak. He can't help interfering.'

'Nice try, Milla.'

'Excuse me?'

'I'm sure a man like Ed Cavanaugh only interferes when and where it suits him,' Heidi remarked archly.

Milla fumed for a moment. 'Ed thinks his family owes me. He's always had a well-developed sense of responsibility.'

'And that's not the only thing that's well developed.'

Milla wisely ignored this. 'Ed also knows business plans inside out and backwards.' It felt weird to be quoting Ed almost word for word, but with Heidi backing her into a corner she was at a loss. And quoting Ed was certainly safer than discussing his physical attributes. After another day of working in his close proximity, answering his endless but surprisingly patient questions about her plans for the bakery, Milla was all too familiar with the way Ed looked and behaved.

All day, while she'd painted window frames, Ed had worked on her business plan, and his presence had dominated her awareness. Mostly, she'd been trying to digest the astonishing reality that a top-flight business magnate from New York was paying such earnest attention to her little country bakery's profit and loss potential.

While they'd talked about the range of goods she might sell, about staff she might need to employ...

While they tossed around ideas like leaving samples of her baked goods in the general store during the lead-up to opening day... Milla had also been stealing glimpses in Ed's direction simply because the breadth of his shoulders was so impressive.

Much to her embarrassment, she'd found herself also admiring the sheen of his dark hair and the neat line it made across the back of his neck as he hunkered over her laptop.

It was mere aesthetic appreciation, of course. Nothing personal. But unfortunately, Ed had caught her peeking. More than once. He'd looked up, their gazes had met, and she'd seen a flash in his eyes that had sent flames shooting under her skin.

She'd tried to cover up with the lamest of excuses, making a comment that she'd never seen him wearing his reading glasses. She was quite sure he'd seen right through her.

But despite these slips, she wasn't *interested* in Ed. Not in *that* way.

'Admit it, Mills,' Heidi persisted with a grin. 'The starry guys have always fallen for you. Remember high school? And Heath Dixon?'

'I'd rather not.' A flash of unpleasant panic scorched Milla, followed by an involuntary shudder.

Heidi seemed oblivious to her reaction. 'You had the sexiest guy in the whole school practically begging you to go out with him.'

'Aren't you being disloyal to Brad by suggesting that some other guy at school was the sexiest?'

'Brad doesn't have a jealous bone in his body.' Heidi's face softened, transformed from plain to exceptionally pretty as her cheeks were warmed by an affectionate smile. 'Brad knows how I feel about him.'

Milla watched as Heidi sent a dreamy, private smile out of the window and she felt a sharp pang of envy.

So, I guess that's what true love looks like.

'But Heath Dixon was something else,' Heidi continued emphatically. 'He was hot-looking and dangerous...and drooling over you, Milla. And every girl in Year Twelve was pea green with envy. You never explained why you went on one date with the guy and gave him the flick. We were stunned and in awe at your heartlessness.'

If only they knew...

Milla had never told anyone, not even Heidi, about what had happened on that one night with the loathsome school heartthrob. 'Heath Dixon was a creep,' she said now, bitterly.

Heidi stared at her with wide-eyed interest. 'Do tell.'

'Actually, no. I'd rather drop the subject of men. I'm afraid it bores me to tears. I'm completely over the male of our species. I'm here to resurrect a bakery.'

'Milla, you can't turn your back on men altogether. Apart from any other considerations, they make up half the world's population.'

Milla shrugged. 'I'm over falling *in love* with them, that's for sure. And I'm certainly over the Cavanaughs. After a disastrous relationship with one member of that family, I have zero interest in getting involved with another.'

'Well, yes, I can see that's fair enough.' Heidi nodded sagely, but it wasn't long before she was smiling again. 'But you have to admit...it was so cute when you arrived here tonight and Ed was so desperately keen for us to admire your cherry lattice pie. He looked so proud…and so *fond*…of you.'

'That's because I remind him of his grandmother.' Heidi hooted.

'No, it's true. He bought me these pastry cutters, you see, and—'

'*Ed* bought pastry cutters?'

'Yes. I told you he was a control freak. He had to make sure I had decent equipment.'

'Sure, sure,' Heidi's voice purred with sarcasm.

'Apparently, his grandmother used to let him cut the pastry strips when he was a kid,' Milla explained.

Heidi's eyebrows hiked. 'Well, there you go.'

Watching her friend's amused disbelief, Milla conceded that the picture of Ed helping her with pastry strips was totally incongruous with his normal persona as Mr Big of the business world.

It had been fun today, teaching him about pastry and explaining how she would plan things when she had to make a dozen pies at one time.

Heidi had said… *He looked so proud…and so fond… of you.*

The word *fond* lingered in Milla's mind, like a favourite passage of soul music.

'Anyway, I'm very glad you brought Ed out to our place,' Heidi continued chattily. Once again, she cocked her head towards the view through the window. 'Brad's certainly enjoying his company. The two of them seem to be getting on like a house on fire.'

Curious, Milla stepped closer to the window, and she saw Ed with Brad, looking extremely relaxed, drinking beer and chatting and laughing as they kept a weather

eye on the sizzling food. Her heart gave a strange little lurch.

Having so recently and vocally avowed that she was
off men, she felt like a hypocrite. This sentimental pang
was a mistake, a momentary aberration.

Perhaps she could blame the perfect setting. Heidi
and Brad seemed to have a knack for making their
home look welcoming and heart-warming, like something you'd want to photograph. Not the perfect shots
of magazines though, but appealing and lived-in and
somehow just right.

They'd built their own barbecue and set it in a pretty
paved courtyard, and tonight there was a wood fire
burning brightly, and the air was filled with the mingled
smells of smoke and frying onions. Heidi had strung
glowing Chinese lanterns between the trees, and she'd
covered the outdoor table with a red gingham cloth and
fat yellow candles.

Despite the cold winter's night, a backyard had never
looked more inviting. And Ed had never looked more
relaxed, Milla thought. He almost looked as if he belonged here.

'Watching from here,' said Heidi, standing close to
Milla's elbow. 'A person could be forgiven for thinking
that those two were old, old friends.'

It was true. Ed's and Brad's backgrounds were worlds
apart, but they were probably around the same age, and
they were both tall and broad shouldered and athletic
and they seemed to be talking and laughing non-stop.

'It's pretty amazing, actually,' said Milla. 'Ed's usually frowning and earnest.'

Just then Brad said something that was greeted by

a crack of laughter from Ed. She wondered what they were talking about.

'So, I'm assuming Ed's keen on your bakery idea?' Heidi prompted as she lifted a potato salad from the fridge.

'I'm pretty sure he thinks I'm mad. But he does seem intrigued by the Save Our Town scheme.'

'Well, Brad's totally committed to *that*. Keeping the town alive depends on keeping the school open, and now that Thomas has started in Year One, Brad's on the Parents and Friends'. Poor Ed's probably copping an earful right now.'

Milla smiled. 'If he is, he doesn't seem to mind.'

'True.' Heidi surveyed her prepared salads with a critical eye. 'OK, these are good to go. Let's get them outside and join the party. Can you bring the bread and the pepper and salt? I'll drag the kids away from their DVD.'

She lifted her voice. 'Thomas! Lucy! Dinner's ready.'

'I want to sit next to the man,' insisted a small, golden-haired cherub as she looked up at Ed with huge brown eyes.

'How about asking nicely, Luce?' her mother reminded her. 'And the man's name is Ed.'

'I want to sit next to *him*,' the little girl said with pointed emphasis.

Heidi groaned. 'Did I hear the word *please*?'

The golden angel smiled impishly at Ed. 'Please, Man.'

'Lucky me,' he said gallantly, but he was wondering what he was in for as he shifted over and made a space beside him on the long wooden stool. 'Shall I lift you up?'

'No, I'm a big girl. I can get up all by myself.' With a certain amount of huffing and puffing, the small person scrambled onto the seat. Once she was in place, she pushed a golden mop of curls out of her eyes and beamed at Ed with a grin of unholy triumph. 'See, I'm up.'

'You are indeed.' He couldn't help smiling. He'd never before been at such close quarters with a diminutive female, and he was intrigued.

'I'm going to have a sausage wrapped in bread with tomato sauce,' she announced importantly.

'And salad,' warned Heidi.

Her daughter's small pink lower lip drooped. 'I don't like salad.'

'No salad, no sausage.' Heidi followed up her stern warning by serving a spoonful of lettuce with cherry tomatoes and cucumber and carrot onto her daughter's plate.

Ed watched, mildly amused, half expecting a wail of protest. Instead, he found two large brown thickly lashed eyes gazing up at him solemnly. 'Do you like salad, Man?'

'I love salad,' he assured her.

Next moment, as her mother turned her attention to her brother, the little girl scrambled to her feet. Standing on the seat, she leaned into Ed with her mouth pressed against his ear. 'I'll let you have my salad,' she whispered in great excitement, as if she were bestowing an enormous honour. 'Don't tell Mummy.'

In a flash, she was down again, sitting demurely as

her father set the desired, crisp and crunchy sausage on her plate. 'You want sauce, pumpkin?'

'Yes, please, Daddy.'

Ed swallowed an urge to chuckle. He'd never realised that feminine wiles started so young. He was enjoying himself immensely, and out of nowhere snuck the most surprising thought. What would it be like to have a small cherubic imp of his own?

He'd hardly given fatherhood a thought, but this evening was having a strange effect on him. From the moment he'd arrived at Heidi and Brad's farmhouse, he'd felt as if he'd stepped back in time. Not that Milla's friends were out of touch with the modern world. They were fully informed and up-to-date, but there was a beguiling, old-fashioned and slower-paced atmosphere about their home and family that took Ed straight back to gatherings at his grandparents' farm in Michigan.

Truth be told, Thanksgiving in Michigan when he was around fifteen was probably the last time Ed had eaten a meal where the adults and the younger generation sat down together. The adults, of course, had been his grandparents, not his parents.

Ed couldn't remember ever sharing a meal with his parents. He could barely remember his mother and father dining together. They were divorced before he'd turned five. After that, whenever he'd stayed in his father's new house, his dad had rarely been home at mealtimes. He'd always been at board meetings, or business dinners or benefit breakfasts.

As for Ed's mother, she'd always slept in late in the mornings, never rising before he had to leave for school, and her evening meals had usually been liquid and consumed on the couch in front of the television. If she'd been awake to say goodnight to Ed, she'd reeked of whisky and slurred her words. He'd been brought up by a succession of nannies and maids.

Sitting here now, pretending not to notice as pieces of tomato and cucumber were surreptitiously deposited onto the side of his plate, Ed watched Milla's smiling eyes and listened to her laughter mingled with that of the others, and he felt unexpectedly, deeply…happy…

And at home.

It was a shock to remember that, no matter how comfortable or welcome he felt here, he was still an outsider. Cavanaugh Enterprises existed in another dimension. It might as well have been an alien planet where the inhabitants had calculators instead of hearts.

Tonight, Ed couldn't help thinking how different everything had been on the one night he'd taken Milla to a social gathering. Harry's glittering, over-the-top birthday party in Beverly Hills had been light years away from this simple, unpretentious backyard barbecue.

Of course, Ed could see now why Milla had been so easily dazzled…

He could also understand why she'd come running back home when the scales had finally fallen from her eyes.

CHAPTER SEVEN

ED DROVE BACK into town along quiet country roads, past starlit paddocks where owls sat on fence posts, waiting to pounce on unwary field mice, or whatever strange equivalent they had in Australia. He drove past dark clumps of gumtrees and over rattling, narrow, one-lane bridges. And in the view through the windshield, a shining full moon bobbed through drifts of gauzy white cloud.

He couldn't remember the last time he'd had such a clear view of a moonlit landscape and sky. The scenery was almost mystical and it seemed to cap off a perfect evening. He felt uplifted. Touched by magic.

Beside him, Milla sat in silence, her bright hair and delicate profile limned by silver light as she stared out at the countryside, apparently lost in thought.

'I really enjoyed tonight,' he said when the silence had gone on a little too long. 'Thanks for letting me tag along.'

'I'm glad you enjoyed it.' Her voice was friendly enough, but she quickly lapsed back into her musings, huddled inside her padded jacket. It wasn't long before she folded her arms, hugging them to her chest. A fencing-off gesture, if ever Ed had seen one.

But he was in too good a mood to let her body language deter him. 'I enjoyed meeting your friends,' he said. 'Brad's a cool guy. Great sense of humour.'

Milla roused. 'Brad's always seen the funny side of life. I suspect that's why Heidi fell in love with him.'

'No doubt.' Momentarily, Ed's happy mood was sideswiped by memories of his brother's laughter and charm. Almost certainly, Milla had been attracted by Harry's broad grin and his love of telling a clever joke, a skill Ed had never mastered.

With an effort, he shook off disturbing memories. 'Brad has a really good head on his shoulders. I'd say he's a very good farmer.'

'Seems to be.'

'I had a good chat to him about growing organic wheat.'

'Really?' Milla sounded incredulous. 'Why?'

Ed shrugged. 'We were talking about your bakery and how there's a growing market for organic products.'

'Oh.' Now she sounded prickly. 'Brad never said anything about it to me.'

'We talked about a ton of stuff,' Ed reminded her. 'But if you did decide you wanted to try organic wheat, Brad would be a good guy to talk to.'

Milla nodded, apparently satisfied. 'Heidi says Brad's very passionate about saving Bellaroo Creek's school.' Unfolding her arms, she sat straighter. 'Isn't it great that they're encouraging those young families to come here by offering farmhouses for a dollar a week?'

'Yeah, maybe. I'm still not sure it will work.'

She turned to him. 'Do you have a better idea?'

Ed couldn't resist the obvious challenge. 'What Bellaroo Creek needs is a proper injection of capital.'

'*Whose* capital?'

'Anyone's. I'm talking in theory, right?'

'I suppose your family could buy the whole town if you wanted to.'

He gave a non-committal shrug as he changed gears and eased the ute around a sharpish corner. 'The thing is, if the place looked more prosperous and was offering solid employment, people would come and pay full rent.'

'Hmm…' Milla sounded doubtful. 'Nice theory. I suppose you might get faster results. But apart from the fact that no one's likely to risk their money on this out-of-the-way place, if one person or a company owned all the businesses in a town, whose town would it be? How would you develop a sense of community?'

'I don't see why—'

'And how could you guarantee that the people you employed would have children to keep the school going?'

'Simple. You'd screen them during the interview process.'

Milla appeared to consider this. 'OK, tell me this, Ed.' She paused as they reached the main road and Ed waited for a truck to pass before turning. Once they were whizzing down the bitumen, she said, 'Do you think the people who came here to work for you would have the same sense of self-worth as someone like me, starting from scratch, doing the hard yards and the renovations by myself?'

'Ouch.' He shot her a sideways glance and caught the almost warrior-like challenge in her eyes. 'That came from the heart.'

'Country towns need heart.'

'And dollars.'

Almost as soon as he'd said this Ed knew it was a mistake. He wasn't even sure he totally believed his own argument. Before Milla could pounce on him, he hurried to cover his tracks. 'Don't get me wrong. I'm not arguing with you. You made a good point. Self-worth is important. In the long run, I'm sure it's more important than fiscal worth.'

'Wow,' Milla said softly. 'Coming from a Cavanaugh, that's a very interesting statement.'

Yeah… Ed had surprised himself, trotting out that little homily. Maybe he'd been down under too long and he was starting to view the world upside down.

But there was no hiding from the bleak truth. Milla was right about his family. The Cavanaughs epitomised the old cliché. Money hadn't bought them happiness. Ed only had to think about his father, obstinately courting his fourth bride-to-be, while knowing that his chances of success were on a par with his previous marriages…

His mother was even sadder. Lonely, bitter and sharp tongued, she had certainly found no comfort in her wealth.

It was hard to tell with his young brother, Charlie, but he was young, so there was still hope.

As for devil-may-care Harry…

Or me?

Ed sighed, while beside him Milla seemed to shrink back into her silent deliberations. Once again she was huddled with her arms folded tightly, her face turned away as she stared out through her side window.

They reached the outskirts of town, slipping past the small white weatherboard church and the endangered little school with its playground and football field, past the straggle of houses that rimmed the main street. Soon, Ed brought the ute to a stop outside the darkened bakery and as the motor died he heard Milla let out a heavy sigh.

All evening at the Murrays' place, she'd seemed to be light-hearted and happy. The return of this low mood bothered him. 'You OK?'

Milla started and frowned at him. 'Sorry?'

'I asked if you're OK. Is something bothering you?'

She shook her head. 'I—I was just remembering… something…'

Whatever she was remembering, it troubled her. One of the few streetlights in the town was shining in on them, illuminating her lovely face, and her anxiety was clear to Ed. He could see its shadows in her eyes and in the sad twist of her mouth.

He was trying to think of the right thing to say when she pushed her door open and hopped out, fishing in her bag for her keys. He climbed out, too, locked the ute and joined her as she opened the door.

The smell of fresh paint greeted them as they went through the shop, carefully skirting the piles of drop sheets on their way to the doorway at the back. The ginger cat came forward with a soft meow and rubbed his sleek body against Milla's legs. Milla gave him a scratch, then turned on the light, bringing the bakery's workroom to life with its thick brick walls and stainless-steel benches and the back section filled by the massive rotating oven.

Ed saw his stretcher in the corner, complete with neatly rolled sleeping bag, and he felt his spirits sink. The stretcher wasn't too uncomfortable, but he knew he wasn't ready for sleep. He hoped Milla wasn't planning to scurry upstairs straight away.

'Is it OK if I make coffee?' he asked.

She looked surprised. 'Are you sure you want coffee at this time of night?'

'I nearly always have coffee at this time of night.'

'Oh? OK.' With a strangely distant smile, she hurried to the fridge and extracted a packet of ground coffee. 'This do?'

'That's fine, thanks. I'm happy to make it. Care to join me?'

She hesitated, and the shadow of whatever was bothering her seemed to hover above her. Ed stamped on an urge to pull her in his arms, to kiss her soft, brooding mouth. But the urge was persistent. He longed to kiss her smooth white throat, kiss any and every part of her till she was purring with happiness and pleasure.

Instead he sent her an encouraging smile, a trick that had worked in the past with almost any woman.

Her answering smile was a shade wistful. 'I won't have coffee,' she said. 'It'll keep me awake, but I could do a peppermint tea.'

'Perfect.'

While Milla collected a tea bag from the pantry cupboard, Ed set the kettle to boil and measured coffee into the pot. As he slipped bright mugs from hooks, she opened the buttons on her jacket and shrugged out of it, letting it drop onto a spare stool before she dragged another stool for herself. Then she slumped forward with her elbows on the bench, her chin in her hands.

Her Renaissance gold hair glowed warmly beneath the harsh fluorescent tube and her face was a picture of mournful self-absorption.

Ed knew it was stating the obvious, but he had to ask. 'That bad memory still bugging you?'

He half expected her to remain sunk in gloomy silence, or to tell him it was none of his business. He was surprised when she lifted her head.

'It's pretty stupid,' she said. 'Just something Heidi mentioned tonight. Something from our high-school days.'

'High school. *Sheesh.*'

Milla's green eyes widened. 'Didn't you like school?'

'It was OK. I guess it's the same for everyone. Some good memories, some I'd rather forget.'

She nodded soberly. 'I wish I could forget this one.'

Ed felt a clutch in his heart. He'd never thought of himself as chivalrous, but tonight he longed to come to her aid, to at least make her smile again. But his gallant thoughts were pierced by the kettle coming to the boil and he made a business of filling her tea mug and the coffee pot.

'Do you want to leave the tea bag in?' Such a safe, practical question.

'For the moment, thanks.'

Then he asked, carefully, 'So you haven't talked to Heidi about this…problem?'

Milla shook her head. 'She doesn't know a thing. No one does. Except—except the person concerned. I—I've never told anyone else.'

Was that wise?

Ed wasn't sure what to say. Unless he was discussing investments or business, his counselling skills were nix. 'I've never been one for baring my soul,' he admitted. 'But they do say that talking about stuff is supposed to help.'

To his surprise, a small smile shone in Milla's eyes.

'Are you offering to be my Father Confessor, Ed?'

The very thought made him nervous as hell. He swallowed to relieve the broken-glass sharpness in his throat. 'Sure. If it would help. It would go no further. I can promise you that. I mean, it's not as if I'll be hanging around after this weekend.'

Milla's hands were shaking as Ed handed her the mug of tea. She was actually feeling sick now. Sick with tension. And fear.

She'd been fine earlier this evening when Heidi had let fly with her chance comment about Heath Dixon. At the time, Heidi had merely stirred a bad memory that Milla had quickly dismissed. Once she'd been absorbed into the give-and-take of lively chatter around the barbecue she'd more or less forgotten about it.

Later, though, when she and Ed were driving home, the memory had stolen back into her thoughts. This time, alone with Ed and the dark night, the memory had turned vicious, rousing a chain reaction of panicky thoughts about dates and boyfriends. Harry and Ed.

Successive memories had spilled, one after the other, stirring her anxiety and guilt till she thought she might burst.

And now...

Why on earth had she thrown that half-smart Father Confessor question at Ed?

Poor man...

Being the conscientious and responsible type, he was now waiting...expecting...

She watched his strong, squarish hands as he lowered the plunger, carefully, slowly, like a true coffee lover.

He had no idea he was actually a part of her problem. How could she tell him?

But perhaps a more pressing question was…how could she pass up this chance to explain the things she'd wanted to explain years ago? In another day Ed would be gone back to America, and this time he would certainly stay there. This was her best and last chance to set the record straight.

But man, she was nervous… And where should she start?

She stared at a spot on the floor, trying to summon her scattering courage. Closing her eyes, she said quickly, 'When I was sixteen, a guy almost raped me.'

It sounded terrible to hear it out loud in the silent, almost echoing space. But perhaps it was like loosening a cork out of a bottle and the rest would come more easily now.

'A guy in high school?' Ed prompted gently.

Milla nodded. 'Everyone looked up to him as the school heartthrob. I was supposed to be incredibly grateful that he did me the huge honour of asking me out.' Nervously, she fiddled with the string attached to her herbal tea bag. 'But on our first date, when I wouldn't play it his way, he turned nasty.'

'You poor girl.'

It was helpful, the soft way Ed said this, as if he really cared. It gave Milla the courage to push on.

'I panicked of course, which made the guy madder, and then he got even more violent.'

She didn't look at Ed, but she heard the *clink* when he set down his mug and out of the corner of her eye she saw his fist clench.

'Does the son of a bitch still live around here?'

'He's long gone, Ed. Don't worry. That was one of the first things I checked when I came back.'

Ed nodded grimly. 'But you've never told anyone about this?'

'I couldn't face the gossip. It's the major downside of living in a small town. And as I said, this fellow was the school heartthrob. All the kids from here travelled to Parkes on the school bus. The other girls were jealous that he was paying attention to me. They knew as soon as he asked me out—he'd spread the word, I found out later. Everyone was waiting to hear what happened on our date.'

'I can imagine,' Ed said quietly.

'If they knew what really happened, it would have been hell. I just couldn't bear seeing the pity or curiosity in everyone's eyes. It was easier to let him tell his mates that I was frigid and he dumped me. I told my friends he was boring.'

Ed was frowning still, watching her with a thoughtful gaze. 'I presume he hurt you?'

Milla nodded. 'It was worse than I let on. I made an excuse that I'd tripped down the stairs. I should have won an Oscar for my brilliant acting. Even my parents believed my story about the bruises. No one ever dreamed the truth.'

Ed made a soft sound, a sigh or a groan—Milla couldn't be sure. 'I assume you told Harry,' he said after a bit.

'No. This was something from my old life and I was trying to reinvent myself after I left here. Besides, it would have been too heavy for Harry. He hated anything deep and meaningful.'

Ed scowled, but he didn't look shocked. 'I'm so sorry

for what happened, Milla. I wish there was something I could say or do to make the memories go away.'

What she needed was a hug—a comforting, platonic, Father Confessor–type hug. But she didn't deserve any further kindness from this man, not after the way she'd so hastily and rudely ditched him in favour of his brother.

What an idiot she'd been.

'Thanks, but I'm OK,' she said.

'I'm not so sure about that,' Ed said gently, and with that he came closer and gathered her in.

And after only a moment's surprised hesitation, Milla sank against him, absorbing the strength of his arms around her as she leaned into the comforting solidity of his chest and buried her face in the lovely softness of his expensive cashmere sweater.

What simple bliss a hug could be! Ed made her feel warm and safe. Comforted. There'd been precious little comfort for Milla lately, especially when she'd most needed it—after she'd lost her baby. In Ed's arms, she felt as if she'd been on a long, exhausting and dangerous journey, and had finally stumbled into a safe haven.

Resting her head on his shoulder, she couldn't remember when she'd felt so thankful.

Careless, selfish Harry had rarely tried to offer her comfort. She wasn't sure he'd known how.

Then again, she hadn't expected Ed to show this degree of thoughtfulness either. And when it came to surprises—the very fact that she could let Ed hug her without getting nervous was another revelation. The calmness she felt in his arms tonight was very different from that first night they'd gone out, when the intoxicating fire and passion of their kiss had frightened her.

But in the very midst of consoling herself with this comforting notion, Milla realised that her hormones had scooted way ahead of her thoughts. Already, she could feel her body reacting. Heat flared along her arms, and in her breasts, her stomach, wherever her body touched Ed's. Coils of longing tightened low inside her.

Perhaps it was just as well that Ed released her. But…oh, how she missed the power and warmth of him. Missed everything, actually, including—no, especially—the stirring excitement.

But she couldn't tell how Ed felt as he moved away to the safety of the far side of the workbench. He kept his gaze averted, although she could see that his mouth was a tight, downward-curving line.

'Thanks for the hug.'

He shrugged. 'My…pleasure.'

An awkward silence fell then, as if neither of them knew what to say. Almost simultaneously, they picked up their mugs.

'I hope your coffee's not too cold,' Milla offered.

Ed took a deep sip. 'It's fine.'

She removed her tea bag, squeezed the excess liquid, and dropped it into the sink. It was so quiet in the bakery she could hear the cat, back in his bed, purring in his sleep.

'So,' Ed said at last, with just the tiniest hint of a smile returning. 'Are *they* right?'

Milla shot him a look of confusion. 'Excuse me? They?'

His eyes glinted with brief amusement. 'They who say confession is good for the soul.'

'Oh.' She let out her breath on a soft sigh. Of course.

She'd told her story and Ed had hugged her better, so he thought her confession was complete.

Unfortunately, the hard part, the important part that concerned him, was still to come.

'Actually, Ed—' Her mouth was so dry now that her tongue wouldn't work, but she couldn't wimp out. She'd wanted to explain about this for so long. 'Actually, I'm afraid there's something else I need to tell you.'

It wasn't surprising that his eyes took on a new, wary alertness.

'It's something that still bothers me…something I feel guilty about.'

Ed frowned. 'There—there weren't repercussions? He didn't make you pregnant?'

'No, no, nothing like that happened. It's just that—'

She looked down at the remains of her peppermint tea, as if somehow the pale dregs could give her strength. Even though she was clutching the mug in both hands, she was shaking. She set the mug down. 'You see…ever since what happened in high school, I've had a sort of phobia. I've—I've always got panicky when I'm out on a first date.'

Her eyes filled with tears, and she blinked hard, desperate to be rid of them. She couldn't afford tears now. This was difficult enough for Ed, without making it worse by weeping. Men hated to see women cry.

Right now, Ed was standing as stiffly as a sentry guard on duty, and his eyes looked agonised. 'And you're telling me this because—'

When he stopped, Milla nodded. 'Because I panicked on our first date, when you took me to Harry's party. That kiss we had was so—' A suffocating heaviness pressed on her chest. Her eyes stung. 'It was so overwhelming,' she managed at last. 'I—I loved it, but it frightened me.'

Ed gave a stunned shake of his head, but in a matter of moments he was beside her again.

'Milla.' Her name was a mere whisper of breath.

'I'm so sorry.' She felt a little braver now that he was close. 'I've always wanted to explain. To apologise. I'm scared of things getting too passionate, you see? Getting out of control with someone I don't really know. I wanted to tell you, but it sounded so childish. I wanted to be sophisticated, like everyone else, but—' She sighed. 'I felt so silly.'

'Don't.' Ed's voice was strangled as he took her hands and clasped them in his.

As his warmth enclosed her she stopped shaking.

'Don't keep punishing yourself,' he said.

'But I've always felt bad about the way I behaved that night. Leaving you and going off with Harry. It was so immature. Stupid.'

'First-date syndrome,' Ed said softly

She looked up sharply. Was he teasing her?

But no. Although he was looking at her with a strangely lopsided smile, there was no sign of teasing in his clear grey eyes.

'It's a well-documented phenomenon,' she said, joining his attempt to lighten the moment. 'And I believe I'm a perfect case study.'

But now, Ed's smile was dying. 'Thanks for telling me this, Milla. It actually means—' His throat worked as he swallowed. 'It means a lot, more than you probably realise.'

For an electrifying moment, as their gazes held, she saw a look in his eyes that almost stopped her heart. If she'd been braver, she would have followed the urgings that clamoured deep within her. She would have taken a step closer and kissed him.

Instead, she merely wondered.

What would it be like to try for one more kiss with this devastatingly attractive man? The mere thought sent excited shivers dancing over her skin. She could already imagine the first touch of their lips, gentle and testing. Then…as happy warmth spread through her there would be a little more pressure…and she would open her lips so she could taste him.

The thought made her dizzy with delicious anticipation.

If only she were brave enough to try.

But now Ed's smile took an ironic tilt as he released her hands. Stepped back. And her lips, her whole body, went into mourning for what might have been.

'So…this begs the question,' he said, still holding that faintly sardonic smile. 'How did my little brother get it right? How did Harry handle your first date?'

'That's the thing,' Milla said with a resigned shake of her head. 'Harry didn't take me on a first date—not just the two of us alone—not for some time, at any rate. At first, there was always a crowd. Parties, sailing trips, night clubs. By the time we got…*closer*…we were more or less friends, and it…didn't feel like a first date.'

A corner of Ed's mouth quirked in a sad, wry little smile. Milla felt sad, too. Sad for the paths their lives had taken, sad because it was too late to do anything about it.

She was almost tempted to tell Ed her one last secret—that Harry had never roused her passions. Not really…

She supposed that was one of the many reasons their marriage had failed. But nothing could be gained by telling Ed about that now.

She watched him go to the sink and rinse out his coffee mug, watched his hands, watched his profile, and the way his shoulders looked so powerful, even performing this simplest action. She watched the way his dark hair fell forward onto his forehead. And a burning ache filled her throat. A terrible sense of loss swept through her, a chilling wave of misery.

It was far too late to realise that she loved him, that she'd fallen for him from the start, from that very first evening he'd swept into The Hedgerow Hotel on a wet London night, wearing his long black coat and looking so dark and dashing.

There was certainly no point in mentioning any of that, and there was only one sensible thing to do now that she'd confessed and more or less received Ed's absolution.

Despite the turbulence of her emotions this evening, she was still basically a prudent woman, so she did the sensible thing.

She said goodnight, and she went upstairs, while Ed got ready for another night on the stretcher.

CHAPTER EIGHT

ED WAS ALREADY awake when dawn crept into the bakery, spreading the first pale glimmers of wintry light. It wasn't so surprising given that he'd been restless for hours, tossing and turning on the narrow stretcher.

What a night.

When he'd first tried to get to sleep, he'd been bouncing from stunned disbelief over Milla's revelations to angry despair that he'd so easily let her slip away. It was patently clear to him now that he'd missed his best, possibly his only chance of true happiness.

Over and over, he'd kept remembering the way she'd looked as she'd told her story—so pale and vulnerable, and yet brave, too, determined to finally throw off the dark shadows of her past.

But as his mind went back to their first date—their one and only date—he asked himself why he hadn't sensed her nervousness at the time. Why hadn't he been more sensitive? Why hadn't he taken things more slowly?

The problem was, of course, that he'd wanted to kiss Milla from the moment he'd first seen her in London, and he'd thought that he'd shown enormous restraint by waiting till the party in California.

But looking back on all this now, the thing that really bugged Ed was the super-lame way he'd let Harry move in on this beautiful girl. Hell. He'd been so miffed and jealous about his younger brother's smooth manoeuvres that he hadn't even tried to reconnect with Milla after that party.

He'd been too dumb to pick up the underlying promise in her kiss, and he'd simply stepped out of the picture. Let her go.

He'd never dreamed that she'd floated around in the party scene for weeks before anything happened with Harry.

What an idiot he'd been. A total klutz. The world's biggest fool. He'd deserved to lose her.

Now, exhausted after a night of remorse, Ed lay watching the first shimmers of morning light. A rooster crowed somewhere in the distance. A car motor started up. Small birds chirped in the tree outside the bakery window. And some of Ed's gloom evaporated.

He knew things were supposed to look better in the morning, and now, with the coming of daylight, he realised that perhaps he could salvage one or two positives from this disaster.

For starters, he now knew that he hadn't imagined the heady passion and heart-lifting wildness of that long-remembered kiss. Call it male ego, but it was a relief to know that Milla's frightened withdrawal afterwards hadn't been entirely his fault.

But this was only a minor consolation, especially now that his feelings for her were growing stronger every minute that he spent with her. After this short weekend, he wasn't just fighting a longing to make love to her. He was beginning to wish he could be part of her life, wanted to make her part of his.

Wanted to throw off their pasts and start afresh.

But that wasn't going to happen. There was no point in wishing they still had a chance. Milla had made her feelings about his family very clear. And she was totally justified.

And if Ed was honest, he had little confidence that he could provide her with the happy-ever-after she wanted, the kind of secure, stable marriage that her friends Heidi and Brad enjoyed. As Milla was only too aware, Cavanaugh men were incapable of providing long-term happiness for their wives.

Ed didn't like to lump himself in the same bracket as his brother and his father, but the sad truth was his longest relationship had lasted six months. Caro, his latest girlfriend, would soon join the others who'd tired of the long hours he worked.

He supposed his main virtue was that he hadn't complicated things by marrying any of those women. But was that really a virtue? Truth was, he'd never been prepared to make promises with his heart. There were times he wasn't even sure that he had one.

Even if he tried to explain any of this to Milla, he couldn't expect her to trust him. Too much had gone wrong for her. She'd married his brother, and his brother had treated her dreadfully. And then, in the midst of heartbreak and separation, she'd lost their baby.

Now, with admirable courage and determination, Milla was digging her own way out of the emotional wreckage. She was finding her own version of happiness. What had she called it? Self-worth.

Free of Cavanaugh contamination.

If she ever contemplated another relationship, she would want a guy she could trust implicitly, and a guy who shared her values—like this self-worth idea.

Ed mulled that over again now. He knew he was trustworthy, but he was pretty damn sure he'd score low on any measure of personal satisfaction.

He wasn't sure if he'd ever truly liked himself.

And yet, if he tried to recall any moments of deep happiness and satisfaction in his life, his mind winged straight back to Michigan. He saw himself as a boy, bringing fresh farm eggs into his grandmother's kitchen, and he remembered the way she had loved him. Looking back, Ed knew that she hadn't loved him because of the exams he'd passed with flying colours, or the races he'd won, or the teams he'd captained.

She'd loved him simply because he was her grandson. Around her, he'd always felt good about himself.

His grandfather had shown him a similar brand of simple, uncomplicated love. Ed could remember standing beside the old man and looking up at the barn they'd painted—the gleaming red walls, bright and solid against a clear blue autumn sky.

'We did a good job, Ed. That's going to last your grandmother and me for years. Might even see us out.'

Ed could still remember the love shining in his grandfather's eyes, could remember the feel of his knobbly hand giving his shoulder an affectionate squeeze.

Self-worth. He'd felt it then. Even in small doses it could make a difference. A huge difference.

Of course, he'd felt it on occasions as an adult, when he'd worked late into the night to pull off a business coup. Yeah, he was proud of the way he'd steered Cavanaugh Enterprises safely through the stresses and

dangers of the recent global financial crises. But that
sense of satisfaction was hard to hang onto when he
came home each night to an empty apartment.

That was the thing about self-worth—it wasn't only
about achievement. It was about making connections
with people who mattered.

He'd had glimpses of that in the past couple of days,
when he'd experienced the heady elation of painting
these bakery walls with Milla...when he'd looked up
from the laptop and seen her smile, and again when
small chubby fingers had pushed pieces of cucumber
onto the side of his plate...

This morning, damn it, Ed couldn't help wondering—just for argument's sake—if fate offered him half
a chance to share his life with Milla, would he grab it?
Should he?

Could he, in all conscience, be certain that he wouldn't
stuff it up for her again?

After the night's revelations, Milla was a little nervous
as she descended the stairs for breakfast. She breathed
a little easier when she saw that Ed was already up and
dressed and busy making coffee.

His manner as he greeted her was friendly but cautious, giving her the impression that he was as worried
as she was about overstepping boundaries. Relieved,
Milla accepted the mug he handed her and joined him
to sit on the back steps in the sun while they drank
their coffee.

The steps weren't wide, so she was way too conscious of her proximity to Ed's massive shoulders, too
conscious of every part of Ed, actually. To distract herself, she waxed lyrical about her plans for the long nar-

row strip of tangled backyard that stretched in front
of them.

'I know it's only a weedy mess at the moment, but it
faces north, so it's perfect for growing vegetables.' She
waved her hand, pointing. 'I'll put the veggie plot right
in the middle with pavers down the centre. And I want
to make a courtyard here at the bottom of these steps,
and I'll get a table and chairs for alfresco dining, and—'

'Hang on,' interrupted Ed, with a grin. 'How do you
plan to make the courtyard?'

'With stone pavers.'

His eyes widened, and he looked both amused and
surprised. 'You? On your own?'

'Why not?' Milla responded airily. 'Pick up any gardening magazine and you'll find instructions.' Before
Ed could pin her down on the engineering details of her
courtyard, Milla hurried on. 'I want to leave sections
between the pavers for growing herbs and I'll have a
chook pen at the far end. And I'll plant nasturtiums.
Lots of lovely, bright nasturtiums. They're so ordinary,
but they always cheer me.'

Ed was watching her now with a smile that held a
hint of disturbing sadness. 'You're really looking forward to all of this, aren't you?'

Puzzled by his reaction, Milla gave a shrug. 'It'll
have to be a long-term project. The bakery will have to
come first, but I'll tackle the yard in stages.'

'You want to make a start this morning?'

Milla gave a laughing shake of her head. 'Heavens,
no, Ed. And I wasn't telling you about this in the hope
that you'll help me. I'm not your responsibility.' She
was pleased that she said this quite firmly.

She still felt thrown by Ed's willingness to help. Until he'd turned up on her doorstep, she'd only ever seen him in business suits that were imported from Milan and came with five-thousand-dollar price tags. Since he'd been here, he'd slept on a stretcher, he'd helped her with her painting and her business plan, but she couldn't possibly ask him to dig up long grass and weeds.

'I think you've earned a day off,' she said emphatically.

Attractive lines fanned from the corners of his eyes as he smiled at her. 'Will you take the day off with me?'

It was the worst moment to blush, but he was sitting so close she could almost feel his body heat, and now as he posed his invitation his grey eyes held a sparkle that lit flashpoints all over her.

'What—what would you like to do?' She looked away as she spoke, in case she blushed again.

'There's a farm near here. I read about it while I was doing the research for your business plan and I saw that they have a display section that's open to the public on weekends.'

Milla frowned. 'Since when have you been interested in farms?'

'This one grows organic wheat. Spelt and other heirloom varieties.' Ed gave a smiling shrug. 'I thought you might be curious. I know there's a growing interest worldwide in organic products. It's not just trendy. There are all kinds of benefits—both for health and economics.'

'That's true. I must admit I've toyed with the idea of making spelt bread.'

Ed was already jumping to his feet. 'Let's go, then.' He held out his hand to help her up.

* * *

It turned into one of those standout days that Milla knew she would remember for ever. A sunny winter's day with the clearest of blue skies and air as sparkling as champagne.

They drove to the spelt farm and Ed spent a surprising amount of time talking to the farmer, asking technical questions about soil and rainfall requirements and the various uses for these crops, including their benefits as stockfeed.

Afterwards, they enjoyed a picnic lunch on the banks of Bellaroo Creek, dining on a loaf of olive bread that she'd baked the day before. They ate it with slices of pecorino cheese and pickled mushrooms and, when they'd finished, they rolled up the bottoms of their jeans and paddled like children in the pretty, clear-running creek.

Milla collected several beautifully smooth, water-washed stones, including a round, smooth piece of red glass.

'I'll put these in a jar on a window sill,' she said, when she showed them to Ed. 'They'll look lovely with the sun shining through them.'

With a thoughtful frown, he picked the piece of red glass from her hand and held it up to the sun, making it glow like an expensively cut ruby.

'Don't you love it when ordinary things are suddenly stunning?' she said. 'A kind of accidental beauty.'

Ed's response was a lopsided smile, but his eyes were so shiny Milla felt a strange ache in her arms. As if she wanted to hold him.

The ache lingered as they sat on the creek bank again, letting their feet dry in the sun.

After a bit, Ed lay back, stacking his hands under his head. 'Forgive me,' he said, staring up through the overhead branches. 'But there's something I don't quite get about you, Milla. I mean, here you are, fitting back into life in the country so easily. And it seems right for you. But it makes me wonder why you took up with Harry, why you let yourself be sucked into the Beverly Hills set.'

'I know.' Milla felt suddenly cold and she hugged her jacket closer. 'When I look back now, I find it hard to understand, too. But we all make mistakes when we're young, don't we? I was hell-bent on getting away and breaking the mould. I suppose I was rebelling, like most young people do. I wanted to be the exact opposite of my parents.'

'Didn't happen that way for me,' Ed said quietly.

'No, you've followed in your father's footsteps.'

'Hoping for his approval.' The hard edge in Ed's voice was at odds with the sadness in his eyes.

Milla felt her heart go out to him. 'Gerry's a difficult man to please.'

'Yeah, just ask his three wives.' Ed grimaced as he said this and he sat up swiftly, leaned forward, propping his elbows on his bent knees.

Milla thought how at home he looked in this bush setting, dressed in a simple T-shirt and casual jeans. She liked the unpretentious way Ed seemed to live in his powerful body as if he was completely unaware of its charms. So different from Harry.

'So what would you like to do now?' he asked.

I'd like to lie here in the sun while you kiss me.

The longing was so strong she almost said the words aloud.

When she remained silent, Ed turned to her and the smouldering grey of his eyes stole her breath.

For a moment, neither of them spoke. It was happening all over again, Milla thought. That spectacular rush of awareness they'd first sensed in London.

But then, with an angry-sounding sigh, Ed got to his feet. And the moment was gone.

'Let's go back,' he said. 'And finish your painting.'

A tense silence hung over them as they drove back to Bellaroo Creek. Ed did his best to stay calm, but he was shaking inside. There'd been a critical moment on that creek bank when he'd nearly pulled Milla into his arms and played out every fantasy that had plagued him since he'd arrived here.

Now, he had to ask himself why he'd stayed this extra day, taking a drive in the country and talking to farmers and paddling in creeks. He'd come here to help Milla with her business and, instead, he'd distracted her, and he'd damn well nearly made a prize fool of himself.

Again.

For the rest of the evening, he would concentrate on practical matters. He would make sure there was nothing more he could do for Milla. For her *business*.

Tomorrow morning he would leave and no doubt they would both say goodbye with a huge sense of relief.

Milla woke to the ping of a message landing on her mobile phone. She yawned and rolled over, rubbed at her eyes and saw pale white light showing beyond the window curtains. It was too early to get up, she decided quickly. She would have enough of early mornings once the bakery opened.

Shivering, she settled back into her pillows and pulled the covers up again. The message on her phone could wait.

But just as she was comfortable another ping sounded. Milla frowned. This was unusual. Since returning to Australia, she rarely got messages, let alone two in quick succession. Could it be her parents?

Fear flared as her mind raced through possibilities. Her mother or father had taken ill during their Mediterranean cruise. They'd lost their passports. A car bomb had exploded in one of the ports—Turkey or Northern Africa.

Having thoroughly alarmed herself now, Milla leapt up and grabbed her phone. There were three missed calls, but they weren't from anyone in her address book, so that was a relief. It was probably a spammer, but just to be sure she checked for a voice message.

'Hi, Milla,' said a woman with an American accent. 'It's Sarah Goldman. I'm trying to contact Ed Cavanaugh. If you know where he is, could you please ask him to call me asap? It's urgent. Thanks.'

Milla stared at her phone in surprise, as if somehow it could provide answers. She remembered Sarah Goldman, Ed's PA. They'd met at a couple of the Cavanaugh gatherings Harry had been forced to attend.

Why hadn't Sarah rung Ed directly?

Milla glanced at the time. It was almost seven. She thought about dashing straight downstairs in her nightie—this was urgent, Sarah Goldman had said. But after a night of dreams featuring Ed in the starring role, she quickly retracted that option.

She hurried through to the bathroom instead, washed her face and ran a brush through her hair. Her curls bounced back stronger each day now that she'd given up the bleach and the straighteners. She liked what she saw in the mirror. It was like rediscovering her true self again.

Back in her bedroom, she pulled on jeans and a sweater that was the exact same shade of grey as Ed's eyes. *Stop it. Stop thinking about him every waking moment.* She shoved her feet into sheepskin slippers, picked up her phone and headed downstairs.

As she expected, Ed was still in his sleeping bag, although he couldn't have been asleep, because he rolled out as soon as he heard her coming, and he was on his feet by the time she reached the bottom of the stairs.

He was dressed in track pants and a T-shirt. His jaw was dark with a five o'clock shadow and his hair was rumpled and messy. He looked unforgivably sexy.

He sent her a sleepy smile. 'Good morning.'

Even his voice was deeper and sexier at this hour.

'Morning.' Milla forced a cheerful smile. 'I was woken by a phone call. Someone's looking for you, Sarah Goldman.'

'Sarah rang *you*?' Ed asked, frowning.

Milla held out her phone. 'She left a message asking you to call her as soon as possible. I've no idea how she found my number.'

'Sarah's a very efficient PA. Better than a bloodhound at tracking me down.' Ed sighed, ran a hand through his hair, making it even messier. 'What the hell's happened?'

He looked as if he hadn't had nearly enough sleep. 'I turned off my phone when I came out here. I wanted to take the weekend off. Obviously it was a *bad* mistake.' Bending quickly, he extracted his BlackBerry from a pocket in his travel bag, frowned at it as he waited for the messages to load.

'I'll start the coffee,' Milla volunteered.

Ed grunted his thanks, without shifting his gaze from the small screen. Then he grimaced, clearly not liking what he saw. Almost immediately, he began to swear. Loudly.

Milla knew it would be begging the obvious to ask if he had a problem, but as she busied herself fixing the coffee she hoped his problem wasn't too serious. After Harry's recent death, she was sure Ed needed a break from bad news.

The news had to be pretty bad, though, judging by the fury in Ed's face as he read his messages, and the string of oaths he continued to let fly.

'I can't believe it,' he groaned. 'Cleaver freaking Holdings. The lying weasels. After the way I bent over backwards to help them last year.'

'So it's a business issue?' Milla couldn't help asking.

Ed looked as if he wanted to hurl the phone into the wall. 'Cleaver's started a hostile takeover.'

Milla had only a vague idea what this meant. She knew the Cavanaughs had floated their company on the stock market a few years ago, but Harry had never been very interested in the business, and she'd been too absorbed with their personal problems to pay it much attention.

Throwing up his hands in despair, Ed paced to the end of the bakery, let out another, louder groan and marched back.

With an air of desperation, he held out the phone to her. 'Cleaver filed a bid for a majority chunk of our stock late on Friday afternoon. It was already Saturday here and I'd turned this damn thing off. They were trying to steal my company while I was out of the country.' He ground the words out between tightly gritted teeth.

Milla felt helpless, but she had to ask. 'Can they get away with that?'

Ed scowled. 'Not if I can help it.'

Even as he said this she could see his mind clearing its initial anger and making plans.

'I have no idea what time it is in the US, but I'll get onto Sarah,' he said more calmly. 'I know she'll answer the phone even if it's two a.m. I'll have to call a few others, as well, but Sarah will give me the latest and she can book me on the first flight home.'

'I can book you a flight.'

Ed's eyes flashed a brief, appreciative smile. 'Thanks, but it's OK. Sarah's used to this. She'll do it in a flash.' Then he was scowling again. 'I'll have to leave for Sydney straight away. Damn it. I wish it wasn't five hours away.' He shot Milla a sharp glance. 'I don't suppose I can fly from here?'

Ed was back to being a business executive, back to his true calling. But Milla knew he must be desperately worried, too. Everything that was important to him could quite possibly be slipping from beneath him. She was surprised by how much this saddened her.

'There's an airport at Parkes,' she said. 'I'll ring and find out about flights.'

'That'd be great. I'll hire a plane. A private jet. A milk crate. As long as it has wings. Anything that can fly me to Sydney.'

'I'm onto it.'

The next fifteen minutes were a whirlwind with both

Ed and Milla on separate phones, at times calling questions to each other as they sorted and settled bookings.

Incredibly, they achieved the impossible, finding flights for Ed that would take him from Parkes to Sydney in time to link up with an international departure direct to JFK in New York.

'How's your father handling this?' Milla asked once everything was settled.

Ed pulled a face. 'He's volcanic, as you'd expect. Blaming me for taking my eye off the ball.'

Before Milla could respond, Ed said, 'Don't worry about breakfast. Coffee will be fine,' and then he disappeared upstairs for a hasty shower and shave.

She felt slightly dazed by all the sudden busyness after the laid-back, relaxed mood of yesterday. When Ed came downstairs again, he looked suddenly too neat with his beard gone and his wet hair slicked back.

'At least I got your business plan sorted yesterday,' he said as Milla handed him his coffee.

'Yes, and I'm incredibly grateful.' But she felt bad, too. If Ed hadn't stayed here to write a plan for her little, unimportant business, his own VIP business might not be in trouble. She knew he would hate to see his company taken over, and now he had to fight for its independence. 'I just hope everything works out for you.'

He nodded unhappily, took another swig of coffee.

She couldn't believe how bleak she felt now that Ed was about to hurry out of her life finally and for ever.

'While you finish your coffee, I'll just check upstairs,' she said, worried that she was about to cry in front of him. 'I'll make sure you haven't left anything.'

There was only the bathroom to check, of course, and Ed had already brought his zipper bag with shaving gear down, but at least Milla had an excuse to splash water on her face, which would hopefully help to keep the tears at bay.

She was drying her face when she looked down and saw the little brush on the floor. It didn't belong to her, but it didn't look like something Ed would own either. It was an old-fashioned shaving brush with a blue and cream ceramic handle and proper bristles. Picking it up, she saw the words *Made in England* printed on the bottom.

She hurried back down, holding the brush in her curled palm and liking the solid, non-plastic feel of it.

'I think you forgot this, Ed. It was in the bathroom.' She held the brush out to him.

He looked surprised, but pleased.

When she handed it over their fingers made contact, and she felt the zap of a small lightning flash.

'Thanks,' he said. 'I wouldn't want to lose this.' For the first time this morning his brow cleared and his expression softened. 'I don't use it much, but it was my grandfather's. I guess it's just a kind of—'

'Keepsake?' she suggested.

He smiled at her. 'Yes. An important keepsake.'

'I'm glad I found it, then.'

'Yeah.' Ed ran his thumb over the soft bristles and for a moment he seemed lost in thought. Then he unzipped his pack and slipped the little brush inside. 'I've kept it as a kind of reminder of the old guy. I—I guess I wanted to be like him.'

When he straightened again, he gave a small, self-deprecating smile. 'But I don't really know why I've kept it. I've paid no attention. I've gone my own way.'

Milla said softly, 'You might be more like him than you realise.'

Ed looked at her for a long moment and he gave her a slow, sad smile. 'I'll hold that thought.'

A huge lump filled her throat and her heart was heavy as she walked outside with him into the cold morning. This was the second time she'd farewelled Ed from Bellaroo Creek, and she'd felt sad enough last time.

This time she'd discovered how deeply she cared for him and the knowledge caused a horrible, aching weight in her chest. She felt fearful for Ed, too, as if she were sending him off to an unknown battlefield.

'There's so much I have to thank you for, Ed. You came back here with the equipment. You helped me with painting the walls and with the business plan. And if you hadn't come—'

To her surprise, Ed silenced her by pressing a finger to her lips. 'If I hadn't come, we wouldn't have had that very important conversation, and I would never have understood what went wrong with our first date.'

He no longer seemed in a hurry as he traced the shape of her chin with the backs of his fingers. 'Believe me, Milla, I have no regrets.'

Her heart was pounding now. She tried to tell herself not to be foolish. Ed was a Cavanaugh. She should be glad he was going back to where he belonged.

But she'd seen such a different side to him this weekend. Against her better judgement, despite everything she knew about his family, she'd fallen for him again. 'I hope everything works out for you.'

Ed smiled. 'Thanks.' He didn't step away.

Now he was framing her face with his big hands,

holding her just so, and looking into her eyes. 'Good luck with everything.'

'You, too.'

He kissed her then. Just the loveliest kiss, sweet but incredibly intimate, and as Milla kissed him back, softly, gently, she handed him her heart, gift-wrapped, with his name on it.

The kiss was over far too quickly. Time was running out, and Ed had to leave.

'You'll do well here,' he said, flashing a quick glance around the bakery. 'Let me know when you have a date for the opening.'

She knew he wouldn't be back, but she said, 'I will, yes.' Her throat was so choked she could barely get the words out, and her eyes filled with tears. 'I hope everything works out for you and the business.'

She thought she saw a damp sheen in his eyes, but he turned away quickly, hurried around the ute, and jumped into the driver's seat.

This time, she didn't stand on the footpath to watch him drive off. There wasn't much point when she was blinded by tears.

CHAPTER NINE

ED DIDN'T WASTE a precious minute of the two hours he had to spend in the international departure lounge before his plane took off. When he wasn't receiving or making phone calls to the other side of the world, he used the time to prepare letters that would be emailed first thing in the morning to Cavanaugh Enterprise's shareholders.

Ed had to persuade their investors against selling their shares to the Cleaver group, despite the tempting, above-market prices that Cleaver was offering.

He felt sick at the thought of their company collapsing, of their employees in danger of losing their jobs. Fortunately, he and his father had established a supermajority clause when they'd floated the business on the stock market, and this meant that eighty per cent of shareholders had to approve any acquisition. Now, Ed desperately needed those eighty per cent on his side.

Sitting in the business lounge, he was oblivious to other passengers as he worked hard at rewriting and refining the message he would send out, searching for exactly the right words. He had to find the perfect, delicate balance that would appeal to his investors' emotions as well as their hard business heads.

At least, there was one good thing in the midst of this disaster—the concentrated work kept his mind off Milla.

Almost.

But there were moments when Ed caved. No matter how hard he tried to resist the temptation, his thoughts flew back to their goodbye kiss, and every time he thought about it he felt echoes of the kiss reverberate inside him like a quivering bowstring after the arrow was released. The simple kiss had been so powerful, had caught him completely off guard.

He hadn't planned to kiss Milla, but everything had unravelled from the moment he touched her. A simple touch to the soft bloom of her cheek had carried such a high voltage, and a man couldn't touch a girl like her without wanting to kiss her.

From the moment their lips touched, her response was so sweet and tender. So apparently innocent and, yet, so potent, as if they'd exchanged a secret message they dared not speak aloud.

Or was he reading too much into it?

Yeah. Surely he was getting carried away?

Damn it, when had he become such a hopeless romantic? There was every chance Milla was happy to see the back of him.

Honestly, it was probably just as well that he'd had no choice but to leave her. As his father had so angrily accused, Ed had taken his eye off the ball for one weekend, and now he was in danger of losing everything that mattered, not just to him but to everyone who worked for him. Cavanaugh's employees and their families relied on him now, more than ever.

He was relieved when his boarding call was finally announced. He wasn't looking forward to the ten-thousand-mile journey, but he was anxious to get back to New York, to get his business problems sorted. And putting distance between himself and Bellaroo Creek would no doubt provide much needed emotional perspective as well.

As his plane took off over the red roofs of Sydney, over the spectacular harbour and the sparkling beaches, he took his last view of Australia.

It was time to realign his priorities.

Mrs Jones beamed at Milla as she came into the general store with a large cane basket on each arm.

'What have you brought for us today?' the store-keeper asked as she rubbed her plump hands in gleeful expectation.

'Two more samples,' Milla told her. 'Whole-grain bread rolls and vanilla slices.'

'Vanilla slices?' Mrs Jones gave a rapturous sigh and dramatically pressed her hands against her heart. 'I can't remember the last time I ate a vanilla slice. I suppose it must have been before your parents left town.'

'Everyone mentions my parents. I'm starting to feel the pressure,' Milla said with a rueful smile. 'Fingers crossed my slices are up to scratch.'

Mrs Jones lifted a corner of the pink gingham tea towel covering one of the baskets and she grinned broadly. 'Ooh, these smell divine and they look perfect.' She gave Milla a fond, almost motherly smile. 'I'm sure you have nothing to worry about, my dear.'

Turning, she called over her shoulder, lifting her voice to reach her husband, who was busy unpacking groceries at the back of the store. 'Bob, come here quickly. Come and take a look at this. You'll never guess what Milla's brought in for us today.'

Milla laughed. 'I hope the rest of the district will be as enthusiastic as you guys.'

'Oh, they are already, Milla. Believe you me. Everyone's talking about your bakery.'

'Well, I'm very grateful to you for helping me to spread the word.'

It had been such a coup when the Joneses had happily agreed to sell samples of Milla's goods in their store throughout the lead-up to the bakery's official opening. To the Joneses' and Milla's mutual delight, the experiment seemed to be paying off.

Not only were Milla's baked goods selling well, but word was spreading. As an added bonus, this marketing strategy had also given her the perfect opportunity to sort out which products were most popular with her potential customers.

In fact, all her plans were coming together beautifully. Since the council had given their final approval, Milla's project had steamrolled ahead. She'd finished painting the shop and the workroom, and she'd set up the baking equipment, working out the most efficient positioning of each item in terms of time and motion. She'd placed orders for bulk quantities of flour and sugar and yeast.

She'd also experimented with recipes for bread, pies, cakes and slices, and she'd made careful notes of timing and quantities. Successes and failures.

Most recently, Milla had placed ads in the bakery's window as well as in the general store, and soon she would be interviewing the applicants who'd responded to the two positions she wanted to fill. She was looking for someone friendly and outgoing to help with shop-front sales, and another person, possibly a teenager, to help her each morning with slicing and packing the bread.

Each day she felt a little more excited, a little more optimistic that she really could do this. And she was touched and encouraged by the number of people who had popped into the bakery to give her the thumbs-up, and to tell her how much they were looking forward to opening day. Already, before the shop opened, she was beginning to feel a part of the town once again.

Now, Mrs Jones positioned Milla's baskets on the counter close to the cash register, and said with a coy smile, 'I don't suppose that nice American fellow will be coming back for the opening?'

Milla's heart thudded at the mere mention of Ed, even though this question was getting monotonous. Almost every day, there'd been someone in this tiny township who seemed to know about Ed. Inevitably they would slip a not-so-subtle question or comment about the nice American fellow who'd made such a stir during his all too brief stay.

Milla was trying really, really hard not to think about Ed. She'd exchanged a couple of emails with him, and he'd told her that he had strategies in place to avert the initial thrust of the takeover threat. He was hopeful that Cavanaugh Enterprises would remain intact.

He'd made polite enquiries about the bakery, which she'd answered carefully, without going too over-the-top with her enthusiasm. After their initial polite exchanges, their emails had lapsed, and she'd decided that was totally appropriate.

They had no reason to write to each other. They lived

on different continents, in different worlds with totally different lifestyles. Ed's hometown was a famous multicultural metropolis with more than eight million people while Milla's was a tiny rural town at the bottom of the world where the population had only recently crept past four hundred.

They had nothing in common... Not. A. Thing.

Apart from a couple of truly sensational kisses.

And Milla was working very hard to forget about those etched-on-her-mind events. Unfortunately, she'd been unsuccessful so far, but she would have to try harder. She didn't want anything to distract her from her goals. This was make-or-break time for her business. It was time to be strong. Time to focus on her preparation and planning.

Of course, now that Mrs Jones had thrown her the difficult question, she was watching Milla carefully as she waited for her answer. Somehow, Milla managed to smile just as she had every other time she'd faced this question.

'Ed won't be coming back,' she assured the storekeeper, and, like all the other times she'd said this, she felt a little chunk of her heart chip off and fall away.

Gerry Cavanaugh stood at the plate-glass window in Ed's penthouse office, grim-faced, hands sunk in his trouser pockets as he stared out at the skyscrapers and busy streets of Midtown Manhattan. 'So we dodged the bullet,' he said, without looking at Ed.

'Yes, it looks like we're finally in the clear.' Last night Ed had been euphoric when he'd realised that Cavanaugh Enterprises was out of danger. This morning he braced himself for the grilling he knew his father was about to deliver. After all, Gerry Cavanaugh never came to Ed's office for any other purpose than to point out his son's errors.

Still intent on the view, his father said, tightly, 'You did well, son.'

Shock erupted in Ed. In thirty-five years, this was the highest praise he'd ever received from his old man. For a moment he was too stunned to speak.

Fleetingly, he wondered if his father was all right. Could he be ill? Could this be the first signs of senility?

Ed was still reeling when Gerry turned from the window. 'But tell me this, Ed.' His voice was cooler now and yet somehow louder.

Ed's brief sense of elation fizzled and died. *Here it comes. The iron fist inside the velvet glove.*

Spearing him with his steely, ice-blue gaze, his father said, 'Why the hell did you think you were entitled to waste so much damn time in Australia?'

Ed let out his breath on a silent groan. 'Give me a break.'

'Give you a *break*? Are you for real?' Now the anger flared, as fierce and volcanic and familiar as ever. 'You took a damn break, Ed. You decided to give yourself an entire week's break, holed up in Sydney. You were supposed to be running this company and you turned your damn phone off.'

'Look, I know it was a mistake to turn off the phone.' Ed spoke quietly, in his most placating tone. He was in appeasement mode now, a role he was well and truly used to. 'I regret turning that phone off. I probably regret it more than anyone. But I wasn't having a vacation in Sydney. You know I went down there to find Milla. And when I found her, I discovered that she needed help. *Our* help. She got a raw deal from Harry. She'd lost her baby. To be honest, I was worried about—'

'I thought she rejected our help,' his father interrupted.

'Milla rejected Harry's money,' Ed said quietly and evenly. 'That's not quite the same thing.'

His father didn't look convinced.

'Another point,' Ed continued. 'Milla's not in Sydney. She's gone back to her hometown. A tiny little place in rural New South Wales.' He watched his dad with narrowed eyes. 'I thought you might understand that. After all, you grew up in a small country town.'

'I don't see how it's relevant.' But despite the snapping retort, his dad looked uncomfortable. A dark stain crept up from his shirt collar.

Ed had never really understood exactly why his father was reluctant to acknowledge his country roots. He must have had a happy childhood, growing up on the farm with loving parents, and yet, as far as Ed was aware, his dad had only gone back for one or two Thanksgivings or Christmas gatherings, and then, sadly, for his parents' funerals.

Gerry Cavanaugh had embraced the big city life and he'd poured all his energy and focus into his business. And he'd made it clear that he expected Ed, as his eldest son, to follow in his footsteps.

It wouldn't be wise to mention Milla's bakery, Ed decided now. Remembering his own reactions when he first heard about her plans, he knew he couldn't expect his father to remotely understand.

'So I assume I can trust you to stay at the helm?' His father's voice carried an all too familiar sarcastic edge now. 'There'll be no more rescue missions down under?'

'No, of course not.' Ed made a show of checking the time.

'Yes, I'm going,' his father growled. But he didn't move. He cleared his throat and looked suddenly, uncharacteristically nervous, almost red-faced. 'By the way, Ed. I guess I should tell you. I'm getting married in a couple of weeks' time.'

He didn't add the word *again*, even though this was Wife Number Four. It wasn't easy for Ed to manufacture the appropriate degree of surprised pleasure, but he managed. 'Congratulations.'

'I guess you should come to dinner,' his dad said gruffly. 'To meet Maddie.'

'Maddie?' Ed frowned. This was a new name. Last he'd heard, his father was dating a former flight attendant, half his age, called Cindy.

'Madeleine Brown. She's…a widow.'

'Right,' Ed said, intrigued. 'Thanks. I—I'd like to meet her.'

'Friday at Spiegel's, then. Eight o'clock. You'll bring Caro, I suppose?'

'Ah, no… I don't think so.' Ed dropped his gaze as he shrugged. 'There's been a parting of the ways.'

'Well, well…another one bites the dust.'

Ed was tempted to snap back that at least he hadn't made a habit of *marrying* the wrong women; he'd merely dated them. But he kept his counsel, and to his relief his father strode off, leaving him in peace.

Peace was a relative term, of course, suggesting a certain lack of restlessness. Truth to tell, Ed had been decidedly restless since his return from Australia.

He'd found the hours spent behind his desk or locked in boardrooms were ambushed by memories of that little bakery in Bellaroo Creek. All kinds of unexpected images had leapt into his focus. He would see Milla's hands, pale and distractingly graceful, even when she was busy with a rolling pin. Remembered her happy smile or her small frown of concentration as she made a lattice pattern with pastry strips over cherries.

He'd remember driving with her through the countryside in the moonlight. Her smile against a backdrop of endless fields of golden wheat. Hell, he'd even called in at a local bakery on Columbus Avenue and tried to peek out the back to see how they'd set up their machinery.

At the oddest moments, he would remember driving out to a barbecue at sunset when the sky was lavender and the wheat fields were pink and gold.

Too many times, he remembered Milla's farewell kiss, the sweetness of her lips, the soft green of her eyes, shiny with tears.

And then there was another thought, one that would have been inconceivable before he left for Australia. The thought shocked him, and he would never admit it to anyone. He could barely admit it to himself. But there were times while he was fighting to save his company when he'd wondered if the takeover would, in all honesty, be such a devastating disaster.

While Ed might have lost his job, he could have fought to save his employees'. In reality, a takeover might have left them better off. And he would have relinquished a shedload of responsibility and hard work. He would have been free to look at other options. New horizons. He'd even begun to understand why Harry had rebelled, and for the first time he was feeling less certain.

These were truly crazy thoughts, of course, and Ed had begun to wonder if the long plane journey hadn't shaken a screw loose.

Milla was standing on the footpath outside the bakery when her phone rang. 'Good morning,' she answered, smiling broadly. 'This is Bellaroo Bakery. How can I help you?'

'Hi, Milla.'

Zap!

At the sound of Ed's voice, a massive jolt almost lifted her from the ground. She had to take a calming breath before she could answer. Why was he ringing? Not another problem, surely?

'Hi, Ed.' Her heart was racing and she was breathless. 'How are you?'

'Fine, thanks. And you?'

'Terrific.' She had to stop to take another breath. 'Everything's falling nicely into place here.'

'Pleased to hear it. So what's the latest?'

'You—you want details?'

'Sure. If you have time… I'd love to hear how the bakery's shaping up.'

And, heaven help her, she wanted to tell him. 'Well… right now, I'm admiring a lovely new sign above the shop. The name's freshly painted in dark green on a cream background, and the writing's slightly curly and olde worlde. I love it.'

'Sounds neat. And you're still using the old name, Bellaroo Bakery?'

'Yes. I played around with other names. Heidi suggested Bun in the Oven, which is cute, but it reminded me too much of…' Milla swallowed uncomfortably. It still hurt to talk about the baby.

Ed made a soft sound of sympathy. 'So when's the opening day?' he asked.

'Next Monday.'

'Wow. So soon.' After a slight hesitation, Ed asked, 'Are you excited?'

'Yes, I am rather.'

'Nervous?'

She laughed. 'Very.' But before Ed could start worrying about her doing everything on her own, she hurried to reassure him. 'I've hired help, you'll be pleased to hear. I have two young mothers working half a week each, and they'll be in the shop, looking after the sales. And when they're not working, they'll be minding each other's babies.'

'OK. That sounds like a good arrangement.'

'I was thinking about someone to help with slicing and bagging, but I'm thinking I might only slice about a quarter of the loaves to begin with, and sell the others as whole loaves. I'm going for a more old-fashioned, wholesome product.'

'Yeah, I think that could work. People often associate tradition with quality.'

'That's what I'm hoping. If I need to do more slicing and bagging, I can. Sherry's young brother Ethan is interested in working for an hour in the mornings.'

'Good plan.' After a beat Ed asked, 'And who'll be helping you with the baking?'

Milla and Ed had discussed, or rather argued about, this when he was here. Even though he couldn't see her now, Milla squared her shoulders. 'I think I'll be fine on my own.'

'You *think*,' Ed said with soft emphasis.

'I *know* I'll be fine.' Now she lifted her chin.

'Those massive bags of flour won't lift themselves.'

'I'll be OK, Ed.'

'Don't forget, your mother had your father's help, Milla.'

'I'm starting on a much smaller scale.'

'That's something, I guess.'

'Please don't start trying to boss me long distance.'

'I won't. I promise.' His voice was gentle now. 'I'll just be concerned at long distance.'

Don't do that either. Forget about me. Hopeless tears stung. She said quickly, 'I thought you must have rung because you had news to share.'

'I do have news, actually. My father's getting married again.'

'Oh.' It was hard to respond to this with enthusiasm.

'I'm meeting the lucky lady tonight over dinner at Spiegel's.'

'Spiegel's? Nice. I'm treating Heidi and Brad and the kids to dinner here.'

'Sounds like fun. Say hi to them from me, won't you? You'll have a great evening.'

'I hope we will, Ed. I know it's a bit stark in the bakery, but I'll fill a few jugs with greenery and I'll have some music going. Some wine. Candles to relieve the bareness. It's really cold here at the moment, so I'm making minestrone soup and ciabatta bread.'

'You know how to make ciabatta?' He sounded incredulous.

Milla laughed. 'I've just taken a big round loaf out of the oven and it looks great. Remember when we went to that organic farm near Parkes, and I told you about the three months I spent working on an organic farm in Italy? Well, the family ended up sharing their four-hundred-year-old recipe.'

'You must have charmed them.'

'I think they were charmed by the fact that my parents were bakers. And I made them my stuffed olive bread.'

Ed's soft groan vibrated in her ear, vibrated all the way through her.

'I want to be there tonight,' he said.

I want you to be here, too.

She knew it was crazy, but she imagined Ed with her friends gathered at her table, imagined his dark, handsome face lit by a happy smile as he chatted with Heidi and Brad, as he charmed little Lucy, as his gaze met Milla's across the table.

Then reality crashed back. She sighed.

'I'll be thinking of you all,' Ed said softly, in a way that made goosebumps break out on her skin.

Don't think about us. You're making this impossible.

Tears filled her eyes and it was only as she began to swipe at them that she realised she was still standing outside her shop and people were watching her.

She hurried inside, closed the door. 'We shouldn't be talking like this, Ed.'

There was a long silence.

'You're right,' he said, and gave a heavy sigh. More abruptly, he added, 'Anyway, I have to go.'

'Thanks for calling. I hope you enjoy the dinner tonight. Pass on my best wishes to Gerry.'

'I will, thanks. And all the best to you for Monday morning. I'll have to work out the time difference so I can think of you getting up at three a.m.'

'I'm sure I'll appreciate your thoughts.'

He said goodbye.

'Goodbye, Ed. Take care.'

'You, too.'

Milla closed the phone and set it on the counter. She felt empty, like a flaking husk of wheat after the grain had been removed. Ed shouldn't have called her. He shouldn't have made her think about him, and he certainly shouldn't have let her know he was thinking about her.

It was time to forget.

She was moving on. This was supposed to be the start of her post-Cavanaugh life.

Madeleine Brown, his father's new fiancée, was sitting alone when Ed reached their table at Spiegel's.

'Your father's been delayed,' she told Ed, 'but he shouldn't be long.'

To Ed's surprise, Madeleine was older than his dad's previous wives, and not nearly as glamorous. But she had the loveliest warm brown eyes, and, despite her unruly, pepper and salt curls and her noticeable wrinkles, her smile was utterly enchanting. Ed liked her immediately.

'Call me Maddie,' she said as they shook hands.

'I'm very pleased to meet you, Maddie.'

'You won't remember me, but I've met you before, Ed.' Maddie's dark eyes held a charming twinkle. 'You were only a small boy. I was home for Thanksgiving, and I called in at your grandparents' place and met you and your mom.'

'Are you from Michigan?' Ed asked in amazement.

'Born and bred,' she responded with a smile. 'I grew up on the farm right next to your grandparents.'

Shock stole Ed's breath. He was completely blind-sided. When he could eventually speak, he felt he had to clarify this astonishing news. 'Are you telling me that you and my father were neighbours?'

'Yes, Ed.' Maddie's smile was wistful now. 'I was the girl next door.'

'That's incredible.' He let out his breath on a whoosh of surprise.

'And your father asked me to marry him when I was just twenty.'

This surprise silenced Ed completely.

Maddie, however, seemed intent on sharing her story. 'I thought I'd had enough of living on an apple orchard, so, although I was sweet on Gerry, I turned him down. I'd set my sights on bigger things, you see. I headed for Grand Rapids where I managed to get work as a doctor's receptionist, and I married the doctor's son. He was a med student about to graduate.'

Ed's mind was racing, taking this in, putting two and two together. He couldn't help thinking that Maddie's departure from the farm must have prompted his father's exit to New York. His father had been in his early twenties when he secured his first job in insurance in Manhattan. After that, he'd studied hard and become an insurance broker and he'd worked even harder to build his business.

Now, tears brightened in Madeleine's eyes as she watched Ed. And the truth of her message dawned in him like a starburst.

When this woman rejected my father, he built his

empire to show her what she'd missed. Cavanaugh Enterprises was all about her.

'You're the love of my father's life,' he said softly.

Maddie nodded. 'So he tells me.' Her mouth twisted as she tried to smile, and then she pressed two fingers to her lips as if she was stopping herself from crying.

Eventually, she said, 'Human beings are strange creatures. Sometimes we spend an entire lifetime looking for happiness in all the wrong places.'

Indeed. Ed was thinking of his father's three unhappy marriages, and his throat tightened on a painful rock of emotion. 'Did Dad ask you to tell me this story?'

Maddie smiled more warmly again. 'He wanted you to know…but you know what a proud, stubborn and uptight coot he is. He couldn't bring himself to tell you.'

That would be right. His father had never been able to express his finer feelings, or to talk about emotional topics. But he must have found the courage to say the right things to Maddie.

Ed was truly amazed by the fond warmth that flooded Maddie's face as she spoke about his dad, even when she was calling him an uptight coot. She was either a very good actor or she genuinely loved the ornery old guy.

'So how did the two of you meet up again?'

'Gerry heard that my husband had died. He waited a year, and then came to Michigan to find me.'

She said this so simply, but it told Ed a great deal about the strength of his father's feelings. He felt shaken. Moved. Happy and sad at the same time.

'How do you feel about living in Manhattan?' he asked, forcing his mind to practicalities.

'Actually, we're looking for a place in Connecticut.'

Maddie held out her wrinkled, sun-spotted hands, free of nail polish. 'Gerry and I both want somewhere with a nice garden.'

'Dad wants a garden?' Ed couldn't imagine his father pruning or weeding, couldn't picture him stopping to smell the roses.

Maddie smiled. 'If you don't believe me, you can ask him. Here he comes now.'

CHAPTER TEN

'ARE YOU ABSOLUTELY sure you wouldn't like me to stay tonight? I'd be happy to hang around on the off-chance that you need help in the morning.'

It was late on Sunday afternoon, the eve of Milla's opening day, and this was the second time Heidi had offered to stay. Milla was beginning to feel bad about turning her friend down, but she knew Heidi couldn't continue to help on a regular basis, so until the business grew this was something Milla had to learn to manage on her own.

She felt confident that she was ready. She'd experimented with dough mixtures and she'd worked out her quantities for water and yeast as well as the timings and temperatures. Already, sourdough loaves were prepared and quietly proving in cane proving baskets. The pastries for the croissants were prepared and in the fridge. Huge bags of flour were lined up beside the big dough mixer. Every bakery surface and piece of equipment was scrupulously clean.

Tomorrow, as well as the sourdough, Milla would make white, wholemeal and mixed-grain bread loaves and buns. Once the bread was baked, she would make three kinds of meat pies—plain steak, steak and onion, and curry.

She'd decided that she would only make one or two sweet things each day to begin with. Opening day, chocolate brownies and fruit scrolls would be the stars.

Every time she thought about the shop filled with fragrant golden loaves, she felt excitement rise like steam inside her. She felt good about doing this. She really did. She knew deep down that a thriving bakery could be an important step in Bellaroo Creek's revival, and she truly wanted to see this town return to the happy, busy place she'd known in her childhood.

She wanted shift workers knocking on her door at six-thirty in the morning, wanted children calling in on their way home from school, hungry labourers lunching on her pies, families making her festive cakes part of their celebrations. Her goal was to see the bakery become the community anchor it had been in her parents' day.

Last week, when her parents had rung from Venice, Milla had finally told them what she was doing. Long ago, before she'd rebelled and left town, it had been their dream to have their only daughter join them in the bakery and carry on a family tradition. So it had felt weird to make this announcement all these years later.

Milla had closed her eyes and held her breath while she'd waited for their reaction, which was, admittedly, slow to come. But once her parents recovered from their shock, they told her how proud they were. They'd rung twice since to repeat this message, and when they arrived back from their cruise they were rushing straight to Bellaroo Creek to offer her any help or advice she might need.

Having her parents onside was important, but Milla also knew she had the goodwill of others in the town. She was encouraged by clear messages that the people of Bellaroo Creek wanted her business to do well. So she felt OK about this venture. Truly OK. And she finally convinced Heidi of her certainty over an afternoon cup of tea and slice of experimental brownie.

After Heidi drove off, with a wave and a final farewell hug, Milla walked around the shop, admiring the smooth, freshly painted walls and the cabinets waiting for her loaves and buns, the stack of crisp brown paper bags ready to be filled and handed over to customers. She admired the decorative terracotta urns filled with ornamental sheafs of wheat, the cane display baskets and shelves.

She smiled at the cute blackboard with a hand-painted floral frame that Heidi had given her as a 'business-warming' gift. It was typical of Heidi's clever taste and it was the perfect touch for this shop, lending it a quaint, rustic air. Milla loved it. Picking up a fresh stick of clean white chalk, she wrote up the details of her opening day specials.

I wish Ed could see all this.

This thought brought a heavy sigh. Since his departure, Ed had muscled his way into her head far too often, and every time Milla felt a sense of loss, like someone who'd lost a limb but could still feel its presence. She kept remembering Ed here—painting walls and working at her laptop, sleeping on the stretcher, or sitting on the back steps and listening to her garden plans. Remembered him kissing her so stirringly.

Don't be stupid. He's gone.

He doesn't belong here and he's not coming back.

You don't want him back. This is the start of your brand-new life.

She was free to carve a new future, and that was exactly what she wanted, so it made no sense that she found it so difficult to let go, especially when Ed had never been hers to hang onto.

Thoroughly annoyed with herself for letting these recurring thoughts spin endlessly, Milla showered and washed her hair. Then she heated leftover soup for her early supper and she carried an oversized mug and a hunk of bread upstairs and curled on her new sofa, dining on soup while she watched a little TV. She went to bed at eight-thirty, praying she wouldn't be too excited to sleep.

When the alarm rang, Milla shot out of bed quickly, remembering exactly what day this was and everything she had to do. Charged with excitement, she dressed in a flash, flew to the bathroom, and then hurried downstairs, flipping switches and filling the gleaming-clean bakery with light.

Wow, this was it. Her big day had arrived. First, a mug of tea, just to get her started, and then she'd dive into the morning's work.

She switched on the kettle and was reaching for a mug when she heard a knock on the shop's front door.

Heidi?

Milla couldn't hold back her smile as she went to open the door. It made sense that her best friend would want to be here to help her, and, of course, she would find things for Heidi to do. She could help keep the place clean, and she could help with lugging trays and carrying bread through to the shop at the front, and she could even help with filling the pie cases.

Milla was grinning as she flung the door open. 'I should have known you'd—'

Her greeting died on her lips when she saw the tall, dark American on her doorstep.

'Hi,' said Ed.

For a moment Milla couldn't move or speak. She could only stare at Ed as a gust of chilly night wind scudded into the shop.

She was dizzied by a rush of emotions. Joy and excitement. An overwhelming urge to leap into his arms.

Ed shut the door. He was dressed in jeans and a dark leather jacket and as he came in from the cold he looked slightly dishevelled and heartbreakingly handsome, like an image on a movie poster.

It felt like an age before Milla found her voice. 'You've got to stop doing this.' She was clutching at a display stand for support, still shaking inside. 'You can't keep turning up on my doorstep when I think you're on the other side of the world.'

'I had to come,' he said as if that were all the explanation she needed.

She gave a dazed shake of her head. 'But I was talking to you on the phone just a couple of days ago. If you were planning to come back, you could have told me.'

'It was spontaneous.' He dropped his duffle bag beside the counter.

Milla still didn't understand. The Ed Cavanaugh she'd known in the past wasn't impetuous. He was careful. He was a planner. She frowned at him. 'Why didn't you ring me?'

'To be honest, I didn't want you talking me out of

this.' With a boyish smile, he shrugged out of his jacket and began rolling up his sleeves. 'I know how fiercely independent you are.' He gave a smiling shrug. 'But now that I'm here, I'm hoping you'll let me help.'

So Ed had arrived, like the cavalry in the old Westerns that her dad used to watch. He'd come to help her.

It meant he cared. For a heady moment, Milla felt her spirits shoot sky high. It was as if the sun had come out already and was shining vibrantly, brightening the long, busy day ahead of her.

But despite her excitement and joy, she was confused. Very confused, actually. And scared that she was merely some kind of intriguing amusement for Ed.

'Don't tell me you've come all this way to help with a few bread rolls and hot pies?' she challenged.

'Why not?' he said, still smiling. 'And I'm here to lift those twenty-five-kilo bags of flour.' His grey eyes gleamed. 'There's other stuff on the go that I need to tell you, but that can keep for now.'

Milla had no idea what the 'other stuff' might be, but the reality was she didn't have time to stand around chatting. She turned her thoughts to practicalities. 'You must be exhausted after your long international flight and driving out here.'

'I arrived a few hours ago and slept in the car. I'm not tired.' His teeth flashed white as he grinned. 'I'm still functioning on New York time. So just tell me when and where you need those flourbags lifted.'

She was torn between an urge to hug him and a strong desire to hit him. She did neither. She had a bakery to open in a few hours' time and Ed was right—his explanations would have to wait.

In the workroom behind them, the kettle was boiling

furiously. 'I'm making tea,' she said, and she hurried back to it and began to pour the hot water into her mug.

Ed followed. 'I'll look after my own coffee.'

'OK.'

OK. OK. Stay calm.

Milla took a sip of hot, strong tea and felt a little steadier. Already, Ed had found the coffee and the pot and he was helping himself.

And it was almost as if he'd never left.

Stop wondering why he's here. Don't get carried away with fantasies. Concentrate on the job.

Preparation and precision timing were the key elements of successful baking. Throwing off her slightly dazed feeling, Milla checked her carefully composed timetable, then measured the yeast and the water she would need. 'OK, Mr Muscles, you can tip the first bag of flour into the dough mixer whenever you're ready.'

Ed certainly made it look easy, and it occurred to her that his big powerful shoulders were designed for physical activity, rather than for hunching over a computer.

Once the hum of the mixer started up, and the flours and water began to combine, transforming quickly into a smooth dough that the mixer continued to roll and stretch, Milla began to relax. The morning was under way.

When the dough was ready, it had to be divided, and moved into the steam prover to rise. That done, Milla set a big pot of simmering beef for the pies on the stovetop, and then worked on shaping the croissants.

To her surprise, Ed's presence wasn't a problem. He was ever-ready to help and quick to pick up on the briefest instructions and, while he didn't have the knack of working with the dough, he could wield a knife and made a fair fist of adding slits in the top of sourdough and bloomer loaves.

He was also happy to help when a bench needed to be covered with flour for kneading and shaping, or when it had to be cleaned again. And he was quick to respond when Milla wanted tins or trays set out, or collected to be carried to the ovens.

His interest and enjoyment in the whole process surprised her. Even more surprising was the fact that, despite Ed's need for instruction, he didn't get in the way, or slow her down, and it was fun to have a partner helping to share the load, especially when that partner's smile made her feel as if she were floating.

But still the questions nagged at her. Why was he here? Really? How long did he plan to stay this time? Could she cope with another fleeting visit from a man whose mere presence sent her heart spinning to the moon and back?

By six-thirty, the first loaves were coming out of the huge, hot oven. First out were the round brown sourdough loaves, followed by the traditional rectangles of white and wholemeal bread, and then the country grains, which Milla had shaped into bloomer-style loaves. They looked perfect and the place smelled sensational!

'They look good enough to eat,' Ed announced with a wink and a triumphant grin as he donned gloves and hefted a huge tray of loaves, ready to carry them through to the shop.

He shot Milla a quick, searching smile. 'You want to supervise where they go on the shelves?'

And that was another thing. Ed understood and shared her excitement, but he was also careful not to overstep the mark. He acknowledged her place as owner and boss.

Now, Milla grinned back at him, and she might have hugged him if his arms weren't laden with hot trays. As she followed Ed through to the shop, she was practically dancing with relief and excitement.

By a quarter to eight, the shelves and baskets were filled with produce and the first customers were already lining up as Heather arrived to work behind the counter.

Milla longed to watch the sale of her first loaf, but she still had too much to do. The meat for the pies had cooled in shallow trays in the fridge and now, with the pastry ready, she laid the strapped pie tins out.

'You can help with this,' she told Ed. 'I'm going to spread the pastry over the tins, and the best way to press it down is with your hands, like this,' she said, demonstrating. 'Then if you get a plastic glove, you can help put handfuls of meat into each pie.'

When they'd finished this, Ed helped Milla to lift another big roll of pastry for the pie tops. They stretched this over the entire line-up, and because the edges of the tins were sharp the pressure of the rolling pin was enough to separate each pie. And they were ready for the oven.

Milla couldn't believe how hard Ed worked, approaching each task with an almost boyish enthusiasm that was contagious. Her energy felt boundless, and while she worked the customers came in a steady stream.

And so the first day rolled happily on.

It was mid-afternoon when Ed hit the wall. As they began to give the workroom a final clean-up Milla could see the exhaustion in his face.

'Go upstairs,' she ordered him, shooing him briskly towards the stairs. 'Put your feet up. Now. Go on, before you drop.'

'I should book into the pub.'

'You can worry about the pub later. I've bought a sofa, and you're welcome to use it, or—or feel free to collapse on my bed.' She didn't look at him as she said this. The mere mention of *my bed* in Ed's presence sent an infusion of heat shooting along her veins like a fast-acting drug. Making eye contact with him would have been a dead giveaway.

It was almost dark when Ed woke, and he took a moment or two to remember where he was. He saw his boots and belt on the floor, a small television screen on a low bookcase, his duffle bag by the door.

The airline tags on the bag brought everything back—his long flight from New York and the drive out to Bellaroo Creek from Sydney, the exhilarating morning.

These were the rooms above Milla's bakery.

When a slight creak sounded, he knew it was the bathroom door opening. A moment later, Milla appeared in the doorway with a towel wrapped around her.

It was then that Ed remembered that the only route from the bathroom to Milla's bedroom was through this small sitting room. Knowing she would hate to be caught out, he quickly closed his eyes, feigning sleep.

At least…he *almost* closed his eyes, but not quite. Only a man in a coma could resist taking a good long peek at Milla Brady wearing nothing but a towel.

She had wound her coppery hair into a knot on top of her head and secured it with a tortoiseshell clip, giving him a perfect view of her pale, graceful neck and shoulders. The towel reached mid-thigh, so there was also a good deal of her bare, shapely legs on display. An added bonus was the hint of her delicious curves beneath the towel. Her skin looked so smooth and pale his fingers ached to touch.

Miraculously, he found the self-restraint to stay perfectly still on the couch. He wanted this woman, wanted to make her his, but he had to play his cards very carefully. It didn't matter that he was going mad with wanting her—he'd promised himself that he wouldn't rush. She was too important to him. He understood her fears now, and he couldn't risk scaring her off.

When Milla was halfway across the room, however, Ed realised that she'd stopped and had turned his way. And she just stood there as if she was looking down at him. With his eyes closed, he couldn't see her next move, but the room was so quiet he could hear his own breathing, and it wasn't exactly calm.

He sensed Milla coming closer, bringing with her the lingering scent of the jasmine soap she'd used in the shower.

He opened his eyes.

Damn it, he had to.

'Oh!' Instinctively, Milla clutched the towel she'd knotted over her breasts, and a bright pink blush spread from her neck to her cheeks.

'What time is it?' Ed asked with a theatrical yawn.

'Ah—around five-thirty. In the afternoon.' She looked delightfully embarrassed. A blushing Botticelli vision in an apricot and white striped towel.

'I went for a run,' she said, her green eyes round and serious, as if it was important that he understood exactly why she was here. 'If I want to stay on top of this new workload, I need to keep fit. And—and then after the run, I had a shower.'

She was talking quickly to cover her nervousness. And yet, Ed noticed with deep fascination, she didn't scuttle away like a startled crab. She didn't rush to her bedroom and slam the door on him. And while he knew he had to take this carefully, Ed had no intention of lying down when his heart's desire was a breath away.

Slowly, purposefully, he got to his feet. To his intense relief, Milla didn't step back from him.

Milla couldn't have moved, even if she'd wanted to. She was mesmerised by the sight of Ed lying there on her sofa, and she would defy any girl not to take a closer look at such masculine perfection.

She had feasted her eyes with a top-to-toe inspection, starting with Ed's thick dark hair, untidily awry, his eyelashes, dark and sooty against his cheeks, the sexy rock-star stubble on his grainy jaw.

She admired his broad shoulders stretching the thin fabric of his T-shirt, and the lovely, manly length of him. His taut stomach. Long legs in jeans. Even his bare feet fascinated her. What a size they were.

And it was absolutely amazing to know that Ed had come all this way to see her. Not to boss her around, but to help her. Again.

She'd run away from him once and lived to regret it, and it was a miracle that he knew this and had still come back to her.

On many levels it didn't make sense, but Ed had told her he would explain. Now, however, he rose from the sofa and stood square in front of Milla. He was touching close, kissing close, and she was naked beneath her towel, and Ed didn't look like a man intent on explanations.

Milla's heart skipped several beats. *Ask him why he's here.*

He smiled at her. 'Am I right in assuming that we're safely past the first date?'

'That's a funny question,' she said, thrown by its unexpectedness. 'Are you angling for another kiss?'

Ed touched her on the elbow, and that simplest contact sent rivers of heat under her towel.

'Must admit, I'm not in the habit of asking.'

She was sinking beneath his spell. *I should be demanding answers. Now. Before it's too late.*

But Ed was already moving in closer and he spoke softly, next to her ear. 'I've missed you, bakery girl.'

I've missed you, too. So, so much.

If she let Ed kiss her now, she knew she would end up in bed with him, and, oh, Lordy, she was melting at the very thought. But she also knew very well that she would end up more deeply in love with this gorgeous man. And how could she let that happen when there were still so many unanswered questions between them?

With huge reluctance, she placed her hands firmly in the centre of his chest, holding him at bay. 'Ed, we haven't talked yet. You haven't told me why you've come back.'

He gave a choked groan.

'It's a fair question,' she said defensively.

His response was a wry, sad smile. 'Milla, give a man a break. You're standing here in nothing but a towel. You're driving me wild, and you want to interrogate me.'

'It's not that I want— It—it's just that—' Her head was swimming. Her hands were still pressed against the brick wall of his chest, holding him away from her, but what she really wanted was to have him close again. Holding her.

She couldn't stop thinking about his farewell kiss. She wanted his arms around her, his lips sealed to hers.

And before she'd properly sorted her thoughts, Ed covered her hands with his own, folding them, holding them against his shirt.

'I have questions, too,' he said softly. 'I need to know if I still terrify you.'

She was sinking fast. 'You don't,' she whispered.

And then…he touched his lips to hers, just the briefest, softest brush… 'What about now?'

Already, she was halfway to meltdown. 'No. Not scared.'

'And now?' he asked, drawing her into his arms.

Now, she was lost in a blaze of longing. She wanted his lips, his hands, his body.

'Not afraid,' she whispered in a breathy gasp as she slipped her arms around his neck, as she looked clear into his eyes and lifted her lips to meet his.

The first mouth-to-mouth touch was magic. It ignited the fire she'd felt on the night of their very first kiss all those years ago, inducing a jolting reaction that rendered her reckless and wanton.

She felt no fear. This was the man who'd worked side by side with her today. The man who'd travelled hemispheres to be with her for this first important day. When he picked her up and carried her to the bedroom, she couldn't find a single reason to resist. She simply gave a soft yearning sigh and pressed her lips against his neck.

Ed lowered her to the bed and he looked down at her, and his eyes were shiny as he traced his fingertips over her heated skin, following the edge of the knotted towel.

'You're so beautiful,' he said softly. 'I'll never forget the first time I saw you in London. I wanted to make you mine straight away.'

She knew she would cry if she thought about the wrong paths she'd taken, so she pulled him down to her and kissed him again, kissed him long and hard till the aching knot of tears in her throat eased.

Oh, how she loved the taste and feel of him. On a wave of rekindled need, she slipped her hands under his T-shirt and slid her palms over his smooth, warm skin, over his muscly shoulders that she'd admired so often.

Impatient now, she helped Ed out of his T-shirt and her heat and longing mounted as he lowered his jeans.

His eyes were smouldering now as he flipped the ties on her towel, and Milla took a deep breath as it fell away. For a scant moment she felt vulnerable beneath his smoky gaze, but as he let his palm glide over the curve of her hip he let out a soft, deeply appreciative sigh. And this time, when he leaned in to kiss her, she felt both safe and triumphant.

She belonged in Ed's arms. He belonged in her bed. They made love with desperate need and with the excitement of new discovery that was interlaced with heart-lifting moments of exquisite tenderness.

With each murmured endearment, with each kiss and touch, Ed took her to new heights of pleasure and release, and she cried from the sheer, piercing joy of it.

Afterwards, she lay for ages with her head on his chest, listening as the drumming of his heartbeats slowed.

And then she turned to him. 'I guess that's answered your question.'

He fingered a tendril of hair from her forehead. 'So you're still OK?'

She'd never had such an attentive and considerate, sexy lover. 'I'm certainly OK, Ed. I'm very OK.' She didn't think she'd ever felt so OK.

He'd made this long day perfect.

CHAPTER ELEVEN

TWILIGHT HAD GIVEN way to night.

Milla turned on a bedside lamp, rolled out of the bed and stood smiling down at Ed. 'You must be hungry.'

He gave a soft laugh. He hadn't given dinner a thought. He was still floating on a cloud of warm elation, still coming to terms with the surprising turn this day had taken.

So much for his plans to take things slowly with Milla...

No wonder people used terms like bewitched and black magic to explain explosive attraction. From the moment he'd touched her he'd been a lost man.

Now, she shot him an exceptionally happy grin as she pulled on jeans and a white sweater.

'Come downstairs, when you're ready,' she said. 'Hungry or not, I'm making dinner.'

From the doorway, she looked back at him over her shoulder and her green eyes flashed a warning. 'And over dinner, I guess you'd better tell me exactly what you're doing back here in Australia.'

Fair enough, Ed thought. He only hoped he could tell his story in a way that convinced her.

There was a storm outside now and sheets of rain

lashed at the windows in wintry gusts as he came down the stairs. The bakery was warm, though, and filled with glowing light as well as the fragrant aroma of simmering tomatoes and herbs.

'Pasta OK for dinner?' Milla asked as she set a pot of water on the stove.

'You must be tired of cooking.'

She shrugged. 'Not really.' She turned the gas high, set a lid on the pot, gave the sauce in the other pot a stir. 'Would you like a glass of wine?'

'To celebrate your successful first day?'

Her eyes danced. 'I think we deserve to celebrate, don't you?'

'Sure.'

They grinned happily at each other once again, and Milla reached for a bottle of rich dark red wine and poured it into two glasses.

'Thanks for your help, Ed.' She handed a glass to him, and her eyes held a dancing smile. 'Thanks for everything.'

A look passed between them that made Ed's heart leap. 'Congratulations to our master baker!' he said.

They clinked glasses and drank, and their smiles held echoes of the new intimacy they'd so recently shared.

'So, I haven't asked,' Ed said as Milla turned her attention to the cooking pot. 'Are you happy with the day's takings?'

'Very happy. We've sold out of almost everything, and people are already starting to leave orders.'

'That's fabulous.'

'I know.' She gave a little skip of triumph. 'I did it! *We* did it.'

But then her expression sobered. She turned from the

stove and picked up her glass, looked down at it, and seemed to study it for a minute or two. Then she lifted her gaze to look directly at him. 'So,' she said quietly, with a worried little smile. 'Are you going to tell me now exactly why you've come back here?'

He knew it was vital that he got his answer right, and he told her the simplified truth. 'As I said before, I've missed you.'

Her eyes widened. And despite their recent love-making, pink bloomed in her cheeks and she took a deep sip of wine.

'I like being with you, Milla. I've always liked being with you.'

Her small smile flickered and vanished like a snuffed candle, and she quickly looked down at her glass again, carefully running her finger around its rim. 'That's nice, Ed. I—I really like being with you, too. But I'd like to understand more. I mean—I'm assuming this is another quick visit? You're an American high-flyer, after all. So what's happening with your business? How can you afford to be here when you've just escaped a takeover by the skin of your teeth?'

'They're all valid questions. And I want to explain. Honestly, I've always planned to explain. It's a long-ish story, though.'

'I'd like to hear it.'

And so Ed told her.

Milla served up their food in deep dishes and they dragged out stools and sat at the bench, sipping wine and swirling rich pasta with their forks, while he told her about his father and Maddie Brown and how their story had lit all kinds of lightbulbs for him. He told her about his grandparents and the farm in Michigan, about the apple orchards and the red barn, and the long summer afternoons beside the Kalamazoo River.

'I've spent my whole life trying to please my father,' he said. 'I've worked as hard as I could at the business, always hoping for some small sign of approval from him. And then I realised in the middle of the Cleaver takeover that my heart wasn't really in it. If I hadn't been so worried about our employees' futures, I could have let the company go.' Ed snapped his fingers. 'Just like that.'

Milla blinked. 'But you were always so dedicated.'

He let out a heavy sigh. 'It was the shock of my life to find out that Cavanaugh Enterprises was all about my father's ego. Or at least, to discover that he could turn his back on it in a heartbeat.'

'For Maddie Brown?' Milla finished softly.

Ed nodded.

She looked thoughtful as she gathered up their plates and carried them to the dishwasher. 'So what's happening to the company now?'

'Just before I left, I settled new negotiations with Cleaver and we're now prepared to let them take over as long as they can guarantee that they'll retain all our employees.'

Milla's face was pale. 'You've handed your company over?'

'Yes.'

'And then rushed straight here?'

'Yes.'

She was shaking her head now. 'But that's crazy, Ed. You can't be thinking straight. You can't have thought this through.' Now she was pacing, wringing her hands.

'Milla, it's OK. Don't get upset about this.' Ed tried to reach for her, but she pulled away.

'I'm sorry. I'm worried. Of course I'm worried. When you first came here and found out about my bakery plans, you accused me of having a knee-jerk reaction to Harry and the baby and everything. Maybe you were right, but I'm happy with my choice. But now, I think you're doing the same thing. You're overreacting to your father's news.'

'Well, if I am, it feels damn right.'

'But—' Closing her eyes, she pressed her fingers to her temples. 'I don't think I can take all this in right now.'

'It's been a long day, and I'm sorry, Milla. The last thing I wanted was to add to your worries.' Ed scratched at the annoying, two-day-old roughness on his jaw. 'Maybe you need a good night's sleep. If you like, I can book into the pub.'

'Actually, I've already done that for you, Ed. While you were sleeping.'

He tried not to mind that she was obviously keen to evict him, but he felt as if everything was unravelling. He'd come here to help her, to take things slowly and to explain the whole situation, to share his hopes, his plans, and instead he'd rushed in and bedded her.

Great work, Brainless.

He wished he could expand on his explanation now, wished he could appease Milla's justifiable concerns, but he knew that she must be exhausted. Her day had started at three a.m.

His only option now was to hope that he could find new and better ways to convince her that he cared. Truly cared. That he would never hurt her. But he would have to leave that till tomorrow.

'I'll get my things,' he said and he was up the stairs and back again in a flash.

At the front door, Milla looked miserable. 'If you'd stayed here, Ed, the whole town would know about it by morning.'

'Of course. Best to avoid the small-town gossip.' He pulled on his jacket.

She opened the door a chink. It was still windy and rainy outside, and she chewed anxiously at her lip. 'The people in this town have already plied me with questions about the nice American.'

He couldn't bring himself to smile. 'It's OK. You don't have to justify sending me to the pub.' He kissed her cheek. 'Don't worry about any of this. Get a good night's sleep.'

She nodded. 'You, too.'

'See you in the morning.' Ed set off, head down, into the rainy night, with the grim sense that he was dangling over a precipice.

Milla closed the door and leaned back against it, closing her eyes, wishing she didn't feel so unbearably lonely now. In her head she knew she'd done the right thing by sending Ed away. She had to protect herself.

She just wished her heart could agree.

Don't think about him. Just go to sleep...

Heaven knew she desperately needed sleep. She'd had a huge day, the biggest day of her life, and there would be another one just like it tomorrow.

But how could she sleep now? she wondered as she trudged back upstairs. In a few short hours, Ed had swept back into her life and he'd completely stolen her heart. But he'd left her mind whirling with a thousand thoughts and questions.

She'd been a fool to start kissing him and more or less lure him into her bed *before* she'd asked *all* her questions. If only she'd heard his impossible story first.

The idea of Ed Cavanaugh walking away from his family business was incredible. The thought of him leaving New York was impossible.

And now she felt guilty and worried that she'd unwittingly lured him here. Had she somehow given him the wrong signals?

Or were they, miraculously, the right signals?

Her mind was whirling with fatigue and nervous exhaustion as she tried to sort out the bare facts.

Ed was attracted to her, certainly. No doubt about that. And he'd amazed her this morning with his help in the bakery.

But what was one morning? One night?

She was planning to put down roots here. She would be working in the bakery day after day, week after week, and Ed's interest could be nothing more than temporary at best.

And yet, knowing this, Milla had helplessly fallen in love with him. Even now, she felt swoony and breathless whenever she thought about his lovemaking. But how could she have made such a foolish mistake?

Arrgh. She had no chance of going to sleep.

The alarm sounded at three a.m.

Milla dragged herself out of bed and didn't allow herself to think about the hours of sleep she'd missed. She dressed quickly, pulled her hair into a scrunchie, splashed her face with cold water and hurried down-stairs.

Just as she had yesterday, she flicked on the lights and filled the kettle, and like yesterday there was a knock at the door.

Her stomach flipped. She hadn't really expected Ed to turn up so early.

When she opened the door and saw him standing there, tall, dark and hunky, eyes holding a cautious smile, she felt her heart twist as if he'd skewered it.

'Top o' the morning,' he said and his breath made a puff of white cloud in the frosty air.

He smiled at her, smiled with his eyes, as if he was asking her to trust him.

I want to, Ed. So much.

She let him in and closed the door quickly. 'I hope you've caught up on your jet lag,' she said.

'I feel fine,' he answered quickly. 'How about you?'

'I'm fine,' she lied, suspecting that he'd lied, too. There were shadows beneath his eyes that hadn't been there yesterday.

'So, is it the same routine today?' he asked as they made their respective mugs of tea and coffee again, and Milla collected yeast and water.

'That's right.' She felt an urge to touch him, to give him a tiny sign of hope, but she made herself be sensible. 'You can put in two bags of flour whenever you're ready, thanks.'

At least, her spirits lifted once again as the ingredients began to mix. She was determined to enjoy this second day, despite her tiredness, despite her nagging worry that Ed was about to shatter her heart.

She knew she loved him, and she suspected that Ed

believed he loved her, but she couldn't take off and spend her life with him. She was committed to this place now and she really wanted to make it work. The alternative option of Ed Cavanaugh settling down in the Bellaroo Bakery was positively ludicrous.

An overwhelming attraction wasn't enough to bridge the huge gap between their lifestyles and allegiances. Even love wasn't enough. Last night Milla had been round and round this problem, rolling and pummelling it like kneaded dough, but this morning she knew there was no solution.

In a way, she was grateful for the hard work ahead of her today. She had to give one hundred per cent concentration to every task, couldn't afford a single mistake. Each loaf and bun and pie had to be perfect.

One thing she couldn't deny—Ed really stepped up to the plate. As an assistant on his second day, he couldn't be faulted. He was a quick learner, of course, and his aim was to lighten her load. Which he did in a thousand and one small ways.

'I reckon you could easily sell at least another dozen bread loaves,' decided Carol, who'd been working in the shopfront, and had made a list for Milla, which she presented at the end of the day.

'White and grainy are the most popular,' she said. 'And pies. By crikey, those Main Roads guys bought up almost all your pies in one hit.'

'What about the sweet things?' Milla asked.

'Well, we have six advance orders for cherry lattice pies for the weekend already.'

Milla laughed. 'I can see what I'll be doing on Saturday mornings from now on.'

'You're going to need to train an apprentice,' suggested Ed.

She nodded tiredly. 'One step at a time.' She rubbed at the back of her neck, trying to ease a nagging headache.

'You should put your feet up. It's my turn to shout dinner,' he said.

'That'd be nice, but I think I should go for a run again. The fresh air will clear the cobwebs.' *And with luck it will tire me out completely.*

'I'll join you.'

That wasn't what she'd planned and she almost protested. All day she'd been super-aware of Ed. Every glance, each exchange, every time they touched, even an accidental connection like bumping elbows, she'd felt a flash of heat, a clutch of longing.

She'd hoped to gain a little clarity and distance on this run. But after the big day Ed had put in to help her, she couldn't reject his company now, especially when she knew he was used to attending the gym and going for regular runs.

'That'd be great,' she said. 'See you in ten.' And she went upstairs to change into a tracksuit and joggers.

At least the rain had stopped, but it was a cold grey dusk with no sign of a sunset as they set off, running down a dirt road and dodging puddles.

Ed matched his stride to Milla's and they jogged side by side along the empty road, past wheat fields and paddocks of sheep where kangaroos grazed in the shadowy verges. When the road dipped to cross a creek, they found stepping stones, then picked up their pace and ran on.

Apart from the thudding of their footsteps, the only sound was the keening cry of a lone falcon circling high above them, floating on the wind.

It was almost dark when Ed saw the sign on the edge of the road. Milla had been pushing herself to keep up with him and she was quietly relieved when he slowed down.

'Hang on,' he said. 'I'd like to check this out.'

'You planning to buy a farm, Ed?' she joked as she stood beside him, hands on hips, panting slightly.

'Just curious.'

'This is the Johnsons' place.'

'You know it?'

Milla nodded. 'As far as I remember, it was a good farm. A mix of sheep and wheat. Lovely homestead.'

He turned to her with a smile. 'I saw the house up on the rise back there. Lots of trees.' There was a silvery flash of excitement in his grey eyes.

'But you're not looking at property, are you?' Milla was suddenly uncertain again.

Instead of answering her, Ed just stood there, staring at the sign.

'Ed, what's this about? Why are you suddenly interested in a farm?'

'I'd like to take a closer look,' he said. 'You know me, always on the lookout for a good investment.' But he said this with a shrug, as if he was trying to make light of it.

She was definitely uneasy now. 'You're not thinking of buying it?' The possibility made her head spin.

'Don't look so worried.'

But she *was* worried. Worried that Ed was getting

carried away. Worried that he was acting completely out of character and rushing headlong into disaster.

'We should be heading back,' she said. 'It's almost dark.'

'You're right,' he agreed, but with clear reluctance. 'We can talk about the farm when we get back.'

Milla worried the whole way back to town.

She deliberately 'dressed down' for dinner, choosing an unromantic turtle-neck black sweater and jeans. It was time for another round of straight shooting with Ed. She couldn't afford another night of emotional turmoil.

She'd agreed to meet him in the pub's dining room, so she was surprised when she found him waiting on her doorstep. Again.

'Slight change of plans.' He gave her a jagged smile as he held out a metal container. 'Hope you don't mind, but I talked the chef into giving me a takeout dinner. Thought we could use a little privacy.'

Privacy...

Milla was slugged by equal jolts of delight and dismay. Privacy with Ed could be fabulous, but also dangerous. At least she was on guard tonight, and she knew she had to seize this chance to set the record straight with him.

'So what are we eating?' she asked as she led him back inside.

'Salt and pepper calamari and Chinese greens.'

'Yum. Good choice. I've just realised how hungry I am.'

She found plates and cutlery and set them on the bench, while Ed grabbed a serving spoon and ladled out generous helpings. The cat came meowing around their legs.

'There might be leftovers if you're lucky,' Ed told Blue, who settled to purr sleepily at their feet.

Milla tried not to think about how cosy and familiar and downright pleasant this dining arrangement was. And she also tried to ignore how attractive Ed looked, showered and shaved, sitting opposite her in a dark V-necked cashmere sweater over a blue and white striped, collared shirt. She had to ignore the enticing whiffs of his aftershave, too, had to forget how positively blissful he'd been in bed.

It was time to focus on setting him straight.

Perhaps he sensed this. He was more subdued as they started eating, and Milla didn't want to spoil their digestion, so she kept their conversation light and easy while they ate, filling Ed in with news about Heidi and Brad and their children, about her parents, about the Joneses in the general store and how helpful they'd been.

But eventually they finished eating and Ed collected their plates and took them over to the sink. Then he came back and sat on a stool, choosing the one beside Milla rather than opposite.

He was smiling, but the smile was a little grim around the edges, and he zeroed straight in on the topic they'd been avoiding all day.

'We've got to talk about us, haven't we?'

'We have,' Milla said softly as tension tightened knots in her stomach. 'I must admit, I'm still very confused about why you're here.'

'I'm not,' he said quietly. 'I know exactly why I'm here.'

Her heart drummed hard.

'It's simple,' Ed said and the look in his eyes was both tender and fierce. 'I want you.'

Those three words *I want you* speared deep inside her, stirring a longing so deep and painful she almost wept. *I want you, too.*

But how was it possible?

'Any terms,' Ed went on. 'Any conditions. You on your native soil. Wherever you want to be, I want to be there with you, Milla.'

Tears filled her eyes. She felt thrilled and scared at once. Ed was reaching for the impossible, trying to make it sound workable.

'I was planning to court you,' he said. 'You know… the unrushed, old-fashioned, patient style of courting.'

She managed to smile at this. 'Isn't that supposed to happen before you rush a girl into bed?'

'That's the general advice.' Reaching for her hand, he looked down at it as he cradled it in his large palm. 'The thing is, Milla, I'm not just crazy in love with you. You've taught me things.'

She knew she looked surprised. She couldn't imagine what he meant.

'When I was here before,' he said. 'You talked about self-worth and you set me thinking. I've asked myself what I needed to change, if I wanted to be someone I really liked. If I wanted to *do* something that felt right. Felt good. Worthwhile. And every time the answer was the same.'

'And it had nothing to do with being CEO of Cavanaugh Enterprises,' Milla guessed.

'Damn right.'

She was remembering now how Ed's eyes had shone when he'd talked about his grandparents in Michigan.

She remembered finding the shaving brush that he'd almost left behind on his last visit.

I've kept it as a kind of reminder of the old guy. I—I guess I wanted to be like him.

At the time she'd told him: *You might be more like him than you realise.*

'So, is this the real Ed Cavanaugh?' she asked softly.

'I think it must be.' Ed gave a shaky laugh. 'We can make it work. I know it.'

The sincerity in his eyes was unmistakable. It filled her with golden light. With sudden glorious courage. 'I believe you.'

She did. At last, amazingly, she truly did believe.

'The main thing is I love you, Milla. I'm hoping against hope that you might love me. I—I know we Cavanaughs have—'

'Shh.' Milla slipped from her stool and took both his hands in hers. 'Let's not talk about Cavanaugh history tonight.'

Ed had gone out of his way to prove his love for her through word and deed, and now she lifted his hands to her lips and kissed his fingers.

Looking up, she smiled bravely, confidently into his eyes. 'I love you too, Ed. I've been scared to admit it, but I know that's crazy considering that I actually fell for you on the first night we met.'

Feeling light-hearted with happiness and certainty now, she slipped her arms around his neck. 'I—I adore everything about you, you gorgeous man. How you look, how you move, how you think, how you kiss. And now you've gone out of your way to help me, and—'

She didn't quite get to the end of her soliloquy. Ed

cut off her words with the most beautiful of kisses, on her lips, on her chin, her neck…

And they didn't finish that particular conversation for a very long time.

By then, their clothes were scattered on the floor and they were curled close in bed, and, having just made love again, they were exceptionally happy and sleepy.

'You realise we now have a second chance to get this right,' Ed said softly.

'Yes.' Milla nestled, deep and warm into the cay of his shoulder. 'This is how we were meant to be.'

'I couldn't let you go a second time.'

Milla smiled up at him. 'I'm so glad you're persistent.'

After a bit, she said sleepily, 'I'm still worried that you haven't thought the bakery part through, though. I can't believe you'll want to work in a bakery for ever.'

'You're right,' he admitted. 'That's why I've checked out the Johnsons' farm.'

'Already?'

He dropped a kiss on her frowning forehead. 'When I went back to the hotel, I stole a quick look on the Internet. The farm has nine dams and a creek, eleven well-fenced paddocks, a machinery shed, three silos…'

Milla tried, unsuccessfully, to hold onto her frown, but a smile broke through. 'And what would you grow in these eleven well-fenced paddocks?'

'Sheep. Organic wheat. Heirloom varieties.'

'So I could bake it?'

Gently, he brushed a strand of hair from her cheek. 'I thought we could employ an artisan baker.'

'But I've only just started.'

'Well, we're certainly going to need another baker when we start our family.'

She'd been on the brink of a yawn, but now her sleepiness vanished in a flash of excitement. 'You want a family?'

'We have to help fill the Bellaroo Creek school, don't we?' Ed drew her into his arms again. 'Isn't it our mission to rescue this town?'

'I knew there was another reason why I loved you.'

EPILOGUE

MILLA SAT ON the edge of the hospital bed, dressed and ready to leave. She was too excited to bother about morning tea. She just wanted to gaze and gaze at the sweet precious bundle in her arms.

Her baby's name was Katie Margaret, named after Ed's paternal grandmother and Milla's mum. She had dark hair like her daddy's and the cutest, neat little nose and ears and the daintiest mouth and hands and feet.

Perfection, in other words, from head to toe.

And now, the little girl yawned and stretched. *Just like Ed,* Milla thought with a happy grin.

Right on cue, her husband appeared in the doorway. 'How are my bride and my firstborn?' he asked, striding into the room proud as punch.

'Ready and raring to go.' Milla flushed with happiness as he came in and kissed her. Ed was still the best-looking guy she'd ever met.

'Has Katie grown while I've been away?' He leaned down to make cooing noises at his daughter.

'I'm sure she's definitely grown cuter and brighter overnight.'

'Spoken like a very proud mom.'

But now, Ed's grey eyes searched Milla's face, as if

he wanted to make sure she really was OK. He'd been a little shaken by the whole business of birthing and he seemed to find it hard to believe she'd bounced back so quickly.

'How's everything at the bakery?' she asked to divert him.

'Absolutely fine. Cooper's managing brilliantly.'

Cooper Jackson, a former shearer's cook, had taken to baking like the proverbial duck to water. Training him had been Milla's latest project. And she and Ed had also sponsored him to have extra experience at an organic bakery in Tasmania. Now he was living in the rooms above their shop and running the show.

'Hey, sweet pea.' Ed touched Katie's hand, watching her tiny fingers unfurl and stretch. 'Ready to come home?'

'Home to a nursery that your daddy has painted from top to bottom and made fit for a princess?' added Milla.

'Home to baby lambs, and a black and white dog and a ginger cat,' said Ed, who was truly in his element now that he was a farmer, a husband *and* a father.

Milla was bursting with happiness, too. She had to pinch herself as she looked around at the profusion of flowers and cards and stuffed toys that had been sent or hand delivered by family members and friends and customers from the bakery.

She couldn't help remembering that other lonely time, over two years ago now, when she'd sat in a bleak, empty hospital room, grieving for her lost baby, and wondering what on earth she would do with the rest of her sad, sorry life.

'I've brought boxes to cart all these things,' Ed said

as he began to gather up the bouquets. 'I'll take them to the car and come back for you. You'll soon be home.'

Home. Their favourite place to be.

They drove from the hospital in Parkes, with Katie safely in her little capsule in the back of their all-wheel drive. Home through the familiar countryside, with fields of wheat shimmering in the soft breeze and with ewes and new lambs grazing in the morning sunlight.

Home to a sprawling low weatherboard house, painted white and surrounded by wisteria-covered trellises, flower gardens and trees.

They adored their comfy, rambling farmhouse with its sunny, north-facing kitchen and its huge fireplace for winter. Together they'd established the vegetable gardens and chickens that Milla had always wanted, as well as a newly planted orchard that meant so much to Ed.

And now a spare bedroom had been painted white with bright colourful trims.

As Ed turned off the main road down the gravel road to their farm Milla felt a rush of happiness and a sense of fulfilment beyond her wildest dreams.

Her parents were arriving in two days' time to admire their granddaughter and to help her settle into motherhood. Gerry and Maddie Cavanaugh were coming the following month. Since Ed's marriage they'd come down under every six months, alternating with Ed and Milla's trips to the US, and each time Milla and Ed saw Gerry he seemed happier and more deeply content.

'All Maddie's work,' he told them with a grin.

'Now,' said Ed as he pulled up at the front of their house. 'There's one more surprise here for you.'

She grinned, thinking of more long-stemmed roses. Or perhaps a bottle of champagne.

'You won't have to cook for the next three months,' Ed said.

Milla blinked at him. 'Are you offering to look after our meals?'

'I don't have to. Our freezer's full to overflowing. Just about every housewife in the district has turned up here with a foil-covered casserole.'

'Wow,' Milla said softly. 'That's amazing.'

'Not so amazing considering everything you've done for this community.'

Perhaps that was true, but it had all been fun.

Milla suspected that she would remember this moment for ever as she climbed out of the vehicle and as she watched Ed carefully extract their baby girl from her capsule. Her heart was as light as a dawn breeze as she hooked her arm through her husband's and the three of them went inside.

* * * * *

PATCHWORK FAMILY
IN THE OUTBACK

BY
SORAYA LANE

Writing for Mills & Boon is truly a dream come true for **Soraya Lane**. An avid reader and writer since her childhood, Soraya describes becoming a published author as 'the best job in the world' and hopes to be writing heartwarming, emotional romances for many years to come.

Soraya lives with her own real-life hero on a small farm in New Zealand, surrounded by animals and with an office overlooking a field where their horses graze.

For more information about Soraya and her upcoming releases visit her at her website, www.sorayalane.com, her blog, www.sorayalane.blogspot.com, or follow her at www.facebook.com/SorayaLaneAuthor

This book is dedicated to my incredible support crew...
My mother, Maureen, because I wouldn't be able
to write one book without you helping me with
the 'little emperor' on a daily basis,
and Natalie and Nicola for our fabulous emails and
chats. I'm so lucky to have you all in my corner.

ARE YOU OUR NEW TEACHER?

- *Do you love children and like the idea of running a small country school?*
- *Do you want a fresh start in a welcoming rural town?*
- *Do you want to be a cherished part of our community?*

Then come visit us in Bellaroo Creek! If you're a dedicated teacher capable of running our small school, then we'd love to meet you. Rent a home for only $1 a week and help to save our school and our town.

CHAPTER ONE

POPPY CARTER STOOD in the center of her new class-room and clasped her hands behind her back to stop them from shaking. Had she taken on more than she could handle?

The desks were lined against the walls with chairs stacked on top of them, and the floor was clean and tidy, but it was the walls that were sending shivers down her spine. Where was the fun? Where were the bright colors that should adorn the room to welcome young pupils?

She sighed and walked to the main desk, pulling out the chair and sinking into it. Her problem was that she'd always been at schools with a half-decent budget, and she knew that this school was barely able to keep the doors open, let alone redecorate.

Poppy dropped her forehead to the desktop before resting her cheek against it instead and staring at the wall. She had a lot to do before tomorrow, and there was no way she was going to start her class in a room like this.

New beginnings, a fresh start and a bright future.

That's why she'd come here, and she was determined to make that happen.

"Hello?"

Poppy sat bolt upright. Either she was hearing things in this spooky old room or there was someone else here.

"Hello?"

The deep male voice was closer this time. Before she could call back, it was followed by a body. One that filled the entire doorway.

"Hi," she said, glancing toward the closest window, planning her escape route in case she needed one.

"I didn't mean to disturb you." The man smiled at her, one side of his mouth turning up as he nudged the tip of his hat and leaned into the room. "We've had a bit of trouble here lately and I wanted to make sure there weren't any kids up to no good."

Poppy swallowed and nodded. "I'm probably not meant to be here myself, but I wanted to have a good look around and see if there was anything that needed doing."

Chocolate-brown eyes met hers, softer than before, and matched with a dimple when the man finally gave her a full smile. "I take it you're the famous Ms. Carter, then?"

Poppy couldn't help grinning back. "Take out the famous part and call me Poppy, and I'd say that's me."

He chuckled, removed his hat and stepped forward, hand extended. There was a gruffness about him that she guessed came with the territory of being a rancher, but up close he was even more handsome than he'd been from a distance. Strong, wide shoulders, a jaw that looked as if it had been carved from stone and the deepest dark brown eyes she'd ever seen....

Poppy cleared her throat and clasped his hand.

"Harrison Black," he said, hand firm against hers. "My kids go to school here."

Right. So he was married with children. It didn't explain his lack of a wedding band, but then plenty of ranchers probably never wore a ring, especially when they were working. But it did make her feel less nervous about being in the room with him.

"How many children do you have?" she asked.

The smile was back at the mention of his children. "Two. Kate and Alex. They're out there in the truck."

Poppy looked out the window, spotting his vehicle. "I'm just heading back to my place for some supplies, so how about I say hi to them?"

He shrugged, put his hat on his head and took a couple of steps backward. The heels of his boots were loud on the wooden floor, making her look up again. And when she did she wished she hadn't, because *his* eyes had never left hers and a frown was hovering at the corners of his mouth.

Instead of acknowledging him she reached for her bag and slung it over her shoulder, and when she looked back he was already halfway to the door.

"Ms. Carter, what made you come here?"

She met his gaze, chin held high, not wanting to answer the man standing in front of her, but knowing it was a question she'd be asked countless times from the moment she started meeting locals—as soon as her pupils began flooding through the door, parents anxiously following them.

"I needed a change," she told him honestly, even if she was omitting a large part of the truth. "When I saw the advertisements for Bellaroo, I figured it was time for me to take a chance."

Harrison was still staring at her, but she broke the contact. Walked past him and down the short hall to the front door.

"And a new haircut or color wasn't enough of a change?"

She spun on the spot, temper flaring. This man, this *Harrison*, didn't know the first thing about her, but to suggest a haircut? Did she look like some floozy who just needed a new lipstick to make her problems go away?

"No," she said, glaring at him, feet rooted to the spot. "I wanted to make a difference, and keeping this school open seemed pretty important to your community, unless I've been mistaken?"

His eyes gave away nothing, his broad shoulders squared and his body grew rigid. "There's nothing more important to me than this school staying open. But if you don't work out? If we've taken a chance on the wrong person? Then we don't just lose a school, we'll lose our entire town." He sighed. "Forgive me if I don't think you look like a woman who could go a week without hitting the shops or beauty salon."

She let him pull the door shut and marched toward his vehicle, desperate to see his children. Right now they were the only things that could cool her down, and the last thing she wanted was to get into an argument with a rude, arrogant man who had no idea what kind of person she was or what she believed in. To even suggest... She swallowed and took a deep breath.

"I think you'll find I know exactly how much this school means to Bellaroo Creek," she said over her shoulder, in a voice as calm as she could manage. "And please don't pretend you know me or anything about me. Do I make myself clear?"

She could have sworn a hint of a smile flashed across Harrison's face, but she was too angry to care.

"Crystal clear," he said, striding past her.

If she hadn't known two little children were watching them from the truck, she would have poked her tongue out. But Poppy just kept walking, and sent up a silent prayer that she'd never have to talk to their father ever again.

Harrison knew he'd behaved badly. But honestly? He didn't care. Speaking his mind to the teacher hadn't exactly been his best move, but if she didn't hang around, then their town was done for. He'd needed to say it now because if she changed her mind they'd have to find someone else *fast*. The future of Bellaroo Creek meant more to him than anything. Because otherwise he'd lose everything he'd ever worked for, just to keep his children close.

He swung open the passenger door. "Kids, this is your new teacher."

They looked out—all angelic blond hair and blue

eyes. A constant reminder of their mother, and probably the only reason he didn't still hate the woman.

"I'm Ms. Carter." Harrison listened to the new teacher introduce herself, watching the anger disappear from her face as soon as she locked eyes on his children. "Your dad found me in the middle of planning your classroom."

"Planning?" he asked.

She smiled and leaned against the open door, but he had a feeling her happy expression was for his children's benefit, not his. "I can't teach young children in a room that looks like the inside of a hospital," she told him. "I don't have long, but in the morning it'll look deserving of kids."

"You're making it look better?"

Harrison grinned as his daughter spoke. She played the shy card for all of a minute with strangers, then couldn't keep herself from talking.

"I want us to have fun, and that means putting a smile on your face from the second you walk through my door in the morning."

So maybe she wasn't so bad, but it wasn't exactly evidence that the teacher would hang around for the long haul. He'd had enough experience to know that an isolated rural town wasn't exactly paradise for everyone, especially for a teacher expected to teach children of all ages.

"If you need a hand…" he found himself saying.

She smiled politely at him, but he could see the storm still brewing in her eyes. "Thank you, Mr. Black, but I'm sure I can manage."

He stared at her long and hard before walking around to the driver's side. "I'll look forward to seeing in the morning what you've done with the place."

The teacher shut the passenger door and leaned in the window. "Your wife won't be dropping the children off?"

Harrison gave her a cool smile. "No, it'll be me."

He watched as she straightened, a question crossing her face even though she never said anything.

"I'll see you kids tomorrow," she called out, walking backward.

Harrison touched his hat and pulled out into the road, glancing in the rearview mirror to see her standing there still, one hand holding her long hair back from her face, the other shielding her eyes from the sun.

She was pretty, he'd give her that, but there was no way she was going to stick it out here as their teacher. He could tell just from looking at her. And that meant he had to figure out what the hell he was going to do if she left. Because staying in Bellaroo wasn't going to be an option for him if the school closed down, nor any of the other families who loved this town as much as he did.

"Daddy, don't you think we should help our teacher?"

Harrison sighed and glanced back at his daughter. "I think she'll be fine, Katie," he told her.

She sighed in turn. "It's a pretty big classroom."

Harrison stared straight ahead. The last thing he needed was to grow a conscience when it came to their new teacher, and he had errands to run for the rest of the afternoon. But maybe his daughter had a point. If he didn't want her to up and leave, then maybe he needed to make more of an effort. They all did.

"We might go back later on and see what we can do. How does that sound?"

"Great!" Katie was elbowing her brother, as if they'd both somehow managed to pull the wool over his eyes. "We could take her dinner and help her do the walls."

Harrison stayed silent. Helping Ms. Carter redecorate? Maybe. Taking her dinner? *Hell, no.*

CHAPTER TWO

HARRISON LIKED TO think of himself as a strong man. He worked the land, could hunt and keep his family alive and comfortable in the wilderness if he had to, and yet his seven-year-old daughter managed to wrangle him as if he were a newborn calf.

"Dad, I think she'll like this."

He stared at his pint-size kid and tried to look fierce. "I am *not* buying a cake to take her."

Katie wrapped one arm around his leg and put her cheek against his jean-clad thigh. "But Daddy, it wouldn't be a picnic without a cake."

"It's not a picnic," he told her, "so there's no problem."

His daughter giggled. "Well, it is, kind of."

He looked at the cake. It did look good and they were being sold for charity, but what kind of message would that be sending if he arrived to help with *cake*? Taking sausages, bread and ketchup was one thing, because he could let the kids help their new teacher while he used the barbecue out back. But this was going too far.

"Daddy?"

He tried to ignore the blue eyes looking up at him, pleading with him. And failed. "Okay, we'll take the cake. But don't go thinking we'll be spending all night there. It's just something to eat, some quick help and then home. Okay?"

Katie smiled and he couldn't help but do the same back. His little girl sure knew how to wrap him around her finger. "Come on, Alex," Harrison called.

His son appeared from behind an aisle and they finally reached the cashier. Harrison had known old Mrs. Jones since he was a boy and was still buying his groceries from her and her husband.

"So what are you all doing in town today?"

He started to place items on the counter. "Had a few errands to run, so we're a bit out of sequence."

"And now we're going to see our new teacher," announced Katie.

"So you've already met Ms. Carter?"

Harrison frowned. He didn't like everyone knowing his business, even if he did live in a small town with a gossip mill that ignited at any hint of something juicy. "We're going to help her make some changes to the classroom, aren't we, kids?"

Katie and Alex nodded as he paid for the groceries and hauled the bags from the counter.

"It's mighty nice to have someone like Poppy Carter in town. Like a ray of sunshine when she came in this morning, she was."

He smiled politely back. He didn't need to feel any worse about how he'd spoken to her earlier, because no matter how much he tried to think otherwise, he did care that he'd been rude. It wasn't his nature, and he realized now it might have been uncalled for. Did he doubt that she'd stick it out? Sure. But maybe he should have been more encouraging, rather than sending her scurrying back to wherever she'd come from before she'd even started.

"So what do you think?"

Harrison looked up and squinted at Mrs. Jones. He had no idea what she'd just asked him. "Sorry?"

"About whether she has a husband? Suzie Croft met her and was certain she had a mark on her finger where a ring had been, but I told her it was none of our business why she'd come here without a husband." The older woman tut-tutted. "We advertised for someone looking for a fresh start, and that's what we can give her. Isn't that right?"

Harrison raised an eyebrow. Mrs. Jones liked to gossip better than all the rest of them combined. "I'd say we'll just have to wait to find out more about Ms Carter, once she's good and ready to tell us her business."

Who cared if she was married or not? Or whether she had a husband. All he cared about was that she was kind to his children, taught them well and stuck around to keep the school from closure. Tick all three off the list and he wouldn't care if she was married to a darn monkey.

"Thanks," he called over his shoulder as he carried the groceries out the door. "See you later in the week."

The little bell above tinkled when he pushed the

door open. He waited for his kids to catch up and race past him.

An hour at the school, then back home—that was the plan. And he was darned if he wasn't going to stick to it.

Poppy was starting to think she'd taken on more than she could cope with. The room was looking like a complete bomb site, and she didn't know where to start. It wasn't as if she could just pop down to a paint store and buy some bright colors to splash on the walls. Here it was do it yourself or don't do it at all.

She sighed and gathered her hair up into a high ponytail, sick of pushing it off her face each time she bent down.

Right now she had a heap of bright orange stars she'd cut out from a stack of paper, ready to stick together and pin across one wall. Then she planned on decorating one rumpty old wall with huge hearts and stars made with her silver sprinkles, before drawing the outline of a large tree for the older children to color in for her. She had stickers of animals and birds that could be placed on the branches, but for everything else she was going to have to rely on her own artistic skills. And her own money.

She didn't have as much of that as she was used to, but at least being here meant she didn't have anywhere to spend it. Groceries from the local store, her measly one-dollar rent and enough to keep the house running—it was all she needed, and she was going to make it work.

"Hello?"

Poppy jumped. Either she was starting to hear things or she wasn't alone. Again. But surely it wasn't…

Harrison Black. Only this time he brought his children with him into the room.

"Hey," she said, standing up and stretching her back. "What are you guys doing here?"

Harrison held up two bags, a smile kicking up the corners of his mouth. "We come bearing gifts," he said.

She grinned at the children as they stood close to their dad, both smiling at her. So this was his way of apologizing—coming back with something to bribe her with.

"You're not here to help me, are you?" she asked them, crouching down, knowing they'd approach her if she was at their level.

It worked. Both children came closer, shuffling in her direction.

"Now, let me try to remember," she said, looking from one child to the other. "You're Alex—" she pointed to the girl "—and you're Katie, right?"

They both burst out laughing, shaking their heads.

"No!" Katie giggled. "*I'm* Katie and *he's* Alex."

Poppy laughed along with them before glancing up at their dad. "I'm glad that's sorted then. Imagine if I'd got that wrong tomorrow?"

The children started to inspect her bits and pieces, so she moved closer to Harrison. She wasn't one to hold grudges, and with two happy children in the room, it wasn't exactly easy not to smile in his direction. Even if he had been beyond rude less than a few hours earlier.

"So what's in the bag?" she asked him.

"A peace offering," he replied, one hand braced against the door as he watched her.

Poppy just raised her eyebrows, waiting for him to continue.

"Dinner for us all."

Her eyebrows rose even farther at that. "Your idea or theirs?" she asked, hooking a finger in the kids' direction.

Harrison sighed, and it made her smile. She guessed he wasn't used to apologies or to being questioned. "Theirs, but it was a good one, if that makes it sound any better."

Poppy was done with grilling him. "I'm just kidding. It's the thought that counts, and I'm starving."

He held up the paper bags and cringed. "I just had a really bad thought—that you might be vegetarian."

She shook her head. "I'd like to be, but I'm not." Poppy took the bags from him and placed them on an upturned desk. "I love that they still use paper bags here."

"Plastic is the devil, according to Mrs. Jones, so don't even get her *started* on that topic." Harrison stood back, letting Poppy inspect the contents. "Although she has an opinion about most things, so that kind of applies for any questions you throw her way."

Poppy laughed and pulled out the cake. "Now, this is what I call a peace offering!"

A hand on her leg made her turn.

"The cake was my idea." Katie pointed at it. "Daddy said no, but…"

"Uh-hmm." Harrison cleared his throat, placing a

hand on his daughter's shoulder. "How about you help Ms. Carter and I'll head out and fire up the barbecue?"

Poppy grinned and let Katie take her hand and lead her back to the pile of things she'd been working on.

Harrison Black might be gruff and forthright, but his daughter had him all figured out.

Poppy looked over her shoulder as he walked out the door, bag under one arm as he strode off to cook dinner. His shoulders were broad, once again nearly filling the doorway as he passed through. And she was certain that he'd be wondering why the hell he'd let his daughter talk him into coming back to help her.

Harrison was starting to realize he hadn't planned this at all. They had no napkins, no plates and an old pair of tongs was his only usable utensil. His one saving grace was that the ketchup was in a squeeze bottle.

He looked up to see his children running toward him. It was still light, but that was fading, the day finally cooling off. He usually loved this time, when he came in for the day and settled down with his kids. And he was thinking that tonight they should have just stuck to their routine.

Poppy appeared then, walking behind his children.

"They couldn't wait," she called out. "Their stomachs were rumbling like they'd never been fed!"

He grinned, then tried to stop himself. What was it about this woman? She had him smiling away as if he was the happiest guy in the world, her grin so infectious he couldn't seem *not* to return it.

"Dad, is it ready yet?" Alex was looking up at him as if he were beyond starving.

"We have a few technical issues, but so long as you're okay with no plates and wiping your fingers on the grass—" he nodded toward the overgrown lawn "—then we'll be fine."

Poppy came closer and took out the loaf of bread, passing a piece to each child. "Sounds fine to me," she said. "Sauce first or on the sausage?"

"Both," Katie replied.

"Well, okay then. Sauce overload it is."

Harrison tried not to look at her, but it was impossible. Even his children were acting as if they'd known her their entire lives.

He knew he should be happy. A teacher who could make his children light up like that should be commended. But there was something about her that worried him.

Because there was no going back from this. If she left, then…it wasn't even worth thinking about.

All he could do was get to know her and make sure he did everything within his power to convince her to stay.

He cleared his throat and passed her the first sausage, which she covered with lashings of ketchup.

If only he could stop staring at the way her mouth had a permanent uptilt, the way her eyes lit up every time she spoke or listened to his children or the way her ponytail fell over her shoulder and brushed so close to her breasts that he was struggling to avert his eyes. Because none of those things were going to help him.

Just because he hadn't been around a beautiful woman for longer than he could remember didn't give him any excuse to look at her that way. Besides, he was sworn off women...for life.

"So what do I need to know about Bellaroo?"

Harrison blinked and looked at Poppy, her head tipped slightly to the side as she looked up at him.

"What do you want to know?"

Poppy wrapped Alex's sausage in bread before doing her own and joining them on the grass. It was parched and yellowed and in definite need of some TLC, but she didn't mind sitting on it. Besides, it was either that or the concrete, so she didn't really have a choice.

"So what's happened to this place? I mean, is it just that too many families moved away from here, or is there something else going on that I don't know about?" she asked Harrison.

He was chewing, and she watched the way his Adam's apple bobbed up and down, the strong, chiseled angle of his jaw as he swallowed.

She needed to stop staring. For a girl who'd moved here to get away from men, she sure wasn't behaving like it.

"Are you asking me if the town is haunted? Or if some gruesome crime happened here and made all the residents flee?"

Harrison's tone was serious, but there was a playful glint to his eyes that made her glare at him mockingly.

"Well, I can tell you right now that I searched the place online for hours but couldn't come up with anything juicy," she teased in return. "So if it's been hidden that well, I guess I can't expect you to spill your guts straight off the bat."

Now it was Harrison laughing, and she couldn't help but smile back at him. His face changed when he was happy—became less brooding and more open. He was handsome, she couldn't deny, but when he grinned he was…pretty darn gorgeous. Even if she did hate to admit that about a man right now.

"Honest truth?"

Poppy nodded, following his gaze and watching his children as they whispered to each other, leaning over and looking at something in the long grass.

Harrison drew his knees up higher and fixed his gaze in the distance. "It's hard to bring fresh blood into rural towns these days, and most of the young people that leave here don't come back. Same with all small towns." He glanced at her, plucking at a blade of grass. "I've stayed because I don't want to walk away from the land that's been in my family for generations. It means something to know the history of a place, to walk the same path as your father and your grandfather before him. This town means a lot to me, and it means a lot to every other family living here, too."

Poppy nodded. "Everyone I've met so far seems so passionate about Bellaroo," she told him earnestly. "And I really do believe that if you fight hard enough, then this town will still be here by the time *you're* a grandfather."

He shrugged. "I wish I was as positive as you are, but honestly?" Harrison sighed. "I never should have spoken to you the way I did earlier, because if you don't stick around, then there's no chance we'll be able to keep our school open. And that'll mean the end of our town, period." He blew out a big breath. "Being sole-charge teacher to a bunch of five- to eleven-year-olds isn't for the fainthearted, but if you do stay? There won't be a person in Bellaroo who won't love you."

Now it was Poppy sighing. Because she didn't need all this pressure, the feeling that everything was weighing on her shoulders.

Before she'd moved here, she'd taken responsibility for everything, had tried to fix things that were beyond being repaired. And now here she was all over again, in a make-or-break situation, when all she wanted to do was settle in to a gentler pace of life and try to figure out what her own future held.

"Sorry, I've probably said way too much."

Poppy smiled at Harrison's apology. "It's okay. I appreciate you being honest with me."

The kids ran over and interrupted. "Can we go back and finish the room?"

"Of course." Poppy stood up and offered Harrison a hand, clasping his palm within her fingers. She hardly had to take any of his weight, because he was more than capable of pushing up to his feet without assistance. But the touch of his skin against hers, the brightness of his gaze when he locked eyes with her, made her feel weak, started shivers shaking down her spine.

"How about I join you in the classroom after I've tidied up here?"

Poppy retrieved her hand and looked away, not liking how he was watching her or how she was feeling. "Sure thing. Come on, kids."

She placed a hand on Alex's shoulder and walked with them the short distance to her new classroom.

Their dad was gruff and charming at the same time, and it wasn't something she wanted to be thinking about. Not at all.

She was here to teach and to find herself. To forget her past as best she could and create a new life for herself. *Alone.*

Which meant not thinking about the handsome rancher about to join her in her classroom.

"Wow."

Poppy looked down, paper stars between her teeth as she stood on a chair and stuck the last of them to the wall. There was already a row strung from the ceiling, but she was determined to cover some old stains on the wall to complete the effect she was trying to create.

"Your children are like little worker bees," she mumbled, trying to talk without losing one of the stars.

"Little worker bees who've started to fade," he replied.

Poppy glanced back in his direction and saw that he'd scooped Alex up into his arms. The young boy wasn't even pretending he was too big to be cuddled, and had his head happily pressed to his father's chest as he watched her.

"It's getting pretty late. Why don't you head home? I'll be fine here." She wobbled on the chair, but righted herself before it tipped.

"How about we give you a lift home?"

Poppy shook her head. "It's only a short walk. I'll be fine, honestly."

Harrison didn't look convinced. "What else do you need to do here?"

Hmm. "I want the kids to walk in tomorrow and not be able to stop smiling," she told him. "So I need to put the glue glitter over the hearts in the middle, and the same with the border over there—" she pointed "—because that's where I'm going to write all their names in the morning when they arrive, in their favorite colors."

She heard Harrison sigh. Which made it even crazier when, from the corner of her eye, she saw him put his son down on his feet and pick up a gold glitter pen.

"Is this what you use for the fancy border thing?" he asked.

Poppy took the remaining paper stars from between her teeth and bit down on her lower lip to stop herself from smiling. She nodded, watching as Harrison walked to the wall and started to help.

"Like this? Kind of big, so it's obvious?"

"Yep, just like that," she said, still trying to suppress laughter.

From what she'd seen of him so far, she had a feeling he'd just storm out and leave her if she made fun of him for using the glitter, and she didn't mind the help. Not at all. Even if a masculine rancher wouldn't have been her first choice in the artistic department.

She stepped down and pushed her chair back behind

her desk before finding the silver glitter and covering some shapes at the other end of the wall from Harrison.

"Daddy, we didn't eat the cake," called out a sleepy-sounding Katie.

Poppy had forgotten all about the cake. She moved back to look at the wall, pleased with the progress they'd made. The children could help her decorate it more in the morning, but for now it looked good.

"How about we finish up and reward ourselves with a piece? What do you say?" she asked.

Harrison passed her the pen as his kids nodded. "Only problem is we don't have a knife."

She gave him a wink. "But I have a pocketknife. That'll do, right?"

He stared at her, long and hard. "Yeah, that'll do."

Poppy pulled it out and passed it to him, careful not to let their skin connect this time. "Well, let's each have a big piece, huh? I think we all deserve it."

And hopefully, it would distract her, too. Because she might be done with men, but she sure wasn't done with chocolate.

CHAPTER THREE

"THANKS FOR THE ride." Poppy swung her door shut and waved to the children in the back. She didn't expect to hear another one open and close.

"I'll walk you to the door."

What? She hadn't ever had a man walk her to the door just to be chivalrous.

"Thanks, but I'm fine. It's not like we're in the city and I'm at risk of being mugged," she joked.

The look on his face was anything but joking. "I'm not going to drive you home and not walk you to the door. It wasn't how I was raised, and if I want my daughter to grow up expecting manners, and my son to have them, then I want to make sure I set a damn good example."

"Well, when you put it like that..." She smiled at Harrison, shaking her head as she did so.

"I know I'm old-fashioned, but then so is this place. You'll realize that pretty soon, Ms. Carter."

"There's nothing wrong with old-fashioned," she said. And there wasn't; she just wasn't used to it. "Except, of course, when it comes to plumbing."

His eyebrows pulled together as he frowned. "You having problems with this place?"

She waved her hand toward the door as they reached it. "The shower produces just a pathetic drizzle of water, and the hot doesn't last for long. But for the price I'm paying I wasn't exactly expecting a palace."

"I'll see what I can do," he told her.

"Honestly, I shouldn't have said anything. Everything's fine."

Harrison stood a few steps away, cowboy hat firmly planted on his head, feet spread apart and a stern look on his face. "I'll take a look myself, check it out. Maybe later in the week."

"If you're certain?" She didn't want him going out of his way, but if he could work his magic on the shower she'd be more than grateful.

"I'm certain," he replied. "You take good care of my kids at school and I'll make sure your house doesn't fall down around you. Deal?"

"Deal." This guy was really something. "You better get those children home. Thanks for all your help tonight. I'm glad you came back."

"So we could start off on the right foot second time around?" he asked, one side of his mouth tilting into a smile.

"Yeah, something like that. And thanks for the lift."

Harrison tipped his hat and walked backward, waiting until she'd gone inside before he turned away. Poppy leaned on the doorjamb and watched him get into the car and drive slowly off, trying hard not to think about how nice he was.

Considering she'd wanted to make a voodoo doll of him and stab it after his comments earlier in the afternoon, she'd actually enjoyed his company. Or maybe it was just that his children were really sweet.

She shut and locked the door.

Who was she kidding? The guy was handsome and charming, or at least he had been this evening, and she was terrified of how quickly she'd gone from hating the entire male population to thinking how sexy the rancher dad was.

And she couldn't help but wonder why the children had never mentioned their mom and why he'd never spoken about the wife that was surely waiting at home for them.

Poppy walked down the hall and opened the fridge, reaching in for the milk and pouring some into a pot to heat. There was no microwave, so it was old-fashioned hot chocolate.

A scratching made her stop. Another noise made a shiver lick her spine.

Poppy reached for another pot and crept slowly toward the back door. She was sure she'd locked it, but… She jumped. Another scratching sound.

She slowly pulled the blind back and looked outside, flicking the light on with her other hand. If someone was out there, who was she going to call for help?

Meow.

It was a cat. Poppy put the pot down and unlocked the door, standing back and peering out into the pool of light in the backyard.

"Are you hungry?" she asked, knowing it was stupid to ask the cat a question but not caring.

She left the door open and walked back for the milk, taking a saucer and tipping some in. Poppy placed the dish inside the back door and waited. It didn't take long for the black cat to sniff the air and decide it was worth coming in, placing one white paw on the timber floor, looking around and then walking to the saucer.

Poppy shut the door and relocked it. The cat was skinny, and she wasn't going to turn him out if he had nowhere to go.

"Want to sleep on my bed?"

The cat looked up at her as he lapped the milk and she went back to stirring her own, adding some chocolate to melt in the pot with it.

"I think we'll get on just fine, you and I," she said. "Unless you go shack up with someone better looking or younger than me down the road. Then I'll know my life's *actually* over. Okay?"

The cat stayed silent.

Black cats were supposed to be bad luck. Heaven help her if there was any more of *that* coming her way. Because she'd had enough bad luck lately to last her a lifetime and then some.

"Come on, kitty," she said, pouring her hot chocolate into a large mug. "Let's go to bed."

Harrison pulled onto the dirt road that led to Black Station and glanced in the rearview mirror. Katie and Alex were both asleep in the back, oblivious to everything going on around them, and he didn't mind one bit. All he wanted was for them to be happy, because if they were happy, *he* was happy.

And they had had a pretty nice evening.

He pushed all thoughts of their new teacher from his mind, but struggled to keep her out of it. She'd been kind, sweet, polite—not to mention the fact that she was the prettiest woman he'd seen in years—but there was still something about her niggling away at him. Something that meant he didn't believe she'd be able to stay. Or maybe it was just that he didn't believe anyone could stick it out here unless they'd been born and bred in a rural town.

His wife sure hadn't. And part of him believed that if a mother couldn't even stay to care for her own children, then Poppy Carter wouldn't stay for other people's children. Maybe he'd expected someone older, someone less attractive. Not a woman in her late twenties with long, straight hair falling down her back and bright blue eyes that seemed to smile every time she looked at his children. Not a beautiful, modern woman who looked as if she should be lunching with friends or shopping in her spare time.

But then, maybe he was being unfair. Just because she liked to look pretty and wear nice clothes didn't mean she wouldn't be able to make a life here for herself. For all he knew she could have her own personal demons that had sent her scurrying away from her former life.

Harrison pulled up outside the house and went to open the door before going back to the truck to carry his children one at a time into their bedrooms. They might be five and seven years old now, but they were still his babies. He'd raised them himself and he was determined to fight to keep their school open. Because he wouldn't ever let them feel as if they'd been abandoned, and that meant boarding school wasn't an option he was willing to consider, not until they were ready for high school.

Their mom had walked out on them, and he didn't ever want them to think he'd do the same. They were his children, his flesh and blood, and he would do anything in his power to protect them. No matter what.

But if he could fix up the teacher's house and make life a little easier for her here in Bellaroo Creek, then he would do it. Because instead of pushing her away, he was going to do everything within his power to convince her to stay.

He'd like to think that his reasons were based purely on keeping his children happy. He had a feeling that part of him, some deep, dark part that was hidden away under lock and key, liked the look of Poppy. A lot. Even if he wouldn't ever be ready to admit it.

Old Mrs. Jones had been right. Poppy arriving in their town was like a beaming ray of sunshine descending upon the place, and they were long overdue for someone like her to be their lucky charm. It wasn't just his children at stake here, it was the future of their entire town.

Poppy Carter was going to keep Bellaroo Creek alive, or she was going to be the final straw that closed the area for good. He just had to believe that she was going to be their falling star—the once-in-a-lifetime teacher that they had only ever dreamed of.

Harrison shook his head and flicked the television on, falling onto the sofa. Maybe he'd been reading too many fairy tales to Katie. Because he was actually starting to believe that maybe Poppy was that person, after all.

Poppy's stomach had a permanent flutter in it. She'd barely been able to eat any breakfast, she was so nervous, and now she was sitting in her chair, thrumming her fingers across the timber surface of her desk.

She sat and stared at the wall they'd decorated the night before, smiling as she thought of big, gruff Harrison using her fairy glitter so they could finish up and head home. She'd met lots of great dads in her time as a teacher, but even she hadn't expected him to volunteer with *glitter*.

The slam of a car door made her snap to attention. *It was happening.* Her first day as sole teacher of Bellaroo Creek School had officially begun.

Poppy stood and crossed the room, pinning the door back to welcome the first of her pupils. A smiling mom was headed her way, three children running ahead of her, straight toward Poppy.

"Slow down!"

She grinned as their mom yelled at them. They skidded to a halt in front of her just before they reached the door.

"Hi, kids. I'm Ms. Carter, your new teacher."

The three boys looked up at her, not saying a word,

but she could tell straight away from their cheeky expressions that they were going to be a handful.

"Hi."

Poppy held out her hand. "You must be pleased school's starting," she said, touching the mother's shoulder before stepping back. "I know how exhausting three boys can be."

"I just hope they don't send you running for the hills. Twenty kids each day would drive me crazy."

Poppy shook her head. "I do this because I love it, so don't worry about a few rowdy children scaring me away." She looked across the yard and saw a familiar truck pulling in close to the curb. "Besides, I'm told the lovely Mrs. Leigh volunteers one day a week as teacher aide." Poppy waved a hand. "Here are the Black children, nice and early."

The other woman followed her gaze. "You've met the Black family already?"

Poppy couldn't look away if she tried. She could see Harrison turn in the driver's seat, talking to his children, before he pushed open his door and went around to help them out.

"I haven't met Mrs. Black yet, but the children seem lovely." She couldn't drag her gaze from Harrison as he strode toward them, schoolbags slung over his shoulder, eyes locked on hers. Katie skipped along ahead of him, little Alex at his side.

"Honey, there is no Mrs. Black," the other woman teased. "Harrison is dad of the year in Bellaroo. His wife left him with the kids when Alex was a baby, so he's kind of a legend around here. We call him Mr. Sexy and Single."

Poppy gulped. He was single?

She looked away and concentrated her energies on the mom she was talking to. "I never caught your name?"

"Pat. And my boys are Scott, John and Sam." She smiled and took a few steps backward. "It was great meeting you. I'll see you this afternoon at pickup."

Poppy waved goodbye and turned to face the next parent...who just happened to be Harrison. Katie gave her a wave and ran straight through the door, but Alex stayed close to his dad.

"Morning," Poppy said brightly. "How are you, Alex?"

He looked a little shy, but managed a smile.

"He had only one term in school last year, so it's all a bit daunting."

Poppy knelt down, pleased to be closer to his son than the man towering over them. "Sweetheart," she said, tucking her fingers gently under his chin to tilt it up. "I'll look after you all day, so you don't need to worry. You can even come and sit with me if you're scared, okay?"

He nodded.

"Why don't you run in and play with the other kids?" Poppy asked him.

Alex threw his arms around his dad's leg before doing as she'd suggested.

"Thanks," Harrison said, his voice gruff.

"No problem. It's what I do."

They stood awkwardly, and she couldn't stop thinking about the fact that he'd raised both his children on his own. It wasn't often she heard of a dad being in that position. No wonder he'd been in no rush to get home last night—it wasn't as if he'd had a wife waiting for him.

Another vehicle pulled up and a few kids climbed out.

"I'd better get in there," Poppy said, nodding toward the classroom.

Harrison touched a few fingers to the rim of his hat.

"And thanks again for last night. I really appreciated your help," she added.

He walked a couple of steps away before turning around and looking straight into her eyes. "I'll fix up that plumbing for you after school when I come to collect the kids."

Poppy swallowed. Hard. Maybe it was because she knew he was available, that he wasn't some other woman's husband.

Because if he were, she'd *never* let herself think about him the way she was right now…not ever. She knew how it felt to be the other woman, so even thinking about married men inappropriately was forbidden as far as she was concerned.

But now… Harrison was as handsome as any man she'd ever laid eyes upon, and the way his jeans clung to his butt when he walked away, the cowboy hat on his head, his checked shirtsleeves rolled up to show off tanned arms…it was making her think all kinds of sin.

"You must be Ms. Carter!"

Poppy blinked and tried to forget all about the man walking toward his truck. She was a teacher, and she had more parents to meet.

She'd be seeing Harrison again after school, and he'd be in her home. In her bathroom.

So no more thinking about him until then.

CHAPTER FOUR

POPPY SAT WITH Katie and Alex, watching out for their dad to arrive. He was only a few minutes late. The other children had all gone right on time, and now she was enjoying the sun and the company.

"Here he comes!" Alex called out, and ran to the edge of the pavement, waving to his dad.

Harrison jumped out and scooped his son straight up and into his arms. "I'm so sorry, Poppy," he said, running a hand through his hair as if he'd just realized he didn't have his hat on. "I had a run-in with a pretty pissed-off bull, and—"

"Daddy!" Katie had her hands on her hips. "You said a bad word," she hissed, "and she's our teacher, so you need to call her Ms. Carter."

He nodded as if she was absolutely right, but when his eyes met Poppy's they were filled with laughter. She had to bite down on her lip to stop from laughing herself.

"Anyway, long story short, he was determined to make his way to the ladies, which wasn't going to happen," Harrison told her.

Poppy did burst out laughing then—she couldn't help it. She was talking to a real-life cowboy when she'd never even been close to a real ranch before. "Do you have any idea how hilarious that sounds?"

He gave her a puzzled look. "Funny now, but not so amusing when you're staring a three-thousand-pound, adrenaline-filled beast in the eye."

She started to walk alongside Katie as they all headed for the truck. "Harrison, the closest I've come to dealing with wildlife is an ant infestation in my old classroom," she told him. "So believe me when I tell you how hilarious you sound to my sheltered city ways. Hilarious, but exciting, for a change."

She could have sworn a dark look passed across his face, but it was gone so quickly she couldn't be certain. Had she said something wrong?

"Although in saying that, I did kind of adopt a cat last night, so maybe I'm getting used to the whole country way of life already."

Harrison opened the front passenger door to his truck, but pointed for Katie to get in the back. "What do you mean, you adopted a cat? It's not like we have shelters for unwanted pets around here."

Poppy rolled her eyes, wishing she wasn't standing quite so close to him. He was at least a head taller than her, and she couldn't stop staring back into his dark brown eyes. They were dark but soft, like melted chocolate.

She snapped herself out of her daydream. Could she really forgive the entire male population so soon after declaring them all to be worthless idiots to whom she'd never again give the time of day? The answer to that question was no.

"I heard a noise last night and a black cat was just sitting there, like it was his house and he wanted to come in."

"But not wild?" Harrison asked. He gestured for her to get in the vehicle. "I'll drive you down the road—you know, so I can fix the bathroom."

Heat hit Poppy's cheeks and she hoped the blush wasn't noticeable. What was it about this guy getting her all in a fluster, especially at the mention of coming into her home? And the thought of sitting beside him in such a close space, despite the fact that his children were in the back.

"I don't think a wild cat would have slept the night on my bed," she told him, glancing down at his hand as he took command of the gear stick. His skin was a deep brown from what she imagined was hours out in the sun each day, and his forearm looked muscular. She tried to switch her focus to the road ahead. "Actually, I take that back. He slept on my pillow."

The children were chatting away in the rear, but she was listening only to their father. The man she couldn't seem to tear her eyes away from no matter how hard she tried.

"You're a real sucker, you know that?" Harrison's eyes crinkled in the corners, gentle wrinkles forming as he laughed at her. "Definitely not a country girl yet."

"I'd like to think I'm kindhearted," she replied.

He shrugged. "Same thing, if you ask me. But it's

weird that a cat just appeared out of nowhere. He must belong to someone."

"I told him he was welcome to stay, but I left a window open so he could come and go."

"And you're not pretending he's yours?" Harrison asked, one hand on the wheel, the other slung out the window.

"Exactly."

"You named him yet?"

"Lucky," she said. "Because I don't believe that black cats are bad luck, and he was lucky to find me and my large pitcher of milk."

"He's yours," Harrison said with a laugh. "Once you name them you're committed. Happens every time."

Poppy laughed with him, because he was right, and because it felt nice not to feel sad for once. She'd spent the past month wondering what the hell she was going to do with her life, how she was going to rebuild everything she'd lost, and that hadn't left much time for just laughing and being happy.

But Bellaroo Creek was her fresh start. It was her place to start over. So if she felt like laughing, then she wasn't going to hold back.

Harrison was lying on his back, squished half inside a cupboard, with his wrench jammed on the fitting he was trying to tighten. He tried to ignore the swear words sitting on the tip of his tongue, shifting his body instead to get a better look at the leak.

"Harrison?"

Crap. He'd been in such a dream world that he

hadn't expected anyone to walk in on him, and now he'd smacked his head on the underside of the cupboard.

"Are you okay? Did you hurt yourself?"

Harrison grunted and shuffled out of the small space. He touched his head. "No blood, so I'll live."

He stared up at Poppy, who was wringing her hands together as if she wasn't quite sure what to say.

"I, um, was wondering if you'd like to stay for dinner? I mean, you've been working in here for a while and I think the kids are getting hungry...."

"I'm not gonna let this beat me. You know that, right?" Even if he still had no idea why this darn plumbing was causing her such a problem every time she switched on anything in the bathroom.

"I didn't mean that you were taking too long, because I really do appreciate it, but..."

"Sure." Harrison shrugged. She was babbling like a crazy woman, or as if she was...nervous. He doubted that, especially after the way she'd stood up to him the day before, sassing at him for speaking his mind. "After wrangling these pipes, I think dinner would be great."

She smiled. As if she'd asked him a tough question and he'd miraculously given her an answer.

"Well, that's settled then. I'll go tell the children."

Poppy turned and walked away, and Harrison sat on her bathroom floor and watched her go. There was something about her, something getting under his skin that he didn't want to acknowledge. Something that had made him offer to fix her plumbing, made him say yes to dinner, all those things.

And it was something he didn't want to figure out.

She was his children's schoolteacher, a new woman in the community, but that was all. Because he wasn't looking for anything other than friendship in his life. His kids meant everything to him, and getting involved with a woman wasn't in his future.

So why was he still sitting on the floor so he could watch her walk down the hall?

Poppy watched the children as they lay on their stomachs, legs crossed at the ankles while they stared at the television. She'd already given them crisps and orange juice, and now she was cooking dinner while they watched a cartoon and their father worked on the bathroom.

The old house was like nothing she was used to, and it was taking all her patience to work in the tiny kitchen, but in a way it was nice. Nice to be cooking for more than just one, to have had a great first day at school and to feel as if her life was finally moving in the right direction again.

"Something smells good."

The deep, sexy voice coming from behind her made her hand freeze in midmotion. Hearing him speak put her almost as much on edge as looking at him did, no matter how much she wanted to pretend that she was just the teacher and he was just the father of two of her pupils.

"It's nothing fancy, just pasta," she told him, resuming her stirring.

She listened as Harrison walked into the kitchen, felt his presence in the too-small space.

"It smells fancy."

Poppy watched as he came closer and stood beside her. He peered into the pan, using the wooden spoon she'd discarded to give the contents a gentle stir.

"Garlic and bacon," she said, moving away slightly, needing to put some distance between them. Anything at all to stop her heart from racing a million miles an hour and quell the unease in her stomach. "I fry it in some oil before adding the sauce and tossing in the pasta."

He nodded and put the spoon back where he'd found it, leaning against a cupboard and watching her cook.

"Anything not working in here?" he asked.

"Ah, no. Everything seems to be fine."

"You don't sound so sure."

What she was sure about was needing him to look away, to go sit with his children instead of fixing his eyes on her while she was trying to concentrate.

"It's fine. Everything works okay, I guess. It's just different," she confessed.

"To what you're used to?"

Poppy sighed, then shrugged. "I've had a fancy kitchen and a modern apartment, and it didn't make me happy, so I'm not going to let a rustic kitchen get me down." It was the truth, and now she'd said it. "Lighting the gas with a match before I cook isn't going to bother me so long as I can do a job I love and wake up with a smile on my face each day."

Harrison was still staring at her, but his expression had lost the intensity of before. There was a softness in his eyes now, almost as if he understood what she was trying to say. What she was trying to get across to him.

"There's something to be said for smiling in the mornings," he told her.

Poppy looked away, not because she was embarrassed, but because she didn't know what to say. When she'd chosen to come here, she'd decided to keep her past exactly that—she didn't want it to define her future and didn't want everyone knowing her business. But it sure was hard to get to know someone without thinking about what her life had been like only a month earlier.

"What's for dinner?" Katie appeared in the kitchen, rising on tiptoe as she tried to see what was cooking.

"Pasta with a carbonara sauce," Poppy told her, using her elbow to playfully push her from the kitchen. "Hang out with Alex for a few more minutes and it'll be ready."

The little girl grinned, gave her dad a cheeky wave and disappeared again.

"You might think this is nothing fancy," said Harrison, pointing at the sauce Poppy was stirring, "but to them it's fun to be somewhere different for dinner. They're usually just stuck with me on the ranch."

She swallowed a lump. It was now or never, and she couldn't help herself.

"So there's no Mrs. Black?" she asked, knowing full well what the answer was going to be.

"No," Harrison replied, his eyes dark and stormy, his expression like stone. "There's no Mrs. Black, unless you're talking about my mom."

If only her question was that innocent, but they both

knew it wasn't. What Poppy didn't know was why she'd asked at all.

Maybe she just wanted to hear it from him, so she could actually believe that he didn't have a wife…that he really was what the mom today had described him as—the town's sexiest bachelor.

Sauce. What Poppy needed to do was focus on the carbonara sauce.

"Anything I can do?" His soft, deep drawl made her skin go hot, then suddenly cold, as if an icy breeze had blown through on a warm summer's day.

"I'd love for you to put those plates on the table," she said, nodding toward where she had them stacked. "And to be honest, I wouldn't mind celebrating my first day at school with a glass of wine."

Plus she wouldn't mind settling her nerves a little with the bottle of sauvignon blanc she had in the fridge.

"Glasses?" he asked, carrying the plates to the table.

Poppy groaned. "Still to be unpacked, I think." One of the few things she hadn't actually transferred from box to cupboard. But if she wasn't mistaken… "Hang on, try the box at the bottom of the pantry," she instructed. "I can't leave this sauce."

Harrison strode across the kitchen in a few long steps, commanding her attention. As if she needed more distracting….

"This box?"

She nodded. "Yep, that's the one."

She dragged her eyes from him and focused on the food again. She took the sauce from the stove, added the cooked pasta to the pot she had waiting and poured all the sauce in, too. She gently tossed it, refusing to give the dinner she'd cooked any less attention than it deserved. This was one of her favorite comfort foods, although she usually did the pasta from scratch when she personally needed comforting, and she was just hoping the Black family would like what she'd rustled up.

Harrison poured wine into the two glasses he'd found and placed them on the table before going to herd his kids in for dinner. They were still mesmerized by the television.

"Let's go, dinner's ready."

Katie had the adopted black cat on her lap, stroking it over and over again, and it was purring so loudly he could hear it from the doorway.

"Put the fleabag down and come sit up," he ordered, trying not to smile at the horrified look his daughter was giving him. "On second thought, perhaps you should wash your hands first."

"It's okay, Lucky," Katie crooned to the cat. "Don't listen to *anything* he says, all right?"

He watched as she placed the cat down gently, as if he was breakable, before standing up and flouncing past him. More teenager than kid.

"He is *not* a *fleabag*," she hissed.

"I was just teasing, sweetheart. Now go wash up, then sit at the table for dinner." Harrison gestured for his son to do the same, then joined Poppy back in the kitchen.

"Finally ready," she told him, her cheeks flushed from standing over the range.

He jumped forward to take the large dish from her, their hands colliding as his fingers closed around it. "Let me take this."

Poppy's eyes met his, blue irises flashing to the food and back to him again, as if she had no idea what to say or why they were standing so close.

"Thanks," she finally said, taking a step back while brushing the hair from her face and tucking it behind her ears.

Harrison transported the dish to the table, wishing he didn't feel quite so comfortable being in this woman's house. He was used to telling himself why he didn't need female company in his life, why he was better off alone, but Poppy was reminding him of all the reasons his thinking could be flawed.

What his wife had done to him, the way she'd hurt him, would never go away. But it didn't mean he needed to feel guilty for spending an evening in the company of the new local teacher. So long as he protected his children from being hurt again, he had nothing to fear.

"Katie seems very fond of animals," Poppy said, making him turn.

She walked to the edge of the table and reached for her glass of wine, taking a small sip.

Harrison pulled out his chair but waited for her to sit down first. His children came bounding back into the room and jumped into their seats before he had a chance to do the same for them.

"Katie loves animals more than anyone I've ever met," he told Poppy, grinning at his daughter across the table. "I tease her about it, but she has a real way with them. Has had since she was little."

Poppy reached for Alex's plate and started to dish out their meals. "Do you like helping your dad on the ranch, Katie?"

She nodded. "Yeah, but I don't like it when it's calving time and some of the babies don't have a mom, 'cause then they're just like me, except they don't have a dad, either."

Harrison's body went tense. No matter how hard he tried, he couldn't help the jolt of anger that hit him just hearing his little girl say those words. "It's one of the reasons we have quite a few pet calves," he said, pushing the fury away and taking a deep breath. "Because Katie is so good at caring for them."

"So you help nurse them?" Poppy asked his daughter.

If she'd noticed the bitterness flashing through him, she did a good job of disguising it. Just when he thought he was over his anger at their mother for leaving the kids, Katie went and said something like that.

"Daddy lets me feed them with a bottle, and we get to name them," Katie said, smiling as Poppy passed her a plate full of pasta.

"Which is why we have an entire field full of pet cows," Harrison explained, smiling across at his daughter. "As I tell the kids, as soon as you name them it's very hard to say goodbye."

"Because they get made into steak," Katie announced.

Poppy's eyes met his. He was certain she hadn't been expecting *that* response.

"That's right." Harrison twirled his fork into his pasta and tasted it. "And this," he said, pausing to swallow his mouthful, "tastes as great as it smells."

Poppy's eyes were still trained on him. "So that's why you told me off for naming the cat."

"Exactly."

She grinned and held up her glass. "I meant to say a toast before we started."

Harrison touched his napkin to his lips and followed her lead. "Sure."

Poppy raised her glass. "To surviving my first day of school and to new friends."

He nodded. "And to me winning the fight with the bull today." Harrison winked at her across the table, then wished he could take it back. Why the hell had he done that?

Because it had come naturally, and he hadn't even thought about it. Even though he hadn't flirted with anyone for longer than he could remember.

Poppy was staring straight down at her plate now, focused on her food, and he felt like a fool for embarrassing her. Especially after she'd been so nice, asking them to stay for a meal.

"So what do you think of Bellaroo so far?" he asked, trying to keep the topic neutral. "Everything you thought it would be?"

Poppy laughed, holding her hand in front of her mouth. He kept eating and waited for her to reply, tuning out the chatter from Katie and Alex. From what he could gather they were arguing about the name for the next orphaned calf.

"I guess I didn't realize how quiet it would be here," Poppy told him frankly.

"You never did visit before you took the job, did you?" he asked, knowing the answer but wanting to hear it from her.

"I just trusted my gut that it was the right place for me," she said. "And I was told there were no other applicants, so I didn't exactly have to audition for the part."

Harrison could tell from the shine in her eyes that she was upset— that just talking about her move here had touched a nerve—yet she'd tried to joke her way out of it.

"At the time, I thought it was a sign, because I needed to get away from…" Her voice trailed off, as if she was trying to decide whether or not to tell him the truth.

"I didn't mean to pry," Harrison said, knowing what it was like to want to keep a secret, to want to keep memories buried.

"You're not," she said, touching a knuckle to each eye, pushing away the first hint of a tear. "They're questions that I'm going to be asked, and I want to answer them honestly."

Was she a criminal? Had something happened in her past that they should have known about before they gave her the job at the school?

Harrison picked up his fork again and continued to eat, more for something to do than the fact that he was still hungry. Because listening to Poppy had taken his mind off his stomach.

"Last year was a little rough for me," she admitted, playing with the edge of her napkin, yet bravely looking at him as she spoke. "I, well, my husband got us into a lot of trouble, and I lost everything I'd worked so hard for."

She was married? "You're married?" How had she not mentioned this earlier, and why the hell did he care, anyway?

Poppy grimaced. "Unfortunately, yes."

Wow. He hadn't even seen that coming. "So your husband won't be joining you here?"

Poppy laughed, but it didn't sound like a happy noise. "Let's just say that me coming here was as much to get away from him as anything." She shook her head and glanced at the children. "One day I'll tell you all about it."

Maybe they had more in common than he'd realized. "We could trade crappy spouse and divorce stories," he joked. Unless she'd walked out on her man, as his wife had him....

"Believe me, mine's up there with the best of them."

Harrison grinned, relieved. "Yep, me, too."

Poppy stood at her front door and waved as Harrison pulled away from the curb and headed for home. It had been a nice evening, and she was pleased she'd asked them to stay, but she was still thinking about their conversation over dinner.

She'd told herself over and over again that talking about her husband wasn't productive, that she'd be better off pretending he didn't exist. But doing so was easier than *saying so*.

After the way Chris had hurt her, the lies, the pain...

Poppy shuddered and shut the door behind her, leaning against it and sliding all the way to the floor.

The man she'd pledged to spend the rest of her life with, the one person in the world she'd trusted above all else, had hurt her so badly that it still took her breath away.

Tears fell slowly down her cheeks, drizzling down her jaw. Poppy shut her eyes, tried to force the memories away, but nothing worked. The cold shiver that took over her body whenever she thought about him descended, as it always did.

And she was alone. After thinking she'd found her soul mate, trusting him like she'd never trusted anyone before, she was alone. And she was broke.

She'd lost her apartment, her husband and everything else she'd worked so hard for. But she wasn't going to let it define who she was, because the one thing he hadn't taken from her was her future. And the person she was, beneath everything she'd lost.

"I'm healthy. I'm a teacher. I make a difference," Poppy whispered, eyes still shut tight as she repeated the words that always got her through her pain.

A meow made her blink away her tears. The cat was sitting near her feet, staring at her as if he was trying to figure out what the heck she was doing on the floor in the hall.

"And I'm a mom," she whispered, pulling herself to her feet and bending to pick up the cat.

Even if it wasn't to the baby she'd been so excited about carrying.

"A cat's better than no one," she told her new furry friend.

And she could tell him everything without fearing the consequences.

CHAPTER FIVE

HARRISON CURSED AT his dog as she ran out and disobeyed his command. He went to yell at her, then stopped himself. Just because he was in a crappy mood didn't mean his dog deserved to be scolded. He could see from the look on her face that she was confused.

"Go way back," he instructed, giving up on his whistling.

The dog glanced at him before following his command, perfectly this time. He walked up slowly, waited for her to push the last few cattle through then closed the gate behind them.

"Good girl," he said, giving her a pat on the head when she settled against his leg, bright eyes connecting with his. "You did good."

Harrison sat down on the grass and stretched his legs out in front of him. The dog lay at his side. He worked Suzy on her own only when they were dealing with a small herd or the odd rogue cattle beast, and she stuffed up only when he stuffed up. And he knew why he was showing himself up today—because there was a certain teacher on his mind he couldn't forget about, and because his daughter was going to be furious with him when she got home.

He was never, ever again going to let her help him with the young stock. What had started as something nice to do together, spending time with his girl and teaching her the ropes, helping her to deal with the confusion of not having her own mom, had turned into him letting her save a heap of calves that he was lumped with for the foreseeable future.

So much for being a tough rancher. One burst of tears from Katie and he'd promised the orphans wouldn't be sent away, even though he knew he couldn't keep them forever.

But he'd solved the biggest part of the problem—separating the bull calf from the females before he became an issue. And lucky for Katie, he was good enough to be considered for stud. Although a half-tame bull might be scarier than a wild one when it came to mating time.

Mating. Why the hell had Harrison thought about that when he was struggling not to wonder why the hell Poppy was living in the middle of nowhere without her husband? Had she left the man? Had he done something to make her want to run? Harrison would be damned if he'd stand by and let the woman be terrified of some lowlife tracking her down.

He let out a big breath and dropped his palm to his dog's head, kneading her fur gently with his fingers. She was his best form of stress relief because he relied on her and she never answered back, and because she was the only female he'd had affection from since his wife had left.

"Come on, girl. It's time for lunch." Then it was school pickup, and he was going to get in and out as quickly as he could. Poppy was a great teacher; his kids liked her, and hell, so did he. But being around her wasn't good for him, made him think all sorts of things that he'd sworn off thinking these past few years, and what he needed to do was distance himself. Before he started thinking up all kinds of stupid ideas and did something crazy like ask her over for dinner.

Maybe he needed to take his helicopter up for a spin, check out the far fields—anything to get his head back in the space he needed it to be in.

Poppy sat at her desk and pretended not to notice some of the girls whispering and passing notes. She wasn't about to ruin their fun, not yet at least, not when they'd already completed the task she'd set them. And besides, she wasn't quite ready to stop her own daydreaming, no matter how dangerous it might be.

Harrison Black. Why couldn't she seem to forget the way his fingers had felt against hers when they'd clashed on the dish? The look in his eyes when he'd been talking about his daughter or the cool way he'd announced there was no Mrs. Black.

Less than two months ago, Poppy had been thinking about her wedding, wondering whether to wear white or ivory, flicking through bridal magazines. Now she was virtually penniless, had had her heart broken in more ways than she could imagine and was already struggling not to think about a handsome-as-hell rancher she'd met only three times.

Poppy smiled to herself. And the first meeting hadn't exactly gone down well.

"What are you laughing about?"

She looked up and saw the girls watching her. They were no longer scribbling notes but eyeing her instead.

"I'm not laughing. I'm just smiling about how nice it is to be here," she replied, cheeks flushing ever so slightly at being caught out, especially with Katie staring at her so intently. The last thing Poppy needed was the young girl knowing she was dreaming about her father.

"Is it different here than your last school?" an older girl, Marie, asked her.

"Yes," Poppy answered, standing up so she could walk around to the front of her desk and lean back on it. "The last school I taught at was in the middle of the city, and we had a big, high fence around the outside and a concrete playground. The children had to be collected inside the gates and signed for by their parents or caregiver."

It couldn't have been more different to the relaxed attitude at Bellaroo, where all the parents knew one another on a first name basis.

"Is it better here?" another child asked.

"I wouldn't have come here if I didn't think it would be better, and I can tell you right now that it's even better than I imagined it could be."

Every child in the room was staring at her now, and

she couldn't help but smile back at their beaming little faces.

"Enough talk about me. It's time for you to share your stories. Let's start with the eldest and make our way down, okay?"

Poppy sat on the edge of her desk and waved to Connor, her eldest pupil, to come forward.

She hadn't been lying to the children; it *was* better here. In fact, old house aside, it was almost perfect.

A phone rang and she looked around. She didn't even recall there *being* a phone in the classroom, and she hadn't bothered turning her mobile phone on since she'd arrived. It had sat dormant from the moment she'd left the city behind, in fact. There wasn't a signal out here, and all the ranchers used satellite phones when they needed to communicate.

"Anyone know where the phone is?" she asked.

A few of the kids pointed to her left.

"In the cupboard?" She wasn't convinced, but sure enough, there was an ancient-looking phone attached to the wall. Poppy picked up the receiver. "Hello, Bellaroo Creek School," she said hesitantly.

"Poppy, it's Harrison."

Harrison? "Is everything okay?" He sounded out of breath and her heart picked up rhythm, starting to beat fast.

"No, I've had some bad news, and I need to head for Sydney as soon as I've given the guys instructions for the cattle."

"Sydney? I don't understand."

He sounded distracted, as if he wasn't really concentrating, not sure of what to say.

"Poppy, my dad's had a heart attack and I need to get to the hospital. I'm trying to organize someone to look after the kids, but is there any chance you could stay with them a bit later today?"

"Oh, Harrison, I'm so sorry." Tears sprang into her eyes because she knew what it was like to receive a phone call like that, to have your day going along like normal and then find out that life had thrown a curve ball that had the potential to break your heart. It had been like that when her dad died, and the only consolation was that he hadn't been witness to her losing everything.

Harrison was silent on the other end, but she could hear him breathing, as if he was running around doing something. Probably packing.

"Harrison?"

"Sorry, it's just..."

"I'll take them," she said without hesitation. "Don't worry about the children, just go. If you're okay with me taking care of them, I'll do it."

He was silent again, a long pause hanging between them before he answered. "Poppy, I can't ask you to do that. You're their teacher, and you hardly even know us."

"You didn't ask me, I offered. And I know you plenty well enough." She kept her voice low, conscious of her students listening to their conversation. "You were kind enough to help me out twice now, and I already adore your children, so just go, and don't worry about them."

"Are you sure?" His voice was deep, husky and commanding. He might be upset and needing to flee, but she could feel his strength without even seeing him. "I'd never ask you to step up like that, and it wasn't why I called."

"Just tell me how to get to your place, leave a key out and do what you have to do."

"You want to stay here?" he asked, clearly surprised.

"Wouldn't that be easier? Then the children can stick to their routine and have all their things around them."

She could almost hear his brain ticking over while he was silent. "There's dogs and chooks and…"

Poppy laughed. "I'm from the city, not another planet," she said. "I have no problem with animals and I'm sure the kids can help me out, tell me where things are, that sort of thing."

Even as she was talking she was wondering what on earth she'd done, but what other option did she have? Harrison was a solo dad with few people to call on, and his children didn't need the extra worry or stress of staying with someone else when she could care for them in their own home.

"I'll swing past on my way out of town, say goodbye to the kids and give you a map for how to get to the ranch," he said after a long pause. "And I'll organize for the dogs to be taken up to the worker's house and for all the chores to be done. I have a family living in the cottage at the moment, and there's a few guys working here full-time at the moment, too, so you won't have to worry about anything."

Poppy said goodbye and took a moment to collect

herself. She glanced at her wristwatch. There was only another forty-five minutes until the end of the school day, which meant she had some time to prepare herself mentally for the children finding out that their grand-dad was unwell and their dad was leaving. She had no idea how long he'd be away for, how long she'd be expected to stay at his ranch without him, but she'd do it.

Because the truth was she missed being part of a family, hated living in a house all on her own when she was used to having people around her every day. And staying at Harrison's ranch would be like a mini-vacation in a way, her first real taste of the Australian outback up close and personal.

Her saying yes had nothing to do with the fact that Harrison had gotten under her skin. That all she'd thought about since she'd made dinner for them was how intriguing he was; how different he was from the man she'd spent the past eight years of her life with. And how easily she could take back the vow she'd made to herself about swearing off men for good.

Poppy drew a deep breath and shut the cupboard door behind her. Every single child in the room was staring at her, no doubt wondering who she'd been talking to and what was going on.

But she wasn't going to say anything to Katie and Alex until their father arrived, because he was their dad and it was his place to explain to them what was happening.

"Okay, back to reading your stories aloud. Who was first?"

Poppy sat down at her desk and fixed a smile on her

face, even though inside she was anything but calm and happy.

She was terrified. Because she'd just volunteered to help out Harrison and his gorgeous children, and the reality of that was starting to set in. She'd be staying in his home, caring for his kids, *being part of his family*.

Poppy touched her stomach with her palm, feeling how flat it was.

If she hadn't had the miscarriage, she'd be close to having her own child, her own family…and there wasn't a day that went by that she didn't think about the child she'd lost.

Poppy kept telling herself that it would happen, that she'd be a mom one day, only she wasn't so sure she'd ever be able to find a man trustworthy enough to be the dad.

Harrison dropped a kiss on his daughter's head and gave his son another big hug.

"I'll only be a few days, okay? I just need to get to Sydney, spend some time at the hospital, then I'll come straight back home."

He felt like crap for leaving them, but what choice did he have? His parents meant a lot to him and he was their only child—he couldn't let his dad die without telling him how much he loved him. It wasn't something he'd ever told him before, and the thought of never getting the chance to be honest and say how he felt? He couldn't let that happen.

"We're going to have lots of fun while your dad's away," Poppy told the kids, meeting his gaze and giving him a reassuring smile. "Late nights, yummy food and lots of television."

Harrison nodded, hoping his smile looked genuine. "I'll be back before you even know I'm gone. It's only a five-hour drive, so if you really need me I can get home pretty fast."

They looked sad, but they understood. Or at least they seemed to better understand now that he'd explained to them why they couldn't join him and what exactly a heart attack was. He knew they'd be scared, but they were in good hands; he couldn't have found anyone he'd trust more with his children if he'd tried, even though they had known Poppy only a short time.

"You're sure then?" he asked, for what was probably the tenth time since he'd arrived at the school grounds.

"Positive."

Poppy had a sunny smile on her face, and when she stepped toward him, arms held out, he didn't back away. Couldn't. Because he was so alone right now, and the pain he was feeling at the idea of his dad hooked up to machines in a hospital was so intense it was starting to consume him. Like a hand around his neck slowly choking him, draining him of all his strength, all his determination.

"Come here," she said, folding her arms around him and enveloping him in a tight hug. "Everything's going to be okay, Harrison."

He mumbled something against her head, into her silky hair, but didn't even know what he was trying to say. What he did know was how great she felt in his arms, how soothing it was to be held. By someone warm and soft and so feminine.

"Thank you," he whispered, his voice low and gravelly as he held back tears he hadn't even known had been waiting to fall.

"I've been where you are and I know how it feels. But you need to believe it's going to be okay," she told him, squeezing him tight before stepping back a fraction.

Harrison looked down into her warm aqua eyes, noting the way soft bits of short hair were wisping around her face. Despite everything—the pain and the confusion—all he could think about when he stared at Poppy was what it would be like to kiss the breath from her, tug her back in tight against him and just kiss the hell out of those plump lips.

Her smile drew him in, made him keep his hands against her back after hugging her. Harrison bent slightly, slowly moving toward her, before he stopped himself. Glancing at his children, he realized they were watching what was happening. And if he hesitated a second longer, if he didn't let go of Poppy, it would move from an innocent hug between friends to something far murkier.

The confusion evident all over Poppy's face told him he'd already hesitated too long, but the nervous smile she gave him? That told him that maybe, just maybe, she'd been thinking exactly what he'd been thinking.

"Uh-hmm." Harrison cleared his throat and put a definite few steps between them this time, needing to get as far away from her as possible. "I'd best be off.

You two be on your best behavior for Ms. Carter, you hear me?"

"Poppy," he heard her say, then turned to watch her mouth as she spoke, drawn in again by the woman he was trying so hard to resist. "I'm more than just your teacher now, so out of school you can call me Poppy."

Maybe inviting her to stay in his home, care for his children, be his *someone* in his hour of need, had been the stupidest thing he'd ever done. *Either the stupidest or the cleverest.* He wouldn't be able to decide until he'd figured out how to resist her. Because they could never, *ever* be more than just friends.

Right now that was the only thing he was certain about.

"Love you," he told his kids, looking from Katie to Alex.

They were being so brave, standing on either side of Poppy now as he walked around to the driver's side of his truck.

"Drive safely and phone us when you get there," Poppy called out.

"Funny, but I said that to my parents when they went away. It was supposed to be their relaxing trip around Australia, taking in the sights, and they only made it to Sydney to enjoy the big city."

Poppy never took her eyes from him, and he spent a moment looking back at her. He could see every bit of the compassion she was feeling for him, as if her arms were around him, comforting him, even though she was still standing on the pavement and he was on the road.

Harrison jumped behind the wheel and waved out

the window, turning the ignition. As he drove away, he alternated between staring at the road ahead and into his rearview mirror.

It had been a long time since he'd seen a woman, aside from his own mom, embracing his children. Comforting them, caring for them, doing the things he'd had to do for so long on his own.

He'd tried to pretend that his children didn't need a mom, that they were doing fine without one and that he was enough.

So why was seeing Poppy with them, so kind and nurturing, making him feel they were missing out on more than he'd ever wanted to admit?

Harrison turned up the stereo until it was blaring and focused on the road. He had a long drive ahead of him, and thinking about his ex-wife, or Poppy, for that matter, wasn't going to make the drive any easier.

CHAPTER SIX

POPPY LOOKED AROUND the kitchen. She was like a fish out of water—less because she was out of her depth and more because it was weird, poking around in someone else's things. Harrison had asked her into his home, told her to make herself comfortable, but it was still kind of awkward.

Plus she'd presumed there would be enough supplies without even checking.

"What do you guys feel like for dinner?" she asked, hand poised on the fridge door.

Alex didn't even look up from the television, but Katie jumped to her feet.

"There should be stuff in the fridge," the girl told her. "Dad's really good at cooking."

Interesting. Poppy had presumed he wouldn't be a good cook, just because he was a guy. That would teach her not to be sexist.

She swung the door open and had to stop her chin from hitting the floor. Her jaw literally fell open when she saw how well stocked it was. There was a heap of vegetables, fruit, bottled things—everything she could think of and more.

"So was your dad just being polite, telling me the food I made was good the other night?" She felt like an idiot now for telling him how and what she'd been cooking when he clearly knew what he was doing in the kitchen. Unless, of course, he just made them eat boiled vegetables all the time? "What does he fix you for dinner most nights?"

Katie shrugged, reaching in for the orange juice. "He cooks, like, spicy stuff," she said, standing on a little stool that was obviously there for the children, so she could get a clean glass from the cupboard. "He said that when he was at university his roommate was from Thailand, and he taught him how to cook, so he either does Thai food or something he's made up."

Poppy couldn't help smiling. So Mr. Sexy and Single wasn't just a single-dad rancher, he was also a gourmet cook. A gourmet *Thai* cook.

"So I guess boiled vegetables aren't allowed?"

"Yuk." Katie pulled a face before going back to drinking her juice. "Hey, do you want me to show you the veggie garden?"

Poppy raised her eyebrows. "Your dad has a vegetable garden?" *When did he have time for all this?*

Katie put her glass down and took Poppy by the hand, leading her across the room. "It's actually my grandma's. She comes here to look after it, and we help Dad water it, but we eat all the vegetables because she has one at her house, too." Katie pointed out the window. "But Dad says the orchard is his because he planted all the trees."

Poppy tried not to laugh but couldn't help it. It was like someone was playing a practical joke on her.

"Hey, do you want to see my room?"

Poppy let Katie take her hand again and pull her along. The kids were coping fine, treating her like a new toy, and so long as she had fun with them she knew they'd be just fine while their dad was away.

"Do you have your own bedroom?"

"Yeah," Katie said, running ahead of her. "And this is my dad's room down here."

Poppy had that uncomfortable feeling again, as if she was doing something she shouldn't be, but she shrugged it away. "Honey, where's the spare room?"

Katie spun around. "Oh, we don't have one. Well, we kind of do, but it doesn't have a bed in it, so you can sleep in Dad's."

Oh dear. Being in Harrison's house was one thing, but in his *bed*?

She cleared her throat, her cheeks burning. "Or I could just sleep in your room?"

Katie laughed and disappeared through a doorway. Poppy followed, but her heart sank as soon as she walked into the room.

"I'm not allowed to sleep on the top bunk yet, but you can if you want to."

Poppy sighed. So it was Harrison's bachelor bed or a top bunk… "It's okay, honey. Your dad's bed will be just fine."

Katie started talking again, showing her toys, dancing around the room as if she were her best friend visiting on a play date. But all Poppy could think about was being in Harrison's room, sleeping between sheets that would smell like him, that he'd been lying in that morning.

She shook her head, trying to push him from her mind.

Did he sleep naked?

If Katie hadn't been watching her she'd have been tempted to slap herself to try to snap out of it.

"I think we should get back to Alex," Poppy suggested, needing to put as much distance between her and the bedrooms as possible. Not to mention she still had to rustle up something for dinner.

And stop thinking about the man whose house she was going to be living in for the next couple days.

"Did Dad tell you about the Aboriginal family living in our cottage?" Katie asked.

Poppy's eyebrows pulled together. "He mentioned there was a family, but not that they were native Australians." She'd never seen their culture firsthand, but was fascinated by their traditional beliefs and way of life.

"They're really cool," Katie told her. "You should come meet them maybe."

"Are there any children?"

"Yeah, two boys. Same age as me. But they don't go to school."

Poppy definitely wanted to meet them. Just because the parents chose not to send the boys to school didn't mean she wasn't prepared to offer them assistance if or when they needed it.

Back in the living room now, she could see Alex hadn't moved a muscle and was still parked in front of the television.

"How about you play with Alex for a while and I'll sort dinner out, okay?" she asked Katie, needing a moment just to collect her thoughts.

Her new little friend ran into the living room, leaving Poppy standing alone. Talk about information overload. A few quiet minutes to process everything was *exactly* what she needed.

Poppy was starting to realize what hard work it was being a parent. She had both children in bed with her, snuggled tight, and she was so exhausted she just wanted to shut her eyes…only Alex was still hiccuping from the bucketload of tears he'd shed on her and her pillow.

So much for being worried about sleeping in Harrison's bed. She'd hardly had time to savor the musky smell of him on the sheets before she was joined by Katie, whimpering and needing a cuddle. Then she'd heard Alex call out, as if he'd been having a nightmare, and she'd run to him as quickly as she could. The poor little boy was missing his dad like crazy and worried sick about his granddad.

"Will he die?" Alex whispered. "Will he disappear like my mom did and never come back?"

Poppy held him tighter, snuggling him so he knew how much she cared. Just because she was exhausted didn't mean she wouldn't sit up all night comforting him if he needed her to. But explaining death to him wasn't something she was comfortable with, and neither was talking to him about his mom when she didn't know the whole story.

"Honey, I don't want you to think about anyone leaving you," Poppy said in her most soothing voice. "Why don't you tell me what you'd like to do with your granddad when he's back here again instead?"

Alex whimpered and wrapped one arm around her neck, as if wanting to make sure there was no way she could leave him.

"I want to make something for him. Something cool."

"Like a poster?" she asked, keeping her voice low to make sure they didn't wake Katie.

"Yeah. Something cool to hang above the door, and a card, too."

She could hear the change in Alex's voice, knew that distracting him was probably the best thing she could do. But getting his hopes up about seeing his granddad again? Harrison had sounded positive on the phone when he'd called, but she knew how easy it was to get your hopes up and then have them come crashing down when something unexpected happened.

"Poppy?"

Hearing Alex say her first name made her smile. Earlier in the evening he'd still been calling her Ms. Carter. She gave him a tighter cuddle to let him know she'd heard him.

"You smell nice."

She dropped a kiss into his hair. Talk about a sweetie.

"And Poppy?"

"Yeah?"

"You're nice to snuggle. Just like what a mom would be like, I reckon."

Now she was struggling not to cry. Talk about a tug on her heartstrings....

"I think we should try to go to sleep now," she whispered, glancing at the clock. It was midnight already and she hadn't slept a wink. "Why don't we pull the covers up and close our eyes, okay?"

Alex nodded his head and tucked down, his little body warm against hers. With Katie tight on her other side, Poppy had never been so hot trying to go to sleep, but she'd never felt so loved, either. Felt as if she actually mattered. There was no pretending with kids, no ulterior motives. Katie and Alex had been comfortable enough to come into bed with her, had trusted that she cared for them and was going to help them.

And that was why she wanted to be a parent so badly. Why she still felt the pain of losing the baby she'd been so excited about carrying. When she'd reached the sixteen-week mark this time, she'd thought everything was okay, that nothing was going to go wrong again. She'd been so looking forward to finding out the gender, counting down the weeks until she'd know if she'd be buying pink clothes or blue, that losing her little baby hadn't even seemed a possibility.

The doctor had said it was the stress of everything, her body telling her it couldn't cope with nurturing a healthy baby and dealing with a divorce and losing all her money, too. Maybe it was a blessing in disguise, even if she couldn't see it now, especially after everything that had happened.

Poppy shut her eyes tight and focused on the pudgy hand pressed to her cheek, on the warm breath against her neck. Just because she wasn't going to be a mom anytime soon didn't mean she wasn't making a difference to the children in her life.

She blinked the tears away, refusing to get emotional.

But with these two in bed with her, she was starting to realize that it wasn't about having her own biological child. She'd just as happily parent these two for the sole reason that she was capable of loving them and they her.

But they already had a dad, and she had no idea what the situation was with their mom. *And she had no right to know.* She was their teacher and a friend of their father's. Thinking dangerous thoughts about how nice it would be to mean something more to them wasn't going to do her any favors.

What she needed to do was sleep. And forget about any fantasies she might have about being a parent, at least for a while. Because she couldn't be a mom without having a man in her life, and she wasn't even close to ready for that. Right now, she was meant to be harboring a grudge against the entire male population. No matter how nice she might think a certain Harrison Black was.

Because she'd thought Chris was nice, too, a man she could trust with her heart. And look how well that decision had turned out.

"I'm healthy. I'm a teacher. I make a difference," she whispered, forcing herself to practice her chant.

She shut her eyes and tried to focus on sleeping, counting every time she breathed in and exhaled.

If she wanted to stay in control, be in charge of her own destiny, then she just needed to take things one day at a time.

CHAPTER SEVEN

POPPY WAS EXHAUSTED. After hardly any sleep for two nights with the kids, then all day teaching, she was ready to drop. But she had two hungry children in the back of her car who were telling her all the things they wanted to show her when they got back to the ranch.

She crossed the almost-dry river, looking ahead to the house. It was beautiful—long and low, with a vine that grew across the front to soften the timber. *A home.* It looked like a home, not a house.

"It's Dad!"

Poppy's heart started to beat faster. Surely Harrison would have called if he was coming home early? "Where?"

"That's his truck," Katie told her, leaning forward. "Right there."

She pointed and Poppy saw where she was looking. It *was* Harrison. Or at least it was his truck, which meant he'd have to be around somewhere.

Oh, my God. She'd left her makeup and clothes in his bedroom, which meant that if he'd... She gulped. There was no point in worrying; they were both adults.

If he'd seen her underwear, it wasn't the worst thing in the world. Even if it felt like it right now.

"Where do you think he'll be?" she asked, trying to keep the alarm from her voice.

But the kids weren't listening to her, more interested in pressing their noses to the glass and searching for him. As soon as she stopped the car they were out, running as fast as they could to the house and racing through the front door.

Poppy took a moment to calm herself, to take some big, slow breaths and prepare herself for heading in. Because after the nights she'd had with his kids, the way she was feeling about them right now, she could easily think things about their dad that were forbidden; things she couldn't consider even if she wanted to.

He was sexy, he was single and he was...*not on her radar.* Or at least that's what she was trying to pretend.

She got out of the car, reached in for the slow-cooked beef pie she'd picked up at the bakery and walked as bravely as she could to the front door. Poppy could hear voices before she even stepped inside—mainly Harrison's deep, soothing tone.

It brought a smile to her face, because it sounded to her as if he was trying to explain that their grand-dad was okay and why he'd come home earlier than expected.

"Hi," she called out as she came into the kitchen. She didn't want to stand in the doorway listening without him knowing she was there. "I'm hoping you're back early because it's good news?"

Harrison gave her what looked like a relieved smile.

"It turns out he didn't even know he had dangerously high cholesterol, or if he did he certainly never told my mom, and he had a heart attack because of blocked arteries."

"But he's going to be okay?" she asked.

"He's going to need a decent period of rest and recovery, but yeah, he's going to be fine." Harrison grinned at his kids. "He told me to get back to these rascals, so I decided to come home."

They looked as relieved as he did, and she knew he'd been downplaying how distressed he'd been the other day for their sake. It was more than obvious that he loved his father, so the relief must have been enormous.

"Is he going to be kept in for long?"

"That's what I was just about to tell the kids," he said, looking from her to them. "I'm going to head back to the city, take them with me this time, then when he's ready I'll drive Dad home. Mom's a bit nervous, and we need to check in with the local doctor in Parkes on our way, too."

Poppy kept her smile plastered to her face, trying hard not to react. It was great that Harrison was taking his kids with him. She had no right to be sad about it.

"I've been trying to explain to them that Granddad had to have stents put in—"

"And it's gross," announced Katie, interrupting her dad and pulling a face.

"It might be gross but it saved your granddad's life," Harrison said, lifting her up to sit on the kitchen counter beside her brother.

"Did they put the stents through his arm?" Poppy asked.

Harrison nodded. "Yeah, they put dye through first because they were pretty blocked, then the stents. It was amazing." He raised his eyebrows, as if he'd just realized that she knew way too much about heart complications. "How did you know about stents, anyway?"

She shrugged, taking the pie over to the counter and placing it there before filling the jug with water for something to do. After the long day she'd had, she was ready for a coffee. A good, strong, black coffee.

"My dad had a heart attack, but he didn't make it. He had to have a triple bypass and there were complications."

Harrison gave her a tight smile. "I'm sorry. I know how lucky we are that Dad pulled through."

She shook her head. "Don't feel bad for telling me your dad made it, Harrison."

He planted his hands on the counter with a thump. The kids had gone quiet, listening to them talk, no doubt trying to understand what they were discussing. Poppy could tell he was trying to lift the mood, distract them.

"Coffee for everyone?" he asked.

"Dad! We don't drink coffee!" Katie squealed as he grabbed her around the waist and set her on her feet.

He did the same to Alex, only kept hold of him a little longer, giving the little guy a big hug. "Okay, so coffee for me and Poppy, and tea for you two."

Katie and Alex were both giggling now, jumping around like silly things.

"Fine, how about orange juice then?"

Poppy watched as he poured them each a glass before opening a container full of cookies and letting them take some.

"Why don't you guys have your snack outside and then play? We'll be out soon."

Poppy stayed silent and watched the kids go. They were such happy children, busy and lovable. Looking after them might have been tiring, but it certainly hadn't been hard.

"You do know what great children you have, right?"

He chuckled. "Yeah, I do. Although it's easy to think all kids are like that and forget how good mine are."

Now it was Poppy's turn to laugh. "Are you kidding me? I don't ever think all children are like that, and I've got *a lot* of experience in that department."

Harrison was staring at her, his body language different than it had been before. Around his children he was open and relaxed, but now that they were gone something had changed.

"I don't know how I'll ever thank you for looking after them for me," he said, pouring the coffee and sliding a mug across the counter toward her. "It meant a lot to me to get to the hospital when I did, and I'm glad they didn't see their granddad looking like that, all hooked up to machines and ghostly when I first got there."

Poppy knew exactly what he was talking about. "They were pretty upset the first night, worrying about him and wanting you, but we were fine. And they *are* great kids, I promise."

He took a sip of his coffee, but he was still staring at her.

"It wasn't until I started driving home today that I realized I'd never told you where anything was, or even which bed to sleep in," he said.

Poppy's face flushed hot and she hoped she wasn't blushing. "I, ah, hope you don't mind, but I slept in yours." *There, she'd said it.* Besides, he'd probably already been in there and noticed, anyway.

"Good. I didn't want you sleeping in the bunks, but I'm just sorry I didn't have time to put fresh sheets on."

She swallowed. Then swallowed again. She was glad he hadn't washed the sheets. His aftershave had been all over the pillows and she wasn't going to pretend she didn't appreciate the scent.

"It was fine, honestly. I'm just pleased I could help out," she said, trying to sound nonchalant when in reality her heart was beating overtime.

"Well, I left my things in the hall, anyway, just in case you had anything private in there."

Poppy's heart slowed then. Her embarrassment died faster than it had appeared. How the heck had she managed to meet a man with manners *this* good? Still, she was ready to change the subject.

"So when are you heading off? I hope you're not going to drive tired." The last thing she needed was to be worrying about him.

"Tomorrow," he said. "We'll leave tomorrow, so the kids will have at least a few days off school."

She shrugged. "No problem. Swing past if you want to take some reading or anything for them."

Poppy cradled her coffee and looked outside. She'd felt a lot of things around Harrison, but never awkward, which was exactly how she was feeling now.

Now? Now she didn't know what to say to him, how to look at him. Because she'd slept in his bed, cooked in his kitchen, cared for his children…and now it was *him* she was thinking about. What kissing him would be like, what touching him would be like, what letting something further develop between them would be like.

Stop! Poppy cleared her throat and just stood there, watching the children as they played outside. She was rebuilding her life here, on her own, to prove that she was capable of starting over. Men were not in her immediate future—not one-night stands, not relationships and certainly *not* Harrison Black.

"Poppy?"

He was standing behind her; she could feel it. Knew that he was too close, closer than he should be when they were nothing more than friends.

"Sometimes I think I could just stand for hours watching them," he said, voice low. "They're pretty good at leveling me when everything feels like it's turned to crap."

Poppy was still staring out the window, but she didn't know what to say, how to respond. But he was right. The way children could make you feel, the way they *did* make her feel, was one of the reasons she loved her job. Why she loved children.

Her body went rigid as metal. Harrison's hand had closed over her shoulder gently, as warm as if there was no fabric between them, even though there was.

She kept staring out the window even though she couldn't see anything, was blind to everything except his touch. Poppy wished she didn't feel this way, wished her resolve about men was stronger, but Harrison was the kind of man she'd wished she'd met all along. The kind of man that might be able to make her trust again, to make her love. And no matter how much her brain was telling her not to think that way, her heart was starting to tell her a different story altogether.

"Thank you, Poppy." His grasp changed then, becoming a soft squeeze that made her shut her eyes, trying to relax and summon enough courage to turn toward him. Because he still hadn't moved, which made her think he was waiting for her. "They've experienced a lot of heartache, a lot of pain over their mom leaving, even though they were so young when she left. It's not often I let someone close to them, so thank you for being there when they needed someone."

She pivoted slowly on the spot, and as she moved his hand fell away, brushing her hip as it skimmed past. But the rest of him seemed carved from stone—unmoving, unblinking, but not unseeing.

Harrison's gaze was steady, yet there was a seriousness in his stare that in equal parts thrilled and terrified her.

"I should go," she mumbled, her voice so quiet she wasn't even sure she'd spoken.

Harrison didn't say anything, but he did move. Now it was Poppy standing as if *she* was carved from stone, still as a statue as he slowly raised his hand, fingers brushing her jaw and staying there. When he pressed lightly, she moved into him, stepping into his space as if he'd asked her to.

Poppy ignored the warning voice in her head, switched it off and refused to be drawn away from something so magnetic, something she instinctively knew was going to feel good.

Harrison's mouth moved closer to hers, lips slightly parted, his eyes no longer looking into hers but staring at her mouth instead. His fingers were warm against her skin, sending tingles through her body that curled into her stomach, and his lips were hot.

Harrison kissed her so tenderly that she had to stifle a moan. She stood still, rooted to the spot, as though if she moved even an inch he might stop what he was doing and...

Oh. He didn't stop. Instead, he reached with his other hand to touch his fingers to the back of her skull, teased her even more with his mouth. Harrison's tongue softly, wetly tangled with hers, and still she didn't move, lost to the sensation of his lips against hers, in the most tender of embraces she'd ever experienced.

And then he pulled away—so slowly that she leaned forward, hungry to feel his mouth back on hers, to lose herself in the moment again.

But he put his hands on her arms then, holding her back, as if *she'd* been the one who'd started this in the first place.

"I don't know where that came from," he said, his voice a husky whisper.

Neither did she. But she did know that she'd liked it, even though her kissing Harrison had a voice in her mind screaming "No!" so loudly that it should have sent her running.

"Daddy!"

Katie's excited call made Poppy jump back a step, not wanting either of his children to catch them kissing. It was bad enough that she'd let it happen without having it complicate things for them, too.

Harrison cleared his throat. "In here, honey."

They were still staring at each other, not saying anything, and Poppy was alternating from having a million and one things to say to him to nothing at all.

"I think it's time for me to go," she murmured.

Harrison smiled, one side of his mouth kicking up at the corner. "You sure you don't want to stay for dinner?"

Did she ever. But she wasn't going to put herself through an evening with Harrison when what she needed was to establish distance between them. To set boundaries and follow through with them. To think about what had just happened.

"Harrison..." she began, not knowing how to say what she was feeling. Not *knowing* how she was actually feeling inside.

"Dad, we found a field mouse." Katie burst into the room. "Alex saw it, too."

Harrison kept watching Poppy, a beat too long, before turning his attention to his children. "How about you show me where you saw it," he said. "That'll give Poppy some time to get her things together."

Part of her liked that he was giving her some privacy, but another part? That part wanted him to ask her one more time to stay.

* * *

"Are you sure you won't stay for dinner?"

Poppy shook her head, but he could tell she'd considered it. The way she glanced around the room and looked at the kids told him she'd given it more thought than she was letting on.

"I really do need to go," she told him, slinging her overnight bag over her shoulder. "I don't want to drive back in the dark and Lucky will be missing me."

"Let me walk you out, then," he said, wanting a moment to talk to her alone before she left, because things were only going to get more awkward between them if he didn't bring up their kiss.

Why he'd needed to cross that boundary, when he had *zero* interest in taking things further with *any* woman, he didn't know. But he had, and now he needed to deal with the consequences.

"Honestly, I'm fine," she said, giving him a tight smile that he didn't buy for a moment. "Enjoy your trip to Sydney, kids."

They called out goodbye to her and Harrison followed Poppy to the front door, leaning past her to open it. She stayed still, as if she was too scared to touch him even by accident, until he stepped aside and she walked out to her car.

"Poppy, about before…" he started.

"You don't need to say anything, Harrison," she replied, not letting him finish.

He shoved his hands into his pockets, watched her as she threw her bag in the back and did everything to avoid making eye contact with him.

"It was a heat-of-the-moment thing and there's nothing to discuss," she said.

If there was nothing to discuss, then why was she trying to flee the scene so quickly?

"Poppy, I'm sorry," he said, needing to apologize before he managed to completely ruin their friendship. "I'm sure you're as hesitant as me to get, ah, *involved*." He paused, not wanting to dig himself a bigger hole than he had already. Nothing was coming out like he wanted it to. "What I mean is you're a beautiful, wonderful woman, but I didn't mean to give you the wrong idea."

She was looking even more embarrassed now than before he'd started to try and explain himself. *Crap!* He was making a complete hash of the entire situation.

"What I'm trying to say is that I got carried away before, but our friendship means a lot to me, and I'm so grateful for what you did, looking after the kids. I don't want to ruin that."

Poppy looked like a startled animal ready to flee, staring at him as if he'd announced he wanted to boil her cat and eat it.

"There's no need to apologize, Harrison," she finally said, breaking the silence. "It just happened, but I couldn't agree more. We're friends, and the last thing I'm interested in is something, well, something happening between us."

Harrison stood on the grass, wriggling his toes into it for something to do, and watched her get in her car.

"Thanks again for helping me out."

She nodded. "No problem. See you when you're back."

He pushed his hands even deeper into his jeans pockets and watched her drive off. Kind, sweet, beautiful Poppy, who he'd managed to thoroughly embarrass after she'd done so much for him. Then he'd talked rubbish, trying to explain his way out of what had happened.

But the problem wasn't what he'd done, it was how she'd responded. How they'd both responded. He'd meant to just touch her, then deliver a soft kiss, but the moment their lips had collided he'd been a goner, and if his daughter hadn't called out and broken the spell between them, he wasn't sure when he'd have pulled away.

Poppy was making him think things that weren't even a possibility for him or his children, not if he wanted to protect them, and it scared the hell out of him.

Harrison watched until her car disappeared from view, then went back inside. He had to heat the pie Poppy had left behind and slice it up for dinner, then pack their bags before they all went to bed. An early night was exactly what he needed before they made the drive back to Sydney. He wanted to leave early in the morning so the kids could just jump in the vehicle in their pajamas and fall back to sleep. That way, they'd make it to the city in time for lunch.

He also had to get on the phone and organize his workers, since he was going to be away for up to a week.

Poppy. Not seeing Poppy for a week? It was playing on his mind. He shrugged the thought away and slid the pie into the oven. Two weeks ago he hadn't even known her name and now he was acting as if he'd known her all his life.

So some time away? That might be just what he needed to get perspective again. Reset his boundaries; reaffirm them. Before he forgot all the reasons why he couldn't let a woman close to him. *Not ever again.*

CHAPTER EIGHT

POPPY SURVEYED THE garden and wondered where to start. She hadn't ever had a lawn to contend with before, or at least not since she was a little girl, and back then all she'd had to do was pretend she was mowing it. In fact, now that she thought about it, she recalled having a tiny pretend lawn mower that had blown bubbles.

The reality of mowing her own lawn wasn't so appealing, but it had to be done and she had nothing better to do.

Poppy looked at the old mower and sighed. She'd got it for nothing from one of her pupils' parents and she doubted it had been used for years. And her lawn looked as if it hadn't been cut in forever.

"Here goes," she muttered under her breath, pushing with all her might.

Five minutes later she was covered in sweat and the lawn looked as if it had been hacked by a machete. The only positive was that pushing the hell out of the mower had taken her mind off Harrison.

And now she was exhausted and thinking about him all over again.

She wanted to know why he'd kissed her, why he'd looked at her like that, why he was acting as if he wanted her one minute and then telling her why nothing could happen the next. She got it; she had to. Because if she was honest, she was the same, like a pendulum swinging hard one way, then zooming back in the other direction a second later. One moment she wanted Harrison to kiss her, to make her think that something could happen between them, and the next she was terrified by the idea of it. Thinking about what could go wrong, how he could hurt her, what had happened in the past... But deep down, she wanted to see if maybe she could make the right judgment call about a man. And whether that man *could* be Harrison.

The phone was ringing. She'd been so lost in her thoughts, and in surveying her stupid backyard, that she hadn't even noticed it bleating.

Poppy ran for the back door, scooted inside and grabbed the phone from its cradle.

"Hello?" She had no answering machine, and it drove her crazy to miss a call and not know who it was.

"Hey! It's me."

Poppy untwirled the cord and jumped up to sit on the counter. It was her sister. "You have no idea how much I needed to hear from you." She sighed down the line.

"You're not getting bored living out there in hickville, are you?"

"Do you have *any* idea how much I miss your teasing?"

They hadn't lived in the same place for years, but she was used to talking to her sister constantly—on the way to school when she'd been in the city, early in the evening, all the time.

"Tell me the goss. Any gorgeous single men?"

Poppy was pleased her sister couldn't see her smile. "You're not going to believe it, but yeah. There is."

Kelly screamed down the line. "I knew it! You little minx!"

Poppy twisted the cord around her finger, feeling like a teenager again just yapping to her sister on the old-fashioned phone. "I'm not interested in a relationship, Kelly. You know that."

She had a feeling that her sister would have slapped her if she'd been in the room. Especially if she'd seen the man they were talking about.

"Who says you need a relationship? Just have hot, steamy sex with him."

Poppy's face was suddenly on fire. Seriously, trust her sister to say something like that. "It's complicated," she started.

"How?"

"I teach his kids, and we've sort of become friends. And it's a really small town, did I mention that?" She was trying to think of every excuse possible, because now that she'd told her, Kelly was never going to back down.

"When are you seeing him next?"

Poppy sighed. "He's been out of town, but Mrs. Jones mentioned this morning that he'd been in to get his groceries."

"Think of an excuse and go see him. You know you deserve to be happy, right? *So be happy.* Not every guy is an asshole, Poppy, and if he is? Kick him straight to the curb."

Yeah, it was easy for her sister to say. She wasn't exactly the type to end up with the wool pulled over her eyes. Come to think of it, she probably tired of men before they had a chance to hurt her.

"He kind of lives a long way out, and I'm—"

"I said make up an excuse to see him, not make up an excuse to give me."

What could she say to that?

"Hey, I have to go. Call me tomorrow after you've seen him," Kelly said. "See ya."

Poppy hung up the phone and stayed seated on the counter, legs swinging. Lucky jumped up and joined her, looking out the window.

"Don't you dare laugh at the state of the grass," she ordered.

The truth was, she didn't care about the grass right now, because her sister had told her exactly what she'd been thinking anyway. And if they both had the same gut feeling...

What kind of excuse could she make to drive up to the ranch? To just turn up out of the blue? And what if she didn't want anything to happen between them?

She'd just come out of a long-term relationship, just dealt with her heart being broken. It wasn't that she didn't like Harrison, but...she wasn't a one-night stand kind of girl, either. And he'd made it perfectly clear that he wasn't interested in something permanent. So unless he changed his mind on that, she was going to have to forget all about him. But first she wanted to give him a chance.

* * *

Poppy was either making the biggest mistake or taking the best risk of her life. Given the intensity of the rain that was falling, she was starting to think it could be a sign, but then again, maybe she was just making excuses again.

The rain had come from nowhere, was bucketing down as if the sky was trying to punish them and her wipers were going flat tack.

It was a stupid plan. Who ever visited someone in this kind of weather? Although it hadn't been quite this bad when she'd made the decision to follow her sister's advice, so at least she had that as a backup excuse.

All she had come up with was something that was truthful, because she wasn't capable of lying or devising a fake reason to visit. It was the Aboriginal family she was going to see. And if she happened to end up spending time with Harrison, then so be it.

Katie had told her there were two children living on the ranch, probably a lot farther out, but still... She was the local teacher, and that meant she had an obligation to provide educational services to every child in the district.

Poppy squinted into the distance, sure she could see someone headed her way. Now that she'd hit the dirt road, she hadn't expected to encounter any other vehicles.

She slowed down, worried about visibility. The oncoming vehicle wasn't going too fast, but it flashed its lights at her. Was it Harrison?

It was. His black truck was almost beside her, and

she slowed even more. Now she felt like an idiot, and would likely end up mumbling a heap of nonsense when she came face-to-face with him. She'd come up with an excuse, but hadn't expected to have to explain herself before she even reached the ranch.

He stopped and wound down his window, and she did the same.

"Hi," she called out.

"What are you doing out here?" Harrison called back, his hair wet and plastered to his face.

She could see the kids in the back, and was embarrassed that she'd even come up with a plan at all just to see their dad. *Their gorgeous, wet, handsome-as-hell father.*

"It seems kind of crazy, given the weather, but I wanted to call in on the family you have living on the ranch. I'm told the children are homeschooled and I wanted to see if there's any way I can help them."

Harrison didn't question her, even though she knew her face was burning. She guessed he couldn't see the change in color through the rain.

"We've had a flash flood, and with the ground this dry our river's overflowing. Must be raining by the bucketload farther inland."

Yeah, really great timing on her part. "I'll come back another time," she said, wishing she'd never listened to her sister in the first place.

"You wouldn't be able to do me a huge favor, would you?"

"Sure." She was having to yell now, the rain was coming down so hard.

"I want to get the kids to my folks so I can deal with the storm and move the cattle to higher ground. But I'm running out of time before the water gets too high."

Poppy didn't need to be asked twice. "Get them in the back," she called to him. "I'll take them now."

"You sure?"

"Of course."

At least she could be helpful. Might take his mind off the fact she'd decided to make a house call to a remote ranch in weather like this. She'd never even thought about the riverbed leading to the property, that it could be flooded.

Harrison jumped out of his truck and grabbed Alex, putting him in the back of her car, then Katie.

"Hey, kids," she said.

They just grinned at her, a little shy from not having seen her all week.

"I owe you big time, *again*," Harrison said, standing out in the gale.

"It's fine. Just get out of the rain and head back home."

He called out some instructions to her, gave her his parents' address then turned around and drove toward the ranch.

Poppy took a deep breath before turning her car around, too. "So do you guys know where we're going?"

"Yes," said Katie. "It's really easy."

She grinned at the children in her rearview mirror, checking that their seat belts were done up.

So much for trying to seduce their father, if that's

what she'd actually been planning. She was much more capable of doing something with his kids.

They pulled up outside a sizable house not far from where Poppy lived. The town was small, so everything was relatively close, but they were on the outskirts and this house had to be the prettiest and nicest maintained of all the homes in Bellaroo Creek.

"This is their place?" she asked.

Katie nodded. "Yup."

Poppy pulled into the driveway, parking as close to the house as possible to avoid the kids getting too wet when they got out. "Okay, let's go," she told them, grabbing their overnight bag from the passenger seat and leaping out of the car.

The front door was open before they even reached the porch. An older, attractive woman was waiting for them, her hair pulled back into a bun, gray but immaculate.

"In you scoot," she said, smiling at the children as they ran past her into the house. "And you must be Ms. Carter."

Poppy held out her hand. "To the children, yes. I'm Poppy."

"Nice to finally meet you after hearing so much about you this past week."

Hearing so much about her? "I hope it was only good things." What else could she say in response to that?

"Of course. Now, dear, I'd ask you in, but my son's

just phoned with a bit of an emergency. He wanted me to go, but…" The other woman sighed.

Poppy's heart sank. "Is he okay?" Surely his mom wouldn't be standing making small talk with her if something terrible had happened?

"Are you any good at delivering babies?"

What? "Um, I can't say I have any experience *delivering* babies, exactly, but I was my best friend's birthing partner when she had both her children."

"Thank goodness." Harrison's mom reached out and touched her forearm. "Did Harrison ever mention the family living in one of the workers' homes?"

Poppy refused to blush, even though her entire plan about seeing Harrison had revolved around the family they were talking about. "Yes, it's why I was heading to the ranch today. To see them." She was getting a lot better at delivering her line.

"Well, she's gone into labor a few weeks early, and Harrison's all in a flap, worried about her, even though I know for a fact her husband delivered her other two at home with no problems."

"So you're asking *me* to go back and assist with the labor?" Poppy took a deep breath. "I mean, well…" She paused. What the hell did she mean? The woman was in the middle of nowhere during a storm, which meant she had no other choice *but* to be capable.

"He said he'd meet me near the river, but I'm sure he'll be pleased to see you instead. He'll take you over the flooding in the helicopter."

This was actually happening. She had a legitimate reason to see him, to spend time with him, and she was so nervous her legs were in danger of buckling beneath her.

"I guess this is another good way to become part of the community, right?" she managed to reply, trying not to let on how nervous she was. So much for the afternoon with Harrison that she'd hoped for.

"That's a girl. Now get in that car and drive safely."

Poppy was numb, but she smiled and walked back to the car. The only consolation was that she got to see Harrison again.

CHAPTER NINE

HARRISON HOVERED THE helicopter, going closer to the car than he had intended but needing to force her to stop. The weather conditions weren't great, but he'd been up in worse and right now his primary concern was ensuring he didn't put Poppy's life in danger by letting her get too close to the river. He was guessing she'd offered to take his mom's place in coming—either that or his mother had seen it as an opportunity to matchmake.

He watched as Poppy stopped the vehicle but she didn't get out straightaway and he wasn't sure if she could see him waving to her or not. Even though the rain was still pelting from the sky he decided to touch down, because the wind had died off and it was probably safest.

Harrison jumped from the chopper once it was clear and ran toward Poppy. She climbed out of the vehicle when she saw him, coat held above her head, and he put his arm around her as they ran back. There was no point trying to talk until they were inside the helicopter.

He opened her door, helped her up then ran around

to his side, hauling himself up, shutting the door and turning to her.

"Hell of a way we keep meeting," he joked, pleased to see a smile on her face even though she was drenched.

"I'm trying to convince myself this whole situation is character building," she told him. "That's the kind of thing I'd tell my pupils, anyway."

Harrison leaned over and helped her with the crossover seat belt, then passed her a headset. "Put this on. I have to get this bird up now while it's safe, and we can keep talking through these." He put his own on, then ignored everything else while he flicked switches and put them up in the air. He knew better than to let anything distract him when there was no margin for error.

"I'll take us close to the barn," he told her as they went up and across the river. "My truck's parked there."

"Oh my goodness, oh my goodness."

Harrison glanced at her. "Are you okay?" The last thing he needed was her freaking out before they touched down. "We'll be grounded in less than a minute."

"I'll be fine," she said, although her voice was wobbly. Even through the headset he could hear how panicked she was. "Just..." She didn't finish her sentence.

"This river is usually dry through this part of the year, but the heavy rainfall farther inland has pushed a lot of water down. The ground's really dry right now, which is why it floods so quickly." He was trying to soothe her, to take her mind off her worries. He loved being in the air, but knew plenty of people were terrified of flying. Especially in a helicopter. "Over winter we're flooded in for a good few weeks sometimes, would you believe?"

She wasn't saying anything now, but he was hoping that listening to him had taken her mind off her fears.

"Here we go, ready to land already."

Harrison brought the chopper down as steadily as he could, even though the rain lashing against them and the wind picking up again wasn't making it easy. One of his ranch hands was waiting for them, running out, head tucked low, to assist. Harrison jumped out as soon as it was safe and went around to help Poppy out, holding her hand and running with her to his truck.

"Give me a minute, okay?"

He didn't wait for her reply but bolted back to the helicopter as fast as he could, securing the rotors down with ropes they had at the ready and manhandling the cover over the cockpit.

"Thanks, Chad," he called out.

His young ranch hand was soaked to the bone— they'd all been out far too long in the wet weather already—but he was jogging back over to him.

"Hey, boss, Sally's had her baby. Arrived while you were gone, and Rocky called it through on the sat phone."

Harrison indicated for him to join him in the barn. "She's had it? Already?"

"Yeah, Rocky went straight back to the cottage, just like you told him to, and he called to say it was their fastest baby yet."

"And they've got everything under control? They

don't need any help with…" he paused, running a hand through his wet hair "…I don't know, women's stuff?"

"Yeah, he said they're all good. Said he'd call you if they needed your mom." The young man laughed. "Although I can see it's actually your *lady friend* come to help."

Harrison glared at him, raising an eyebrow. "She's not my *lady friend*, Chad. She's the kids' teacher."

He received another laugh in response and he shook his head. Clearly he'd been way too lenient with his young worker for him to tease him like that, *especially* about a woman.

"Whatever you say, boss."

Harrison started to walk off, then spun around again. "What did they have?"

"Little girl," Chad called out, walking backward through the barn.

"Hey, you guys may as well call it a day. Warm up and dry off before you catch a cold. And don't forget to feed the dogs."

Harrison put his head down and ran for the vehicle. Now that the baby was safely delivered, there was no reason for Poppy to be here. But he had no intention of taking the helicopter up again, and the river was way too high to cross even in his truck.

Which meant Poppy was stranded here for the night with him.

He could see her sitting inside, watching him, until he yanked the door open and jumped in. "I have good news," he said, smiling. Or at least he hoped she thought being stuck with him, and not having to help bring a baby into the world, was what she'd consider good news.

All Poppy could think about was how reckless she was being, listening to her heart instead of her head. Either reckless or stupid. She couldn't decide which.

The fact that, instead of looking pretty and serene, she was soaking wet and freezing cold, was running through her mind, too. She was stuck at Harrison's ranch until she didn't have a clue when, which meant she needed to get over her embarrassment at being here and looking like a drowned rat. Or at least start to believe the lie she was stating — that she'd headed in the direction of the ranch to see the family. The family whose baby she was also meant to have helped deliver.

Arghh. Nothing about today had turned out as planned.

"So how's your dad doing?" she asked, unable to think of anything else to say.

"Great. He's doing great," Harrison replied.

They stayed silent again, as if he was as troubled for words as she was.

"I'll pull up right against the house," he told her. "Although given how wet we are—" he looked at her and then down at himself "—I'm not sure it's going to help any."

Poppy hadn't dared to look at herself in the mirror, even while she'd been in the vehicle alone, because there wasn't much she could do. Except perhaps rub any smudged mascara from beneath her eyes.

"Okay, run whenever you're ready. Just don't slip on the brickwork."

If he hadn't warned her, she probably would have done exactly that.

Poppy moved quickly up the steps and into the shelter of the porch and Harrison was right behind her. His body knocked hers, pressing into her for a second before he slid back out of the way.

"Sorry," he said, pushing the door. "It's not locked. I don't think anyone would bother to burgle us."

She laughed, but it came out all nervous sounding. She seriously needed to get a grip. Poppy focused on walking into the house, waiting for Harrison to flick on the lights, before realizing she was making a puddle on the floor. Thank goodness she'd had a coat on to keep her top relatively dry, but her lower legs were soaked and she sure wasn't going to strip off her pants.

"I'm making your floor all wet."

"Ditto." Harrison laughed, but at least he had wet-weather gear on. "I'm going to hit the shower and change clothes. Is there anything I can get you? You know where the main bathroom is if you want to grab a shower, too."

She shook her head. "No, I'm good. I'll just…" What? She wasn't exactly sure what she was going to do. "You go have a shower and I'll try to dry off."

Poppy watched as he peeled off his jacket, sweater and socks, rolled up the bottoms of his jeans then crossed the room and disappeared.

"I'll crank up the fire, make it warmer in here," he called out.

Hopefully, it would warm enough for her to dry out quickly, because she wanted to take as few clothes off as possible. She stood, listening to him putting logs on the fire, hearing the flames hiss, then his footfalls as he walked to his bathroom. She stripped off her shoes and socks, removed her sweater and carried them all into the living room. Water was still dripping from her jeans, so she rolled up the denim.

At least she had her handbag, although it held only tissues, lip gloss and some mascara. Maybe some old mints, too, if she was lucky, but probably not much else.

On second thought, maybe she should use the bathroom. She could tidy up a little, try to wring some of the water from her jeans and make sure her tank top wasn't indecently tight. Not that she had any other options if it was, given that she'd never planned on anyone seeing it.

If her mobile phone worked out here, she could have called her sister for a pep talk, a confidence boost, but technology wasn't her friend in Bellaroo

She heard the pipes groan and then go silent. Which meant Harrison was out of the shower.

It also meant she didn't have long before she had to face him…for the rest of the night.

Harrison could hear Poppy in the living room. He pulled his shirt on and started walking, finding her standing in front of the fire and looking at some photographs on the mantel.

"Warming up?"

"Yeah," she replied, turning to face him.

She was beautiful; he couldn't deny it, even if he was trying to stop thinking about her like that. After their kiss…

He pushed the thought away. It didn't matter how much he liked her; it wasn't a possibility. Which meant he had to treat her like the friend she was and nothing else.

"Is this your wife?" she asked.

"Ex," he snapped, instantly wishing he hadn't answered quite so quickly or with such a bitter tone.

"She's beautiful," Poppy said, still staring at the photo. "And it's nice that you keep a photo here after, well, you know. I'm sure it was difficult."

Yeah, he knew. "It's not the kids' fault that she left, but she still brought them into this world." He paused, watching Poppy. "I'll never understand how she did it, but now when I think about it, I'd like to believe she wanted to give them a better life. That maybe she did it for them, because she couldn't be the mom she thought they deserved."

Poppy was staring at him now, the photo forgotten. "I know it's not my place to say anything, but I just don't get how a woman can leave her kids. I mean, to completely walk out on your own flesh and blood seems…"

"Cold?" he finished for her. "Cruel, unbelievable?"

Her expression was sad. "Exactly."

A moment earlier he'd been feeling exhausted but happy. Now he was just annoyed that they'd somehow ended up talking about his past when for once he'd forgotten about it.

"When I said to you the other day that I wasn't ready for anything, that I couldn't take what I started with you any further," he told her, forcing himself to meet her eye, "*that's* why. Because I don't trust that someone else won't hurt my children again. No matter who that person is. And that means I can't let anyone into my life. It's why I'm so protective."

Poppy sighed. He couldn't read her expression, but he could tell she disagreed with him about something.

"Believe me, I have trust issues, too. But maybe we have to move forward in order to let go."

No, she was wrong. "Or maybe we have to hold on to it," he said, anger starting to thump through his body. "Instead of making the same mistake all over again."

CHAPTER TEN

"I'm not your ex-wife, Harrison, so you don't need to speak to me like I am."

He glared at her, so angry she could feel it. His jaw was clamped so tight she could see a flicker in his cheek.

"You have no idea what you're talking about," he growled. "I'm trying to be honest with you, not pretend that you're *her*, but you don't seem to get the reality of what happened."

Now it was Poppy's turn to glare, to be furious with him, because she *did* get it, and it was about time he listened to her.

"I know that she left you, and I know that you've raised your children alone. If you want to elaborate, then by all means," she said, refusing to raise her voice. He could get as angry and loud as he liked, but she was not going to get into a yelling match with him, any more than she was going to let him speak to her like that. "All I'm saying is—"

"My wife left me as if our marriage vows meant nothing," he interrupted, his voice a low hiss. "I don't care that she left me, but I do care that she left our children. Don't get me wrong, I cared plenty at the time, but seeing the pain in their faces, seeing the confusion in their eyes when I had to explain to them why she didn't want anything to do with them anymore… It doesn't matter that I've made peace with raising them on my own because they'll never understand what she did." Harrison shook his head and strode away before turning and pacing straight back in Poppy's direction. "How do you think your husband feels? Did you just walk out on him, too? What would he think if he knew…" Harrison's voice trailed off.

How dare he turn the conversation around like that and try to make *her* into a villain? This was about him, not her.

"If he knew what?" she asked, knowing full well what he was going to say.

"If he knew that you'd been unfaithful? That we'd kissed?"

She laughed—a weird, evil laugh that she'd never heard come from her own mouth before. "You think *I've* been unfaithful?" Oh, if only he knew the half of it.

Harrison was staring at her hard, his eyes never leaving hers, almost as if he was trying to set her on fire with his gaze. She had no idea why he was taking so much of his anger out on her, why he'd somehow made all this *her* fault.

"Unfaithful is finding your husband in bed with another woman," she said, refusing to back down now she'd started, not prepared to let him think that what had happened to her was *her* fault. Not when she'd finally managed to believe the truth herself. "Sorry, in *my* bed," she corrected. "Naked and in bed with another woman, and only discovered because I decided not to stay late and mark term papers but went home instead. So if you wanted to hear about *unfaithful*, now you have."

The look on Harrison's face had changed. Gone was the anger, the wildness in his eyes that had taken over his entire expression only a minute earlier. But he'd asked. He'd accused her of being, what? An *adulteress*? Just because she hadn't received her divorce papers in the mail yet?

"My marriage is over, Harrison. And you'll find that it was my husband's choice to ruin things between us, not mine."

Poppy watched as he swallowed, almost enjoying how uncomfortable he looked after the way he'd spoken to her.

"Poppy, I'm sorry. I never should have said anything when I had no idea what you'd been through." His voice was deep, commanding.

She shrugged. "Your wife hurt you, *badly*. I get that. But it doesn't mean that every other woman who walks away from a marriage is at fault."

Harrison stood so still he seemed to be carved from marble, a statue in the room facing her.

"My husband not only cheated on me, Harrison, he took everything from me."

"I don't understand."

Poppy looked up at the light, staring at it, forcing her emotion away. Refusing to succumb to the tears that were threatening, so close to the surface she didn't know if she had the strength to fight them.

"I've worked so hard all my life to have somewhere nice to live, to afford the little luxuries I wanted, and when my dad passed away, he left me half of everything he owned. My sister and I received equal shares of his estate, and I didn't waste a cent because I know how hard he had worked for everything he had."

Harrison just stared at her, but now his gaze was soft and caring, as if he was feeling every flash of the pain that was going through her body and truly regretted his burst of anger.

"I'd been with my husband for years, had known him since we were at school together, and I'd never known he was a gambler," she confessed, ready to tell Harrison everything. "It turns out that he'd slowly been getting us further and further into debt without me knowing. And because we owned everything together—" Poppy shrugged and took a deep breath "—he managed to lose our house, our cars, *everything*. He'd drained my bank account without me even knowing, all because I'd trusted him too much."

"Oh, Poppy, I'm so sorry."

She bravely tilted her chin up, blinked the tears away again and held her head high. "So that's why I'm here, trying to start over and forget the last year even existed."

"I never should have been so hard on you. I'm sorry, I…" Harrison looked torn, as if he didn't know what to say or how to go about comforting her.

Poppy squared her shoulders. "So now you know all

my dirty secrets," she said. "I'm an almost-divorcee, I'm broke and I managed to spend all my married years not knowing my husband was screwing around behind my back, with my money and the woman who lived across the hall from us."

"I guess we have more in common than we realized," Harrison said, his voice soft now, which seemed to soothe the thumping of her head and the shaking of her hands.

"Yeah," she muttered, crossing her arms.

But it was too late. Harrison had already seen her hands shaking and he was stepping forward and reaching for them, interlacing their fingers.

"You know what I'm wondering?" he asked, pulling her so slowly toward him that her body obeyed without her consent.

"What?" she whispered, staring at his hands instead of his face.

"How any man could ask another woman to his bed when he already had you to come home to."

Poppy didn't believe him, not for a moment, but his words still put a smile on her face. "I don't believe you, but thanks," she said, braving his gaze and wishing she hadn't, staring at him now as if she was stuck in the web of his eyes, hypnotized, with no chance of reprieve.

"If you don't believe me, then how about I show you?" Harrison's voice was so low, so husky, that she was powerless to resist him.

His hand left hers and slowly reached for her face, his palm cupping her cheek, fingers tucking beneath her chin and raising it. Poppy complied, more because she couldn't *not* than because she consented.

Harrison dipped his head, eyes dropping to her mouth, and she did the same. Because his lips were moving toward hers and she wasn't going to pull away.

His mouth was inches from hers, his breath warm against her skin, but still he hesitated, as if waiting for her to accept, to make the final decision.

Hell, yes. The words ran through her mind at the same time as she stepped toward him, just one step, but enough for their bodies to touch and their lips to meet in a kiss that stole her breath away and made her arms snake around the back of his neck. Her fingers found their way into his hair as his hands enclosed her waist, holding her still as their mouths danced, as his tongue so gently played against hers.

So what if she'd promised to stay away from men? Harrison Black had been on her mind since her first day in town, and if she didn't get this out of her system now, then she'd probably never get a good night's sleep ever again. Besides, maybe she didn't need long-term. Maybe one night was enough.

Maybe he'd gone mad. It was the only reason to explain why his lips were currently locked on Poppy's and why he wasn't capable of pulling away even if he'd wanted to.

Her mouth was soft yet firm against his, her hips pulled in tight to his stomach, and he couldn't keep his hands off her. They were skimming her waist, touching her hips, running down the curve of her—

"Stop." Poppy's voice was breathless, but his hands froze at the same time his lips did.

She said *stop*, he stopped. No questions asked. But…

"You okay?" he managed to rasp.

Poppy was nodding, as if trying to convince herself that she *was* okay. "It's just…" Her sentence trailed off and she touched her fingers to her mouth, as if remembering what they'd been doing, touching where *his* lips had been. "I'm not sure… I mean, I don't know if I'm ready for this."

"Poppy, I don't know if either of us is ready for this, not mentally," he said, inching closer again, reaching out slowly to touch her arm. But he was sure ready *physically*.

"Then why are we doing this?" she asked, her eyes connecting with his.

"Because it feels so good?"

Harrison was smiling; he couldn't help it. Because it was the truth. Did he want to be with another woman again, theoretically? *No.* But the pull he'd felt toward Poppy, the amount of time he was spending thinking about her? That was telling him he didn't really have a choice. If they kissed, they kissed, and he'd have to deal with the consequences later.

Poppy was grinning now, and he started to laugh. She did, too.

"How did we end up here?" she asked him, stepping into his arms and dropping her head to his shoulder.

"I have no idea," he replied truthfully, pressing a kiss into her hair.

"How about something to eat?" she murmured.

Harrison took a deep breath, then blew it out slowly. "Sure, why not."

Eating wasn't exactly what he'd had on his mind, but what else were they going to do? For now, the power hadn't gone out, but they were stuck, and would be at least until morning.

So he needed to get his head straight, forget about what had happened and go back to thinking of Poppy as a friend.

She stepped out of his embrace and made for the kitchen, and he couldn't take his eyes from her body. Her sweater was slung over the back of a chair, damp from the rain earlier, so she was just in her jeans and a skintight tank top. Everything clung to her body, showing off every single curve she possessed.

Harrison groaned. It was time he started being honest with himself, and the first step was admitting that he'd never, ever thought of Poppy as just a friend.

In the beginning, she'd infuriated him because he'd needed someone to be angry at and she'd given him a tongue-lashing for being rude. Ever since then he'd been fighting something else entirely, and tonight, if he'd had his way, he'd be giving in to those desires in a heartbeat.

"Are you coming?" Poppy called.

Harrison marched out to the kitchen after her. Food was better than nothing, and she was a pretty good cook.

CHAPTER ELEVEN

POPPY WAS TRYING hard to concentrate on dinner, but it wasn't easy. She could feel Harrison watching her, knew he was staring at her, tracking her every move, and it was making her feel…nervous. This man—this gorgeous, sexy-as-hell man whose house she was stranded in, and who she'd pulled away from earlier when all she'd wanted was to kiss him over and over again—was so tempting it was killing her. And the more she thought about how she'd pushed him away, the more she wanted him. Even though it went against everything she'd vowed not to do.

"Where did you learn to cook like this?" he asked.

"I love being in the kitchen, and I was pretty addicted to the food channel for a while." It was true; sometimes she'd preferred to stay home, glued to the television. Although in hindsight, she might have been more sensible keeping an eye on her husband. "But don't get too excited, it's just a French omelet. I know you can do better."

"Well, it smells fantastic. I can only cook Thai, remember?"

A sudden loud bang sent her sky-high, dropping the pan with a crash to the counter.

"Crap!" Poppy's hand was heating up already from where the pan had burned her, but she couldn't see anything. The lights had gone out, leaving them bathed in darkness. A complete blackout.

"It's okay," Harrison reassured her.

She could hear him but couldn't see him, and she was starting to panic. She was used to having streetlights, not this kind of midnight dark.

"Just wait for a minute until your eyes adjust," he said. "There's a flashlight in the top drawer and I've got one at the back door."

"What the hell just happened?"

"The storm has killed the power. Must have been a fuse blowing to make that kind of bang. I'm going out to check it, so you sit tight."

The last thing she wanted was to be left alone, but Harrison was right. Her eyes were slowly starting to adjust, enough for her to shuffle to the top drawer and find the flashlight. She flicked it on, took a deep breath and held the light to her hand. It was only a tiny patch on her finger that had burned, but it was stinging and she wanted to get it under cold water. At least doing that might take her mind off the fact that she was starting to feel like they were in a horror movie.

Poppy pushed the pan away from the edge of the counter and held her finger under the faucet, shivering as the cold water touched her skin.

"We've definitely lost power."

She turned at the sound of Harrison's voice, making out his silhouette, then seeing him more clearly as he came closer.

"So we're stuck in the dark for the whole night?" she asked.

She didn't know whether it was not having any power or lights or the fact that she was stranded with a man who in equal parts terrified and excited her, but her skin was covered in goose pimples, and not just from the cold water.

"This kind of thing happens out here more often than you'd think, so we're prepared." Harrison walked into the kitchen like a man on a mission, but he stopped dead when he saw her with her finger immersed in the water. "What happened?"

"Burned myself when the lights went out," she told him.

Harrison put down whatever it was he was carrying and turned the faucet off. He held her finger up to the light and inspected it, so tenderly she could scarcely feel his touch.

"How badly does it hurt?" he asked.

"I've had it under water this whole time. It's no big deal." She couldn't even feel the pain any longer. Although that probably had more to do with the proximity of the man standing in front of her than anything else.

"Poppy?"

The way Harrison said her name made the blood pump through her veins as fast as if she'd just finished a marathon. He'd said it as a question, as if he wanted something from her, only she wasn't sure quite what he wanted, and all sorts of thoughts were racing through her mind.

But he didn't bother saying anything else.

Instead, Harrison closed the gap between them and grabbed the back of her head, fisting his hand in her hair and kissing her so hard she could hardly breathe. But she had no intention of resisting, was powerless to.

He grabbed her around the waist without breaking their kiss, hoisting her up onto the counter and pushing his body between her legs. His face was damp, his hair wet from being out in the rain, but she didn't care.

Instead, she obliged. Poppy tucked her legs around his waist, keeping him close and holding on to his shoulders, running her hands down his back and letting her fingers explore his muscles, the curve of his shoulder blades, the back of his arms.

"Are you sure this time?" He'd pulled back just enough to murmur against her lips, was kissing her again before she had time to answer.

Poppy tried to nod, but it was useless, and she was so focused on his tongue against hers, on the way his lips were moving softly one moment, then roughly the next, that she couldn't even comprehend talking.

Because that would involve putting distance between them, and she didn't want that. Not at all. What she wanted was for Harrison to kiss her and kiss her until that was all she could remember.

A crash outside sent her leaping off the counter and into his arms, legs knotted tightly around his waist.

"What was that?"

The storm was raging, with rain teeming down so

hard now she figured it was a wonder water wasn't pouring through the roof.

"Just a tree," he said, trailing gentle kisses down her neck while her attention was diverted. His arms cupped beneath her bottom, held her locked in place.

Poppy sighed and tried to relax again, giggling when he nibbled the edge of her collarbone.

"It doesn't matter what's out there, Poppy," he murmured in between kisses, plucking at her skin so softly that she didn't even realize he'd sat her back down on the counter. "I'll protect you."

She shut her eyes and tipped her head back, the touch of his mouth on her neck and chest enough to make her moan. But she knew he was telling the truth.

Whatever his downfalls were, he would protect her, no matter what. She'd seen firsthand how much he loved his children, had witnessed his strength and determination, and that told her she was safe. That he'd do whatever it took to protect her in the truest sense of the word.

"I think," he whispered against her skin, gently inclining her head forward so he could find his way back to her lips, "that we should take this somewhere more comfortable."

Poppy slid her arms around his neck. That sounded like a very, very good idea.

So much for staying strong and resisting her. Harrison carried Poppy to the fire, gently placing her on the big leather sofa in front of it. The room was almost dark, the red glow from the flames casting a low light and creating shadows.

"I still can't believe I'm stranded here."

Harrison smiled down at Poppy, sitting on the edge of the sofa as she snuggled back into the cushions. "If I didn't know better I might think you'd planned it."

"Yeah, I called on Zeus for some help up there in the sky, and he had someone cut the power," she said sarcastically.

Harrison lay down alongside her, length to length, their bodies just touching. He watched as Poppy sucked part of her bottom lip between her teeth, her eyes dancing from his lips to his eyes and back again.

Wow, she was sexy.

"Hey," he whispered, reaching out to touch her face, smoothing a few loose strands of hair back before trailing a finger down her jawline.

She giggled. It was so soft and unexpected it made him chuckle in turn.

"A few years ago I promised myself never to let a woman into my heart or my home ever again," he told her. It was the truth, but he'd never told anyone, never shared how determined he'd been not to be hurt again or experience what it was like to lose all faith in another human being and be prepared to do anything to protect his children.

"Sounds kind of familiar to me," she replied in a low voice. "I came here because I thought it'd be country hicks and old guys."

Harrison gave her a soft punch to the arm. "Who are you calling a hick?"

She shook her head and sucked in her bottom lip

again as she stared straight into his eyes. "Not you," she said.

Poppy barely moved, just the smallest wriggle of her hips, but it was enough to press their bodies more tightly together, for the tip of her nose to be touching his, for her mouth to be so near that he couldn't think of anything other than kissing her. Again. And again.

Screw it. Why was he holding back? When there was a beautiful woman lying beside him, telling him with every bit of her body language that she wanted him as badly as he wanted her?

Harrison skimmed his fingers along her side, down her torso and to her thigh, at the same time as he brought his lips closer to hers. He tasted her mouth, their lips meeting, tongues colliding so delicately that it made her moan. And when she moaned, she thrust her body tighter to his, one hand gripping his shirt as if she was holding him in place, refusing to let him move, taking charge.

He hadn't been with a woman in…way too long. Had tried to pretend that he was fine on his own as a bachelor, that he didn't need the comfort of a woman. But Poppy? She was telling his body an entirely different story.

She was warm and soft against him, her touch gentle. Poppy's mouth was yielding to his, but the way she was holding on to him told him he was a fool to think he was the one in control here. And he didn't care. Not one bit.

But he was scared. Scared that he'd let a woman into his home, into his life. Because the only women he'd been with since his wife left had been one-night stands when he'd been in the city. Poppy? Poppy was no one-night stand.

She held his face between her hands now and had flipped so she was sitting astride him. Harrison couldn't think, not about *anything* other than the woman looking down at him. She'd broken their kiss, but was leaning forward again, her long hair falling over one shoulder and curling on his chest, her full lips kissing his jaw, then the side of his mouth, before he grabbed hold of her arms, forced his lips to hers.

Poppy kissed him over and over, and he complied, lost to everything except the way her body felt in his hands, the flash of her aqua eyes as they met his every so often before shutting again, as if she was as lost to pleasure as he was.

Harrison couldn't take it any longer. He needed to touch her skin, to see her bare, and he wasn't going to wait.

He pushed her top up, smiling when she sat back and finished the task, tugging it over her head and throwing it to the ground. Her bra was black, plain but pretty, and he wanted it off.

"No," she whispered, when he went to unhook it. Poppy was shaking her head, so he stopped, not wanting to push her.

"Why?" he asked, needing to know. "You don't have to be embarrassed, Poppy. You're beautiful."

She had a wicked look on her face, a grin that told him she was feeling more confident that he'd realized. The light flickering from the fire was making her blond hair into a golden haze, an ethereal effect that left him wondering if he wasn't dreaming about having his children's teacher poised above him in her bra.

"You first," she whispered, wriggling down his legs and pushing his T-shirt up. Her tongue followed her fingers, trailing across his skin. He could hardly stay still. It was torture.

"You're the devil, you know that?" He sucked back a breath as she nipped at his belly with her teeth.

Harrison yanked his T-shirt off and flung it away before grabbing Poppy and flipping her so she was beneath him.

"Hey!" she protested.

"You *are* the devil," he whispered, teasing her the same way she'd teased him, but holding her down by the wrists so she couldn't squirm away even if she tried. *"And I like it."*

Poppy had no idea where her confidence was coming from, but she wasn't going to waste time questioning it. She'd been terrified at the thought of being with another man after so long with her husband, but she needn't have worried. Because Harrison was so kind, so sexy, so *consuming* that she wasn't even having time to worry.

"Off," he ordered, fiddling with the top button of her jeans, lifting his weight just enough to pull them down, but not enough to let her escape.

Poppy tugged at her pants until they were around her ankles so she could kick them free, watching as he did the same, sitting up and discarding his until they were both clothed in only their underwear.

This was actually happening. She sucked back a breath as he lowered himself over her again, with care this time, so unlike before when he'd flipped her and pinned her down. Now he was back to being careful with her, to touching her as if she was so delicate she was in danger of breaking.

"You sure about this?" Harrison's voice was gruff, so unlike his usual tone.

Poppy nodded. "I'm sure." And she was. Nervous, definitely; hesitant, yes. But there was no part of her that didn't want Harrison. And she wasn't going to let a sudden jangle of nerves get in the way of her enjoying herself.

They were stranded at his ranch house, in the dark, and she was lying in the arms of a man who could literally steal her breath away with one touch or kiss. So she was *not* going to back down now.

Harrison was staring into her eyes, waiting for her. As if he wasn't convinced.

So she showed him. Poppy reached behind her and flicked the hooks on her bra, shrugging out of it so she was lying there bare. Harrison's eyes flashed brightly as they stared from her breasts to her eyes and back again.

She reached for him, cupped the back of his head and drew him closer until his warm chest was pressed against her skin, firm against her breasts.

Then she kissed him, lightly at first, teasing him, then pulling him harder against her, her mouth firm against his. His lips touching hers sent licks of heat through her body, and his hand reaching to cover her breast, the roughness of his skin against the softness of hers, was making her think all kinds of wild thoughts.

If she was going to break her promise to herself, she was glad she was breaking it with Harrison.

"Thank you," she whispered.

"For what?" he murmured, pulling back to look at her.

"For making me feel wanted again."

Harrison grinned and snapped the elastic of her panties, making her squeal. "Baby, I couldn't want you any more if I tried."

CHAPTER TWELVE

POPPY OPENED HER eyes, blinking until the blur cleared. She snuggled deeper beneath the blanket, tucked so tightly against Harrison that they may as well have been one.

The light from the fire was orange now, the flames dull compared to their earlier brightness, but the room was still warm and she wasn't going to get up and throw more wood on. She'd never been in a house with a real fire before, but there was something soothing about watching flames lick against wood. Even the smell of the timber burning was kind of comforting.

"Hey, beautiful." Harrison was stretching out one arm, the other still pinned beneath her. "What time is it?"

She had no idea, so she just shook her head, then leaned toward him and placed a soft kiss to his lips before wriggling down a little to press her face into his chest. There was no way she wanted to get up, no matter what the time was.

"This," he said, dropping a kiss into her hair, "is a nice way to wake up."

"Uh-huh," she murmured, not letting go of him.

"The rain sounds like it's stopped, too," Harrison said.

They lay there in silence, the early-morning light starting to filter in.

"Will the power still be out? I'd offer to make pancakes or French toast, but I can't do much without power." Her stomach was rumbling so loudly that it was going to embarrass her if she didn't eat something soon. "I can't believe we didn't eat dinner, when I had it almost ready."

"Poppy, there's something I need to tell you."

She groaned. "If you have a deep, dark confession to make, it's a little late."

Harrison tugged her up so they were lying nose to nose. His body was still pressed to hers, legs tangled beneath the blanket.

"It's nothing terrible, but I think you'll be angry with me."

What was he talking about? "Harrison, if you're not cheating on a spouse, and you didn't secretly video what we did, then I think I'll be able to cope." So long as it wasn't *actually* something even more terrible than that.

"It's about the power." He was grinning now, clearly unable to keep his face straight, and she was starting to get suspicious.

"What about the power?" she asked.

Harrison looked guilty. A cat-caught-with-feathers-in-his-mouth kind of guilty.

"Well, I wasn't lying when I said the power had gone out. That a fuse had blown. We both heard it blow."

She pushed back from him, holding the blanket tight to her and glaring at him. He was grinning again, so she knew it wasn't something hideous, but the look on his face…

"Harrison?"

"The power goes out here all the time, usually over winter, so we have a backup generator."

"So let me get this straight," she said, shaking her head.

He laughed and interrupted her. "I'm not going to lie. I could have flicked one switch and fired up the generator and we would have had power in the house almost instantly," he admitted.

"Harrison! You purposefully left me in the dark and then pretended we were stranded so you could, what? *Seduce* me?"

He reached out to touch her face, but she playfully slapped his hand away.

"Sweetheart, I'm just a bloke. I had a beautiful woman in my house, an excuse to keep the lights out…"

"I can't believe you did that to me," she exclaimed, trying hard to sound angry and completely failing.

"Oh, but you can," he said, refusing to let her get away this time, holding her wrists locked in place against his chest.

"Harrison," she warned.

"What?" he whispered, his voice silky and seductive.

Poppy just shut her eyes and let him kiss her. So he'd lied about the lights. So what? It wasn't like he'd had to force her into anything. And this Harrison, the laid-back version of him, she was liking a lot.

* * *

Harrison stood under the water, eyes shut as it hit his face. It was hot, almost to the point of burning, and he didn't want to get out. Maybe he should have asked Poppy to join him....

He stepped back and blinked the water from his eyes. What had happened last night had been fantastic, exactly what he'd needed, but he was starting to think it might have been a mistake. A good one, but a mistake nonetheless.

But if it was a mistake, then why was he thinking about calling her in to get naked under the water with him?

Harrison submerged his face again, trying to clear his head. It was just one night; one crazy, heat-of-the-moment kind of night that didn't have to happen again. *Unless he wanted it to.*

"Harrison, ready when you are!"

He held his breath for as long as possible before turning off the faucet. There was a part of him that wished what had happened could turn into something more, that it wasn't just a fun, one-night thing. *A big part of him.*

The truth was, Poppy was a great girl, and if he'd met her ten years ago he might have thought she was *the one*. But his wife *had* left him, he *was* divorced and he had two children who meant the world to him. Not to mention the vow he'd made not to let them or himself get hurt again, if it was at all within his power.

Poppy might stick it out, or she could stay a week or a month or two, then head back to her old life. Nothing was keeping her here other than her desire for a fresh chance and to feel she'd made a difference.

"Harrison?"

Her voice was closer this time, as if she'd come looking for him. He dried himself, then slung the towel around his waist and knotted it.

"Oh, sorry." Poppy stood in the open doorway, eyes downcast, cheeks pink.

Her shyness struck him, made him forget all about his rationale and think only about her.

"After everything we did last night, *now* you're shy?"

She laughed, but she was still avoiding him, even though they'd been naked under a blanket less than thirty minutes earlier.

"I don't exactly do this kind of thing," she told him, folding her arms across her chest and bravely staring back at him.

"What do you mean by *this*?" he teased, unable to stop himself.

"You know what? How about you get dressed and I'll see you in the kitchen for breakfast?" Poppy said, starting to back away.

Harrison had hold of her arm in less than a second, his fingers closing around her biceps. She didn't turn, but stayed dead still.

"You," he said, scooping the hair from her neck so he could breathe on her skin, run his lips across her warm flesh, "are doing something to me." Harrison stood close to her, his front pressed to her back, fitting against her. "And I don't know how or why, but I feel like every time I try to hold back, you reel me in."

"Really?" she whispered.

"Really," he replied. "Like witchcraft."

Poppy chuckled and spun on the spot, looping her arms around his neck and leaning back slightly. "Funny, but I feel like you're doing the exact same thing to me."

Harrison shut his eyes when she kissed him, wishing he was stronger.

"You do realize I have animals to check and feed?" he asked, rocking back to put some distance between them.

"Let's have breakfast and then you can show me how I can help," Poppy offered. "Deal?"

"You're actually going to come outside and try to help me?"

She shrugged. "Why not? I'm not some city princess. I just need to be told what to do."

Harrison shook his head. "Deal, then," he agreed.

Poppy grinned at him over her shoulder before disappearing, leaving him half-naked, staring after her.

Déjà vu. That's what it felt like to him. Because one day his wife had said the same thing, been so eager to see what living on a remote ranch was like. Then out of the blue she'd blamed exactly that in the note she'd left him, before running out on him and their children in the middle of the night and never coming back.

Poppy was so different, though. A kind, loving person he could never imagine behaving that way, let alone walking out on children. But he'd never thought his wife would, either. Which meant he couldn't read women as well as he'd once liked to think he could. And what if he made the wrong call again? It wasn't worth it. Not to him. Not to Katie. And not to Alex.

He needed to talk to Poppy, burst the fun, carefree bubble they had been living in since he'd rescued her from the river the night before. He didn't want to hurt her any more than he wanted to hurt himself, and the longer he let himself behave like this the harder it would be to walk away.

Poppy cleared the plates from the table and put the maple syrup back in the fridge.

"You know, you half deserved to lose everything in your freezer for playing that trick on me last night," she told him. It wasn't like she hadn't enjoyed herself, but still. She didn't like that he'd tricked her, or that she'd so blatantly fallen for it.

"I already had that one sussed out," he said with a grin. "So long as you don't open them, freezers are good for at least twelve hours with no power. I had all my bases covered."

He thought he was so clever. Poppy gave him what she hoped was a withering look. "So how about these animals? You still game for showing me the ropes?"

Harrison was giving her a weird look, one she couldn't read. "Am *I* game?" he asked. "I thought you were just saying that to be polite."

She laughed. "Would it surprise you that much to know that I actually *want* to learn? I'm part of a rural community now, so I can't exactly have the children I'm teaching know more about ranch work than their teacher, can I?"

"All righty, then." He stood up and stretched, looking her up and down. "But you do realize you'll need to wear something more…" he paused "…*appropriate* than that, right?"

If he was trying to intimidate her or put her off, then she wasn't going to take the bait. Poppy walked up close to him, standing in his space, eyes never leaving his. He wanted to intimidate her? Then she'd do the same straight back at him.

"Let's go saddle up, cowboy," she said, in her impersonation of a drawl.

His face showed no expression, but his eyes were glinting, and she knew he was trying hard not to smile. Harrison bent slowly, teasingly, and pressed a barely there kiss to her lips. "You have no idea what you're getting yourself into," he whispered.

"Try me."

He stayed in place, hands moving gently up and down her arms, before he backed away. "I'm not intentionally being hard on you," he said. "Well, I guess I am, but it's only because I don't think you should try to change who you are."

Her eyebrows rose in question. "I'm not trying to change who I am, Harrison. Is that honestly what you think?"

He shrugged. She could tell he was uncomfortable, from the way he was standing to the look on his face.

"I came here because I wanted to, Harrison. I came because I wanted a new beginning, and if the people of Bellaroo are prepared to give me that, then I'm prepared to push a little out of my comfort zone to embrace life here."

"I'm sorry." He was staring out the window as if he was a million miles away, even though he'd just apologized.

Poppy stayed by the table, not sure what was happening and wishing they could go back to how things had been a few moments earlier. When they'd been having fun and pretending they were both just two people with no issues and no ugly pasts to ruin their chances at anything great happening between them.

"I thought we'd already had this conversation," she said, her voice so low she was almost surprised he heard it. "I'm not *her,* Harrison."

"Don't you think I know that?" His own voice was louder than usual, pained in a way she'd never heard it. She'd seen him sad and stressed—when he'd been rushing to visit his dad in hospital and fearing the worst—but this was different. Now he looked tortured, as if he was struggling hard to fight his inner demons and didn't know how to stop them from haunting him. "You are *nothing* like her, Poppy. Nothing at all like her. But having you here, having a woman in my home after so long being on my own…"

Poppy crossed the room, touched Harrison's elbow and propelled him forward.

"Let's go outside and just enjoy hanging out. It doesn't have to mean anything more than you showing me around, okay?"

He nodded, but the anger and pain were still there—in his eyes and written all over his face.

"Yeah, you're right," he said.

Poppy looped her arm around his waist and gave him a squeeze. Maybe she should have been angry with him, should have told him at length how wrong he was about her. But Harrison wasn't trying to offend her or hurt her. He was trying to stop from hurting himself, and she understood that more than anyone else in the world right now.

"Harrison, you forgot about your dogs! Why weren't they crying at the door to come in?" Poppy dropped and gave the big dog a cuddle, arms around him. The other one held back a little, but she coaxed him over.

"My dogs are pretty lucky, Poppy. They don't get locked in kennels, they're well fed and they get treated well. And last night they were up at the worker's house, so they've only been down here waiting since this morning."

She shook her head. "They should have been inside, in front of the fire."

Harrison ran a hand through his hair before pulling on his boots and reaching for a jacket. "I'm already called the soft rancher by most of the men around here, so I think I'll pass on pampering the dogs."

"You're considered soft because you feed your working dogs properly and treat them with the respect they deserve?"

He laughed and this time it hit his eyes, making them shine the way they usually did. "They call me soft because I have an old sofa at the back door for my dogs and because I let my daughter convince me not to send a bunch of cattle she's fallen in love with to the slaughterhouse. So, yeah, that's considered pretty pathetic around these parts."

Poppy completely disagreed, but at least they'd moved on to a new discussion.

"Okay, what do I wear?" she asked, giving the dogs one last pat each.

"Anything you like, just take your pick."

Poppy liked looking nice, but contrary to what Harrison thought, she couldn't care less about throwing some boots and a warm top on, even if the latter was five times too big for her.

"Ready when you are," she said, grabbing the closest jacket and zipping it up. "Let's go."

Harrison was starting to see a pattern where Poppy was concerned, and he didn't like it. Not one bit. He hated being rude to her, acting as if she was somehow deserving of the stupid comments that he just couldn't seem to hold back, but she wasn't. Which meant he had to learn how to hold his tongue, get used to the hurt look on her face when he offended her or stay the hell away.

He clenched his fists. The last one wasn't something he wanted to do, but he knew it was the logical choice.

"Do we go through here?" Poppy was striding on ahead of him, hand poised on the latch to the gate.

"No!" he yelled. Harrison sprinted the short distance and slammed his hand over hers. "No," he said, more softly this time.

Poppy was frozen, her body like stone, and he gently lifted her hand from the gate.

"I didn't mean to hurt you."

"I'm fine," she mumbled.

He could see how strained her face was, as if he'd finally managed to push her that one step too far. Only this time his rudeness had been warranted.

"I have our stud bull in this field," he explained, pointing him out. Poppy followed his gaze, and he placed his hand on her shoulder, trying to reassure her, show that he actually did care. "The fences are all electric, but if you'd gone through that gate…" He blew out a breath. "On second thought, let's not even think about it."

Poppy was slowly starting to nod. "So you kind of saved me, huh?"

He grinned, could see she was seeing how amusing the situation was. "Yeah, I guess I kind of did."

"Maybe I should let you lead the way. You know, so I don't make some massive blunder that ends up with you needing to resuscitate me."

Harrison slowly removed his hand and started to walk again. Him having to resuscitate her was not something he needed to be thinking about, not with the thoughts of Poppy in his arms the night before still playing through his head like a movie stuck on repeat.

"Let's go through here. We can check on Katie's herd, walk down to the river and see how high it is."

"This might be a silly question, but don't you have hundreds of cattle that need to be checked?"

"I do, but with the size of this place we let the cattle do their own thing because they're on massive blocks rather than just in fields. They have hectares and hectares to roam, so we make sure they're okay, but in general they're just left to do what cows do." Harrison glanced at Poppy, made sure she wasn't bored to tears. "We do our mustering with helicopters these days, and I have a few guys working here full-time, so they'll be out doing the grunt work for me already."

"You love it here, don't you?"

Poppy's question made him turn. "What made you say that?"

"It's true, isn't it? I can see it in your eyes and the way you talk about the place. I don't even think you're aware of how your face lights up when you're looking at the land."

Harrison dropped to his haunches, scratching one of his dogs on the head. "That's why I'm so protective," he said, knowing he had to be honest right now, that he needed to answer more than just the question she'd asked. "I love Bellaroo Creek more than anything because it's the land I grew up on, and it's the land I want my children to grow up on."

Poppy's face was soft, her eyes locked on his, tears glistening. "I understand, Harrison. Not because I have a ranch or get your connection with the land, but because I know what it's like to have the home you love and the people you love snatched away without having any control over it happening or not."

He tried to smile and failed. "I need you to know that the Harrison you met that first day at school, that's not who I am. But the idea of having to sell this place and move to stay near my kids, to keep them out of boarding school…" He shook his head. "It's eating me up, one day at a time. It's all I think about, why I'm so sure you'll bolt and leave us. Because someone like you coming here and sticking it out just seems too good to be true."

He wanted to touch her, to connect with her physically and show her that he did care about her. That he wanted to think she *would* stay, but that he couldn't let himself believe it.

"Harrison, I'm not going to let this community down. Not if I can help it."

He didn't doubt her intentions, but past experience told him he wasn't always the best judge of character. "Poppy, what happened last night was great." He shut his eyes for a beat, trying to get his head straight, wanting to say this right.

"Geez, Harrison, I feel like you're breaking up with me."

She was trying to be lighthearted, but he could see she was hurting, and he hated being the cause of that. He'd already attempted to have this conversation last time they'd kissed, and now…now it was much more than just a kiss.

"When I met my ex-wife, I thought I'd met the person I'd spend the rest of my life with," he told her, speaking as honestly as he could. "When we moved here, she said she'd do it for me, that she wanted to give our life here a chance, and when we had Katie and then Alex, I thought everything was going great."

"So what happened?" Poppy asked.

Harrison leaned against the timber fence and looked up at the sky. "I knew she was struggling, but there was nothing more I could do for her." He recalled the day when he'd woken to find her gone and the reality of raising two kids on his own had set in. "When she left, it was so final. A note on the kitchen table, the car and some of her things gone, and that was it. For a while I thought she'd come back, that there was no way a mom could leave her children, but it never happened. And then I became so angry, so furious about the way she'd left and what it had done to my kids, especially to Katie at the time, and I couldn't see past it."

"But you did, you must have," Poppy said. "If you were that filled with anger still, then you wouldn't be the father I've witnessed firsthand with his kids."

Harrison nodded. "Yeah, that's true, but the anger is still there somewhere. It's never really left." He took a deep breath. "I mean, I can see now that maybe she wasn't cut out for motherhood or living here, but it still hurts me to see my kids grow up without a mom. I would do anything for my children, *anything* to protect them, and keeping our family unit together and free of any more pain is the most important thing in the world to me."

Poppy had tears in her eyes now. "And it's why you'd sacrifice your family's land to move away with them if they had to change schools. Why you'd give up what you love."

"Without a moment's hesitation."

CHAPTER THIRTEEN

HARRISON FELT AS if he'd been broken all over again, dredging up the past and reliving it.

"Do you know what it's like, to hold your baby in your arms, to look into his eyes and whisper to him that his mommy has gone, that she's never coming back?" Harrison choked, emotion ripping his throat and making him so angry he could have bellowed like a bear. "What it's like to want to do everything in your power to love and protect this little child when you have *no idea* where to even start? How to do it on your own? Not to mention having a heartbroken little girl sobbing in your bed night after night?"

He stared into Poppy's eyes and then wished he hadn't, because he could see how his words were hurting her, as if he was accusing *her* of something that she most certainly wasn't guilty of. But now that he'd started, he couldn't stop. He'd kept his feelings bottled up inside for years, locked it all away, and now that he was talking about it, everything was crashing back. The way it had been at the time, alone with two children, thrust full-time into solo parenthood.

"When you have a child, all you want is to give them everything. But there were so many times, late at night, when I'd only just managed to get Alex back down after walking him around the house for what felt like hours, then would get into bed and have Katie crying for her mom, that I almost gave up. Thought I couldn't give them what they deserved, the love they needed that only I could give."

Tears started streaming down his cheeks and he couldn't do anything to stop them. Because his children weren't here, he was talking about the past and he couldn't hold it back any longer.

"I had to be everything for those kids, two parents rolled into one, and it made me like a protective papa bear. And it's why I'll never be able to let anyone close to me or them again." Harrison wiped at his eyes, furious with himself for breaking down since he was usually so good at keeping his composure. "They mean everything to me, Poppy, and I'm all they've got. And while they're little…" he paused and stared out at the field, the young cattle Katie loved so much putting a smile on his face "…then I'm going to make sure I protect them the only way I know how."

Poppy had started to walk away. Harrison rubbed the back of his hands over his eyes and down his cheeks, refusing to let his emotions take over again. "I'm sorry, I don't know where that all came from."

She didn't stop, so he jogged to keep up with her, touched her elbow to make her halt. When she didn't turn, kept her face down, he stepped around her to force her to stop moving or crash into him.

"Hey, I'm sorry." Why the hell had he gone off the handle like that? Acted as if it was somehow her fault, that he had a right to just burst out with something he'd been sitting on for five years? Poppy hadn't deserved it, not when she'd been there for him this past week more than anyone else in his life. "Poppy, honestly, I don't know where all that came from, why I…" *Crap.* She was crying.

When he reached for her arm, she just shook her head, but he wasn't going to give up. Why the hell did he have to go and ruin everything? Upset the one person who deserved more than anyone *not* to be hurt?

"Poppy?" Harrison tucked his fingers under her chin, gently lifted until her eyes met his. They were swimming with tears, tears that hit him so hard because it was his fault she was crying.

"You're right, I don't know what it's like to hold my own child," she said, her voice cracking even though he could see how hard she was trying to be brave.

"I didn't mean it like that, Poppy. It's just that I've been sitting on all that crap, the past, for so long, and it just came spewing out of me."

She was looking out into the distance now, but her eyes found his again before she spoke. "Something I do know, though," she told him, wrapping her arms around herself, "is what it's like to want a child so badly only to lose it. To be pregnant and so excited, then find out you've lost that baby you've been so desperate to have."

Double crap. How the hell had he screwed up to such an extent, talking as he had without even thinking that

Poppy might have been through a tragedy of her own? "You lost a child?"

"I've miscarried twice in the past couple of years, but then, I guess, given everything that happened, some people might call it a blessing." She cleared her throat. "The last one happened not long before I moved here, most likely from the stress of everything, because aside from what I was going through, I'm as healthy as can be."

Harrison frowned.

"My wife said she wanted children, Poppy, but the way she left them tells me she didn't ever love them like I do." He was trying to say the right thing, make the situation better, but he felt he'd put his foot in it again.

"Just because your wife walked out and left your children doesn't mean every woman in the world would, Harrison. And it certainly doesn't mean that *I* would."

He groaned "That's not what I meant. I know you wouldn't do that, Poppy. I was just ranting, saying things I should have talked about years ago instead of holding on to it for so long."

"I want a child more than anything in the world, Harrison. Children to care for and love, to be their everything, and I would never, ever walk away from them."

"I know that, Poppy. I don't believe you would."

"I get that you want to protect your kids, and I *know* that you're a great dad, but you need to stop looking at everyone like a potential threat." She'd blinked away her tears now, her strength growing as she spoke, her voice more confident than before. "Be careful, Harrison, but don't isolate your family so much that you find yourself completely alone. Because by then it'll be too late."

Harrison knew she was right. Every inch of his body, his mind, was screaming out to him that what she was saying was true. But he still couldn't admit it. If he did, it would be acknowledging that he'd been wrong all these years, that *he'd* been the one at fault.

"And what if you're right? That I'm wrong?" he asked, because he couldn't not.

Poppy touched his arm. "I know what it's like to lose something you love, and I know how hard it is to admit to being wrong. But you have to make up your own mind, Harrison. About what's right for you and for your family. Only you can do that."

"I know, but sometimes it's easier to push everyone away than take a chance on letting someone close." He swallowed, hard, and stared past her, because it was easier than meeting her gaze. Easier than acknowledging the truth of her words.

"Last night was great, Harrison, and I appreciate you showing me around this morning, but I think it's time I went home."

Crap, he'd pushed too far and said too much. He was usually guilty of the exact opposite, yet today he hadn't been able to hold back.

"You don't have to leave," he said, not ready to say goodbye to her, not yet. "I don't want you to think that…"

"What?" she asked, shaking her head. "That you have the same opinion of me as you have of your ex, just because I'm a woman? That no one else understands what it's like to have their heart ripped out by someone they loved and trusted more than anyone in the world?"

He shut his eyes, pushing back the anger so desperate to escape from within him. But this wasn't a fight he needed to have with Poppy. It wasn't her who had damaged him, who had left him, who had ripped his heart out and left him with two little children who'd become his entire world.

"I can't help the way I am, Poppy. Don't you think I'd do anything to wipe out the bitterness that's plagued me since she left? To take away the pain and protectiveness I feel for my kids?" He ran a hand through his hair, tugging at it, barely managing to keep the bite of fury back as it gnashed its teeth and threatened to emerge. "I don't *want* to be this person, Poppy, but I can't do anything about it. It's who I am and I have to deal with it."

She was the one angry now; he could see it in the flash of her eyes and the clench of her fists as she glared at him. "You're not the only person who's been hurt and left with a rough deal," she snapped. "Do you think I wanted to start over, to see everything I'd ever worked for snatched away from me? Do you have any idea what it took to come here to a new town, *alone*, and make a fresh start? With a stupid smile on my face, as if I was the happiest person in the world and not a woman who'd lost *everything*?"

"I know you've been hurt, Poppy," Harrison said in a low voice, trying his best to sound as sympathetic as he felt. "I'm not saying you've been hurt any less than I have, I'm just *saying* that this is the way I am. That

I can't get past what happened to me, what happened to my children."

"Try harder, Harrison," she said, her voice quiet but seething. *"Try harder."*

Poppy spun on her heel then, marching back in the direction of the house, and he let her go. Because what was he going to say to her?

Especially when the only words going through his head were too hard for him to admit to.

She's right.

He did a quick head count of the cattle and checked the fences, then walked up to the barn to get his quad bike. Climbing aboard, Harrison accelerated and headed toward the river, checking fences as he passed to make sure there hadn't been any major damage after the storm. He slowed as he neared the water, surveying its height.

Harrison turned the bike around and headed toward the house. There was no way anyone was going through that in a vehicle, which meant taking up the helicopter to get her safely over to her car. And after last night's experience, he wasn't sure she was going to like that idea at all.

He shut off the engine and went inside, taking off his jacket and walking in. Now he just needed to figure out what the hell to say to her.

CHAPTER FOURTEEN

POPPY STARED INTO Katie's room. She hadn't walked in, but she couldn't move away from the door frame. It was girlie, but not over-the-top—pink walls so soft in color that they were almost white and pretty polka-dot curtains that reminded Poppy of her own room when she was a child.

It was the room she'd like to give her own daughter one day, but the thought of losing another baby still hit her with the force of a heavyweight punch. Finding out she was pregnant, *twice*, imagining holding her own child and then miscarrying. Her skin broke out in goose pimples as it always did when she thought about it. The rooms she'd planned, the tiny white clothes she'd bought as soon as she'd found out she was expecting…and here was a little girl with a pretty room and no mom. One day it would happen for Poppy, because it wasn't as if she couldn't get pregnant, but it seemed like a pipe dream right now.

She got why Harrison was so messed up about women because she couldn't imagine how any mother could walk out and leave two little children. But she hadn't deserved to hear all that. Not when she wanted to be a mom so badly, when she'd done nothing but be there for his children and for him. Not because she wanted anything or expected anything, but because she genuinely cared about every single child in her class that she taught each day, and because she cared about Harrison, too.

A tear escaped from the corner of her eye and she quickly brushed it away. She wasn't going to cry over a man. She wasn't even supposed to *be* with a man. So she most certainly wasn't going to blubber over this one.

"Poppy?"

She squared her shoulders and turned away, trying to forget the perfect room she'd just been staring into. Harrison was back, which meant it was time to go, and she didn't want to stay here a second longer than she had to.

The helicopter was hovering and Poppy was trying not to look down. They only had to go up and across the river, but after last night's experience she was still terrified.

They landed without so much as a bump, but her hands were shaking.

"Better than last night?"

Poppy glanced at Harrison and gave him a quick smile. She didn't want to be rude, but this was awkward and they both knew it.

She waited for his signal, not opening her door until he did his and keeping her head low just as he'd shown her the night before. Harrison ran around, grabbed her handbag and helped her down, but she kept her distance. She didn't want to look at him, touch him, *nothing*. Because then she'd only regret what had happened, the way she'd opened up to him and let herself just *be* with him. When she'd been scared and unsure, she'd pushed past it because it had seemed like the right thing to do. Because she'd trusted him. Now? Now she wasn't so sure.

"Poppy…"

She shook her head, more to tell herself no than him. "Harrison, don't. Please just…don't." As if this wasn't bad enough, standing here with him. The last thing she wanted was an apology or to talk about anything. All she wanted was to go home. To just get in her car and drive as far away from Harrison as possible. Because she should have known when they'd argued last night not to let things go so far between them.

"I just wanted to say I'm sorry."

He crossed the space between them so fast that she never saw it coming. One second he was passing her bag to her, the next he was grabbing her by the shoulders and kissing her so fiercely that she could hardly breathe.

Harrison's hands held her in place, his body solid like stone. She wanted to pull away but was powerless to, even though she knew it would be their last kiss. That she wasn't ever going to let herself be put in this position again.

He pressed his lips to hers over and over again, his touch desperate, as if he were a death-row inmate stealing the last kiss of his life. *With the woman he loved*.

Poppy pushed her hand between them, had to stop it

before it went any further, before she lost the strength to say no to him.

"Goodbye, Harrison," she said, her palm flat to his chest to keep him at arm's length.

Poppy turned her back and walked to her car, refusing to look over her shoulder. Her chest heaved, unshed tears, gulps of emotion tearing through her body. She fumbled in her bag for her keys, knowing that Harrison had to be staring after her still because she hadn't heard the helicopter fire into life yet. Could almost feel his eyes on her back, watching her leave.

Harrison was a good man—a strong human being and an amazing father, too. And that's why it hurt so much. Because the last man she'd been with had hurt her beyond belief, and in the end hadn't cared that she was leaving. Hadn't cared that he'd stolen all her money, that she'd lost their baby, *nothing*.

But Harrison? He was the exact opposite, and that's why he wouldn't let her close. That man loved his children so much that he would do anything to protect them, and was so guarded that he wouldn't take down his defenses for a moment.

Poppy started her car and tried to keep her eyes downcast, but she couldn't. Harrison was standing where she'd left him, his face unreadable, his mouth a grim line that she'd never forget. But he never took his eyes from hers, his gaze unwavering.

She turned the key, praying the engine would start, and then slowly pulled away and headed down the dirt road for home. In her rearview mirror she could see him walking away, turning his back and heading for his helicopter, but he was so blurred she wouldn't have recognized him had she not just seen him up close.

Tears fell in a steady stream now, curling down her cheeks and into her mouth, falling on her sweater. Poppy turned up the volume of the radio and tried to drown out the voice in her head telling her to turn around.

And the one telling her what a fool she'd been to ever let herself be intimate with him in the first place when she knew better than to fall for a man. Any man. Especially one as easy to fall for as Harrison Black.

Harrison waited for his children on the other side of the river, in the exact place he'd stood watching Poppy leave earlier in the day. A swirl of dust told him his mom was close, and the last thing he needed was her asking why he looked sullen. Telling her that the weather had gotten to him wasn't an excuse she'd buy, not for a second.

The car came into view then, and he fixed a smile and waved to the kids, knowing they'd be pressed to the window looking for him before he could see them. His mom flashed her lights and Harrison made his smile even wider, trying to convince himself that he was fine. That he'd had a pleasant morning instead of feeling as if he'd gone ten rounds in a boxing ring.

"Daddy!" The car door was flung open the moment the vehicle was stationary.

He bent down, arms out as Katie and Alex ran toward him. "Hey, guys." He was smothered in cuddles within seconds.

This was what he needed. Because this was what

he was trying so hard to protect, what he was giving up everything else for, to keep these little people safe.

"Hello, darling."

Harrison stood, one child in each arm. "Hey, Mom." He laughed. "I'd kiss you if I could."

She smiled back at him, shaking her head. "I was just telling your father that there probably isn't a dad in the world as loved as you are. Most kids like getting away from their parents for some fun, but these two just want to get back to Dad all the time."

He swallowed hard, refusing to acknowledge that one word—*parents*.

"It's good to know I'm wanted."

His mom sighed. "Darling, you're *wanted*. I don't think you need to worry about that."

Harrison wished he hadn't said it like that. "Dad okay today?"

She smiled. "He's spent most of the morning telling me he needed to come and help you."

Harrison put the children on the ground and watched as they ran to inspect the river. "Not too close," he called out.

When he turned back to his mom, she was staring straight at him, her mouth pursed as if she was trying to figure out whether to speak her mind or not.

"Just say it," he said.

She sighed. "You know I don't like interfering, Harrison, but the young lady who dropped the kids off last night seemed, well, lovely."

"She's just the kids' teacher." He *did not* want to discuss this with his mother.

"Sweetheart, she's more than just their new teacher. I can tell that from the look on your face, and it was written all over hers last night, too."

"I'm not talking about Poppy with you, Mom."

"And you don't have to." She touched his face, looking into his eyes so there was no escape. "But I've seen you struggle all these years, Harrison. I'm so proud of the dad you've become, but I know you could be an amazing husband to someone, too."

He took a deep breath to push away his anger, refusing to let his mom see him lose his cool. "I've already been a husband, and look how that worked out for me, huh?"

He turned to check on Katie and Alex, watching as they laughed and played together.

"I'm not saying you need to get married, but seeing you happy, seeing you spend some time with someone lovely who deserves your company, that would make me so happy."

Harrison swallowed his groan. "Point taken, Mom."

"You called her Poppy."

He raised an eyebrow. "So?" That was her name. What was so unusual about that?

"I was just wondering if the fact she stayed here last night was the reason you'd stopped calling her Ms. Carter?"

"How did you…?"

His mom was laughing. *The old fox.* Talk about cunning.

"I'm going to get these two back to the house," he

told her, leaning forward to drop a kiss on her forehead. "Thanks for looking after them."

"See you soon, sweetheart."

"Say goodbye to Grandma," he called to the kids.

They came running over to hug her goodbye while he watched. He'd all but admitted Poppy had stayed the night, which meant his mom would never give up until she knew more about their relationship.

Pity he'd made such a hash of things, because maybe his mother was right. Maybe he *did* spend too much time on his own.

"Is Poppy at the house?" Katie was looking up at him like an excited Labrador.

"No, sweetheart, she's home now."

"Did she stay in my room?"

Harrison held back a laugh. If only it was as un-complicated as that. "Come on, let's get you two in the helicopter, okay?"

He lifted first Alex and then Katie, secured the door, then walked around to the other side. His kids had grown up around big machinery and helicopters, but they still grinned like crazy every time he took them up in the air.

"Copilots, prepare yourself for takeoff," he said through his mic.

The children were already wearing their headsets, seat belts done up and big smiles beaming at him.

Harrison took them up into the sky until they were well above the river. But he didn't want to go back to the house, to park the chopper just yet. He needed a release, a reason to remember why the land he worked was so important to him. Why he loved his life here, what he had to be grateful for.

"What do you think of a scenic flight around the ranch?"

The two happy faces peering out the window gave him his answer. They might not have a mom in their lives, but his kids were happy. They were loved and nurtured and growing up in an environment that most children could only dream of.

Maybe he was too hard on himself. Maybe he worried too much about what Katie and Alex *didn't have* instead of what they *did*.

Being up in the air was good for him. It was his addiction, and it had been far too long since he'd just enjoyed flying with his children by his side.

CHAPTER FIFTEEN

Poppy held the envelope tightly and sat down. Her hands were shaking, unable to push beneath the seal to open it.

"Hey, Lucky," she said, watching the cat as he jumped up on the table and stared at her, his tail flicking back and forth as if he was equally anxious about the contents of her envelope. "What do you think?"

She hadn't been expecting it. That's what the problem was. What she'd been expecting was a pleasant trip to the store, trying to decide what she needed to buy for the week. Not Mrs. Jones telling her there was some mail for her, and getting *this* letter.

Poppy sighed and slapped the envelope down before picking it up again and sliding her nail through the seal.

She'd done it. Now she just had to read it.

The paper was crisp, and there were a number of pages. The cover letter bore the emblem of a Sydney law firm, one she didn't recognize, and she had no idea how he'd even managed to pay for it.

Poppy glared at the page. Of course—he'd probably tricked his poor girlfriend into doing so, and she wouldn't realize she'd end up fleeced of everything she'd ever owned.

Poppy closed her eyes, took a deep breath, then slowly released it.

Chris in bed with her friend, her bank account at zero, credit card maxed out, her home up for mortgagee sale.

They were all thoughts she'd pushed away, refused to dwell on, but the memories were still there. Still so fresh and raw and painful when she let herself remember, still capable of sending a shivering shudder through her entire body.

Poppy opened her eyes and forced a smile. This could be what she'd been waiting for, the final piece of the puzzle she needed in order to move on with her life and leave those memories behind. Forever.

She was divorced.

She scanned the document over and over again, reading the words, studying the signatures.

She was divorced! She'd asked for a speedy dissolution of their marriage and it had actually gone through!

"Lucky, it's happened!" She jumped up and grabbed the cat, dancing around the room with him. "It's finally happened!"

The cat looked beyond alarmed, going rigid, but she didn't put him down. Because right now she needed a warm body pressed tightly to hers, needed someone to share the moment with. And if a cat was all she had, then a cat would do.

"Wine, that's what we need," she announced, heading for the fridge. "I want wine and I want it now."

Tonight she was going to celebrate. She wasn't going to think about her *ex*-husband, and she wasn't going to think about Harrison. All she needed to think about tonight was herself and what it meant to have a real fresh start, to forget she'd ever been married and just enjoy being Poppy Carter. Thank goodness she'd never changed her name.

Poppy unscrewed the bottle, poured herself a big glass and made for the living room. A night of wine, ice cream and *Sex and the City* was what she needed. Because after all this time, she was finally free.

And being alone had never felt so good.

Poppy held up the wine bottle and found it empty. She slumped back on the sofa and stared at her glass. Also empty.

She was starting to think that being alone wasn't so great, and seeing Big leave Carrie at the altar hadn't exactly made her feel great about herself. Unless she counted the cat curled up beside her.

A loud knock made the cat jump even higher than she did. Who the heck would be banging on her door at this time of the night? She stood and held on to the back of the sofa to gain her balance, not used to drinking so much alcohol. She usually stopped after her second glass, no matter what or where she was drinking.

Poppy headed to the kitchen first, grabbing a fry pan, then leaned against the wall as she walked to the door. The person knocked again, making her heart beat even faster. Who would hear her scream if she needed help?

She held the handle of the pan tighter, wishing she hadn't drunk so much.

"Who is it?" she called, her voice unsteady.

"Harrison."

Oh, dear. He was the last person she needed to see, but at least she knew he wasn't here to burgle her house or murder her.

"Just a minute." Poppy looked at herself in the hall mirror and almost burst into tears. Her hair was a mess, her mascara had smudged and she was dressed in a baggy sweater and ugly sweatpants.

She tugged her hair down and smoothed it, pulling it up into a more respectable ponytail.

"Poppy?"

She flicked the lock on the door and slowly opened it. "Hi."

Harrison stood in the half-light cast by the old cobweb covered bulb hanging at the front door. His hair was messy, as if he'd been worrying it with his fingers, but his eyes were bright. They locked on hers the moment she looked at him.

"Coming here seemed like a really good idea when I left home," he said, shoving his hands into his pockets. "Now I'm starting to think I should have called first."

Poppy kept her hand against the door frame, steadying her body. "Are the children okay?"

He nodded. "Fine. They're asleep in the truck."

"Harrison, I need to tell you something—"

He interrupted her. "Me, too," he said. "Any chance I can go first?"

She held on tighter to the door, the lightness in her

head making her wonder if she was actually going to be able to stand and listen to him. "Ah, sure."

"It's just, well, I've had some time to think, and I feel like crap for the way I spoke to you earlier."

Poppy sucked her lip back between her teeth and stared at him. He wasn't exactly hard to look at, and she wasn't used to men apologizing to her.

"You were right about me being too scared to move on, that I needed to protect myself less and just, well, you know, you said the words."

"It's fine, Harrison. I know you've had a rough time, and you're a great dad."

"But that's just it, Poppy."

He stepped forward, into her space, his body too close to hers for comfort, or maybe just close enough. Harrison touched her cheek with such tenderness, such surprising softness, that she didn't know where to look or what to say. What he expected, if he expected anything at all.

"I don't just want to be a dad. I want to remember what it's like to be a man, too."

Shivers ran up and down her body, curling down her spine and across her belly. Was he talking about her, about last night, or had the wine just gone to her head?

"Harrison…"

He put his fingers over her mouth and the words died on her lips. "Let me finish," he whispered.

Poppy nodded. She wasn't capable of anything else, especially not with his hands on her, his body *way* too near.

"I want *you*, Poppy. I'm scared as hell, and I've

driven all the way here in the dark because I needed to tell you," he said, his voice so low she had to tilt her face up to hear him. "I don't want to think about the past or pretend like I know anything about you other than what you've shown me to be true. *I just want you.*"

He started to swim in front of her as if he was swaying, and she had to grip the timber frame harder.

"Are you okay?"

She shook her head. "No."

"I shouldn't have come here. I just, hell, I don't know what's happened to me, Poppy, but I can't stop thinking about you and I needed to tell you what was going on in my head."

"Harrison?"

He raised an eyebrow in question.

"It's not that I don't feel the same, but . ."

"Was it something important you wanted to tell me? Sorry, Poppy, I just started talking and I couldn't stop. Do you have someone here?" He peered around her, as if he expected to find a visitor in the house.

"Two things, actually," she mumbled. "But no, no one's here except for me and Lucky."

He was waiting, silent as he watched her.

"I'm officially divorced," she announced, warmth touching her body as she said the words. "The papers arrived while I was at your place. I collected them earlier."

"That's a good thing, right?" he asked, a cautious look on his face.

"Yep, it's brilliant."

"What's the second thing?"

She laughed, unable to help herself. "I think I'm drunk."

Harrison checked the kids before jogging back to the house and taking Poppy's hand.

"Still sound asleep," he told her.

Poppy linked their fingers, but he pulled away in favor of wrapping an arm around her to steady her. She was a little wobbly on her feet.

"Do you want to carry them in?" she asked.

"No." Harrison steered her in the direction of her bedroom. "I'm going to put you to bed, then I'm getting straight back in that truck and driving back to the ranch."

If the water level hadn't retreated so fast he'd never have been able to visit her, and he didn't want an excuse to stay. Besides, he didn't trust himself around Poppy, and he didn't want to take advantage of an intoxicated woman.

He held her hand as she sat down on the bed, then bent to kiss her on the forehead, lips staying against her skin longer than he'd intended. But the truth was she smelled so good, *felt* so good, and moving away from her wasn't something that came naturally to him. No matter how much he'd tried to fight it before now.

"Did you mean what you said before?" she murmured.

Harrison knelt down on the floor in front of her, taking her hands from beside her and placing them on her lap, clasped in his. "Every word, Poppy. And if you don't remember them in the morning, I'm going to tell you all over again."

She was blushing, a warm red stain making its way up her neck and across her cheeks.

"I think I was a bit hard on you today," she said. "I mean, I was so annoyed with my ex, and when I got the divorce papers I wondered if maybe I was angry at you because I didn't want to be angry at him. So I didn't have to think about the past." She sighed. "I know, that doesn't even make sense, does it?"

He leaned forward, arms on her legs to steady himself. Harrison kissed her gently, softly touching his lips to hers. "I think we both need to forget about our pasts. Why hold on to something that could ruin everything in our future?"

He'd never found it easy to talk, especially about his feelings, but Poppy had done something to him. Had made him want to talk just to see the smile on her face.

"Does that mean we have a future?" she asked, her voice barely a whisper.

"Tomorrow," he said, kissing her one last time before standing up. "Our future starts tomorrow."

She smiled, lay back and pulled the covers up, snuggling beneath the quilt, eyes closing as soon as her head hit the pillow.

"I'll lock the door on my way out," he told her, bending one more time to touch her face, pressing his fingers against her cheek and then her hair before pulling the covers up a little higher.

Harrison made himself walk out. Reminded himself

that his kids were in the car. Because it would have been way too easy to lie beside Poppy and hold her, sleep beside her all night.

But he couldn't. Because if what he'd just told her was true, their future wasn't starting until tomorrow.

So he'd just have to wait until then.

CHAPTER SIXTEEN

POPPY SMILED AT the children as they laughed at her. She was reading aloud, the smaller kids tucked close to her feet, the older ones lying or sitting on the floor.

A tap at the door made her look up, book fallen to her lap. The door wasn't closed—she rarely pulled it shut—so she could see exactly who was waiting there. *Harrison.*

She'd wondered when she'd see him again, had been disappointed when he'd dropped Katie and Alex off and left in such a hurry earlier before she'd had time to say anything. To apologize for being tipsy when he'd visited; to try to figure out if she'd misheard him or if he'd meant it when he'd—

"Daddy!" Katie jumped up and ran to her father, giving him a hug around the legs before scooting back to her spot on the floor.

Poppy stood and held the book tightly in one hand, the other anxiously smoothing her hair back. "Hi."

He was standing in her classroom, or almost in it, as if waiting to be invited to enter.

"Sorry to interrupt, kids, but I need to talk to Ms. Carter."

She had to bite her lip to keep from smiling. When he said it all official like that... Poppy put the book on her desk and walked toward Harrison.

"I won't be a moment," he added.

She had no idea why he was here, but she wasn't going to tell him to come back later. She needed to hear what he had to say.

The smile he gave her was so genuine, so full of happiness that it took over his face, made his eyes crinkle at the corners and his dark brown irises even darker.

She grinned back, trying to stay nonchalant and failing. The butterflies fluttering in her stomach, as if caged and ready for release, wouldn't let her do anything different.

Harrison took his hand from behind his back and held out a bunch of flowers—wildflowers in bright purples and pinks. "I would have brought you roses, but it's a long drive to Sydney and back."

She laughed; it was impossible to do anything else. "You didn't steal these from anyone's garden for me, did you?" Poppy took them and dipped her nose into them, holding the modest bunch as if they were the most beautiful flowers she'd ever been given. And in a way, they were.

"I'll have you know I picked these myself, from my own garden, for you," he said in almost a whisper.

Poppy knew the children were listening, their ears all flapping like an elephant's, so keeping her voice low wasn't going to keep their conversation private. But talking quietly, intimately, felt right.

"Thank you," she said. "Nothing makes a girl feel more special than flowers."

Harrison stepped into her space, touched his fingers to her elbow in a caress that seemed more intimate than any she'd ever experienced before. It was as if a magnet was drawing them together, refusing to let them part until what needed to be said was said.

"Do you remember what I said last night?" he asked.

Poppy nodded. "I had a feeling it was a dream, but…"

"No," he said, shaking his head. "It wasn't a dream, Poppy. I meant every word, and I can honestly admit I've never felt the need to say something so badly that I've had to bundle my kids in a vehicle and drive in the dark because it couldn't wait until morning."

She held her breath, not wanting to believe the words he was saying. She'd been so deeply hurt by a man only months before, had felt so damaged and used at the time that she'd thought trusting another human being would be impossible for her. But Harrison… Right now she knew in her heart that she could trust him with her life.

Because Harrison was a protector, a man who would risk his life willingly to save those he loved. Would do anything for his children to make them happy, no matter what the sacrifice.

Her ex-husband… He'd been a taker, only she hadn't realized it until the bitter end.

"What does this mean?" she asked, not wanting to

believe what Harrison was hinting at until he spelled it out.

"What it means," he said, inching closer and taking her face into both of his hands, "is that I want to start a new chapter of my life. I want to trust again, and I want to love again."

Poppy swallowed, staring into his eyes, waiting for the words.

"And Poppy?" he whispered.

She nodded, hardly able to breathe.

"I want that person to be you."

She silently let out the breath she'd been holding, scared beyond belief, but happy, too. Exhilarated by his words.

"Are you sure we're ready?" she asked.

"All we can do is try," he said, his fingers brushing her skin while his palms rested against her cheeks. "I don't want to look back and wish I'd taken a chance with you, and know that the only reason I didn't was because I was scared."

"Okay," she murmured, nodding. "Okay."

"Yeah?" Harrison asked, his own voice a low whisper.

"Yeah," she whispered back, leaning into him as he bent down to her, mouth covering hers in such a gentle kiss she could feel only warmth as his lips brushed hers.

Poppy let him hold her, one arm tucking around her waist and drawing her in, the other still soft against her face.

A burst of giggles and laughter made her break the

kiss, but she couldn't bring herself to step from the circle of Harrison's arms.

"I think we have an audience," she told him, pressing her forehead to his for a moment before facing her pupils.

"Show's over, kids," Harrison said, blowing his daughter a kiss and giving his son a thumbs-up. "I'll come back for Ms. Carter after school."

She watched him go, laughed when he winked over his shoulder at her then picked up the book she'd been reading and settled back into her chair.

"Where were we?" she murmured, finding her place.

She had their attention on the story again, but hers was wavering. Because even as she started to read, trying to focus on each word on the page, all she could think about was Harrison. The man who'd just changed her world, her future, and was making her stomach flip as it hadn't in years.

Harrison stood outside the school, leaning on the bed of his truck, hand up to shield his eyes from the sun. He glanced at his watch. It was right on three o'clock, which meant he had a few minutes to wait before he knew how Poppy really felt about what he'd said.

And he'd never been more scared in his life.

Opening up to someone—putting everything on the line when he'd spent so long protecting himself and creating a safe little world for Katie and Alex—was terrifying. But he couldn't shield his kids all their lives. After talking to his mom, thinking about what Poppy had said…it had made him question everything.

Just because one woman, one cruel, heartless woman, had left them, didn't mean he had a right to punish everyone around him. *Especially someone like Poppy.*

He looked up as children's laughter and chatter filled the air around him. Poppy was walking behind them, like a mother duck herding her babies, and he stood dead still, didn't take his eyes from her. Her hair was loose and hanging down her back, her slender arms folded across her chest.

Parents were arriving, some walking and some by car, but Harrison didn't move. He wanted to watch the woman who had changed everything about his life, who'd made him change the way he thought and the way he wanted his future to be.

And if he had anything to do with it, she'd be the one to save their town, too. He wasn't going to let her go without a fight, and he wanted her to stay. Forever.

Harrison stood back, giving her space to take leave of all the children. His two came running toward him, jumping in the back of the truck.

"I'll just be a minute," he said, so distracted he wasn't even paying them the attention they were used to.

"Dad, that was kind of embarrassing before," Katie told him, leaning out the open window and flicking his back with her fingers.

"Why?" he asked, trying hard not to laugh. "Haven't your friends ever seen grown-ups kiss before?"

She giggled. "Yeah, but *you kissed our teacher.*"

He glanced in at Katie and Alex and they both smiled

back at him. He doubted they were that embarrassed, but he knew they'd want to know what was going on. They hardly ever asked about their mom anymore, but he knew a day would come when they'd want to know more about the woman who'd given birth to them. Even if right now she was just someone who sent money and a card each birthday.

The money he sent back, but the cards he read to them before tucking them away in a box beneath their beds, in case one day they wanted to read them again.

"Harrison."

Poppy said his name as a statement, not a question, but the shyness in her eyes told him she was as nervous as he was.

"I hope I didn't embarrass you before," he said, standing up straight and holding out his hands, palms up. "According to Katie it was all *very* embarrassing."

Poppy placed her hands in his, grinning up at him. She leaned in and stood on her tiptoes, her lips brushing his cheek in a gentle kiss.

"Kind of embarrassing," she said, her voice low, "but in a good way."

Harrison put his hands on her waist, staring into her eyes. He needed to know how she really felt, needed to know if he'd made a fool of himself to the one woman he'd opened up to.

"You're not going to abandon our school, are you?" Maybe he should have thought about that before he'd turned up and blurted out his declaration.

Poppy laughed. "You haven't scared me off, Harrison," she said. "I'm not going to run away with my tail between my legs just because you were honest with me."

"You're not?" He shuffled forward, holding her hands against his chest now.

"If anything, you've made me more sure about staying."

He raised an eyebrow, making her laugh again. "I have?"

"Yeah, you have," she whispered, standing on tiptoe once more and kissing him, smiling against his mouth.

"So you're going to save our town *and* me?" he asked.

"Yeah, I think I might just do that."

Harrison grabbed her around the waist and wrapped her in his arms, pulling her clean off the ground.

"How the hell did we find a teacher like you?"

She laughed and threw her head back. "Keep flattering me like that and I'll never leave."

He hoped so.

"So what would you say if I asked you to marry me?"

Poppy giggled like a child. "I'd say that I've only been divorced twenty-four hours and that you're moving a little too fast."

"Huh," he said, kissing her neck when she tipped her head back again. "How about moving in with me?"

"No," she replied, swatting him away. "But I *will* date you."

"Kids, we're going on a picnic," he called out, putting Poppy back on her feet and opening the door for her. "I think we'll get one of those cherry pies from the bakery."

"We are?" Poppy asked.

"We are," he said with a grin. "Because if you want to be courted, then we're having our first date right now."

EPILOGUE

POPPY STRETCHED OUT in the hammock, unsuccessfully stifling a yawn. The sun was just starting to disappear, but it was still more pleasant in the shade of the tree.

"Hey, gorgeous."

She looked up at Harrison's voice, pushing her hair back and searching for him. He was walking toward her, the kids running alongside to keep up with his long, loping stride.

"What are you guys doing?" she asked, sitting up and trying to get out of the hammock as gracefully as she could without tipping it.

The kids were giggling and grinning. Poppy narrowed her eyes and tried to look stern, knowing something was going on that they were in on.

"Why do you all look like you're up to something naughty?"

Harrison bent down and whispered something to the children, and they were practically wriggling on the spot now, smiles stretching their little faces.

"Harrison?" she asked. What was going on?

He started walking again, reaching out for her hand

and grinning at her. "There's something we'd like to ask you."

If they just wanted to ask her something, why were they all acting so strangely? "Okay."

"Poppy Carter," Harrison started, nodding to the children. They scurried up beside him, staring upward as if expecting to hear something so exciting they couldn't wait. "You're the best thing that's ever happened to us, and we want to tell you how much we love having you in our lives."

Tears welled up in her eyes, but she fought them, not wanting to ruin the moment. Because she might be special to them, but she couldn't even begin to describe how much they all meant to her. How much they'd changed *her* life.

She watched as Harrison nudged Katie. Poppy turned her face and smiled at the little girl.

"I love having you here because now it's like I have a mom," she said, her arm wrapped around her dad's leg, but her smile all for Poppy.

"And I love having you here because you bake yummy cakes and give me nice cuddles," Alex said, his voice a whisper.

Harrison cleared his throat and she looked at him, shaking her head. She knew he hadn't told them what to say, because it wasn't something he would do, which made it all the more special.

"I love having you here, too, Poppy," he told her. "There's nothing I don't like about having you in my life. In *our* lives."

She did cry then, couldn't stop the tears from falling

down her cheeks. "They're happy tears," she mumbled, wiping them away, not wanting the children to think she was sad. "It's just, well, I still can't believe that I'm here. With all of you."

Harrison squeezed her hands. She could see his eyes were glinting with unshed tears, too, and it wasn't something she was used to seeing. Her rugged rancher wasn't exactly the emotional type, so it hit her even harder, made her swallow an even bigger lump in her throat.

"Poppy, we have something we'd like to ask you."

She tilted her head, looking from Harrison to Katie and then to Alex.

"Poppy, I didn't want to rush things with us, but I know in my heart that you're the most amazing, kind, loving woman I'll ever meet," he told her.

"And we think you're the best mom we could ever have found, too," said Katie.

Poppy's heart had started to race. She could hardly breathe, her chest somehow constricting all the air in her lungs and holding it hostage. Surely he wasn't going to…

"So I'd like to ask for the honor of your hand in marriage," Harrison said, not even blinking, his eyes never leaving hers.

Katie was jumping up and down she was so excited, and prodding her brother.

"Oh, yeah," Alex said. "And we want to ask you to be our mom."

Poppy couldn't contain herself; she was so excited she thought she might burst.

"Yes," she said, throwing her arms around Harrison and kissing him, before tilting her head back and looking up at the sky. *Maybe someone up there did care about her, after all.* "Yes to being your wife," she told Harrison, before bending and opening her arms to Katie and Alex. "Yes to being your mom, too." They hugged her back, tightly. "I promise to love you forever and never, ever leave you." It was a big promise, but one she knew in her heart she'd be able to keep.

Harrison cleared his throat again, making her look up. He was holding something, waiting for her to stand up again.

She kept a hand on each child, but her eyes were for Harrison.

Oh, my goodness. He had the most beautiful ring in his open palm, sitting there glinting in the sunlight. A large solitaire diamond set on an intricate band.

"This was my grandmother's, and my mom has been holding it for years," he told her. "She has given it to me with her blessing, for me to give to you."

"Are you sure?" Poppy asked, letting Harrison slide it on to her finger.

"We want you as part of our family, Poppy. *For life.* So yes, I'm absolutely sure."

"I'm sure, too."

He took her into his arms, holding her carefully, as if she was the most precious thing in the world.

"We love you, Poppy, and we can make this work."

"I know," she whispered against his skin, loving his lips against her mouth, brushing her cheek when she pulled away.

"You saved our school, and you saved my life," Harrison said. "And I'll never take that for granted."

"You might have to find another teacher one day," she whispered, "because I think a place like this needs a big family, you know."

Harrison laughed, hoisting Katie and Alex up so they were all at eye level.

"I think you could be right," he said, stepping in so they could have a group hug.

Poppy closed her eyes and hugged her little family, knowing in her heart that she'd done the right thing. In coming to Bellaroo, in meeting Harrison—in everything.

This was her home now, and she couldn't have been happier.

"I just passed Sally and Rocky on my way here," Harrison told her. "I asked them to join us for a little celebration."

Poppy raised an eyebrow. The children were looking mischievous again. "Tell me what's going on," she insisted.

"Daddy said we're having a little party," said Katie with a giggle.

Poppy looked at Harrison and he just shrugged.

"You were that sure I'd say yes?" she teased.

Harrison put his kids down and grabbed Poppy instead, sweeping her up into his arms, dropping a quick kiss to her lips before carrying her inside, the children running beside them. "We have champagne and some treats from the bakery," he confessed. "Nothing fancy, but I thought you'd like to see Sally and have another squeeze of that baby girl."

Poppy couldn't exactly argue with that.

Seeing her new friend walking to the door, she wriggled until Harrison put her down. Once, she'd worried about being lonely in Bellaroo, but now she knew better.

"Hey, little one," Poppy cooed at baby Arinya. She gave Sally a hug. "Nice to see you, too."

The other woman grinned and gave her a hug back. "Are we celebrating?"

"We are." Poppy laughed and held out her left hand, showing off the ring on her finger.

She took Arinya to give her a cuddle and almost walked smack bang into Harrison.

Poppy met his gaze, felt the heat traveling from his eyes to her body. Next time it would be them with the newborn, would be them starting on the journey of parenting a new baby. But for now she just wanted to spend every minute with the family she already had.

* * * * *

MILLS & BOON®
By Request

RELIVE THE ROMANCE WITH THE BEST OF THE BEST

A sneak peek at next month's titles...

In stores from 8th September 2016:

- **Bound by His Vow** – Melanie Milburne, Michelle Smart & Maya Blake

- **Her Sweet Surrender** – Nina Harrington & Nina Harrington

In stores from 6th October 2016:

- **Seducing the Matchmaker** – Joanne Rock, Meg Maguire & Lori Borrill

- **It Happened in Paradise** – Liz Fielding, Nicola Marsh & Joanna Neil

Just can't wait?
Buy our books online a month before they hit the shops!
www.millsandboon.co.uk

Also available as eBooks.

0916/05

MILLS & BOON®

18 bundles of joy from your favourite authors!

2 free books

Get 2 books free when you buy the complete collection only at
www.millsandboon.co.uk/greatoffers

PECIAL DELIVERIES_0916